BLOOD
GAME

Also by David Lyons

Ice Fire

BLOOD GAME

A Jock Boucher Thriller

DAVID LYONS

EMILY BESTLER BOOKS

—

ATRIA

NEW YORK LONDON TORONTO SYDNEY NEW DELHI

ATRIA PAPERBACK

A Division of Simon & Schuster, Inc.
1230 Avenue of the Americas
New York, NY 10020

First Emily Bestler Books/Atria Paperback edition August 2013

EMILY BESTLER BOOKS / ATRIA PAPERBACK and colophons are
trademarks of Simon & Schuster, Inc.

For information about special discounts for bulk purchases,
please contact Simon & Schuster Special Sales at
1-866-506-1949 or business@simonandschuster.com.

The Simon & Schuster Speakers Bureau can bring authors
to your live event. For more information or to book an event,
contact the Simon & Schuster Speakers Bureau at
1-866-248-3049 or visit our website at www.simonspeakers.com.

Manufactured in the United States of America

10   9   8   7   6   5   4   3   2   1

Library of Congress Cataloging-in-Publication Data

Lyons, David.
  Blood game : a Jock Boucher thriller / by David Lyons.
      pages   cm
  1. Judges—Fiction. 2. Police—Louisiana—New Orleans—Fiction. 3. Suspense
fiction. I. Title.
  PS3612.Y5745B57   2013
  813'.6—dc23   2012050303

ISBN 978-1-4516-2932-3
ISBN 978-1-4516-2934-7 (ebook)

To my family,
who shared the dream and made it possible.

I also want to thank my good friend,
the late writer and sailor Doug Danielson,
expert on all things nautical,
who provided invaluable advice and counsel.
He now sails that never-ending sea.

Those who forget history are doomed to repeat it.

—GEORGE SANTAYANA (1863–1952)

The longer you look back,
the farther you can look forward.

—WINSTON CHURCHILL (1874–1965)

In addition to combat of all kinds, possible operations in
the next several years will include everything from helping
victims of a flood to restoring order in a collapsed state
with large-scale criminal activity, violence, and perhaps
even unconventional weaponry.

—GENERAL RAYMOND T. ODIERNO, CHIEF OF STAFF OF
THE U.S. ARMY, *FOREIGN AFFAIRS*, JUNE 1, 2012

Si vis pacem, para bellum.
(If you wish for peace, prepare for war.)

—ANONYMOUS

PROLOGUE

MAC HALLEY DESERVED A better death.

He'd known failure, more than his share. Three marriages had ended in bitter divorce. Failed husband. Three kids from those marriages were grown and on their own. Not one kept in touch with him. Failed father. He had owned a small barge company that plied the Mississippi River and Intracoastal Waterway, but it went bust. Then he had a seafood restaurant overlooking the gulf, but Katrina smashed it flat, and after he'd spent every last dime getting it back on its feet, the oil spill fouled the neighborhood beaches and robbed him of the regular trade he had built up. Failed businessman. Alicia, his latest live-in, had dumped him; walked out with her suitcase—and his Rolex. Failed lover. At fifty-five years of age, he didn't have much left, but it helped when he gave himself credit for his one consistent success in life: survival. His failures were not all his fault, and the fact that he got back on his feet over and over reinforced his sense of self-worth. His resilience had helped him land the job he had now; a shit job but one that kept him alive. Halley's present occupation was a galley cook on one of the many offshore service vessels owned by Dumont Industries, one of the Gulf Coast's biggest conglomerates. It was a curious combination of his former lines of work, only now he was a grunt, not a proprietor. Big difference.

The 350-foot high-capacity vessel had finished a run deep into the gulf and was now on its way back to shore. It had been his first trip. Except for sack time in his bunk, he'd spent all his time in the galley cooking, as he'd expected. What he hadn't expected was to be ordered to remain in the galley unless permission was given to go topside. This ship was not running personnel to and from the offshore rigs, as most of them did, but taking out drilling equipment. Were they worried he'd hurt himself? He probably knew the business better than most of the crew.

On the second day of rolling seas, he said to hell with the orders. He needed some air. Looking for an access to the main deck, he passed an entrance to the ship's hold, opened the door, and took a peek. He wasn't sure what he saw, but he knew what it wasn't. It wasn't offshore drilling equipment. One item was uncovered. It was a tripod and stood chest-high. Painted olive drab. Halley forgot about going on deck. He hastened back to the galley. Where he stayed the rest of the day.

That night he was in his bunk alone. All the crewmates quartered with him were on duty. The ship was slowing down and, without speed, was rolling in moderate swells. Being cooped up inside was enough to make any sailor seasick. He got up, went to the head, and splashed cold water from the sink on his face. He then went to the cabin door and found it locked. They'd locked him in the crew's quarters. The engines rumbled, gurgled, then stopped. He heard another ship for just a moment, then its engines died too. It was close by. Then it was alongside. There wasn't a lot of noise, but he knew the ship's cargo was being transferred. The silence was odd. He'd never offloaded a vessel without yelling orders; it was part of the process. When he finally did hear voices, they were speaking Spanish. Half an hour later, the engines started up. Halley got back in his bunk. He feigned sleep when his mates returned.

The next day, he waited for his chance and took another peek at the hold. There was a new cargo. The hundreds of rectangular packages were easily identifiable. That night after dinner, he complained about the restriction on his movement. A man needs fresh air.

"Go on up," the captain said. "Have a smoke."

He was standing at the stern of the vessel, one hand on the railing. It was a still night with a half-moon, and by its light he gazed at the dark water, phosphorus blinking like fireflies. He took a drag from his cigarette, leaned over the rail, and exhaled smoke. He did not know what sent him over and into the ship's wake. His head hit the stern as he fell, and Halley was unconscious when he hit the water. Reflex actions took over, his pulmonary system seeking air. Half a liter of water was swallowed with the first gasp and flooded into his lungs. Then six liters of ocean water filled his respiratory organs. His throat constricted with rigor, cutting oxygen to his brain. Survival, his one success in life, now eluded him.

The body sank quickly; fifty feet, one hundred, till it danced on underwater currents. Inside the cadaver, nature's forces began their slow but inexorable process. Bacteria feeding on dead flesh in the belly and chest began to produce gas, carbon dioxide, hydrogen sulfide, methane: gases that caused it to rise like a balloon, though not all body parts rose at the same time. The torso was the first to bloat, as it contained more bacteria than the head, arms, and legs. The body was turned facedown in the water, limbs dragging below and behind. Passing fish took their nibbles. About a week later, the bloated corpse of Mac Halley rose to the surface. It wasn't pretty. He had deserved a better death. He'd worked hard for it all his life.

CHAPTER 1

"WE'RE NOW TRAVELING AT the speed of a rifle bullet," the fighter pilot said, "twice the speed of sound, over fifteen hundred miles per hour. We'll arrive in Washington less than two hours from takeoff."

"What plane is this?" asked the passenger in the second seat, directly behind him.

"F-15 Strike Eagle."

The voice of the pilot was audible but tinny, transmitted into the earpiece of the flight helmet. Jock Boucher stared at the complex instrumentation in front of him, astounded by where he was at this instant and where he had been just thirty minutes ago. Wrapped in a towel in his hotel room in Puerto Vallarta, Mexico, his evening shower interrupted, he'd been greeted by a U.S. Air Force colonel telling him he had orders from the president to fly him back to Washington without delay.

He'd been rushed to Puerto Vallarta's international air-port, given a flight suit, and practically carried onto the tarmac, where he'd found this winged devil cleared for immediate departure.

"How did you get permission to fly a fighter aircraft into Mexico's airspace?" he said into the helmet's mouth-piece.

"Our president spoke to their president. It's unusual for a jet fighter, but our navy pulls into Mexican ports all the time."

"This must be costing taxpayers a fortune. I could have flown coach."

"I needed to log the flight time," the pilot said. "I would have been up in this bird anyway; the president's orders just gave me a mission. At least this is one thing they can't assign a UAV." The acronym was muttered with a sneer evident even through the lousy audio.

"UAV?" Boucher asked.

"Unmanned aerial vehicle. A drone. They're taking more responsibilities away from fighter pilots every day. I'm glad I'll be retiring soon. I hate what's coming. Took me two and a half years and cost the government ten mil-lion dollars to train me to fly this aircraft. Now they're teaching twenty-year-old kids to play video games. After a few weeks they're guiding drones over Afghanistan from a cozy cubicle in Las Vegas. Not what I signed up for. Yogi Berra said it best. 'The future ain't what it used to be.' He should have been our national poet laureate. Anyway, sorry to ruin your vacation."

"Well, thanks for picking me up, I guess."

Boucher had one thought. The President of the United States must *really* be pissed off at him. A federal judge from the Eastern District of Louisiana, Boucher had let it be known he was leaving the bench only months after assuming the position. His first case had caused him to question whether he was fit to sit in judgment of others. In self-defense, he had taken the lives of two men with his bare hands. He had no remorse; in fact, he would do it again if given the chance. Bringing his girlfriend on vacation while he pondered the ramifications of his decision, he had been forced by this unexpected presidential command to leave her to make her own way home. The unheard-of abandoning of his judicial post must have caused anger and embarrassment to the man who had nominated him, and now the president was going to chew him up and spit him out in little pieces. He had sent supersonic transport in order to do it without delay. Jock Boucher was nervous.

"How high are we?" he asked.

"We're climbing to our cruising altitude of forty-five thousand feet, over eight miles high. You can see the curvature of the earth from up there."

"Am I in the copilot's seat?" He wondered if the controls in front of him needed attention that he would not be able to give.

"That's the WSO's position," the pilot said. "Weapons systems officer. Don't worry, I don't think we'll run into any hostiles between here and the nation's capital. You do have a throttle and stick back there, and they have all the controls you need to fly the plane. HOTAS—hands-on throttle and stick. Do you fly?"

"Does a Piper Cub count?"

"Same principle. Grab the stick. Get the feel. Got it? Great. I'm going to take me a little nap. Wake me up when—"

"Don't you dare!"

The pilot laughed. "Just kidding."

Boucher repeated the question he'd asked the colonel on first meeting him. "Is the president pissed off at me?"

"Like I said earlier, you'll have to ask him. We'll be touching down at Langley. There's ground transport waiting to take you to the White House."

"That seems kind of late. Maybe I could just find a place for the night and meet him in the morning."

"I have my orders. Sit back and enjoy the flight."

"Yeah, right," Boucher muttered.

Despite his misgivings, it was a fascinating flight. The pilot explained the function and purpose of the screens and monitors and impressive equipment that were the responsibility of weapons systems officers, or "wizzos," as they were called. The WSO station had four multipurpose displays, MPDs, including a moving map that could show a TSD—

tactical situation display. It showed the area over which the plane was flying, as well as the location of any enemy aircraft and its exact position and direction of flight.

"Wizzos are damned good instrument fliers," the pilot said. "They have to be, with their restricted vision back there. There's probably not a closer team in the military than a Strike Eagle pilot and wizzo."

They landed at Langley AFB, Virginia. A long black limo was waiting on the tarmac, as were two assistants to help Boucher discard his flight suit, stripping him out of it like mechanics in a Formula 1 pit stop. Dressed in his civvies, Boucher looked down at his feet. He was wearing his well-worn loafers with no socks. Not the way to meet the president. It was also damned cold. He'd started this journey in the tropics.

It was after nine p.m., but there was still plenty of traffic on the George Washington Parkway. Boucher recognized Key Bridge as they crossed the Potomac and spotted the spires of Georgetown University on the other side. They turned onto M Street, which led to Pennsylvania Avenue, but a series of turns before nearing Lafayette Square meant he was not being taken into the White House through the front door. Instead, the limo parked outside an entrance to the Executive Office Building, where handlers as efficient as those who had disrobed him at the air base hustled him inside to an elevator that took him down to a basement corridor. They rushed through it to a smaller elevator, then pushed the button and the door closed. Boucher rose alone. The door opened, and a Secret Serviceman awaited him, wearing an earpiece attached to a white spiral cord that ran behind his neck and inside the back of his sport coat.

"He's here," the agent said into a microphone clipped to his lapel. As these words were spoken, a door opened and two men in suits and ties stepped out, both olive-skinned with black hair, one with a small trimmed mustache. The president was right behind them. He was herding the two men toward the elevator and frowning as if mulling over a deep thought that required perfect organization before speaking—this from a man whose extemporaneous communication skills were legendary. He stopped, turned, and stared at the new arrival. "You're Judge Boucher."

"Yes, sir, Mr. President."

"And you just flew up from Mexico."

"I was in Puerto Vallarta, yes, sir."

"I think that's quite a coincidence. Let me introduce you. Gentlemen, this is Federal Judge Jock Boucher of the Eastern District of Louisiana. Judge Boucher, this is Tony Torres, our ambassador to Mexico." The gentleman with no mustache offered his hand. "And this is His Excellency Candelario Cuellar, the Mexican ambassador to the United States." Boucher shook the Mexican diplomat's hand, and they gave each other a respectful nod.

"I hope you enjoyed your visit to our country," the Mexican ambassador said.

"Very much, Your Excellency. I only wish I could have stayed longer." Boucher did not look at his commander in chief as he said this.

"Then you will have to return."

"I am already looking forward to that."

"Gentlemen," the president said, "Judge Boucher is a friend, and this is just a social visit, but we'd better get started with it so I can have my family time."

"Of course, Mr. President," Ambassador Cuellar said, "I am sorry for the imposition. Please forgive the late hour."

"Not at all, Your Excellency. Thank you for coming. When you live above the store like I do, you keep later hours, but you don't have a problem finding time for the wife and kids." He turned to the U.S. ambassador. "Tony, it's always good to see you. We'll talk."

"At your earliest convenience, Mr. President."

The Secret Service agent held the elevator open for the men, and they both gave slight waves as the doors shut.

The president sighed and shook his head in the silent corridor. "Hell of a mess down there. I don't suppose you saw any of it where you were."

"Saw what, sir?"

"Cartel violence. Decapitations. Torture. Gruesome murders. God, the death toll down there exceeds our combat losses in Vietnam."

"Sir, I saw sandy beaches, blue skies, blue water—and friendly people."

"Yeah, well, I'm sorry to have cut your vacation short. Come into my office."

Boucher walked behind the president, took a few steps inside the Oval Office, then closed the door behind him. He stood in place as the president walked to his desk, leaned against it, then faced him with arms folded across his chest.

"Like I said outside, with due regard to the separation-of-powers provisions of our Constitution, yours is purely a social visit."

"Of course, Mr. President."

"So tell me, what is this shit about you wanting to quit after being on the bench for only a couple months?"

"I don't think I'm suited for the job, sir."

"The United States Senate thought otherwise; so did I. You know how much time and effort goes into a judicial appointment, and I stake my credibility on each and every nominee I send to the Senate for confirmation. Quitting so soon? You're making me look like an ass. I'm trying to get the highest qualified men and women on the bench— jurists who'll serve their country for the next two, maybe three decades.

"I'm familiar with your background, Jock. You grew up in poverty, a Cajun raised on a Louisiana bayou in a town so remote you spoke French before you learned English. Your parents struggled to make a living, and you achieved a fine education, professional success as a lawyer, then as a well-respected state judge before your appointment to the federal bench. Believe me, I know how much you had to overcome to achieve what you did. You're a credit to your family, your state, and an example of the promise this nation offers every man and woman regardless of creed or color. And you want to throw that all away? What the hell's the matter with you?"

"I'm sorry, Mr. President."

"'Sorry' doesn't cut it. I want to know why you want to quit."

"I killed two men," Boucher said, "and given the opportunity, I'd do it again. I'm not fit to be a judge."

"When you screw up, you do it big-time, don't you? I know you acted in self-defense, and I understand the dilemma you're facing. On the other hand, I can't just let you walk away. There are too many young men and women out there facing challenges in their lives, like you did throughout your professional career. You're an example to them—at least you were. I am not going to have you regarded in their eyes as a failure or, worse, a dilettante. I fight a partisan battle with the Senate with every judicial nomination I make. They're not approving my choices, and there are far too many vacancies on the federal bench. Some judgeships have been vacant for over five years. Even the chief justice of the Supreme Court is pleading with men of his own political party. If a judge I appointed tries to quit after a few months, they won't blame themselves, that's for sure. They'll be screaming that my selection process is a failure, and I may not get another judge approved for the rest of my term in office. I'm not going to let you do that to our justice system. You're not leaving public service yet. I've got another job for you, and it's not a promotion.

"You will remain a judge of the Eastern District of New Orleans, but you will not try cases until you are told otherwise. You will handle any administrative task that any other judge in your district decides to give you, and they're going to pile it on. I also want you to see if you can help that poor judge who was swamped with all the oil-spill litigation. I understand most of the lawsuits have been settled, but if there are any complaints, I want them going to you. It's a no-win situation for you, Jock. The poor people affected by that tragedy are going to hate the process for going too slow or for not giving them enough money. But because a federal judge who has no connection to the offshore energy industry is involved, the people will know the matter is being taken seriously. Have I made myself clear?"

"We had a judge impeached in our district. He was given a similar penance while his proceeding went forward."

"You're not being impeached, at least not yet. This assignment was at the advice of your chief district judge. He'll oversee your work. I'm at arm's length here."

Jock said nothing.

"Look," the president said, "I couldn't fill your slot if you left now. There's been a death and an impeachment in your district. One of your judges has had no time for anything but oil-spill litigation. Help me out here, Jock. When the political landscape shifts and I can get an appointment approved, you can go back to full duties, or you can quit. Do you agree to my terms?"

"Yes, sir."

The president looked at his watch. "Then we're done here. I've got family duties. There's someone waiting outside to show you to your sleeping quarters. You scared of ghosts?"

"I beg your pardon?"

"You're sleeping in the Lincoln Bedroom tonight. I figure that's a good place for you to think about the duty you owe to your country. Don't worry, there haven't been any sightings in forty years."

"Maybe I'll get lucky," Boucher said.

The president shook his hand, looking deep into his eyes. "Yes," he said, "I'm hoping you will."

Boucher called his girlfriend, Malika, on her cell. She answered after the first ring.

"Well, I've had a few dates cancel with fancy excuses," she said, "but dumping me in Mexico for a meeting with the President of the United States, that's a first. Where are you?"

"I'm in the White House," Boucher answered. "Specifically, I'm in the Lincoln Bedroom, where I'll be spending the night."

"Isn't that where they see his ghost?"

"No. This room was Lincoln's study and his cabinet room. It's where he signed the Emancipation Proclamation. I'm getting goose bumps just thinking about it. When President Truman moved Lincoln's bed in here, they started calling it the Lincoln Bedroom. I'm sitting on the bed right now. It's huge: eight feet long and six feet wide."

"Wow. I can't imagine Lincoln's spirit isn't hanging around that. There can't be too many beds that size in heaven."

"You're trying to scare me, aren't you?"

"Yes, I am. Just because your country's leader calls, you think that's sufficient reason to leave me stranded in Puerto Vallarta all alone with the sound of the gentle surf and the soft strumming of guitars . . ."

"I'd be on the next plane if I could."

"I know. What did the president want? Are you going to be shot at dawn for leaving the bench?"

"I have a mission. I'll be going back to New Orleans in the morning. Maybe it would be a good idea if you got a flight out tomorrow and met me there."

"Juan, could I have another margarita?" Malika was holding the phone away from her face, teasing him. At least he hoped she was teasing him.

"Malika, look. I'm sorry."

"I know you are, Jock. It's not your fault. Your country needs you, and I need a vacation. I was hoping we'd have a chance to talk about our relationship and where it's going, but I guess affairs of state trump affairs of the heart. Don't worry about me. I'm going to stay till the end of the week, then I'll be back in New York. Call me when you can."

"I will."

He heard music in the background. Damn those guitars.

Jock Boucher was a collector of antiques, and for someone with this particular passion, the Lincoln Bedroom was nirvana. He used his cell phone to surf the Web and educate himself about the famous collection. First the bed itself: Mary Todd Lincoln bought it in 1861, along with a suite of bedroom furniture. Originally, it was placed in what then was called the Prince of Wales Room. There was no evidence that Lincoln ever slept in it, but his son Willie probably died in it in 1862, at eleven years of age. It was moved around over the years, and there was no doubt that several subsequent presidents slept in the bed.

Pieces whose use by Lincoln was documented included four Gothic Revival walnut side chairs—the only ones remaining that had been used at Lincoln's cabinet table; a French portico mantel clock purchased in 1833 by

President Andrew Jackson; and a slant-front desk transferred from the Soldier's Home—Lincoln's summer residence—and on which he was known to have worked on drafts of the Emancipation Proclamation. A complete restoration of the room was completed under the guidance of First Lady Laura Bush in 2005. Boucher stared in awe, hardly daring to run his hands over the items that had witnessed one of the most meaningful acts in the history of America—especially to *his* forebears.

But it had been a long and draining day, and he was tired. When Boucher pulled down the sheets and climbed into Lincoln's bed, he thought of the mind-numbing boredom that faced him with his new job description. It put him right to sleep.

CHAPTER 2

NEXT MORNING, JOCK WAS brought breakfast and informed that a car was waiting to take him to the airport. He was to make his own way home. Waiting for his flight at Dulles airport, he bought a newspaper and mused over a small article stuck in the back pages. In a Mexican village not far from the border, thirty-nine bodies had been found dismembered and decapitated. There was a time when such a heinous crime would have been international front-page news, but no longer, so callous and accepting had people become to cartel murders. Even the president had asked if Jock had seen any violence from his vantage point at an idyllic resort on the Pacific coast. He discarded the paper and shopped for another necessary purchase, a pair of socks. His loafer-clad feet were freezing.

It was late afternoon when he arrived at Louis Armstrong New Orleans International Airport and hailed a cab home. An antebellum house in the French Quarter, Jock's home was his castle, and as he walked the steps to his porch and front door, it felt good to be the king. He'd certainly been knocked off his throne yesterday. As he unlocked the door, he thought again about the responsibilities the president had given him. He decided the punishment fit the crime, then opened his door and forgot about the challenges ahead, focusing his thoughts on where in the Quarter he would have dinner. It was good to be back.

A shower, a nap and change of clothes, a bourbon with bitters, and Jock was ready for his evening meal. The night air was cooled by the breeze blowing off the river, but his sport coat was enough protection from the elements. He walked from his house on Chartres Street, a couple of blocks, then right on Dumaine toward Bourbon. Mardi Gras was over, and though there was still plenty of pedestrian traffic, the annual crush with all its chaos and color was gone. With no specific destination in mind, he knew something would speak to him, and the accent was Cajun. He called the game restaurant roulette, and the odds were in his favor. It was impossible to lose when his love of the French Quarter and its restaurants was so absolute and consuming. As he walked, he admired the eighteenth-century facades, looking up at the decorative hand-wrought iron filigree on the narrow second-floor balconies of the Creole town houses. The larger of these extended farther out from the building. These were add-ons built in the 1850s, called galleries. They were supported by columns cast from molds in local foundries. He was gazing up at a second-floor gallery when he bumped into a fellow pedestrian and began to beg pardon, though the collision had not been his fault. The man blocked his path.

"Keys, wallet, cell phone, credit cards. Quick," the man said.

"What?" Boucher was stunned. He was on one of the most public streets in the Quarter, only blocks from his house, his neighborhood, in the early evening. His reaction was visceral, primal, and territorial. But not a muscle in his face twitched.

"I gotta spell it out for ya?" the gunman said.

Boucher froze; the barrel of a pistol a foot and a half from his gut. The man wore a hoodie pulled well over his head. The face was hidden, but a pair of eyes glared out, the whites opaque, almost yellow. High on something. His right hand held the gun. It shook. From the left hand, palm up, fingers fluttered like feathers in a breeze; the classic "gimmee, gimmee" motion. Boucher slowly raised his hands to his chest.

"What're you doin'?"

"My wallet. It's in my jacket pocket."

Boucher was wearing one of his two-button patch-pocket blazers. Making sure his eyes engaged those of the robber, he grabbed his lapel with his right hand, slowly pulling the garment from his body; he slid his left hand inside to retrieve the billfold. It was a ruse. His intention was to get his arms above those of his assailant. Boucher had spent most of his military career as a member of the All-Army Boxing Team and had added to his martial arts skills over the years. He was fast, and now he was angry. Anger added an edge. As he continued to stare into the man's eyes, his motions were a blur. His left hand, fingers extended as if preparing a salute, chopped down on the assailant's right wrist with enough force to shatter bone. The right hand pulling the blazer lapel was already formed into a fist and a short distance from the gunman's head, too short for a hook but enough for a jab. Elbow next to his body, Boucher extended his right arm straight out, rotating his fist, turning the thumb inward as he dropped his chin. He stepped forward with his right foot, connecting with his target at the same moment his right toe struck the ground, magnifying the force of contact. Caught on the chin, the man's head snapped to his right with enough force to break his neck. The pistol clattered to the sidewalk. Boucher crouched, ready for another swing, but it was unnecessary. The man fell back onto the sidewalk like a toppled tower, his head hitting the cement. It sounded like an egg thrown on the pavement.

Boucher pulled the silk kerchief from his breast pocket, draped it over the pistol, picked it up, and stuck it in his belt. Though not an expert in firearms, he knew that this was a lot of weapon for a common street criminal. He bent over the unconscious man and pulled back the hood for a look at his face. Blood oozed from the assailant's left ear, dripping down to form a scarlet pool on the sidewalk.

Boucher stood up. "Everything's fine," he said to those within earshot who had stopped to watch the street drama as if it were no more than a page of flash fiction played out for their amusement. The attempted robbery and takedown had happened so fast that those over twenty feet from him hadn't known what was happening. He pulled his cell phone from his sport coat and dialed 911.

"I need an ambulance. Now!" he hollered into the device.

"Let the bastard die." A man had walked up and was standing next to Boucher, who ignored him.

"A man is injured," he reported, giving the address, then answering the expected questions. "It was an attempted armed robbery. I knocked him out. I think he's seriously hurt. My name? Jock Boucher. Federal District Judge Jock Boucher. I'll wait right here, but hurry." He hung up.

"Guys like him are ruining the Quarter for the rest of us," the spectator said. "I think you did a good thing."

Jock Boucher didn't share that opinion. He'd already killed in self-defense. It was not something he wanted to repeat. Ever.

He bullied his way into the ambulance and accompanied the injured man to the Interim LSU Public Hospital on Perdido Street, then paced back and forth outside emergency while the man underwent treatment. When a doctor finally came out, Boucher stopped him in the hall. "How is he?"

"You family?"

"I put him there. He tried to rob me at gunpoint. I hit him. I'm Judge Jock Boucher." He offered a hand in greeting, which the doctor refused with a frown. Handshakes were discouraged during the course of intensive procedures.

"Go wait where you're supposed to. I'll keep you informed."

Boucher found a chair within sight of the emergency room, and whether it was an approved waiting area or not, he sat. No one bothered him. Well over an hour later, the doctor came out, saw him sitting there, and walked over.

"He has expired," the doctor said. His selection from the number of words available to convey the passing of a human being was his only concession to compassion. Death was commonplace here, its description blunt as a matter of course.

"My God, I killed him."

"Not unless you punched him in the kidneys. He died of acute renal failure, the result of a long history of drug and alcohol abuse. You knocked him unconscious, but that was not life-threatening. You ever do any boxing? You must have quite a haymaker."

Boucher turned and walked away.

* * *

"I see you're back in town."

It was Saturday morning. Boucher had hoped to sleep late. The jarring phone ring ended that plan. The speaker was Fitch—just Fitch—a detective with the New Orleans Police Department and his best friend.

"I'm looking at the *Times-Picayune*, page one, above the fold," Fitch said, then sighed. "They've cut back on the number of editions they print. I guess I'm going to have to read about your exploits in their online edition."

"Shit." Boucher rubbed his eyes with his free hand. "What does it say?"

"You disarmed a gunman who tried to hold you up on one of the busiest streets in the Quarter at seven p.m. on a Friday evening. We've had a dozen calls already."

"What?"

"Verdict's still out, Your Honor, on whether you're a hero or a villain. Businesses say the attention is scaring the tourists. Others wish you'd shot the bastard with his own gun. Here in the department, we're concerned that your act is going to encourage copycat vigilantes. Not everyone has your martial arts experience. You should have let him have what he wanted. You can always cancel credit cards and change your locks."

"I wasn't thinking. I was out enjoying an evening walk just a few blocks from my home. I reacted instinctively."

"I'm not criticizing you," Fitch said. "Probably would

have done the same thing myself in your position—if I was your age and had your expertise. Understand you went in the ambulance and sat with the guy most of the night."

"He died. You have anything on him? He had ID, but it was fake."

"Wasn't fake; just wasn't his. He'd hit a guy earlier. Probably spent the cash to score some crack, was coming down from his high when he took you on. He might have done that over and over all night long. You ruined his evening."

"I ruined more than his evening," Boucher said. "He altered my plans a bit too. You know who he is—or was? How old was he? He looked in his mid-thirties."

"He was twenty-five. The street life ages one fast. Record as long as my arm. Habitual."

"He has no habits now. Look, Fitch, I'll talk to you later, okay?" Boucher was about to hang up, but he heard Fitch holler at him.

"Don't you *dare* hang up on me. You there?"

"I'm here."

"I've got to work today, but I'm off tomorrow. I'm going to pick you up at five a.m. Got that?"

"What the hell are we going to do at five in the morning?"

"We're going fishing. Today I suggest you go for a walk in the Quarter, make up for that dinner you missed last night, and try to get whatever guilt you're feeling out of your system. You're moping over this already. I know you. Sometimes you liberal bleeding hearts need a right-wing boot up your butt. This man was an irredeemable recidivist. Now he's off the street. I'm not going to have you feeling guilty about the loss of one dirtbag. Tomorrow we're going out in the gulf, catch some fish, and do some talking, man to man. You got that?"

"I'm not a bleeding-heart liberal," Boucher said, "and it's too cold to go fishing."

"The chill will help keep your mind off self-pity too. Dress warm. See you in the a.m." Detective Fitch hung up.

Walking and dining in the French Quarter always lifted Boucher's spirits, but not today. His brooding concern for the man whose life had met with a violent end did not mix with the savory sachets of Cajun cuisine. His mood was such that the chef came out and inquired whether there was a problem with the food. Realizing he was ruining the evening for those around him, Boucher returned home and went to bed early, not at all looking forward to the Sunday plans Fitch had made.

CHAPTER 3

BOUCHER WOKE SECONDS BEFORE his alarm sounded and turned it off, glad to have avoided the annoying buzz. He got up and had already completed a comprehensive inner monologue of invectives before reaching the bathroom. *Fishing,* he cursed. It was still cold, even though there had been a temporary warm spell. Why hadn't he just said no? He could have done that. He was still a federal judge. By order of the president. His thoughts turned to audible grumbling as he showered, dressed, then fixed some coffee and toast. He heard Fitch pull into the driveway; he gulped his coffee, then grabbed his coat and walked out the back door, locking it behind him. Fitch waited in his car, an unwashed Ford Taurus missing a hubcap on the front wheel, passenger side.

"You had your coffee?" Fitch asked as he turned down the volume on his police scanner.

"Yes," Boucher said.

"Then we're off."

They headed out of town to Route 90, Chef Menteur Highway to Fort Pike. They pulled off at Lake Catherine Marina, where Fitch kept a 1978 thirty-eight-foot Chris Craft Commander. The boat was gassed up and ready. Coolers of bait and beer were waiting, as Fitch had requested of the marina staff. All that was left was to jump aboard and motor out. A large thermostat on the pier showed the temperature to be sixty degrees, which meant the day might get into the low seventies. That was tolerable. Boucher felt his frown soften into a more neutral expression. The air was fresh. The morning held promise.

He studied his friend, remembering the first time he met Detective Roscoe Fitch. In the cop's dank office with stains on the wall from bad plumbing, the air full of stale tobacco smoke, Fitch had sat with purple bags under his deep-set eyes, loose flesh hanging from his jowls. On this brisk morning, Fitch looked like he'd had a face-lift. It wasn't a plastic surgeon's knife; it was a new attitude.

"What's so bad about this?" Fitch asked as they made their way to Lake Borgne, past Gamblers Bend, then toward gulf waters. They watched the coastline in silence. Much of this area had been closed during the oil spill, rescue crews cleaning beaches, treating oil-soaked wildlife. "Some are saying the long-term damage won't be as bad as originally feared."

"I've read contrary findings," Boucher said. "Passing through these waters, I feel like a sea monster's going to raise its ugly head out of the water and swallow us whole."

There was a sense of danger lurking, unseen, biding its time. The next disaster. But the dawn rising on the gulf was something to behold, the gray sky and morning mist turning a soft pink. The water was calm, and warmth soon followed the early light of day.

"We haven't talked in a while. What's new with you?" Fitch said.

"Not much. Malika's pissed off at me because I had to cut our vacation short and leave her alone in Mexico when the president sent a fighter jet to take me to the White House so he could personally chew me out for wanting to leave the bench. Then I came home, went out for dinner, and killed some thug who was trying to rob me. By the way, what do we know about him, and what kind of a gun was he carrying? I've never seen one like it."

"His name was Tyrone Manley, in and out of jail so much you'd have thought we offered frequent-flier miles. Last known address was before Katrina, apparently homeless since then. He was just a common drug addict and street criminal. The pistol he carried, now, that's more interesting. It was made in Romania for the Soviet army's special forces in Afghanistan. It fires steel-core armor-piercing ammunition. A rifle caliber is bad news when it's used in a handgun. Some call it a cop killer."

"That was the most lethal-looking handgun I've ever seen. How did a homeless drug addict get ahold of a weapon like that?"

"That's something I'd like to know. I've seen a couple of them before. We took down a Mexican narco last year. He had one. That gun is real popular with the cartels."

"You arrested a member of a Mexican cartel here in New Orleans?"

"It's not that surprising. They operate all over the States, keeping tabs on their market—and their money. They've got cells in Laredo, Dallas, and Houston, so I've been told, and some are saying they're in Chicago. Not surprising that they show up on our doorstep from time to time. We've had a warrant out for one of the Mexican bosses here since before you were on the bench. So you flew supersonic to the White House. What did the president say?"

"I can't quit. If I do, he might not get another judicial appointment passed in the Senate."

"Makes sense. What else?"

"I'm not to try any cases, just do whatever administrative work the other judges dump on me. He wants me to help with the disbursement of compensation from the oil-spill settlement."

"I like it," Fitch said. "You'll get fed up with all that shit, and after a while you'll beg to serve in your full judicial capacity. Looking after all those folks damaged by the oil spill will probably arouse your compassion more than anything I can think of, and it will teach you the most important thing you need to know about being a judge: that it's not about you. I think his idea is effin' brilliant."

"Effin'?"

"I'm trying to watch my language," Fitch said.

"I'll be damned," Boucher said. "You've met a woman."

Fitch turned and smiled sheepishly. "Yeah," he said.

"Tell me about it."

"Not much to tell. I was coming out of a grocery store. This woman parked next to me said I'd lost a hubcap, and I said, 'Fuck.' She took offense at my language. I apologized. Next thing, I was asking her if she wanted to have a cup of coffee, and she said yes, and we did. We're having dinner Friday. She's a middle-school principal. Name's Helen."

Detective Fitch had lost his wife to Katrina and had spent the years since going through the motions of life. This simple meeting was a real breakthrough.

"I think that's great," Boucher said.

"It's no big deal," Fitch said, but they both knew different.

The next hour passed with small talk. Though the sun was out, the horizon was hazy, creating the optical illusion that distances were greater than they actually were. Even in the broad expanse of the gulf, traffic could be heard long before it was seen. A ship was speeding toward them, seemingly on a collision course. Fitch grabbed the air horn he kept next to the wheel and gave three blasts. The ship changed course after coming close enough for them to recognize the logo of Dumont Industries on the bow.

"We need traffic cops out here," Fitch said.

They were several miles out in the gulf when Fitch finally cut the engine. He joined Boucher in the second of the two fighting chairs on the aft deck. They baited their hooks and cast their lines. It was nearing midday, and the sun was high. Once they'd stopped moving, the water was like glass, so smooth that the mere plop of their baited hooks cast ripples.

"Never seen it this smooth," Fitch said, "especially this time of the year."

The two fighting chairs were complex pieces of new equipment that at first glance seemed to suit a dentist's office rather than an older sport fishing boat. Fitch grabbed a couple of beers from the plastic cooler, popped them both, and handed one off. He set his rod in the center gimbal, holding it lightly in his free hand, more intent on his beer. "It don't matter to me if we don't catch a thing. I like being out on the open water."

"Yes," Boucher admitted, "this was a good idea."

An hour later, they hadn't had a single bite. Fitch rose and went back to the captain's station and started the engine. They cruised, then tried another spot, chatting in low tones on the still waters about nothing in particular. It was pure escape. It was an affirmation of their friendship.

"I think we're going to have to chalk this up as a dry run," Fitch said as the afternoon deepened. "You ready to call it a day?"

"What's that over there?" Boucher said.

Fitch turned. "Where?"

Boucher pointed off their starboard side. "Over there. Something's floating on the surface."

Fitch squinted, then retrieved his binoculars. "Can't quite see. Let's check it out." He started the engine and turned the boat about, slowing when he was about fifty feet from the object. Standing at the wheel, he had a better view. Fitch was frowning. He slowed even more, the engine barely above idle. "Looks like a floater," he said. "Don't know if you want to see this."

"Floater?"

"A body. Shit. I can smell it."

"Remember your language."

"I'm warning you, Jock. A floating corpse is not a pretty sight."

"Don't worry about me."

They pulled alongside, and Fitch confirmed his sighting. He stepped down to the deck, reached into a storage compartment, and pulled out an armful of netting. "I use this to catch baitfish," he said. "Hope it's strong enough." He went to the side, started to cast the net, then stepped back. "God, it is rank. That compartment." He pointed without turning around. "There's a blue tarp folded inside. Get it out and spread it on the deck right here."

Jock spread the tarp.

"This thing touches my deck, I'll never get the smell out," Fitch said.

He leaned over and tossed the net, walked the railing till he'd enclosed the corpse, then began pulling. Fitch pulled the body in, threw it on the spread tarp, covered it up, then gagged, leaned over the rail, and vomited. He had dry heaves as he started the engine. Opening the throttle wide, he grabbed his ship-to-shore radio mike, identifying his ship and asking that a coroner meet him at the marina. And someone from NOPD forensics.

"White male, mid-fifties," the forensics expert said. As requested, a team had been waiting when Fitch returned to his slip. "This your case?"

"Naw," Fitch said. "Way out of my jurisdiction. But I did discover the body, so I imagine I'll be asked some questions."

"I'm going to get it to the lab. Guess you want to rinse off your boat."

"You got that right."

Boucher and Fitch didn't say much on the way home, just listened to the mellow jazz guitar of Pat Metheny on the radio. Boucher's choice; it was fine with Fitch. They arrived at Boucher's house. He got out of the car, then leaned back in. "You have a great time on Friday with that schoolteacher."

"She's a principal. Anyway, I'll be talking to you before then," Fitch said.

"About anything in particular?"

"That body we just fished out of the gulf."

CHAPTER 4

BOUCHER ARRIVED AT THE Hale Boggs Federal Building on Monday morning. He felt sorry for the security guard who had to give him the bad news that some higher-up coward didn't have the courage to do himself.

"I'm sorry, Your Honor, but your parking space has been reassigned."

Wow. A federal judge with no parking. They might as well have sent him to the gulag. The same hapless guard gave him a slip of paper. On it was the number of his new office. Boucher took it in stride. He'd been away, and jurisprudence went on. No doubt senior and retired judges from this and other districts had been called in as temporary replacements, had been assigned his office and his parking space. He was being punished, and they knew how to make it sting. He parked in the nearest public lot and addressed the attendant. "I'm Judge Boucher, and they don't have a parking space in the federal building for me right now. I was wondering if you could—"

"Keep a good spot open for you? Sure. No problem. I do that for a couple attorneys."

Who no doubt pay him well for the service, Boucher thought. They made a lot more money than a judge.

He found his new office after some searching and discovered that, presumably, he'd also been given a new assistant. This assumption was based on the fact that there was a small desk in the outer office of his tiny windowless two-room suite. There was no one seated at it. His few personal possessions had been moved down from his former chambers, so he knew he was in the right place. Three hours later, his phone had not rung, and no one had knocked at his door. He went out for lunch. No one spoke to him in the hall or the elevator. The afternoon was the same. He figured the other judges needed time to determine what assignments they were going to give him. Maybe he'd be asked to negotiate plea arrangements; maybe draft motions. Perhaps he'd be asked to serve some of the functions of administrative law judges, like immigration matters, Social Security, and federal housing complaints. He sat alone in the charmless office, waiting and wondering what he'd be given to do and how much time his fellow jurists would need before calling on him. By midafternoon, he decided to give them all the time they wanted and left the federal complex.

Angry and frustrated in equal measure, he was listening to a local radio station while he drove home. A commentator named Cal Fellows was taking calls and had struck a nerve. Citizens were complaining, mad as hell. Lives had been ruined. Businesses had been ruined. There were children to feed and clothe. There were mortgages to pay. Victims of the oil spill. Boucher made a promise to himself. Tomorrow would be more productive.

His cell phone vibrated with an incoming call. It was Fitch. Boucher pulled into a gas station and answered.

"The floater we fished out," Fitch said, "could be a homicide. Blunt instrument to the back of the head; unconscious when he hit the water. The guy worked for Dumont Industries, one of those boats that almost ran us over. They reported him missing and presumed drowned about a week ago."

"Is there any commercial activity in this state that the Dumonts are *not* involved in?"

"Nothing comes to mind," Fitch said. "You doing okay?"

"I'm being given the silent treatment by my judicial brethren. I'm switching gears tomorrow. I'm going to try to meet some of the victims of the oil spill. Anything on where the guy who accosted me got his gun?"

"I got a call from someone at ATF about fifteen minutes after my first inquiry. He said they appreciated my help but they'd handle it. Remind you of anything?"

"I don't even want to go there," Boucher said. He hung up.

Later that afternoon, Cal Fellows received a surprising phone call at the radio station. The receptionist told him a federal judge was holding. A radio commentator, Cal couldn't remember ever taking a call from a judge; in fact, he couldn't remember ever speaking to one. He might have asked a news-related question of a jurist once or twice in his career but either was put off with a brusque "no comment" or was courteously but firmly told that judges did not discuss pending cases. But here was one calling him. On line two.

"This is Cal Fellows."

"Mr. Fellows, this is District Judge Boucher. I was listening to your show earlier today about victims of the gulf oil spill."

Cal said nothing. Not a clue where this was going.

"I was thinking I might talk to a few of these aggrieved persons to see if there is some way to help matters."

"Just a question of money," Cal said. "More and sooner."

"Yes. Do you know of anyone who would talk to me?"

"Some will talk to anyone who will listen. But I wouldn't want to waste their time or yours."

"I would try to be sympathetic to their needs."

"Let me ask a couple of them," Cal said. "If they agree, I'll put you in contact. If anything comes of it, I want to be the first to know. I have a radio news talk show, remember."

"Fine. Here's my home number. You call me or they can call me. I want to hear what they have to say. Thank you."

After hanging up, Cal stared at the paper in his hand. This was the home number of a federal judge? He dialed it and was stunned.

"This is really Judge Boucher? I thought it might be a prank."

"This is really me. But please don't give out this number over the air."

"I certainly won't, Your Honor. Thank you for taking an interest in the matter."

"It's not just me. I'm acting under orders of the president."

"Well, I'll be damned."

Though warm spells teased, spring had not arrived. Boucher tried to enjoy a tranquil moment in his courtyard, but a late-afternoon chill chased him inside. He berated himself for not thinking to make a grocery run earlier. He'd done no shopping since his return, and staples were low. There was nothing in the house for dinner. He didn't feel like going out, then asked himself if he was cowed by the recent incident. That decided it. Out he went.

Dinner was close to home and a pleasant meal. Companionship would have added to the flavor. Jock returned home, not as distracted as before, watching everyone who shared the sidewalk with him. He walked up the steps to his house, turned the key in the lock, and opened the door. A caller was leaving a recorded message on his answering machine.

"Well, I'm not surprised to find no one there; guess it was too much to hope for. We're getting used to nobody answering—"

"Hello. This is Judge Boucher. Who is this?"

"Ah, a real voice. I understand you want to help us, Judge."

"May I please know to whom I'm speaking?"

"Fred Arcineaux is my name. You want to know how to help? Meet me tomorrow. You know where Pointe à la Hache is?"

"Across the river from me, south of Gretna."

"Right. Come to my boat. Ask anyone for the *Sans Souci*. Everyone knows where it is. I'll be on it. Come by anytime. I ain't gonna be out workin', that's for sure."

He hung up. Boucher recognized in his voice a malady that frequently accompanied financial travail. The man was quite inebriated.

On his second day back at work, Judge Boucher found that at least his existence was now acknowledged. His new assistant was an older woman named Mildred French who, he noticed immediately, had a strong attachment to talcum powder. The scent was strong enough to create the illusion of a dainty white cloud dispersing as she rose to greet him and again when she sat down. She was delighted to be working for him, she said, and gave him her professional profile. She had been laboring in the catacombs of the bankruptcy filing room for twenty-five years and saw her posting to this small windowless suite not as a lateral move but as a promotion and recognition of her true worth. There was a small stack of files on her desk. The top one had a blue Post-it stuck to the corner with a handwritten note welcoming him back and asking for his help on the matter contained within. He recognized the signature of the district's female judge, the opposite gender, as always, more inclined to courtesy than his own. Mildred followed him into his office, carrying the files, clutching them to her breast as if they were photo albums of her life's most precious moments. She set them on his desk and smiled. He thanked her, and she returned to her station, turning in the doorway separating their work spaces for one last smile before closing the door. Boucher picked up the first file. It reeked of talcum powder.

It was a timid beginning; his assignments easily could have been given to the judges' own law clerks. Obviously, his judicial brethren had concerns for his longevity in his current post and were not going to give him anything too demanding, certainly nothing that might be challenged on appeal, and their concerns were valid. This was a waste of his expertise and the taxpayers' money. He wouldn't be here long—either he'd be given back his full role as judge, or he would resign, despite the president's admonition, or ultimately be forced to quit. Federal judges were not intended to suffer plebeian indignities. Judge Boucher was feeling sorry for himself.

The busywork was completed in short order. The phone had not rung. He returned the files and bade Mildred a good day. She was unsure how to handle her remaining hours, and he told her she should bring a book tomorrow. It would not be inappropriate. It was just the two of them. Behind closed doors.

He drove his pickup from the parking lot and headed across the river, replaying in his mind the phone call of the previous evening. Fred Arcineaux, good Cajun name. Pointe à la Hache, point of the ax. The name of the boat? Oh yeah, the *Sans Souci*. Without a care. Obviously christened in better days.

The locale was found easily enough, and a garage attendant pointed him in the general direction of the river, indicating where the boat was moored. Boucher had to locate the exact site without further directions because no one was about. The small marina was home to a number of oystermen and their craft, and those boats were secured. The oil spill had been especially devastating to oyster beds in the region, depriving many of livelihoods that had supported generations. But the *Sans Souci* was not an oyster lugger. It was a shrimp trawler. Boucher guessed it to be about fifty feet in length. On its aft deck was a hand-painted sandwich-board sign positioned so it could be seen from the river as well as from the shore. Its two words spoke volumes. FOR SALE. The vessel's owner was slumped in a canvas folding chair on the aft deck, beer in hand. Next to him was a tin washboard tub with melting ice and beer cans both empty and unopened.

"You Judge What's-his-name?" the beer drinker asked.

"Boucher."

"I'm Arcineaux. This bucket is mine. Come aboard."

The reference to bucket might have applied to the ice-filled beer container positioned next to him, as the boat owner had an obvious attachment to its contents. Boucher stepped carefully aboard, care required because of all the loose debris, much of it garbage, covering the deck.

"Pull that over and have a seat." Arcineaux motioned to a closed hard plastic cooler suitable for sitting, and Boucher dragged it close enough for conversation. At this point, a general compliment about the boat might have been offered as an icebreaker, but not in this case. It was a wreck. The same observation applied to its owner. Fred Arcineaux was a man somewhere in his early fifties. He was overweight, his beard merely the consequence of not shaving, and the hair that stuck out beneath his ball cap was likewise unkempt. The cap was filthy, its logo faded and unrecognizable, with the bill black from dirty fingers and frayed so badly at its tip that threads hung and fluttered in the wearer's line of sight.

He wore a sweatshirt, the perspiration rings around the neck so eaten into the gray cotton that they could never be washed out, over which he wore a rough denim long-sleeved shirt, light blue in rare patches where there weren't oil and grease stains as permanent as if they had been sewn on. He wore jeans that hadn't seen soap and water so far in this calendar year, and rubber slop boots.

"Wanna beer?" he offered.

"No, thanks. You're selling your boat, I see." It was the only observation about the craft that could be made without offending.

"Got to."

"May I ask why?"

The response was a sigh accompanied by a long draft from the beer can, which he upended, emptied, then crushed. This was a prelude to his narration; not literary, perhaps, but not without drama.

"Used to make a decent livin' at this," Arcineaux said, staring over the side in the direction of the gulf. "Know anything about shrimping?"

"No."

He shook his head with pity, as if Boucher were an illiterate locked in a great library. "My wife was my striker. We made a good team. She died before the oil spill. Glad she didn't have to see the old girl like this."

"Mr. Arcineaux, I'm here to talk about—"

The shrimper waved away his interruption. "Show

some respect. I don't talk about my life without including Dora."

Boucher sat back and relaxed.

"The spill hit, and we lost shrimp grounds. Had to go out further and further away from home port. Spent more on gas, had to hire me a new striker. We were all trying to help with the spill any way we could. We offered to track the oil. We volunteered to help with the cleanup, but nobody'd hire us, who knew the gulf better than anyone. Had to let my striker go, went out alone. Caught next to nothin', and no one would buy what catch I brought back, saying everybody was afraid the oil contaminated it. We're all out there like loose corks bobbin' on the water, catching nothin', comin' back in at the end of the day, gettin' drunk together because we needed each other. Oystermen, shrimpers, captains and crews of offshore service vessels with no work, 'cept one. Boy, how we cussed them. No jobs for anybody in the gulf but the bastards from Dumont Industries. Arrogant pricks. They had runs every day, plenty of work, but would they buy a thirsty man a beer? Hell, no. They was careless too, not good seamen. In such a hurry to get everywhere, there were near collisions 'bout every day. 'Cept in my case. Wasn't near; they ran me over. Ripped my outrigger and nets clean off and left me there. That was all she wrote. I couldn't afford to buy new nets and replace the outrigger. So here I sit. Got enough cash to keep me in po'boys another couple of weeks. Then what? What am I supposed to do?"

"Did you make application for compensation from the settlement?"

"Of course I did. It got denied. They said I had a damage claim against the company that wrecked my boat, that I had to get a lawyer and go to court. Fuck that. I got money for a lawyer? And how long will that take? Hell, if it weren't for that damned spill, I'd have had money to replace my nets, hire a striker, and be out there catching shrimp. Now I have to sell my boat. Where am I gonna live then?" He looked up at the overcast sky and spoke to his dearly departed. "Dora, I miss you, honey, but I wouldn't want you to go through this."

"I'll look into the matter," Boucher said. He stood.

"That's it?"

"For now. I'll let you know what I find out."

"All I want to know is when I'm going to get any money coming to me from those who ruined my business and my life."

Boucher rose and nodded. He disembarked, stood on the pier, and waved good-bye. They had not shared a handshake, he realized. He had not offered that basic gesture of good faith, not wanting to soil his own hand. He walked to his car and took a last look at the man slumped in his chair, who did not raise his head, staring down at his litter-strewn deck. The letters on the stern were faded but still legible. *Sans Souci.* Without a care. It was easy enough to say.

CHAPTER 5

FROM THE STATELY MANSION on Saint Charles Avenue, upstairs, right-hand corner window, the one closest to the two-hundred-year-old magnolia, came the sound of glass shattered by forceful contact with a wall, which, over its 150-year history, had been repaired, rebuilt, and tricked out with crown molding and exquisitely detailed boiserie panels. The crash was accompanied by a shrill screeching voice with enough power of its own to shatter glass. The house was set back far enough from the street that the sound was not likely to reach pedestrians passing by, nor was proximity to neighbors a concern. The lot was huge. Finally, the magnificent trees on the grounds provided no small degree of soundproofing. All of which helped to keep Elise Dumont's frequent rages a family matter.

"This is one of René Lalique's earliest pieces," Ray

Dumont said, picking up shards of glass, remains of a perfume bottle over a century old. "At least it was."

"If you devoted half the attention to your business that you do to the antique crap you stuff into every corner of this old barn, you'd know why we're losing money," Elise growled.

"We're not losing money. We're just not making as much as we used to. Darling, I know you are aware of the world's economic situation, the—"

"Don't give me that financial-crisis crap again, Ray, or the next thing you'll be cleaning off the floor will be . . ." She looked up from her vanity table. On her nightstand stood a Chinese enamel ewer and lid that dated back to the fifteenth-century Ming Dynasty.

"Oh, God, no." Her husband rushed to the nightstand and cradled the piece as if willing to die for it.

Elise returned her gaze to her mirror as she applied gloss to her thin lips. She no longer focused when looking at her reflection; too many procedures had left her with a face she barely wished to acknowledge as her own. Cosmetic surgery had not given her the youthful appearance she had fought to keep, unless the taut skin of a drumhead connoted youth. There was not an ounce of excess flesh anywhere on her body. Her high metabolic rate from worrying about money was better than an anorexic diet.

"The offshore service company's profits are down," she groused. "Our oil and gas production is down. Our car dealership's profits are down. The bank doesn't make us any money, our real estate is costing us a fortune in carrying costs, and we can't sell a damn thing. Our stocks are in the toilet while everyone else's securities portfolio has doubled. Ray, our casinos' profits are down. Broke people find money to gamble, just like poor drunks find money for liquor. There is no reason we should not be making more from our casinos. We are losing on each and every one of our businesses because everyone thinks you are an idiot they can walk all over. You're getting screwed, Ray. And if you're getting screwed, I'm getting screwed. I don't like getting screwed, Ray."

His antique vase secure, Ray Dumont walked over and stood behind his wife, bending over till he could see himself in her mirror. He tied his tux bow tie—no clip-on for him—with deft expertise born of decades of experience, or possibly heredity. The Dumonts were the closest thing to aristocracy one could find in the state of Louisiana, or the entire nation, for that matter. Formal evenings had been a regimen since he was toilet-trained. Now Ray Dumont was at last beginning to lose the trim figure of his youth. A modicum of diet and exercise—and less alcohol intake—would have kept him fit, but his attitude toward aging was like his attitude toward life itself. Let it roll, the good and the bad. Though his hair was still full, his mustache still black, his chiseled jaw now drooped with jowls, and belts were loosened a notch or even two, cinching in an expanding and overhanging gut.

"You know," Elise continued, "I read that four hundred Americans have more wealth than half of all Americans combined. I know something else. We're not on that list." Her makeup complete, she took the Tiffany diamond necklace she had selected for the evening and draped it around her neck.

Ray assisted with the clasp. "What would you have me do, darling? Fire everybody working for us? Replace them with whom? You want me to put you in the showroom selling Chevys? I can't see you working on one of our off-shore rigs, or one of the service vessels. Maybe you could deal blackjack on the riverboat, or you could waitress. I don't think I could let you wear this necklace, though. I'd have to hire extra security just so you could serve Sazeracs. That would not be cost-efficient."

"You're mocking me, Ray." She glanced again at the Ming vase. He put his hands on her bare shoulders and restrained her from moving too quickly. Her temper had cost enough for one night.

Elise Dumont suffered from bipolar II disorder. Periods of elevated energy and impulsiveness could be followed by bouts of extreme depression. The symptoms had begun after the tragic death of their only son, on whom they had placed their hopes for the continued success of the family dynasty. Ray's reaction was no less acute, maybe even more debilitating because it was not given expression. The father internalized the wound to his soul. He did not speak of his deceased son but thought of him often. He remembered his last visit home. Thanksgiving. Well over a year ago. The two had sat in his library. Rain had thrummed against the beveled glass windowpanes as they spoke, a couple of armchairs pulled close to the room's blazing fireplace.

"Dad," his son had said on that early-winter afternoon, "I've discovered what could be one of the greatest hydrocarbon reserves in the western hemisphere." Charles Dumont was a geologist, an independent consultant under contract to the U.S. Geological Survey, exploring a field in Mexico. "Did you know Mexico used to be number two in oil production after Saudi Arabia?"

Dumont nodded and sipped his Scotch.

"The USGS undertook a study of the area where I've been working almost a decade ago. I was retained to update their earlier findings. There's a continuing U.S. government effort to determine how Mexico's resources might meet our future energy needs. We've always been their biggest customer, and their production is down. At current estimated reserves, in ten years they'll have nothing left to sell us if they don't start investing to increase production. We need them. If we're going to import energy, it should come from Canada and Mexico. Dad, we must end our dependence on Mideast oil."

"You said you made a discovery."

"The Eagle Ford shale formation. You know what that is."

"I know it's in Texas and that every domestic and international energy company has a piece of it except me."

Charles put down his drink and leaned forward in his chair. "The Eagle Ford shale continues south from Texas. Geologic formations don't conform to international boundaries, and Eagle Ford deepens and thickens, the farther into Mexico it goes. It might hold more oil and gas than any field in the Middle East. Dad, we've got what could be the world's largest hydrocarbon play, and it's just over the Rio Grande. Another thing—we're finding that these source rock shale formations are stacked. Below each one is a similar formation from an earlier geologic era. There's enough energy in them to last for centuries."

"I can't believe you're the first geologist to discover that the formation goes beyond our border."

"That's not my important discovery. Dad, I found the sweet spot. Sweet spots are the biggest secrets in shale oil and gas production. You know what they are."

"Optimum location for drilling. You found one?"

"I found several."

"That's great for oil, but there's a glut of natural gas on the market right now."

Charles sat up. "That's normal after a huge discovery. The price is fluctuating. Right now it's seventy percent up from its market low and continuing to rise. In the past, most natural gas went to fuel electric plants. Now that we have a secure supply, we're beginning to create the infrastructure that will ensure demand. We're finally beginning to use natural gas in transportation. It's cheaper, cleaner, than oil. The glut on the market you mention is temporary. It will evaporate in no time, and we'll be scrambling to firm up long-term supplies. Right now city buses are converting from gasoline to natural gas. DHL has converted its truck fleet to natural gas. Shell produced more natural gas than oil last year, and they are installing liquefied natural gas pumps in truck stops across the entire country for long-distance heavy-duty eighteen-wheelers. Detroit has already designed cars that can run on natural gas. In some countries it's the exclusive fuel for all cars. It will displace oil. You know it, and I know it. It's a question of time, and those who get in now will be the next Rockefellers."

"I'm glad you're keeping yourself informed on developments in the industry while you're away."

"We have satellite TV down there, Dad. I watch Jim Cramer's *Mad Money*, just like you. He's been bullish on natural gas for years."

"If this play is so big, why isn't everybody running down to Mexico like they did to Texas?"

"The first reason is that I haven't turned in my findings yet. The second is because at the moment it's dangerous as hell down there. Cartel violence has practically shut down much of the production in that part of the country and scared off further investment and development."

"The drug cartels?"

"It isn't just about drugs anymore. It isn't even just about Mexico. There's a criminal insurgency along the northern tier of the country, but they operate up here too, I guarantee you. They kill their rivals, they kill law enforcement, and they kill elected public officials. They've become transnational criminal organizations and are also active in Central America, Europe, and Africa. They've diversified into almost every criminal endeavor you can think of. They're killing machines."

"What you have down there is gang violence, pure and simple."

"The criminal insurgents are organized armed forces fighting against the state for control of specific regions. They have their own secure mobile phone networks. They've built antennas in every state in the country for their own encrypted radio communications. They've forced the government to resort to the use of federal troops to combat them. They coerce civil authority to bend to their will, or they kill them."

"Are you suggesting we intercede in another country's gang wars? Hell, we've got our own."

"You're damned right I'm suggesting we intercede if necessary. How long do you think it's going to be before terrorist suicide bombers cross that dried-up old creek we call the Rio Grande? It sickens me to see the criminal element perverting that society. Mexicans are the friendliest people I've ever met. They are hard workers, passionate about their country and its customs, faith-based, and intensely focused on family."

Dumont chuckled. "You just described a typical Republican. Anyway, it sounds too dangerous. I don't think I want you going back there."

"I'm only a geologist, and I don't take chances. I'll finish my report next week, and then I'm done. Dad, with your contacts, I know we can dial ourselves into that play when the time is right, and that time will come. We have the technology to develop shale oil and gas deposits. Mexico is sitting on some of the most massive resources in the world, and they've got an energy shortage. Because of bad planning—and, of course, the violence—they can't supply their own domestic market. We can help their oil and gas industry, their economy, and we can make a fortune doing it. You missed out on the Canadian tar sands oil and the plays in Texas. Don't miss out on Mexico."

Dumont looked at his son with pride as he spoke with such knowledge and confidence. His legacy was in good hands. "I'll give it some thought," he said. "You finish your work, then get out of there. Just make sure I get a copy of your findings. Now let's wash up and tackle that turkey."

It was about two weeks later when he got the phone call in the middle of the night, and since then, any late call caused his heart to stop. He remembered each word of the brief conversation.

"Mr. Dumont, I am sorry to have to tell you that your son, Charles, is dead."

"What? Who is this?"

"My name is Bill Patterson. I worked with your son and was asked to call and inform you."

"What happened?"

"I don't know the details, but he died instantly. We are arranging to have the body flown back to New Orleans. I have one thing to ask—actually, beg. Please, Mr. Dumont, do not open the casket. You will regret it for as long as you live."

The caller hung up. Dumont sat on the side of his bed, the receiver in his hand until the beep of the disconnected line jarred his consciousness. He hung up the phone and looked at his wife, lying on her side, her back to him. He let her sleep, got up to pace, to ponder, and to weep. He recalled the words he'd said to his son: "You finish your work—and make sure I get a copy of your report." How those words now haunted him.

Dumont failed to follow the advice he'd been given that night and opened the casket when it arrived, to his everlasting regret. His son's head had been severed from his body. The face was bruised beyond recognition. He sought out others who had worked with his son, who had abandoned the project in Mexico and returned to the

States. He found Gus Schmidt, the man who had been with Charles when he was killed, and extracted from him details of the killing.

"We weren't forty miles across the border from McAllen," Schmidt said. "There was a narco blockade."

"A what?"

"That's what they call them when one of the organized criminal gangs hijacks a couple cars or trucks, then sets them on fire to block the road. They do it when the police are chasing them; sometimes they do it just to show they can, like a territorial thing. It's a way of demonstrating to the police, to their rivals, even to the local civilian population, who's in charge. Anyway, we were stuck in this stalled line of traffic, trying to turn around and get the hell out of there, when we were dragged from our car. They marched us out to this field. They'd also forced some of the poor folks from the pueblo to come out; men, women, and children lined up on the side of a football field like they were there for a game. They were all so scared they could hardly stand. This guy with a machete picked a couple boys for his gang. Mothers started crying. Charles started yelling at him in Spanish and the guy walked up to Charles and cut off his head with one swing of his machete. He is the head honcho in that part of the country. They call him El Jimador."

"I speak some Spanish," Dumont said, "but what's a *jimador?*"

"It's a traditional farmer who harvests the blue agave

plant used to make tequila. Machetes are the tools of their trade. Please, sir, you don't need to hear any more of this."

"No," Dumont had insisted. "Tell me everything."

The man sighed. "He cut off your son's head, then played soccer with it, in front of all those women and children. Why? To terrify them."

"With so many eyewitnesses to my son's murder, why didn't the police do anything?"

"They wouldn't even take my statement. The police are powerless against the big guns."

"I can't let the man who murdered my son—"

"If the Mexican authorities are helpless against these criminals, there's not a thing we can do. If El Jimador ever crosses the border, let me know, and I'll cap him myself. But as long as he stays on his side of the Rio Grande, we can't touch him."

Dumont thanked him and hung up, nauseated by waves of anger and futility. It was in this moment that the seed of an idea was sown.

He'd managed to keep details of his son's death from the media and his wife. After the tragedy, she began to berate him for the slump in their financial standing and the degradation of their life in general, a roundabout way of blaming him for their loss. Her bouts with depression and the other effects of her bipolar disorder upset him. He dealt with her impulsiveness as best he could, even if it meant destruction of art pieces he had bought to keep her happy in the first place. Elise's fixation with finances seemed to be bordering on mania, and he did not want to see her slide into a more serious phase of the illness. Her mental instability had provided an unusual incentive of late, he had to admit, inducing him to work harder and in ways he had never thought of and in ways he could not speak of, least of all to her.

"Elise," he said. "I wish that you would not worry about our finances. I'm in just about every viable business that exists in this state, and I'm doing better than most. I kept everything going after Katrina, the oil spill, and the offshore drilling moratorium. You lack for nothing, and I make sure you live like a queen. What else do you expect from me?" He loosened his hands. The marks from his fingers were red impressions on her pale skin. "I'm sorry," he said.

"That's all right, dear. Fetch me a stole from the closet. I'll wear the sable tonight."

She stood and examined herself in the full-length mirror. Ray put on his tuxedo jacket and stood beside her. They were once a handsome couple. Time marches on and over everyone. As they looked at themselves, they shared the same unspoken thought. No amount of wealth could compensate for what they had lost, for what had been so brutally taken from them.

Rosario closed the drapes to the drawing room as Sr. and Sra. Dumont pulled away in their limo. When the car was out of sight, she went to the kitchen at the rear of the house and switched the lights off and on twice. Soon there was a soft rapping at the back door. She opened it, and a swarthy man stepped in, closed the door behind him, and took her in his arms. His kiss was urgent, penetrating, and lengthy. She pulled away only when the need to breathe required, then fell into his embrace, whispering into his neck over and over, "*Mi amor, mi corazón,*" until she could stand his body odor no longer.

"Javier, you stink. Come."

She led him to her maid's quarters and drew him a bath. His clothes, even the jacket he wore, she took and threw into the combo washer/dryer with which she was so familiar.

"I would die for something to drink," he called out to her. She smiled at the sound of him splashing in the tub like a child.

"Water? Iced tea?"

"No, a drink. I'm sure your *patrón* has something I could tolerate."

Indeed he does, Rosario thought. There was a wine cellar that she hated because the dank, dusty cavern with fifteen hundred bottles made her sneeze. There was the liquor cabinet that contained an extraordinary collection of expensive spirits and liqueurs with which she was totally unfamiliar; then there were the two kitchen cabinets that held their everyday "utility" alcohol. There were several bottles of tequila that she assumed were quite good, having seen them on dining tables of tourists in Acapulco, her hometown and that of the man splashing in the tub. She found a shot glass and filled it, leaving the bottle on the counter.

"Please don't make too much of a mess in here," she said, serving him the glass in the tub. "I will have to clean up before they get home."

He caught her wrist as he sat in the steaming water, threw back his head, and had her pour the tequila down his open throat. He swallowed with one gulp, took the empty glass from her, and kissed her fingertips one by one. "Someday you will clean only what is ours."

She smiled, having no such illusions, then left him to finish. Rosario went to the kitchen and fixed a simple meal, knowing that he would be hungry. Though she was not concerned that any food would be missed, still she chose with care. Two eggs, some presliced ham, bread and butter. She was about to serve his plate. He stood in the kitchen wrapped in a towel. His body was well defined, with the reflection from the overhead light bouncing off his damp skin. His thick black hair glistened, droplets falling on his shoulders. She felt weak at the sight of him and rushed to his arms. She sat him in the kitchen chair, then, without undressing, spread her skirt and straddled him, grabbing the back of his neck, not kissing . . . devouring.

Javier ate his eggs cold.

"Your clothes will be ready soon," Rosario said as they sat at the kitchen table. "They are drying now."

Javier pushed away his empty plate, poured himself a glass of tequila from the bottle he had retrieved from the counter, downed the shot, then poured another.

"I will have to replace that," Rosario said, "or they will think I drank it."

Javier shrugged, threw back his glass, and handed her the bottle. "Just water it down and stick it in the back. Gringos won't know the difference."

Javier had a simple solution for everything. "Want to show me this place?" he asked.

"I don't mind. As soon as you're dry. We can't stain the carpets or furniture."

"It's ridiculous to have possessions that control you. When we have our home, there will not be a table or a chair, certainly not a carpet, where I cannot make love to you any time I choose, wet or dry." He reached out to grab her arm, but she pulled away with a smile.

"Maybe a little walk would do you good," she said.

She toweled him dry, got his clothes, he dressed, and they left the kitchen, Rosario leading the way, closing blinds and drapes, or guiding him through the dark when they walked past windows where they could be seen from the outside. They knew they were surrounded by objects that represented great wealth, though neither could put a monetary value on anything, and the craftsmanship or antiquity made no impression. Javier just tutted constantly about the lack of functionality of everything. Even the master bedroom was inappropriate for its two highest and best uses, he thought. They returned to the kitchen.

"Where does this go?" he asked, passing a closed door just off the kitchen.

"The cellar. Señor Dumont keeps his wine collection down there and, uh, other things."

"I want to see it."

"I don't like it down there. It makes me sneeze."

"You're probably afraid of ghosts. Are there ghosts down there?"

"Javier, please."

"I want to see." He opened the door. The stairwell was steep, but a light switch illuminated the descent. He stepped in. "Are you coming?"

"Javier, it's time to think about them coming home."

"Then we'd better hurry." He walked down the stairs. She followed.

The light at the foot of the stairs cast dim but sufficient illumination to allow them to walk through corridors of wine racks. Javier's gait was unsteady, the result of poor lighting and rough flooring, perhaps, but just as likely from the tequila shooters. Rosario begged him not to touch the wine bottles, but he ignored her, pulling out one, then another.

"These are older than me. This one's older than my father. This is ridiculous."

The wine collection holding no allure, he returned to the stairway but spotted a small separate chamber. He stepped inside, feeling the wall for a switch. There was none.

"Javier, please. Let's go."

"Just a minute. Here it is." His face brushed against a hanging chain in the center. He pulled it, and a single naked bulb cast a blue light in the small space. "*¡Caramba!*" Javier said.

Against the wall were glass-enclosed gun racks with rifles stacked. Waist-high display cases held pistols of every size. He lifted the glass of one and pulled out a gun. "*¿Cazador? No. ¿Bandito? Sí.*" He examined the gun in his hand with a smile.

"Put that back," Rosario said. "Now."

"Or what? You will take it from me? How will you do that, my little parakeet?" The barrel pointed unsteadily in her direction. "What if I told you to take your clothes off right here, right now. I would like to see you naked in this light. You look like a Madonna."

"You don't need a gun to fuck me, you ass. Put it back now."

Javier's eyebrows arched almost to his hairline. "You would speak like that to me?" He pointed the gun at her. "I said I wanted to see you naked."

"You're drunk. Give me that." She stepped toward him, reaching out. Javier raised the gun.

The explosion in the small underground space was deafening. The single blue-tinted lightbulb hanging from its cord swung, buffeted by the sound waves. He had been holding the pistol loosely, having had no intention to fire it, and the recoil nearly broke his hand. He dropped it, and a second discharge went off. He fell back against a glass display case, shattering it. But in the second between the first and the second shot, he stared at a vision that seared itself into his brain. He would go to his death with the image of Rosario standing before him, arms outstretched, bathed in blue light. Gone was her smile, the dark eyes. Gone was her head above the jawline, the bottom row of teeth visible over a lower lip curled in a grotesque grimace. The body began to fall. Before it could land, Javier was running from the room, up the stairs, through the kitchen, across the backyard, flinging himself at the wall at the rear of the property, clawing his way to the top, then over. Dropping to soft ground and running, running, knowing that he would be running till the end of his days from the ghost of the woman he had murdered, a spirit that would haunt him till he drew his final breath.

CHAPTER 6

LIGHTS WERE ON LATE in the Dumont home that night. The kitchen light was on when they got home, and Ray could feel air circulating from the open back door as soon as he entered the front.

"Stay here," he ordered his wife. "Rosario?" he called out. "*¿Dónde estás?*" In the connecting hallway, the door to the basement was open. Rosario never would have gone down there at night. But before checking it out, he peered into the kitchen. The remains of a meal were on the table, as well as a bottle of his tequila, well sampled, which meant he'd have to fire her. Damn. He needed to check out the basement but first went to a large locked cherrywood cabinet in the dining room. He kept a key to this piece of furniture on his key ring; he fished it out of his pocket and opened it. From a drawer he took a small pistol.

"What are you doing, Ray?" Elise called to him.

"Just stay there," he said.

Dumont descended the stairs. The basement was dim with the ambient illumination coming from below. He held the pistol before him like a flashlight. He ignored the wine cellar; the blue glow from the man cave that held his gun collection beckoned. He approached.

"Aw, goddammit," he said when he saw the body. He heard noise at the top of the stairs. "Elise, don't come down here. I mean it. Don't come down."

Lights were on late in the Logan home that night. Walt Logan was chief of the New Orleans Police Department. Logan valued influential friends. Ray Dumont was one of them.

Lights were also on late in the home of Detective Fitch. He growled at the late-night call from Chief Logan.

"Sorry to bother you this late, Roscoe," the chief said.

Roscoe? Logan hadn't called him by his first name in the over twenty years they had worked together. If they had shared anything more than an arm's-length working relationship, Logan would have known that Fitch hated the name.

"What is it, Chief?"

"Ray Dumont and his wife returned home from an evening with the governor to find their maid in the basement with her head blown off. She might have known the killer. No sign of B and E. I need you to get over there. I don't want the Dumonts embarrassed by this, uh, situation. Understand what I'm saying?"

"Right. I'm on my way. The big house on Saint Charles Avenue, right?"

"Yeah. Come see me in my office when you get in tomorrow morning."

"Will do."

Embarrassed? Why would they be embarrassed by the death of a domestic? Fitch asked himself. They could not have had a better alibi than an evening with the governor. *Well,* he thought as he dressed, *a rich man's home is a labyrinth of secrets.* He knew he was being called out on a cleanup detail. Ray Dumont was waiting at the door, having heard Fitch's car arrive. Introductions were curt.

"'This way, Detective. The body is in the cellar."

Fitch followed him down the stairs. Basements were rare in older New Orleans homes for the same reason that graves in cemeteries were elevated—another reminder that much of the city was below sea level. He followed Dumont into the room of blue light. The body was on the floor, untouched. The loss of blood was massive and filled the floor of much of the room, a reflective black pool.

"You step in here?" Fitch asked.

"Had to," Dumont replied.

"Why?"

"To take inventory. I have some valuable weapons in here."

"Anything missing?"

"No. The murderer must have had his own gun and taken it with him."

"You go in there in those shoes?"

"No. The ones I wore are right inside here." He pointed to the floor just inside the door. "I didn't want to track blood through the house."

"Good. You touch anything?"

"No."

Fitch knew this was a lie, a lie he would be forced to cover up. This was why he'd been called. "Has your wife seen this?"

"I wouldn't let her downstairs. She's in bed."

Fitch took a deep breath, and wished immediately he hadn't. There was so much decay in the air. Aerated blood. The dank musk of long-fermented juice of the grape seeping through the rare imperfect cork. Mold spores so fecund in dark, humid subterranean caverns. Mostly, it was the rank scent of death.

"Got to get the body moved." He pulled out his cell.

"You won't get a signal down here," Ray Dumont said. "Shall we go upstairs?"

They went to the kitchen, and Fitch made the necessary calls.

"She knew the killer," he said, looking at the empty plate. Everything on the table was just as it had been.

"Yes," Dumont said. "She probably let him in through

the back. I know he left that way; the door was open when we got home. You can look in her quarters. I think she let him take a bath."

"You seem sure it was a man."

"Look in the bathroom."

Fitch did. The team would be busy in there, as well as the kitchen. A glance was all that was necessary. "It was definitely a man, and they probably knew each other well," he said, "though I doubt their relationship would have stood the test of time even if she hadn't been killed."

"Why do you say that?"

"The state he left the bathroom. Women might excuse a guy not rinsing the tub when he's done taking a bath, but not rinsing the sink after shaving? That's disgusting. Anyway, they're going to remove the body, then go through the basement first. Anything down there you don't want them to see?"

"No, Detective, nothing."

To Fitch, this confirmed the previous lie. "Mind if I take another look?"

"Certainly not."

The cave was no more inviting on the second visit. Fitch sidestepped the pool of blood in an attempt to stand where the shooter had been. In the ghostly light, he calculated the height of the body, then extrapolated that of the killer; only slightly taller. Which meant he was holding the gun waist-high, pointed up. Which meant a good possibility that the shooting was an accident. An aimed gun would have been held higher. He glanced at the far wall, at the height where the woman's head would have been before it was blown off her body. There it was. He stepped around the gore and pried the bullet from the wall without damaging it too much. A penknife was enough; the concrete was softened and slowly rotting from humidity. He stepped back to his previous position and noticed a chink in the cement floor, close to and possibly right between the feet of the gunman. He bent over. It was recent. Something hard had fallen and chipped the cement. The gun? Yes, Fitch surmised, it had been a horrifying accident. The man had dropped the gun. Fitch got down on his knees and took his mini Maglite out of his pocket. There was a chip in the cement floor and powder burns. The gun had fired when it dropped. The second bullet could be anywhere, and the team would soon be here. Now he'd have to stay with them and oversee every last detail until they finished and left, taking custody of the second bullet if they found it before he did. It was going to be a long night. He stood up, cursing his creaking joints, and went upstairs.

"Can you make some coffee?" Fitch asked Dumont.

The owner of the estate home just looked at him.

"I know how to make a pot of coffee, if you'll just show me where everything is," Fitch said.

Again Dumont was dumbfounded. "I wouldn't know where to look. The maid always prepared the coffee. I could fix you a drink . . ."

Vehicles were heard in front of the house, adhering to Fitch's instructions—no lights, no sirens. He went to the front door. Two paramedics rushed forward with a stretcher.

"Body's in the basement. There's no need to rush. It's not going anywhere."

From a patrol car, two plainclothes officers got out and approached the house. Fitch let them get to the front door, then held up his hand. "Something you need to do before you start," he said.

"Sure, Detective, what is it?"

Fitch stuck his hand in his pocket and pulled out a ten-dollar bill from his money clip. "Go buy me some coffee. Black. Master of the house doesn't know where it's kept."

It was late the following afternoon when Fitch made it to Chief Logan's office on South Broad Street. The chief sat behind his desk in his white shirt, looking like he had just put it on. Fitch, on the other hand, wore a shirt he had ironed himself and a tie with stains from the energetic shaking of a bottle of Tabasco sauce, the stains concealed only when he kept his sport coat buttoned. But he had showered and shaved, and his hair was combed. That was the best the chief was going to get from him after he'd been at a crime scene all night.

"I appreciate it," Chief Logan said.

"And?" Fitch said.

"I won't forget it."

"That's better."

Fitch threw a Ziploc bag on the chief's desk. Had the bag not landed on the simulated leather top, its contents might have dented the wood, but Fitch knew what he was doing. He was making a point.

"What's this?" Logan asked.

"One is the bullet that killed the maid. The other, a random shot I dug out of the wall about eight inches up from the floor. I think the shooter knew the victim and the killing was an accident. He had drunk a lot of Dumont's tequila. Probably dropped the gun in shock after he killed her, and it discharged. Hence the second bullet."

"What do you want me to do with them?"

"Chief Logan, it's not my case, and in the immortal words of Rhett Butler, 'Frankly, I don't give a damn.'"

"Do you have the gun?"

"No. Had I gotten there before your friend Mr. Dumont, I might, but he got there first. No gun."

"You think he's hiding the murder weapon? His alibi is airtight. Why on earth would he—"

Fitch held up his hand and gave a slight nod. It wasn't

exactly a command for silence from his superior, but it was damn close. "Do those bullets look familiar to you?"

Logan reached for the Ziploc. He held it up in front of his face. "What caliber are these?"

"Bingo," Fitch said. "They're cop killers, rifle caliber made for a pistol. Your friend kept a small collection of weapons in the basement. I did not examine them, and I kept the investigation away from them as best I could. There were gun cabinets and display cases. I think the shooter fell back on the one where he'd taken the gun and broke it. It looked to me like Dumont might have cleaned up and removed the damaged case, and the other display cases looked like they might have been moved to cover the gap. I think he took the murder weapon. I don't believe he had anything to do with the murder, but I think your buddy might be in possession of illegal firearms. If he's hiding the murder weapon . . ."

Fitch did not need to finish the sentence, and from Logan's next words, he knew it wouldn't have mattered anyway.

"Thank you, Detective. I'll take care of it from here. You've done a fine job."

Fitch took a deep breath, then stood up to leave. He got to the door and turned around. "A buddy of mine was stuck up in the Quarter a few nights ago. We got the perp, who has since died from complications of drug and alcohol abuse, and we got his gun. It was an odd weapon for a strung-out street thug, made in Romania. It used the same

ammo. Kinda makes you wonder. Kinda makes me worry.
Body armor would be about as much protection against it
as a T-shirt."

Fitch left the office of the superintendent of the New
Orleans Police Department as Chief Logan stared at the
contents of the Ziploc bag on his desk.

CHAPTER 7

CURLY FREEMAN HAD BEEN an investigator with the Louisiana State Police for six months. He still chafed at the nickname bestowed on him his first day, finding it neither clever nor humorous. There were other skinheads on the force, though they generally weighed in at 250 and over. Monikers for the big guys were bestowed carefully if at all. Curly was five-six and punched the scale at 140. Since he didn't want his size disparaged, he put up with Curly.

He'd been assigned the case of a body found in the gulf, within three miles from shore, which made it his department's jurisdiction. He'd already talked to the ME, who had declared death by drowning, no doubt about it; no other possibility; don't waste your time. Curly had thought this finding was a little too pat, especially since somewhere along the forensic trail, an early examination of the body had mentioned head trauma. It was worth a question or two. That was what he was paid to do.

He was driving from state police headquarters in Baton Rouge to Houma, seat of Terrebonne Parish, southwest of New Orleans. Houma was home to a newly expanded port facility with access to the Intracoastal Waterway and the gulf, and it even had its own airport. It was also home to Dumont Industries, the largest offshore services company in the state and the employer of the deceased. Curly estimated the drive time at about an hour and a half, if he didn't run over any gators. Like Baton Rouge, Houma was bayou country, Cajun country. If nothing interesting was learned on this trip, at least he'd treat himself to a good meal. Curly hadn't called ahead for an appointment.

Dressed in plainclothes and driving an unmarked car, he showed his badge at the gate of the complex and was given directions. He passed the shipyard on the way to the corporate offices. The hull of a huge vessel, at least three hundred feet, was being laid. Several smaller ships were also under construction. This was quite an operation, and Curly guessed that possibly two thousand people were employed in this location alone. Economic importance meant political importance, and that meant he'd have to be polite today. The receptionist was a heavyset black woman with a smile in proportion to her size. "Why sure, hon" was her response to almost any query. After making a phone call, she took him in tow and personally led him to the head of personnel.

"My sister lives in Baton Rouge. Name's Ruth Corey. She plays piano and sings in a bar called King Porter's. You know her?"

"I don't believe so."

"You ought to check her out. She sings like Billie Holiday. On Fridays she has other musicians with her. But if you don't like jazz . . ."

"But I do. I know where King Porter's is. I'll check it out when I get home tonight."

"I'll call her and ask her to save you a special table." She stopped at an open door and beckoned him to walk in. "Sam Matthews is head of personnel. Have a good day, sir."

"Thank you. You've been very helpful."

"That's my job." She and her smile returned to the front desk.

Sam Matthews had seen Curly from his windowed office and had come out to meet him. He introduced himself.

"If that woman ever wants a job in Baton Rouge, you tell her to look me up," Curly said, handing him his business card.

"She's not going anywhere if I have anything to say about it. Lois greets everybody who comes in this building the way she greeted you, and if you arrive in a bad mood, it's gone by the time you reach your desk. We all love her. What can I do for you, Officer?"

"Just a routine inquiry"—Curly never started an investigation with those words—"and I don't want to take up much of your time. It's about an employee of yours whose body was found floating in the gulf."

"Mac Halley. You won't be taking much of my time, because there's not much I can tell you about him. He had just been hired and was out on his first trip. Terrible accident."

"It was his first time out?" The ME's words rang in his ears: "Don't waste your time." Curly was thinking he should have listened.

"Yes, on this job. But he'd had experience. He owned a coastal transport company at one time. Guess the guy had a run of bad luck. I've got a copy of his résumé in my files. Would you like to see it?"

As Curly read the résumé, Matthews continued, "Guy did okay in the end."

"How do you mean?"

"Life insurance. We've got perks in that job you wouldn't believe. For his two days of service, his beneficiaries are going to come into a small fortune. Policies cost us, but Mr. Dumont is very generous to his offshore service workers."

"You think it might have been a suicide to get the insurance?"

"Don't think so. I doubt he even knew about it. Halley was hired on the spot because we needed a cook and the ship was going out. We usually set up a counseling session with new employees to explain their benefit packages, which can be a bit complicated, but Halley wasn't with us long enough for me to arrange a meeting. You might ask the crew what they thought about him. I never met the man. I could check and see who was on that trip, it won't take a minute." He went to his desk, tapped on his keyboard, and the printer spat out a document in less than thirty seconds. "You know," he said, "the only thing that amazes me about computers anymore is how we take them for granted. A couple years ago, that little task could have taken hours. But talking to any of those guys is going to be another matter. They're all at sea right now. No, wait. Ken Self, he's here. He's in the dispensary. He called me a few minutes ago to confirm his medical coverage. I could check with him."

"That would be very helpful."

But it wasn't. Curly met the seaman as he was getting a prescription filled. "Didn't know him," Self said. "He was the cook on that one trip. I don't go in the galley. I'm on deck when I ain't sleeping."

"Well, thank you for your time," Curly said. He was done here.

He returned to where he had parked but stuck his head in the reception area with a final essential question. "Could you recommend a good restaurant?" he asked the ever smiling Lois.

"Why, sure, hon."

He ate jambalaya like a bear gorging before hibernation, wondering not for the first time if his mental and digestive processes were somehow linked. Curly often ate out alone, which was good in a way, because he would have ignored anyone sharing a meal with him. When he ate, he thought. When his thoughts were deep, he ate till he could burst. His questioning of the seaman had brought on that familiar feeling in his gut, and Curly went with his gut—even when it was bloated with beer and boudin. The guy hadn't wanted to talk about his dead shipmate; that was obvious. The decedent had experience with boats, and such men didn't accidentally fall over railings. Suicide was possible, but one generally doesn't take on new employment with the idea of ending it all. And the first to examine the body had found head trauma. Curly paid his check and walked to his car. There was someone he needed to talk to in New Orleans before heading home.

"Hey, Fitch, there's a guy here wants to see you."

"What guy?"

"Come see for yourself. I ain't your secretary."

Fitch didn't move fast for anyone, least of all unnamed strangers. Before he got up from his desk, the man was standing in his doorway, leaning against the jamb. The face looked familiar, but Fitch didn't know him. He was sure of that. He had no acquaintances that bald. This guy had no hair, not even eyebrows.

"I'm Chris Freeman," he said. Fitch stared hard at the face. "My dad told me to come by and say hello."

"You Tom Freeman's boy?"

"I am. The guys on the force call me Curly."

"They would, those assholes. Come on in and sit down. How's your father?"

"He bought a fishing shack that backs up on Lake Verret; never leaves the place. Just throws his line off the porch, catches what he wants to eat. A neighborhood woman comes by to clean up and bring him groceries."

"Can he get around?"

"He's in the wheelchair, if that's what you mean. Bullet busted his backbone."

Fitch said nothing, recalling a joint mission and one man's bravery. "I heard you were following in his footsteps," he said.

"Criminal investigation. Been away for a while, just got back."

Fitch tried not to stare, but Curly saw the question in his eyes.

"Stage four cancer," he said. "Lost my hair with the chemo. They say it'll grow back. I'm starting to have my doubts."

"Sorry. What brings you to the Big Easy?"

"You found a body in the gulf. I got the case. I wondered if you might tell me anything about it."

Normally, Fitch would have reached for a cigarette long before now. Testaments to his abstinence were scattered on his desktop in the form of chewing gum wrappers. The urge to do something with his hands was strong, and he took an inner wrapper from a stick already chewed and folded it lengthwise repeatedly. "Not much to say. We were fishing, caught nothing, and were about to head back in."

"We?"

"Me and Federal District Judge Jock Boucher."

"Whoa. That's uptown."

"He's a good friend. He spotted the body. I motored over, picked it up, called for a crew to meet us, and brought it in. The body had probably been in the water for several days, maybe a week. It was little more than a gasbag."

"The forensics guy was from here?"

"The first one, yeah. He told me he thought he saw evidence of a blow to the back of the head, but the ME overruled him, and it was put down as death by drowning."

"Did he contest the ME's finding?"

"That isn't done here if one wants to keep one's job. Especially now."

"Yeah, I heard you guys got some shit flung at you."

"The department has been found to be 'dysfunctional.' We're operating under a consent decree while we clean up our act." Fitch shrugged. "There'll be some new icing, but it'll be the same cake."

Curly leaned back in his chair as if changing position could add comfort to the government-issue furniture. "Reason I came by, I was just at Dumont Industries over in Houma. Decedent was their employee. Met with the personnel director, he was cooperative; then I happened to meet a seaman who was on board when the fellow went over. He definitely did not want to talk to me about it. I got this feeling."

"Uh-oh."

"Yeah. So I was wondering if maybe something did happen on that ship. Maybe the guy did get one upside the head, and maybe the ME's got a reason for wanting to play it down. I know who Dumont Industries is, and the 'dysfunctionality' you guys are catching shit for ain't exactly a singular phenomenon in this state."

A folded copy of the *Times-Picayune* was on Fitch's desk. He pushed it toward the man sitting across from him. "Take that," he said. "Check out the employment section. Guy thinking like you is going to be looking for a new job soon."

Curly ignored him, staring unblinking over Fitch's head.

Fitch sighed. "Well, if there's no talking sense into you, what I'd do, if it were my case"—Curly leaned forward—"I'd get that cooperative personnel director to tell me when the ship will be back in port, and when it docks, I'd interview every man on board before they can go anywhere. If I still had that 'feeling' after talking to a couple of them, I'd get some tech guys to go over the ship as a possible crime scene.

After doing all that, I'd buy me a small ranch in Montana, 'cause I'd sure be throwing away my chances for a peaceful retirement in Louisiana."

Curly took the business card out of his coat pocket and made the call from his cell phone. "Mr. Matthews, this is Trooper Freeman. Can you tell me when that ship is going to be back in port? I want to interview the captain and crew. Tomorrow? Great, I'm going to bring an investigative team to go through the vessel. Shouldn't take too long. But if we find something, I've got to tell you that we may have to keep the ship in port. I'll see you tomorrow. Thank you, sir, your cooperation is appreciated."

"I wouldn't have told him you'd arrest the ship," Fitch said, "even though they know you can."

"Arrest the ship?"

"Maritime law term. Means the same for ships as it does for suspects. That ship is a huge investment, and it doesn't make money sitting at a pier. You've given them a reason not to like you very much, and you're still just trying to confirm your 'feeling.'"

Curly nodded and stood up. "You've been helpful, Detective."

"Say hi to your dad for me."

Fitch stared at the back of Curly Freeman's shiny bald dome as he left the office, shaking his head at the impertinence of youth while blessing the courage of the father passed down to the son.

* * *

Curly Freeman used his cell for half the journey on his drive back to Baton Rouge. He set up a team to accompany him to Houma for the interviews and the possible arrest of the ship. Otherwise, it was an uneventful drive. His lunch was still with him when he reached the Baton Rouge city limits. He didn't feel like dinner or going home to his empty apartment. He thought of the invitation extended earlier in the day. Maybe the woman's sister sang at cocktail hour.

The bar was genre Louisiana icehouse, on a back road nestled alongside the Mississippi. As he pulled into the gravel parking lot, he hoped the seminal 1920s Jelly Roll Morton composition "King Porter Stomp" was the establishment's namesake and that the singer included songs from that era in her repertoire. Turned out the barman/owner's name was Porter, and he had crowned himself king when, as a younger man, he'd tried his hand at vocalizing.

"She don't come on for another hour, but you're welcome to have a drink and wait," he said, as if there were some other purpose for a bar.

Freeman took a beer to the jukebox and studied its offerings. Jackpot. From the twenties through the fifties, it was a jazz collection to match his own. Remastered box sets offered rare early recordings of the greats: Morton, Hines, Armstrong, the big bands. He was fishing in his pocket for some money when the owner came up to him.

"Just got a call. You met Ruth's sister today, right?"

"That's right."

"Music's on me. Make your selection. It's a pretty good group."

"It is that."

Curly consumed three beers while waiting, and another six listening to the chanteuse. It was close to midnight when Curly finally called for the check. He dropped fifty dollars in the woman's tip jar. Though she reminded him more of Dinah Washington than Billie Holiday, she'd sung a dozen of his requests and performed them well. But he was wobbly and would be up early in the morning.

The parking lot was dark, the only light coming from the neon name over the door. Freeman got in his car, checked his cell, and turned it off. He started the car and turned to look into the black void behind him, his backup lights adding no illumination as he did a reverse U. His headlights pointed toward the road, and he headed home. The road was narrow, dark, and winding, and he'd been drinking. He reduced his speed to a crawl. He was humming "King Porter Stomp" when the lights of another car came up behind him. The damn fool began riding his tail with brights on, though there was plenty of room to pass on the deserted blacktop. Freeman adjusted his rearview mirror to reflect the blinding beams back into the idiot's eyes. He reached for his warning lights, and then another glare hit him from the front, this car appearing out of nowhere and aiming at a head-on collision. He slammed on the brakes and the car behind him scrunched into his rear bumper. The driver in front hit him full-force. The air bag exploded and pushed his chin back like a roundhouse punch to the jaw. He was jolted, rattled, and all that beer sloshed in his belly. He puked all over himself and gasped for air, grabbing his neck with both hands in a vain attempt to clear his constricted throat. Unable to draw breath, he lost consciousness.

Freeman's door was jammed shut, and when it was finally wrenched open, he was bent over the steering wheel, his air bag having deflated almost immediately after being deployed. The man reached in, grabbed the trooper's arm, and pulled him out, laying him on the road. He bent down and looked at eyes staring up at him, felt the neck for a pulse, then pulled out his cell phone and punched numbers. "Boss," he said, "we got a problem."

"What is it?"

"We sandwiched the guy, you know? Front and rear. Not much more than fender benders. I thought it would soften him up, maybe knock him out, but the guy's gone."

"What do you mean gone?"

"I mean he's fucking dead! Maybe he had a heart attack or somethin.'"

"Oh, shit."

"Yeah, that's what I said. What do you want us to do?"

"Any traffic?"

"Ain't seen a single car."

There was a sigh on the other end, then crisp commands. "Leave him and his car just as they are. Wipe off anything you touched and get out of there now. Drive to the warehouse and park in the back."

"Okay, we're going."

Two crumpled cars left the scene of the accident. In the big house on Saint Charles Avenue, a single light in the upstairs bedroom was extinguished.

The Russian gunrunner was known in his small professional circle as Clean Hands, and it was not a physical description. In the tight world of illicit arms dealers, he would not do business with just anyone; he demanded pedigree. He had refused to sell arms to Saddam Hussein, but he did sell them to King Hussein of Jordan, who then turned around and resold the very same weapons in a more circuitous route to the Iraqi leader. Islamic extremists from Nigeria had been clients. The pirates of Somalia had not. With expertise in fraudulent end-user certificates and forged shipping documents, he had an enviable network of intermediaries who were above suspicion and never questioned. No illegal trades implicated him. His hands remained clean.

It was coincidence that the shipment was being sent air freight from an oil-producing region of Turkmenistan and that the contents were labeled OIL DRILLING PIPE AND EQUIPMENT and that they were being sent to an oil-producing region of the United States. The actual contents had nothing to do with the hydrocarbon industry. The cargo's forged shipping documents were printed in the Cyrillic, Roman, and Arabic alphabets. Even Hanyu Pinyin, the adopted alphabet of the People's Republic of China, was represented on the otherwise nondescript papers. To be sure, drill pipe was found in abundance in Hazar, the small town on the Caspian Sea where transit originated. Used pipe was even stacked up on the shoreline and used as a makeshift seawall, corroding, staining the waters and pitiful beaches of the stark outpost, but there was no drill pipe in the containers loaded aboard the aging transport plane.

Hazar, Turkmenistan, was a collection point for weapons because of its location and its malleable, dependable bureaucracy—one of the cheapest to bribe on the global trail of the illicit arms trade. Here were gathered consignments of AK-47 assault rifles, rocket launchers and mortars, and large-caliber military hardware of every size and description. These were purchased from remote corners of Russia, from Afghanistan and Pakistan, from China, even from Israel, though Hebrew script was not represented on the bogus documents of transit.

The plane was heavy with freight, the weather not promising, but that did not deter the captain or his copilot.

Neither rain nor snow nor sleet nor dark of night would stay these couriers from their appointed rounds. The compensation at the end of the trip was enough to overcome fear. A few such runs could set a man up for life, and both members of the crew were looking forward to joining their pilot predecessors as owners of newly purchased condos on the beaches of Marbella, where they would live out their days in sun-drenched luxury and leisure. The flight plan called for them to land at the small airport in Belgium before dawn. There they would collect their cash and be sleeping in a five-star hotel by this time tomorrow in the European capital of their choice while someone else flew the final leg of the journey.

The plane left Bruges, Belgium, late that afternoon, an unusual departure time for westbound flights, but not without reason. Its arrival would be in the dead of night, that being more suitable for offloading contraband cargo. The flight plan stated New Orleans as the destination, but Houma was its target, and the minor correction would be made at the last minute. Air traffic control had been taken care of. Everything was in order. Logistics of this magnitude were expensive and time frames short. Only one representative was needed from each of the numerous federal agencies involved in an international arrival, but once these essential persons were in place, there was no going back. Plans could not be changed just because a green state trooper had decided to stick his nose where it didn't belong.

CHAPTER 8

ROYAL STREET ART-AND-ANTIQUE WALKS, called "strolls," had become a much favored event in the French Quarter, with each one surpassing the previous. Local chefs were invited to prepare specialties, and they upped their game with each occasion. Wines offered for tasting were premium choices. Admission tickets weren't cheap but sold out quickly. It was a fun crowd that created not a carnival atmosphere—Mardi Gras too recent for that to be desired—but more like a lively auction without the competitive bidding. Good food and wine inspired lookers to browse the shops, and more than a few were buyers. Boucher walked the aisles of M. S. Rau, a nearly hundred-year-old antique emporium. He stopped to admire a nineteenth-century campaign desk.

"They didn't have much of a concept of portability back then, did they? I pity the poor soul who had to haul that around at a capricious officer's whim."

The speaker standing beside him was not an employee; that was obvious from his cashmere sport jacket and Italian loafers. He held a glass of wine, in contravention of numerous signs prohibiting food or drink anywhere near the antiques.

"I was thinking," the man continued, "I've got just the place for it—unless you're interested, of course." He offered a handshake. "I'm Ray Dumont."

"Jock Boucher."

"You're Judge Boucher?"

"I am, and I know who you are, Mr. Dumont. Yours is one of the oldest and most revered families in New Orleans."

"Luck of the draw. I had an ancestor who arrived early. He was probably on the run and didn't have the fare for the next leg of his journey." Dumont looked around. "I'd like to introduce you to Mrs. Dumont, but she's wandered off again. That could cost me." He smiled. "I hope you won't mind if I go find her."

"Not at all," Jock said.

"And you're not interested in this campaign desk?"

Jock shook his head.

"Then I'm going to buy it. Maybe you'd like to come see it at our house one evening. I know Elise would enjoy meeting you. We know most of your colleagues, Judge

Boucher. Look for an invitation soon." He waved and was off in a flash, still holding the glass.

It was late when Boucher got home from the art walk, at least late to be getting a call on his cell—unless it was coming from a time zone two hours earlier, he thought hopefully.

"Malika?"

"Hi, Jock. Sorry to be calling so late, but I'm going to finish my L.A. business, and I want to come see you. I was thinking Friday. Is that all right?"

"That would be wonderful."

"Good. I'll text you the flight and time when I have it. I've got to run. See you soon. Okay?"

He smiled. It was a high note to end the day.

Next morning, Boucher arrived at his office to find flat carts with boxes of files parked in the hallway right outside his door. Business was picking up. Mildred was on the elevator just behind his.

"I guess I won't need this after all," she said, holding the romance paperback she had brought to pass the time. "Shall we get to work, Your Honor?" She was positively gleeful, and her attitude was infectious.

"That's what the taxpayers expect of us," he said, opening the door for her and hefting the first box of files.

By midday, they had cleared everything out of the hall, and Mildred had devised her own filing system utilizing the cardboard boxes, which now lined the walls of his office.

"I'm guessing you want to show them you can make do with just what they've given you," Mildred said.

"How did you know that?"

"I know men."

She was right. He would ask for nothing. He'd show them, or rather, the two of them would. The diminutive matron took control, telling him what to pick up and where to set it down. The vignette of the two would have been more comical only if he had been wearing his judicial robe as she ordered him about. The phone rang and gave him a needed break from her commands.

"It's a Mr. Arcineaux for you," she said.

Boucher's eyebrows rose involuntarily, and he heaved a sigh. He took the phone. "Mr. Arcineaux. How are you today? No, I haven't. Yes, I plan to. Actually, I was talking to the owner of the company just last night. Uh, no, not about your case specifically, it was our first meeting, but it's a start. Yes, I will. Of course. Thank you, Mr. Arcineaux."

Mildred stared at him. "Judge, there was about as much truth in your voice just then as there are cat claws in a snow cone. Was that one of those fishermen hurt by the oil spill that you're supposed to be trying to help?"

He looked around, longing for a window, anywhere he could look out and avoid meeting her piercing eyes. "I really was with the owner of the company last night, who—"

She raised her right hand. "Do you swear?"

He felt two feet tall. "I haven't had time yet to—"

Again she held up her hand. "Then we need to work harder to give you the time you need to help them. You can't lie to the poor man. You're a judge."

Blessed relief came with another phone call. Two so close together were notable after days of solitude in the makeshift office.

"It's Detective Fitch," Mildred said, handing him the phone and getting in one final remonstrative glance.

"Hey," Fitch said. "Sorry to call you at the office, but something's bothering me, and I was wondering when we might talk."

"We can talk now," Boucher said, grateful for a diversion. He smiled at Mildred. She read the sign and returned to her own desk, closing the door. "What's up?"

"I had a visit yesterday from the son of a friend of mine. State trooper investigating the body we found."

"Yes?"

"I sort of advised him to interview the crew of the boat the dead guy was on; to keep the ship in port, if he had to, till he was satisfied. I wish I hadn't done that."

"Why?"

"I got a call from the father a few minutes ago. His son didn't show up for work this morning. He and his unmarked squad car are missing. Hasn't checked in or anything. The father's worried. He remembered he'd told his boy to pay me a call."

This was turnabout: Fitch seeking reassurance from him. "I know what you'd be telling me," Boucher said. "You'd be saying it's too early to be concerned and that there's probably a logical explanation."

"I would never waste such drivel on someone I respect," Fitch said. "The kid was going to organize a tech team to go over the ship and interview the crew. Instead, he's missing, and I feel responsible because he did just what I told him to do. I thought you of all people would understand. I'm feeling like shit. He was a good kid."

"Was? You're jumping to that conclusion already? Fitch, the guy might have been in an accident and is lying in a hospital somewhere. Maybe he found the love of his life, packed in his job, and flew to Tahiti. Fact is, Detective, it's too soon to be assuming what you're assuming, and that is exactly what you'd be saying to me if this situation were reversed."

"Kid said he had a feeling. Now I've got a feeling. It's not a good one."

"Do you know where he was going after he left you?"

"Home to Baton Rouge. I spoke with his lieutenant. He was in constant communication with them on the drive back. He must have gone somewhere last night and found trouble. And no, no one has any idea where that might have been."

"What do you want to do, Fitch?"

"I'm going to see the boy's father. I was hoping you

might want to go with me—that is, unless all that busywork is really important. There's something else I need to tell you. Not on the phone."

"Fitch, I'm about as useful here as tits on a bull. When do you want to go?"

"Can you get away now?"

"Meet me at my place in an hour."

Mildred frowned as he left.

Fitch pulled up in front of Boucher's home. Ready and waiting, Boucher locked his front door, then descended the porch stairs.

"I appreciate you coming with me," Fitch said when Jock got in the car. There was an odor of fried chicken, Fitch's carry-out dinner of the previous evening, but the more prominent aroma was of freshly brewed coffee. Fitch sipped his; and a second cup, with a thin column of steam rising from its sip hole, was set in the two-cup holder between them. Boucher lifted it almost as if offering a toast.

"Did you know this fellow well?" he asked.

"The trooper? Met him for the first time yesterday. But his dad and I were on a joint operation a few years ago, a takedown. He caught a bullet in the back and is confined to a wheelchair. I think he has people looking after him, but I want to make sure. I also want him to know that I care about his son, whatever happened. He was still MIA, last I heard."

Fitch turned to face Boucher. "Might do a little sight-seeing too. There's something I've been wanting to tell you." He gave a narration of his cleanup job at the Dumont mansion. "The caliber of the bullet that killed the maid in his basement was the same as that of the gun used in the attempt to rob you. Now we have a trooper missing after asking a few questions about a boat owned by none other. This Ray Dumont's got me curious. I thought we might pass by his company headquarters in Houma on our way back."

"It's funny how his name keeps popping up. I met him at an art walk. He said he was going to invite me over to his place. You know, now that you mention it, I'm in the mood for a little sightseeing too." He leaned back in his seat.

They left New Orleans on Route 90 east, then turned north on 70 just outside of Morgan City. They said nothing. Boucher knew these bayous. He'd almost been murdered in one near here and had the detective next to him to thank for saving his life on that occasion. Fitch either knew where he was going or had memorized an impressive number of directions: a flurry of lefts and rights. There was water all around them. Lake Verret was actually a shallow system of waterways east of the Atchafalaya levee system. The day was clear, and the sun could be seen in brilliant patches through the leaves and branches of cypress trees along the shoreline. It was too pretty to be on such a sad mission. They passed competing real estate agents' signs offering waterfront lots for sale. Fitch turned in to an overgrown drive. Dense low-hanging branches completely hid the house from the road. The driveway was not deep. It ended about ten yards into the brush, right in front of the house. The covered porch had a ramp built for the owner to enter and depart. It was unscreened and wrapped around the right side. This section was supported on stilts and built right over the water. The front door had been widened to accommodate a wheelchair. The lord of this manor could just roll out his front door, take a left, and hang his fishing line over the balcony. It was almost like living on a houseboat. Tom Freeman sat in profile, staring over the lake. He didn't turn when the car pulled up, when the doors opened and closed, not even as the two men approached.

"Tom, it's me, Fitch. I brought a friend."

"Come on up, Fitch."

They climbed the porch and walked slowly toward him. Anyone could see from his face that worry had already given over to expression of life's most profound grief.

"Thanks for coming," he said.

"Have you got anybody looking after you?" Fitch asked.

He nodded. "Yeah, yeah. Don't worry about me. Pull up a chair."

There were two collapsible lawn chairs folded and leaning against the wall. Boucher grabbed and unfolded them, and they sat next to him. Fitch reached out and put his hand on the man's forearm. The touch brought on the tears.

"It's okay, Tom," Fitch said. "It's okay."

"They found him," Tom Freeman said. "They found my boy's body." The father sobbed.

Fitch's complexion turned from gray to white. "Oh, God, Tom. I'm so sorry."

"It was a car wreck, but it wasn't an accident." He ran the back of his right hand over his eyes, then forced a smile. "This is really thoughtful of you, Fitch."

"Nonsense. You don't have to talk about it if you don't want to."

"Actually, I do. Once a cop, always a cop, you know? They called me and told me what they know so far. There were simultaneous collisions, front and rear. Two other cars were involved. They fled the scene, left him lying on the road." Tom lifted his head and looked at Fitch. "They estimate from skid marks that all three cars were barely doing a crawl. My son always wore his seat belt, and his car had air bags that deployed on impact.

"He was in chemotherapy: one week on, one week off. Had a catheter surgically implanted in his chest, and every other week his oncologist hooked it up to a pump the size of a tennis ball that he carried in his pocket. The pump injected the chemo over a two-day period, so instead of spending that time in a clinic, he could work and live almost normal. During the chemo weeks, he couldn't drink any alcohol; during the off weeks, he could have a little. They say last night he had more than a little. Then with the shock from the collision . . ."

There were no more sobs, but the tears silently flowed. On still waters, a largemouth bass broke the surface. A great white egret skimmed over the ripples. Boucher studied the grieving man. He wore blue denim, both shirt and trousers, fabric softened and beginning to fray from many washes but spotless. His upper torso was brawny and his belly still flat, no beer gut, which so many sedentary men acquired with much less justification than this gentleman. His jeans rode up to reveal withered ankles, but he wore socks rather than skip the effort of putting them on, and his shoes, not slip-ons but black leather oxfords, were shined. The only concession to his limited mobility was a Velcro overlapping strip on his shoes in place of laces. His short dark gray hair was neatly trimmed, and his nails were clean and manicured. His appearance was one of pride, not surrender, though his slouching posture warned of a possible change in this attitude. After minutes of a silence to be found only on a woodland lake, he straightened up and asked, "Fitch, what did you two talk about?"

It hit Boucher that he'd been deaf and dumb to his friend's dilemma before this moment and only now understood the courage, perhaps the necessity, of the journey. The father was voicing the doubt Fitch himself was wrestling with—did he say something that had led the young man to his death?

"Wait a minute," Freeman said, "I'm being rude. You haven't introduced me to your friend."

"This is Jock Boucher, federal district judge in New Orleans," Fitch said.

"Pleased to meet you, sir. Excuse my manners." His handshake was firm, perhaps a sign of the strength and resignation that would be needed to carry him through this tragedy.

"It's a pleasure to meet you, sir," Boucher said. "I'm sorry for your loss."

Fitch began his response to the unanswered question. "The judge and I took my boat out and went fishing in the gulf last Sunday. We found a body floating and brought it in."

"You know, I was real pleased when they assigned him to criminal investigation," Freeman said. He was staring, it seemed, right into the sun above the cypress and mangrove trees that encapsulated his private world. "I knew they'd arrange it so he would run less of a chance of coming under fire. They could have let him go after his cancer. I'm sure they kept him on because of what happened to me." He turned to Fitch. "I interrupted you. I'm sorry. You two went fishing."

"Decedent had been working an offshore service vehicle. Body was found in state jurisdictional waters, and your son got the case. He came to me after visiting the company that owned the vessel. He happened to catch one of the seamen who'd been on the ship. When he and I talked, he told me he had this 'feeling' after talking to the guy, and"—Fitch paused and took a deep breath—"I told him he should talk to the entire crew, even arrest the vessel if he thought there was sufficient reason. He was going to do just that, he said, then he left my office."

"Who owns the vessel?"

"Dumont Industries."

"Aw, fuck," Freeman said. "That's like screwing with God. You don't screw with God. Not in Louisiana."

For this assertion, no explanation was needed, no dissenting opinion expressed.

Fitch had borne his burden and laid it down. There was nothing more to say, nothing more to be done.

"Can we get you something?" Fitch asked. "Go to the store, maybe?"

Freeman ignored the offer. He spoke barely above a whisper. "My son was dying of cancer. I felt so fuckin' helpless." He looked at the men sitting with him. A sneer curled his lips. "I couldn't do nothin' against that killer, but I can make life hell for those bastards who left my boy lying there on the road.

"I appreciate you coming, Fitch. I really do. You too, Judge. You're both busy men. Why don't you go along and do what you're paid to do. I got me some fish to catch."

Fitch stood and said, "I'll do what I can, Tom."

"You won't do a damn thing," Freeman said, not a challenge but an order. "It's not your jurisdiction. Those responsible will do what they can. I'm going to make damned sure they do. Now, go on. Get out of here."

It was hard to leave him there so alone, his mantle of grief visibly pressing down on his shoulders. Fitch took one more look at the profile of Tom Freeman as he sat behind the wheel.

"I just gave him a new lease on life," he said bitterly. "Now he's got something to hate."

"You told him what he wanted to know, what he needed to know. And he was right. It's the responsibility of the state police. Not New Orleans Eighth District and not Roscoe Fitch."

"Don't call me Roscoe. It's Fitch. Just Fitch."

"Okay, Fitch just Fitch. Let's go home."

"I want to see that ship," Fitch said.

"Where are you going?" Boucher asked.

"The Houma Navigation Canal runs into the Intracoastal Waterway and extends about thirty-seven miles southward to the Gulf of Mexico. Dumont has their shipyard alongside the canal. We won't have to go on their property. I'm going to find a spot on the other side. We'll just park and watch for a while. Maybe we'll see something, maybe not. It'll be like a picnic. You up for a couple po'boys?"

"I don't have much of an appetite."

The name of the vessel was the *Gulf Pride*, and finding

it could not have been easier. Fitch used Google Maps on his cell phone to locate the company's private docks. There was no problem finding a spot on the other side of the navigation canal where they could watch. Larger than most of the gulf's offshore fleet, the ship was easily spotted.

"It's loaded," Fitch said. "Look at the waterline. It's going out with the tide, what do you want to bet?"

"I wonder what it's carrying. And where it's going."

"As to the second question, that should not be too difficult to find out. With the size of that vessel, it's not cruising the shore. How many deep-water offshore rigs are operating right now?"

"That shouldn't be too hard to find out either."

"Should be a piece of cake."

CHAPTER 9

IT WAS LATE AFTERNOON by the time they got back to New Orleans. Fitch dropped Boucher off at his house.

"I'd better show my face at work," Fitch said.

"I'd better get to the office too," Boucher said. "By the way, isn't tomorrow night your date with that woman you met?"

"Don't remind me. I'm nervous as hell about it."

"I'm sure it will go fine. What have you planned?"

"Dinner." Fitch told him where.

"That's a bad idea for a first date. I know it's popular. That's the problem. It's crowded, too noisy for conversation, and the service is fast because they're trying to turn tables. The owner told me they try to do three covers per table a night. You need something at least a little more sedate, if not romantic."

"I don't want any romantic shit. This is a dinner, that's all."

Boucher picked up a scrap of paper from the console, took out a pen, wrote something, then handed it to Fitch. "This is where I suggest. Call and ask for Ted and tell him I recommended his place."

"Is it expensive?"

"No. If this woman is worth your time, she's worth the price of a nice dinner. Look, Malika is coming tomorrow. I don't know how long she'll be staying, but I'm sure there'll be an evening we can go out together. Maybe you should postpone your plans till we can arrange a double date."

"Listen to us," Fitch said. "We've got dead people everywhere we turn, and I'm talking like a high school kid with a zit on his face before prom night. No, I'm going out tomorrow. Thanks for the advice. I'll be fine."

"I know you will. Just watch your language." Boucher got out of the car. He looked at his watch, then ran to his pickup. He had to get to the office without delay and face judgment from a sweet little lady with the scent of talcum powder.

The peace offering of fresh flowers in a reusable vase helped, but Mildred still had something to say about his unexplained absence. "Everything has been properly filed, Your Honor, but the work isn't going to do itself."

"You are absolutely right, Mildred. I plan on staying

late tonight. If you have a few minutes to explain your filing system to me, I'd really appreciate it."

"I've already written this guide"—she held up a piece of paper. "It explains everything, but sure, let me show you. Oh, wait, I almost forgot. This came for you by messenger."

She handed him a sealed envelope. Fine stationery. Not office supply. Certainly not a government document. He opened the gummed lip and pulled out an invitation with a coat of arms embossed in gold, beneath which, in florid script, was one word: DUMONT. He and a guest were invited to dinner Saturday. Smoking. RSVP. He stared, puzzled.

"Something wrong?" Mildred asked.

"It's a dinner invitation. It says 'smoking.'" He showed her the card. "I don't smoke."

Mildred tittered. "It means that you are requested to wear a smoking jacket. I haven't seen this term used in quite a while. A smoking jacket is what Hugh Hefner wears with his pajamas, but in Europe—on the continent, at least— what many call a 'smoking' is what we would call a tuxedo jacket. Like the white one Humphrey Bogart wore in *Casablanca*. I would say the dress requirement is a step up from a business suit. Who are these . . . Oh, the Dumonts. Now I understand. They were never ones to shy away from pretension, those Dumonts."

"So you think I should rent a tuxedo for this dinner?"

"If you don't own a white tuxedo jacket, I would suggest you purchase one. I think every gentleman should have both a black tuxedo and a white tux jacket in his wardrobe. White is especially useful in this climate. You can wear it with black dress slacks if you don't own a tuxedo."

"Thank you for your advice."

"I do have another suggestion. Do you plan to bring a date?"

"Yes."

"Then you should encourage her to bedazzle them. The Dumonts are hard to impress, but when it happens, they don't forget."

"It sounds like you know them."

"Ray Dumont's uncle was mad about me when I was young. I led him on, then dropped him for the man I married." She tossed her head and looked up for a moment, gazing somewhere in her distant past. Boucher recognized the aspect of one who once was the belle of the ball. The reminiscence faded. "This day is almost done," she said. "May I respectfully suggest that you get busy?"

"Yes, ma'am."

"Don't call me 'ma'am.' 'Ma'am' is for old maids."

Mildred explained her filing system, which was logical and simple. She offered to work late, but Boucher was adamant in his refusal. He was looking forward to a little solitude and some hard work. The total silence heightened his concentration, and though the tasks were insulting to his intellect and ability, they had to be done. They would have been just as demeaning to the judge who assigned

them. He gave his best effort to chores that he too would
have delegated to others. More than once he came across a
seemingly insignificant detail that could have had larger re-
percussions in a case. Several times he caught minute errors
that could have sent a contested matter in a wrong direction. And over the hours he once again came to appreciate
the details of jurisprudence, the intricacies that seemed so
tedious but, when ignored, could lead to errors, even abuse
of the system. Once again he was honing that tool he'd valued as a younger man, but which had become dull due, he
had to admit, to his own arrogance. That invaluable tool? A
fine-tooth comb.

It was after three a.m. when the ink began swimming
before his eyes and he had to call it quits. The federal marshal looked at him curiously as he left the building and
walked alone to the parking lot. Boucher's Ford F-150 was
right there in the prime spot, under lights, safe and sound.
Earlier that evening it had been under surveillance by a man
who was unable to match Judge Boucher's late-night stam-
ina, a man who had already gone to his rest. His mission not
accomplished this evening, he would bide his time.

Boucher had set his internal clock to wake him the next
morning, and it did almost to the minute. Having worked
as late as he had, he felt no compunction to race and instead
fixed himself a breakfast of fried egg with runny yolk, one

piece of buttered toast, and freshly ground coffee made with his French press. The only thing missing was fresh juice. After sponging his plate clean of yolk with the toast, he slowly enjoyed a second cup of coffee while he watched news on the small TV he kept in the kitchen. Then it was the morning mechanics, push-ups, sit-ups, shower, shave, and dress, then out. Mildred was beaming when he got to his office. She didn't need to say a thing; "that's more like it" was written all over her face.

"I'll need to return some of these files to the respective judges now that you've finished them," she said, swooping an armful of manila folders into her arms. "I'll be gone a while. Is there anything I can get you?"

"Do you think they have orange juice in the cafeteria vending machines?" Boucher asked.

"I'm sure it's not fresh, but I'll see what they have," she said. "You don't mind answering your phone while I'm gone?"

"Not at all."

Boucher had no problem making his own calls either. He picked up the phone and dialed the number of the oil-spill claims administrator. He identified himself. The woman put him on hold, then came back online.

"I'm sorry sir, but Mr. Thompson is—"

"You tell Mr. Thompson that District Judge Jock Boucher will be in his office at ten o'clock Monday morning to review each and every disbursement he has made to date and to review his procedures as well. If he is not there, he will be meeting me on my territory, the subject of a bench warrant. Is that clear?"

"Yes, sir."

"Fine. See you Monday. Have a nice weekend." He hung up the phone rather forcefully. It felt good.

He neither made nor received another phone call for the rest of the working day, with the exception of a text message from Malika, confirming her flight arrival time that evening. With new application to the work he had disparaged, Boucher basked in the adulation of his assistant for the remainder of the day as he churned out document after document. The hours sped. It was five o'clock.

"Mildred," he said, "I think we've earned our salaries today. Let's close up shop."

"I can stay," she offered.

"But I cannot. My girlfriend is flying in this evening."

"Oh" was all she said, and began clearing her desk.

His ears perked at what might have been the flat tone of disappointment; then he realized it was Friday syndrome. Lonely people whose jobs are the center of their lives don't always look forward to weekends.

"I'll have to come in early Monday," he said, "and get a few more things finished. I have a ten o'clock meeting with the administrator of the oil-spill funds."

"I can be here early if you need me."

"It would be helpful, but I don't want to impose."

"It's no imposition at all. I'll be here at eight."

He bade her a good weekend and left her to lock up. She was already gearing up for Monday's early start.

He walked to the parking lot. The man who'd missed him last night now walked right past him, looking down, his hat covering his face. Their shoulders almost touched. At any spot along the city blocks between the federal complex and the public parking lot, he could have done it. A gun or a knife; either would have worked. Each had pros and cons. The gun's benefits were obvious, but heads turned instinctively at the sound of a gunshot. They'd be turning and staring at him the moment the bullet was entering Boucher's body. The knife was silent, but the physical aspect made many shun its use as a murder weapon. Boucher was fit, that was obvious. Against the judge's fitness weighed the element of surprise. Fitness was not a factor when you didn't see it coming. He watched Boucher drive away in his gray pickup. He knew where the judge was going, and at his own pace, he'd follow him there. There was no hurry. Trying to conceive, to construct, the perfect opportunity had given him a sense of purpose he'd never known. He'd almost hate to see it come to an end. But it would. And soon.

They had reached an understanding early in their relationship. Malika did not expect to be picked up at the airport.

She traveled light and had no problem with taxis. Their reunions took place not in public but behind the closed doors of Boucher's home. All was ready when he heard the taxi pull up out front. He'd chilled the champagne; an assortment of fruits and cheeses were plated and prepared to serve. He had bought and arranged flowers, putting the roses aside for special use. From the vermilion blooms, he'd plucked petals and strewn them in a trail from the doorway, across the living room floor, and down the hallway to the bedroom. He turned down the duvet and scattered rose petals across his fine cotton sheets. On the nightstands were two scented candles. Their purchase had caused him no small amount of reflection as he had stood in the small specialty shop and asked himself: Was cinnamon sexy? It reminded him of breakfast as a child, saved for special mornings. Bread going stale was toasted rather than thrown away, spread with soft butter, and the spice mixed with sugar was sprinkled on each warm slice. Running to the table whenever it was served was a delightful memory. He lit the candles. Once again the scent of the spice inspired a hunger—but this time not one born of childhood reminiscences. He was dressed simply in chinos, blue oxford shirt, and loafers, no socks—one less article of clothing to remove if this reunion held true to form. He would know soon enough.

"Hi, stranger." Malika stood in the doorway for a second and stepped inside. The taxi driver was right behind her and set her single piece of luggage inside the door, then closed it and departed.

Beyond radiant, the woman glowed. Her dark brown hair fell over her shoulders, on which was draped a red scoop-neck dress of layered silk, no jewelry. Her footwear: six-inch stiletto pumps, the bold color matching her dress. She reached behind her back, and the dress fell to her feet like a feather, revealing her in all her loveliness. Jock stood in stunned silence as he stared at her soft skin, the hue of cinnamon, the color that had subliminally dictated his candle choice. He raised his hand to his chin to make sure his mouth was not gaping, recalled that breathing was an essential life function, and gasped at her beauty.

"You'll have to come to me," Malika said. "I'm not taking another step in these things."

He fumbled awkwardly at his shirt, then ripped it from his body, sending buttons flying in all directions. He was more adept with his trousers, which fell to the floor as he slipped off his loafers and walked to her. He picked her up in his arms and carried her along the red-petal trail to the bedroom, placing her gently on the bed against a mound of pillows.

"Candles and rose petals," she said. "Very well done, Jo—" The last consonant was lost as his lips came crushing down on hers.

Hours later, passion spent, they sat before the fireplace in terry-cloth robes, sipping champagne, the traditional finale to their reunion and commencement of their "together again" stage.

"I've missed you so much," Boucher said.

"I was beginning to wonder."

"Well, wonder no more. To prove my love, I'll sip champagne from your slipper." He picked up one of the six-inch heels.

"Sip away. I won't be wearing those again."

He examined the shoe. "I can't believe you wore these in the airport."

"I didn't," she said. "I slipped into the dress in the ladies' room after we landed, and I put the shoes on in the taxi. I wanted to get your mind away from wherever it's been lately. You've sounded so disconnected."

Boucher sighed. "Can we talk about it in the morning? You just got here."

She ran her fingertips across his cheek. "We don't have to talk about it at all. What I was saying is that I want to pull you away from that world, if I can. There's a sadness in your eyes, Jock. I don't know how it got there. Maybe I don't want to know."

He kissed her fingertips and changed the subject. "We're invited to dinner tomorrow night at the home of the richest family in New Orleans, the Dumonts. The invitation calls for a smoking, which my assistant tells me really means a tuxedo jacket."

"They call them that in Europe. Jock, I don't have anything formal."

"And I don't own a tux. I know it's an imposition, but

would you mind if we spent our first day together shopping?"

Malika smiled and reached for her champagne. "I guess every relationship requires sacrifice, doesn't it? Besides, I need to buy you a new shirt."

The man had been watching the house when the taxi pulled up and the woman got out. He sauntered away, unhurried, unfazed. Time was on his side.

CHAPTER 10

SHOPPING IS A GOOD test of a relationship. Enduring the ordeal, even finding humor in it, is a good indication of how a couple will fare with sterner challenges. They survived their day at the malls. For the evening with the Dumonts, Malika chose a black silk strapless gown and black satin flats with a crystal ornament. The lady did protest but then accepted Jock's gift of a diamond necklace with matching earrings. His jacket was a perfect fit. He remarked on the number of pockets in the lining.

"It's a smoker," Malika said. "You have a pocket for a cigarette case, one for your lighter, and one for your cards of introduction, usually carried in a case of gold or silver. There are often pockets for a *portefeuille*, that's French for billfold, for glasses, and pen."

"I do have a billfold. I guess I could carry my cell phone in one of the other pockets."

"There you go."

His new white tux jacket brought on a very bad Bogart impression when he put it on that evening. "Here's looking at you, kid," he said upon the arrival of the chauffeured limo the Dumonts had sent for them.

"I hate myself every time I use the word, but wow," Malika said as the limousine pulled up to the entrance of the Dumont home. They rang the bell and were granted entry by a uniformed butler who could have walked off the stage of a British sitcom but for his pure New Orleans accent, distinctly Southern but with an insouciant elongation of vowels that reminded her a bit of the South Jersey shore.

"Cocktails are being served in the solarium," the butler said, and motioned for them to follow.

They passed through a large salon, then a dining room with mural-covered walls. Doors were almost hidden, as the murals were painted over them also, and crystal doorknobs were barely visible. The butler opened a door and led them to the solarium. It was a glass-paneled pavilion and the largest room yet, verdant with plant life. There were potted palms of numerous varieties and hanging planters filled with orchids. White rattan furniture was placed throughout. The room was filled with the scent of blooming flowers. The Dumonts stood in a far corner, looking out toward their massive backyard, where dancing lights played on a huge fountain. They turned when their guests were announced by the butler. Ray Dumont held a martini glass in his right hand, and his left was slipped into the patch pocket of his black tuxedo jacket, thumb overhanging. Elise Dumont sipped through lips frozen in a half-smile. Her diamonds sparkled from fifty feet away as if a spotlight had been beamed at her for just that purpose. Ray Dumont put his left index finger to his lips and motioned for them to come forward. His greeting was whispered. "Welcome. There's a raccoon at the fountain. Look."

It was hard to tell just what the creature was doing— washing, preening, or drinking—but it stood on the ledge of the fountain in a proprietary manner, either oblivious to or unconcerned with the fact that it was so visible. A light rain had just begun, and the grounds were a glistening wonderland with uplights strategically placed at the trunks of ancient magnolias, casting filtered beams of blue, pink, and purple on the green canopy. It looked like a Disney animation. The raccoon raised its masked head, looked directly at the two couples, then scampered away. Ray continued to stare in wonder as Elise spoke.

"He's a nature nut. He'd have an African safari out there if the city would allow it. Hi, I'm Elise. My, you two are a striking couple."

A more cordial beginning to an evening could not have been imagined. Prepared for an icy formality to match the dress code, Jock and Malika were immediately won over by their hosts' easy manner. When Malika hesitated at the offer of a vodka martini from the ready-to-serve premixed pitcher, Elise didn't miss a beat. "Hon, you look more like the champagne type." She motioned to the butler, and before you could say Cristal Brut, Malika was holding a Baccarat flute.

"Judge Boucher is our most recently appointed federal judge," Ray said to his wife, a fact obviously intended to draw a respectful response.

"And an expert in self-defense," Elise said. "I read about your little sidewalk altercation. I bet our street scum will think twice before tangling with you again, Judge. I hope you're as decisive with them in the courtroom."

"I'm not trying cases at the moment," Boucher said, his discomfort obvious.

"Why not, for heaven's sake?" said Elise. "A man who puts criminals in their place as effectively as you did? We need more like you."

"I'm sure the judge doesn't want to talk about his professional duties," Ray Dumont said.

"I don't mind," Boucher said. "I'm restricted to administrative matters temporarily."

Dumont turned to Malika and changed the subject. "That's such a pretty name. Where are you from?"

Malika told them she'd been born in Mumbai and schooled in London and New England. Her unique multinational background became the focus of the cocktail conversation, till the butler informed them that dinner was ready. When all were seated, Ray took charge, first stating that everything on their plates was locally produced: homegrown vegetables, gulf seafood, and a saddleback of venison, the deer shot on one of his properties. The wines had both domestic and international provenance; Dumont was an oenophile, delighting in his knowledge. Each selection had been chosen with care, and he explained the reason for each choice. Far from pompous, his discourse added an element of enjoyment to the meal and expanded the knowledge of his appreciative guests. Even the liqueurs he offered after dessert were selected with purpose. When the cordial glasses were served, he asked Boucher, "Would you like to see that campaign desk I bought at Rau's? I haven't confirmed it yet, but I might have an historical piece."

"I'd love to see it."

The gentlemen left the ladies involved in a conversation of their own.

Dumont's study was on the ground floor, and though it did not look onto the backyard, the side view was well landscaped and equally attractive. There was an alcove off the study, a sitting area where the desk was placed. He turned on a light, and they examined the piece.

"Did you know," Dumont began, "that from 1810 to 1840, New Orleans had more free black craftsmen than any other city in the United States? An artisan by the name of Jean Rousseau had the most apprentice contracts with freemen of color. This piece might be one of his earliest. But look here." Dumont pulled out the central drawer. On the inside of the drawer was carved something barely legible. "I looked at it under black light. It says 'Capt. W.S. U.S.A. 1811.' In 1811, Winfield Scott served as a captain under General Wade Hampton. Right here in New Orleans. Winfield Scott. He became the greatest general of his age, maybe better than Napoleon. In March 1847, with a force of eighty-five hundred men, he landed at Veracruz, then marched to capture Mexico City, the largest capital in the Western world at the time. He later governed the country, and his leadership was exemplary. I can't help but think that if we had someone like him now . . ." He let the thought dangle. "Anyway, if this desk was his . . ."

"You'd have a national treasure," Boucher said, excited at the possibility and sorry that he had passed it by.

"It's a guess at this point," Dumont said. "But just the thought: the desk that might have belonged to General Winfield Scott."

The two men stood in silence. Dumont put a hand on Boucher's shoulder. "Judge, may I ask you a personal question?" Boucher nodded. "I heard frustration in your voice earlier over your current assignments. Hypothetically, if you were to leave the bench, what would you do?"

"Go back to practicing law, I guess. Though the thought of the years involved in building a practice doesn't hold much appeal for me."

Dumont stroked his chin. "The general counsel of

Dumont Industries is nearing retirement. I'll be looking for a replacement. Would that appeal to you? It's as diverse a workload as most law firms, I can guarantee you that. It would be far better than the administrative penance you are now forced to endure."

"It's an interesting proposition."

"Think about it. Shall we rejoin the ladies? Malika is absolutely stunning. I can tell Elise likes her too, and that's not an everyday occurrence. I do hope we'll be able to spend more time together, the four of us."

"I'm sure we'd enjoy that."

They arrived back at the dining table.

"Ray, guess what?" Elise said. "Malika has never been to a casino. Never. We've got to take them to the showboat."

"That's a great idea," Ray said. "How about one night next week?"

"I've got a lot of work—" Boucher said.

"Oh, come on. We'll have an early dinner, catch the show, and lose a little money in any way you choose. You've got to lose, though; in this economy, we're having a hard time keeping the old tub afloat. Set yourself a limit, that's what I do, and when it's gone, the evening is over, and we've all had a good time. What do you say?"

"Monday's fine with me." Boucher looked at Malika. She nodded.

"Monday it is, then. We'll pick you up. The party starts in our limo."

"No," Jock said. "If you're coming to my home, we'll have drinks there before going out. Malika and I insist."

"That's fine too."

There was a shared exuberance, the high point of the evening having just been reached. Ray called for the driver, and they said good-byes at the door. The rain had stopped.

"See you Monday," the Dumonts said as their guests bundled themselves into the limousine. They waved as the car pulled away from the house, then they stepped inside, closing the door behind them.

"How'd we do?" Elise asked.

"Brilliant. We worked our magic."

"Was it worth it? I mean, he's just another judge."

"Maybe more than that," Ray said. "He might leave the bench; he's not happy there. A former federal judge with his contacts? I could always use a man like that."

They were silent on the short drive home, but Malika spoke the instant they entered the house. "I was confused by what you said when we were introduced. What was all that about?"

"Something happened the night I returned from Washington. We'll talk about it later. What did you two discuss?"

"Ayurvedic medicine and transcendental meditation," Malika said, walking away from him toward the bedroom.

"She assumed I knew all about them because I was born in India."

"Do you?" He locked the front door and followed her.

"Jock, my father is a doctor of nuclear medicine. I tried to be polite."

"You didn't like her."

"I wouldn't say that. I just thought they were trying too hard. Didn't you think it was all a bit much?"

"I thought they were acting like rich folks do."

"You're not exactly poor. You don't act like that."

"I'm not in their league, not by a long shot."

"I think they're too concerned with wealth. For some people, there's never enough. But I liked them fine. I'll be happy to spend time with them, if you want."

Jock got into bed and turned out the light. In the dark, Malika said, "She said something curious to me."

"Hmmm?"

"She said to excuse her husband if he drinks too much. It's the way he compensates for the loss of his son."

"That's strange," Jock said in the darkness. "He said exactly the same thing to me about her."

"Let's go to sleep."

Next morning Jock fixed a pot of coffee and sat at the kitchen table while Malika showered. The sun was rising over the former slave quarters at the rear of the property. Boucher stared at the second-story banister, recently repaired. He had crashed through it, taking two murderers intent on killing him to their well-deserved deaths only a few months ago. He thought of the street criminal, now dead, against whom he had defended himself. He thought of the man they had fished from the gulf. He had not even thought to ask his name. Then there was the crippled father whose son was dead, the circumstances curious. He poured himself a cup of coffee and noticed his hand was shaking.

"Good morning," Malika said. She sat down and put her hand on his arm. "If you want to talk, I'm ready, Jock."

As if he'd been given a reprieve by a higher power, his landline rang. He got up to answer the retro kitchen wall phone with its spiral cord.

"This is Fitch. I didn't want to bother you, but I thought you should know this. I had a friend do some research for me. There are hundreds of active offshore rigs in the gulf and many others shut down, due to lack of production or destruction by Katrina or Rita. There are lots of offshore service vessels, but Dumont is the big player. He's got a lock on servicing the deep-water rigs."

"If that's what the ship we saw is being used for, then it's perfectly legitimate."

"Guess so. Something's still bugging me, though. Anyway, sorry to interrupt, I know you've got company."

"Is anything being done concerning that young man whose father we met?"

"I'm sorry. Jock, I'm shut out on that one."

"I had dinner with the Dumonts last night, and we're going to their riverboat casino with them tomorrow evening."

"No shit. You be careful around that guy."

"I will. Thanks for calling, Fitch." He hung up the phone. "Malika, there's something I try to do on Sundays. I'd like to have you join me."

"What's that?"

"I drive around storm-damaged neighborhoods. Sometimes I pick up trash and haul it off. Sometimes I see somebody trying to patch together what they can, and I try to help. I never have a grand plan, just drive out, do a little something, drive back. That's all."

"I'm ready when you are," she said.

Driving through St. Barnard Parish, they spotted a group of volunteers rebuilding homes. Jock asked if they could join in, and they were graciously welcomed. At the end of a satisfying afternoon, he wrote them a check for their charitable efforts.

"That was rewarding," Malika said on their drive home. "Jock, folks in this town are certainly resilient."

"I have my own word for the people of New Orleans."

"What's that?"

"Indomitable."

CHAPTER 11

BOUCHER GOT TO HIS office early Monday morning. There were new boxes of files inside his office, stacked high against the wall. Mildred was at her desk.

"They say be careful what you pray for," she said. "I'm afraid my prayers have been answered."

"I'm glad the good Lord's taken a liking to you. You can put in a word for me."

He hurried through documents, then made his exit for his previously scheduled appointment. He was on time. The administrator wasn't. Boucher was fuming when the man arrived half an hour late, and it only got worse. When the meeting was concluded, his blood pressure was off the charts. He feared for his driving and pulled off the road into the empty parking lot of a restaurant not yet open for business. He pulled out his cell phone and punched numbers.

"Fitch, I have to talk to somebody, and right now that somebody is you."

"I would say 'be still my beating heart,' but it sounds like you're just pissed off at something."

"Boy, you've got that right. It's a travesty. That guy administering the funds from the oil spill paid himself millions in his first few months on the job, and he hired his own law firm, and they're getting paid millions more. Guess what else? He lost a computer with the applications and personal data, including Social Security numbers, of thousands of claimants."

"You're not behind the wheel at the moment, are you?"

"No. I pulled into an empty parking lot."

"Good. Now get out and lean against the car. Lift up your head and shout, 'I have stood still and stopped the sound of feet,' as loud as you can, as many times as you can in a single breath."

"What good will that do?"

"It's Robert Frost. He always calms me down. If it doesn't work that way for you, then at least you'll feel like an idiot for hollering poetry in an empty parking lot. That's better than being pissed off."

"I've got another idea. I met a shrimper whose claim was denied. I think I'll pay him a visit."

"That'll work. Just drive carefully."

Boucher called Fred Arcineaux and told him he was coming for a visit. The shrimper's response was not enthusiastic. Then he reported in to Mildred and told her where he was going. She was more encouraging. As he drove, he smiled at the thought of the crusty New Orleans detective and his surprising affection for the New England poet. Fitch and Frost. Roscoe Fitch and Robert Frost, same initials. He chuckled. At least his blood pressure was dropping.

"Come aboard. Watch your step," Arcineaux said.

Nothing had changed since the last visit, save perhaps a few more empty beer cans and paper wrappings from sandwiches. Boucher wasn't sure if the man had bathed. He definitely hadn't changed his clothes. Boucher stepped carefully onto the littered deck, pulled over the same cooler, and sat down. "You look like shit," he said. "So does your boat."

"If you came here to tell me that, you wasted a trip, and now you're wasting my time." Arcineaux threw back a large gulp of beer.

"You sit here wallowing in this filth," Boucher said. "How do you expect anyone to help you? You and this stinking floating shithole are a disgrace to your profession. You said you were glad your late wife wasn't here to see you like this. Amen to that, brother. Your surrender to self-pity would break her heart."

Arcineaux sat up in his chair, his back stiffening. "You son of a bitch. Nobody comes onto my boat and talks to me like that. How dare you mention my wife? How dare—"

His face reddened and his hands blanched, the knuckles turning white as he dropped his beer can and gripped the armrests. He tried to stand but fell back in his chair, gasping for breath.

Boucher stood and grabbed the man's wrists and bent toward him, their faces inches apart. "Take a deep breath and repeat after me: 'I have stood still and stopped the sound of feet.' Say it."

"What the fuck? Let go of me."

Boucher did. He backed away from Arcineaux's beery breath. "You okay?"

"No. I'm mad as hell. Who are you to talk to me like that?"

"I want to help you, but I can't if you won't help yourself. Look at you. Look at this mess around you. I might be able to do something for you, but you've got to take the first step."

"Do something for me like what?"

Boucher sat down again. "I just came from my first meeting with the claims administrator. I don't like the guy, I don't trust the guy. And I've got to be honest, I think pursuing your claim would be a waste of effort."

"Tell me something I don't already know."

"I think you might have a cause of action against Dumont Industries for collision and damage to your boat if you can prove it, but a lawsuit can take years, and they have deep pockets. You might lose."

"You're just full of good news today, aren't you?"

"Listen to me. I was thinking about getting you a job."

"A job? Working for who?"

Boucher took a breath. "Dumont Industries."

"You're joking."

"You're a seaman, Fred. You have skills, experience."

"They'd never hire me. Look at me."

"Why don't I step off and come back aboard. That was my point. I was trying to shake you up so you would take a look at yourself. Take a shower. Shave. Put on some clean clothes. Clean up this filthy boat like you have some pride in it, then shower and put on clean clothes again. When you start to feel like your old self, I think I can get you an interview."

"You really think I could get a job?"

"I might be able to pull a string or two."

"You know somebody?"

"I told you, I know the owner of the company. I'll ask him personally."

The shrimper studied his dirty fingernails. "I haven't worked for anybody in a long time. I been my own boss." He paused, then looked up. "But if you'd do that for me, I'd do my best for you."

"I know you would."

They both stood. Fred excused himself and went below. Boucher could hear the sound of water running in the head. The shrimper came back on deck and offered a handshake. A clean hand.

* * *

Boucher called Fitch. "Ours is an unusual friendship, you know?"

"Yeah, we're a regular odd couple. You feeling better?"

"It came to me as I was talking to the guy. I can get him a job. Dumont wrecked his boat. I can get Dumont to give him a job."

"That has a certain symmetry to it," Fitch said, his mind obviously elsewhere. "Wait a minute. What did you say?"

"I was thinking like a lawyer. In tort law, there's—"

"No. You said something about Dumont giving him a job."

"I thought I'd ask him to find the guy something. He owes him."

"Do you really think you could get Dumont to do it?"

"Of course. Low-level, but the guy's capable. I'm sure Dumont would do it for me. He'd probably love to have me owing him a favor."

"Are you on your way to your office?"

"Yes."

"I'll meet you there." Fitch hung up.

When Boucher got there, Fitch was waiting, sitting uncomfortably in a small chair placed a little too close to Mildred's desk. She was looking at him as though he didn't pass the admissions test, and she wasn't about to let him into the judge's office to wait unobserved.

"I guess you two have met," Boucher said. "Come on in, Fitch."

As soon as they were in his office, Fitch closed the door and sneezed hard enough to burst a blood vessel. Boucher had a box of tissues on his desk, and Fitch grabbed one. "Talcum powder." He sneezed again. "I'm allergic to it. Sitting there so close to her. In that little room."

There were four more nasal explosions before he could regulate his breathing. Boucher was laughing. "You called this meeting. What can I do for you, Detective?"

"You said you could get this guy, the shrimper, a job with Dumont. Maybe you could get him a job on the *Gulf Pride*."

Boucher frowned. "I wasn't thinking along that line. I don't want to put him in any danger. I was really just trying to get him an income."

"Yeah, I know. I'm not sure I'd want to do it either. I just thought it was a chance." Fitch started cracking his knuckles.

"Don't do that," Boucher said.

"Look, we don't really need him to get a job on the ship. Maybe he could get an interview with the captain or mate. It might be enough if they'd give him a tour of the vessel."

"Are you thinking of planting a wire? A camera? That's too dangerous."

"I was thinking more like shoes. He wouldn't even have to know."

"Shoes?"

"The soles of his shoes. They'd be treated to pick up trace chemicals. If we could get him aboard and they gave him a tour of the ship . . ."

"I don't know, Fitch."

"Then ask your buddy Dumont to give you a personal tour, and we'll treat your feet."

"I like the first option better."

CHAPTER 12

BOUCHER RETURNED HOME TO an exotic treat. Malika had prepared Indian snacks to accompany cocktails with their guests.

"Smells delicious," he said as he kissed her in the kitchen. "What is it? No, don't tell me. I smell red chili powder, coriander, and cumin. What else?" He sniffed the air.

"Mango powder," Malika said. "That's the samosas. I've also made tamarind chutney and mint-coriander chutney. They go with dhokla, a steamed biscuit of gram flour made from crushed chickpeas. Why don't you mix a pitcher of martinis, since we know they drink those."

"I will later. First I need to take a shower. Better idea: why don't *we* take a shower?"

"Water conservation is a part of Indian culture too," she said, unfastening her apron.

* * *

They heard the Dumonts' limo pull up out front. They stood in the open doorway to greet them. The couple walked up the stairs to the raised porch.

"This is one of the finest historical homes in the Quarter," Elise said.

"Thank you. Please come in," Boucher said. "I hope you don't mind my wearing my smoking jacket again. I thought it would suit a casino."

"You look great, Judge," Elise said.

"Wow!" Ray Dumont's exclamation was immediate. He knew antiques, and Boucher's collection was the result of over a decade of devotion. Dumont went from piece to piece, studying each one with a practiced eye. "These are museum-quality," he said. "I can't tell you how impressed I am."

"You have hit on his first love," Elise said. "I live in fear of the day he'll move me and my few meager possessions out of the house because he's found yet another French provincial commode."

"What should I say, my love—that it will never happen because I prize you the most, of all my antiques?"

"You say that, and your prized wife will communicate with you through her prized divorce lawyer."

"Uh, I've made martinis," Boucher said.

"What is that marvelous smell?" Elise asked.

"I've made some Indian hors d'oeuvres," Malika said.

"Aren't you a dear. And look at you. You look lovely!"

Malika had tried to dress down for the evening, not knowing what attire was expected on a Mississippi riverboat casino. She wore a simple saffron-colored cocktail dress and mid-heel pumps. These were set off by the diamond necklace and earrings Boucher had given her, and at any rate, Malika could look stunning wearing a pillowcase.

They had a few drinks and bites to eat, during which the Dumonts' repartee was reminiscent of Taylor and Burton in *Who's Afraid of Virginia Woolf?* There was no argument when Ray said it was time to get to the casino. "We don't want to miss the show," he said.

They arrived at the riverboat, the limo pulling right up to the ramp. Moored to the dock, floating on the grand, gently flowing Mississippi, it looked like a Christmas tree. No, a circus. No, a whorehouse. Or a combination of all three. The owners were given due deference by employees as they were led to the ballroom and shown to the ringside table. Ray looked around before sitting, saw faces he recognized, and waved. "There are some people here tonight that I'd like you to meet later on," he said to Boucher.

The show began in circus fashion—"Ladeees and GEN-tlemen"—but the spectacle was professionally done and geared to the escapist crowd. A cabaret singer embarrassed Boucher, wrapping her boa around him while singing suggestive lyrics, until Ray Dumont warned her away with a raise of his eyebrows. But all enjoyed the dinner and show. Again, the Dumonts were attentive and gracious hosts, only this time they had a lot more help.

"Okay, let's go lose some money," Ray said when the floor show was over. "What's your game?"

"I wouldn't mind playing some blackjack," Boucher said.

"I'd like to try roulette," Malika said. "But I must warn you—when I went shopping in the French Quarter earlier today, I ran into a fortune-teller on Jackson Square. She not only told me I was going gambling, she told me to play eight and five."

"Then, honey," Elise said, "bet the ranch."

"Fine," Ray said. "You two go play roulette, and the judge and I will try our luck at blackjack. I wish everyone good fortune."

As the men were making their way through the crowd to the tables, a man approached. Boucher recognized him from somewhere.

"Judge Boucher," Ray said, "do you know Senator Jim Farmer?"

"Senator," Boucher said. "I thought you looked familiar. No, we haven't met." The senator had voted against his confirmation.

"Jim is one of our more enlightened senators," Dumont said.

"Thank you, Ray," Senator Farmer said. "When are

you going to have one of your—" He stopped himself in midsentence.

"It's okay, Jock's a friend," Dumont said, clapping Boucher on the shoulder. Then, turning to him, he said, "We get a game of Texas Hold 'Em going once in a while. It's a pretty exclusive group of players. You play poker, Jock?"

"The last time I played poker, I don't think Texas Hold 'Em had been invented."

Ray laughed. "Maybe you'd like to join us one evening." He turned to the senator. "I'll let you know when, Jim. We'll get a game up soon."

There were two more introductions before they made it to the blackjack tables. Both of the men were federal agents of separate but related agencies.

"Damn," Jock said after meeting the regional head of one of the major forces in the fight against drug trafficking. "If a terrorist were to blow up this boat, he'd take out the national security apparatus for the whole gulf coast."

"Not a chance in hell of something like that happening, Judge. Not a chance in hell."

They played for half an hour, and Jock was up five hundred dollars.

"You hold at fifteen," Ray said after studying his play.

"Always," Boucher said. "Look, Ray, I have a personal favor to ask you. I met this shrimper who lost his shirt because of the oil spill, and he's been denied reimbursement from the fund. He says his boat was damaged in a collision with one of your boats, and I talked him out of suing. He needs a job. I was hoping—"

"Don't say another word. Of course I'll help him. Can he cook? I know we need a cook for one of our offshore service vessels."

"I'm sure he can cook. He lives on his shrimp boat."

"You tell him to contact Sam Matthews at our personnel office in Houma and say he's a galley cook. I'll call Sam and tell him to get this guy an interview with the ship's captain. What's his name?"

"Fred Arcineaux."

"Good Cajun name. Got to help a fellow Coonass, right?"

"Thanks, Ray."

They rejoined the women to find that Malika had won fifteen thousand dollars.

"I want to find that fortune-teller," Ray said, "and get her a job somewhere. Like Brazil. She'll ruin me if she stays in New Orleans."

Malika was excited and giddy with success. Nothing like this had ever happened to her, and it was impossible to begrudge her good fortune. It was with the best of humor that Ray Dumont said, "We're going home. I've got to get both you winners out of here."

In the backseat of the limo, champagne was open and on ice. The party never stopped, and the Dumonts were not to be refused. Fortunately, it was a short drive to Boucher's house, because Malika began feeling queasy.

"It's all right, hon," Elise said. "It's always the last glass that does it. We just pushed this little darling over her limit. We'll be home soon."

They pulled in front of Boucher's house, and he walked Malika to the door. "You okay?"

"I'll be fine. Go back and thank them for a wonderful evening."

She stepped inside, sat at the dining table, and put her head on her arms.

"Is she all right?" Ray asked.

Boucher leaned into the open window of the limo. "She had too much excitement, that's all. But we had a great time. She asked me to thank you both for a wonderful evening."

"We'll get together again soon," Ray said, with Elise nodding and sipping her champagne.

"And thank you for helping Mr. Arcineaux," Boucher said. He backed out of the window and stood on the curb, watching as the limo pulled away, then turned to go back to the house.

A pedestrian was passing. He stopped alongside Boucher. Boucher nodded in greeting, then froze. "You?"

The gun exploded. Boucher felt heat searing his body, followed immediately by a cold, cold chill. He fell to his knees and toppled over facedown on the sidewalk. As he fell, he took a last look at the light shining from inside his house. He saw Malika's silhouette.

CHAPTER 13

MALIKA DIDN'T NEED TO look out the window to confirm what she knew in her soul, but she did so in hopes of seeing the gunman. All she saw was a fleeting glimpse of a shadow. She did not scream. She didn't know whether her heart was beating or had stopped in one breathless suspension. She grabbed her cell phone from her purse and yanked an old wool knit blanket from the back of the sofa, not caring whether it was an antique or not. She was dialing 911 before she was out the front door.

"There's been a shooting," she said with a calm that surprised her. "Judge Boucher has been hit. We need an ambulance." She gave the address. "Please call the NOPD and ask them to get the message to Detective Fitch immediately. No, I don't know his first name. Good-bye. I'm busy now."

Boucher was facedown on the sidewalk. There was blood coming from his side.

There goes his new white jacket was the involuntary absurd thought that zipped through Malika's brain, a defensive reflex to keep from facing things so much worse. Boucher seemed to be vibrating, his head shaking against the sidewalk, his body trembling. She felt his neck for a pulse. It was beating very fast, and she realized her own was thumping just as rapidly. His skin was cold to the touch. She covered him with the blanket. Pedestrians stood gaping, indulging their morbid curiosity. She leaned over and whispered in his ear. "Jock, an ambulance is on its way. You're going to be fine." Then she said she loved him and knelt next to him, her cheek on his to warm him, thinking abstract thoughts of time and its capriciousness. "Thank God," she whispered when she heard sirens in the distance, coming closer, getting louder, screaming as they turned onto the block and raced to the house. The ambulance pulled up and paramedics jumped out, equipment in their hands. Two went immediately to work, wasting no time asking questions, the situation obvious. They turned Boucher over, then lifted him onto a stretcher and loaded him into the ambulance. Malika followed them. As she was getting in, a car squealed to the curb, and Fitch got out.

"How is he?" he asked to anyone who could answer.

"We'll know when we get him to trauma," a paramedic said.

Malika and Fitch locked eyes, sharing silent prayers.

The ambulance pulled away. Fitch was forced to wait for a patrol car. When the two officers arrived, he transmitted the few known facts, then got back in his car and rushed to the hospital. Malika was sitting in the hall outside the trauma center. Fitch sat down beside her. "Do we know anything yet?"

She shook her head and began talking. "We had just come back from an evening with the Dumonts at their riverboat casino. I wasn't feeling well, and Jock walked me to the house, then went back to their limo to thank them for the evening. I heard the Dumonts' limo pull away, then I heard the shot. I did see someone running away, but it was too dark. It was just a shadow. I called 911 and asked them to call the police and you. That's all I can tell you."

He put his hand on hers. She gripped it. Tight. A doctor came from the emergency room. "You friends or family?"

"Yes," they replied in unison.

"He's a lucky man," the doctor said. "The bullet hit his cell phone. It's more than a superficial wound, which he exacerbated with his fall, but it could have been much worse."

"Can we see him?"

"No, not at the moment. He has suffered a rather extreme form of acute stress reaction—in layman's terms, shock. We've given him a sedative and something to regulate his heartbeat. We would prefer that he receive no external stimulus of any kind until tomorrow at the earliest. These symptoms may disappear within hours, sometimes days, but occasionally, they last longer and lead to more serious complications. We'd rather be safe than sorry."

"You say the bullet missed him?" Fitch asked, identifying himself.

"It grazed him. A direct hit would have killed him instantly at that range. The bullet was deflected by the cell phone he was carrying in his jacket pocket. It busted the phone, which caused lacerations and substantial blood loss, but as I said, he's a lucky man."

"Can I see him in the morning?" Malika asked.

"No promises. But come back tomorrow at noon. I'll be on duty, and I'll decide based on his condition at that time. All right?"

"We'll be here," Fitch and Malika said, again in perfect unison.

"You two practice that routine?" the doctor asked.

They were both at the hospital at noon the following day.

"He's still unconscious," the doctor said, "and it's not due to any sedative. I have to confess I'm a little worried. He keeps mumbling about being shot by a dead man."

"Shot by a dead man?" Fitch repeated, to make sure he'd heard right.

The doctor accompanied them to Boucher's room. They stood just outside the open door. Jock was twitching like a puppy having a bad dream.

"Lengthy unconsciousness is not typical with the kind of wound he's suffered. I'm concerned about damage to the hypothalamic-pituitary-adrenal axis, a possibility with extreme stress response."

"What can we do?" Malika asked.

"There's not much to do but wait," the doctor said, then excused himself.

"Let me drive you home," Fitch said to Malika after the doctor left them. She sniffed and said nothing during the drive, and when they got to Boucher's house, Fitch said, "I have some work to do, but I'm coming over with a friend this afternoon. We'll bring something to eat. I'm not going to leave you alone this evening."

Malika dabbed a tear. "I'm sorry." She sniffed. "Who's your friend, another policeman?"

"No, it's a lady I'm seeing. I think you'll like her."

"I'm sure I will." Malika forced a smile, then got out of the car.

Fitch watched till she was inside the house. He drove to his office and called Ray Dumont.

"How's he doing?" Dumont asked with obvious concern.

"The injury is not life-threatening," Fitch said.

"Can we visit him, Elise and I?"

"The doctor would prefer that you wait awhile. Can I ask you some questions about that evening?"

"Of course, Detective."

The questions were routine and the answers satisfactory. There was no reason to call the couple in for a face-to-face. They had not heard the shot—entirely logical, inside a hermetically sealed limousine with air-conditioning, top-of-the-line sound system, and clinking champagne glasses—and they had not seen the shooter. Fitch thanked him, hung up, then put his feet on his desk and thought about Boucher's mumbled words. A dead man had shot him. There had been too many dead men around Jock Boucher of late, entirely too many.

It was five that afternoon when Malika looked out the window to see who was knocking at the front door. It was Fitch and his lady friend.

"Malika, Helen," said the man of few words.

"Pleased to meet you." She welcomed them in. "I've made some chai. Why don't we sit at the dining table?"

The guests took their seats, and Malika brought out a tea service, studying the woman Fitch had brought with him. Helen was compact, about five-three. She wore a wool robin's-egg-blue skirt with a matching jacket over a white cotton blouse. Her hair was silver, wavy, and brushed back from her face. There was not an iota of fashion to her ensemble, but her face was kind, her slight smile full of empathy.

"I appreciate you coming over," Malika said, "but I'm doing fine. I'm going to the hospital in an hour, and I plan to stay with Jock this evening. They won't get rid of me so easily this time. I think he needs me."

"I agree," Helen said, pouring herself a cup of tea. "I think loved ones are always the best medicine. Fitch has told me what Jock has been through lately. I can understand him being under stress."

Malika looked at Fitch. "You know more about what he's been through lately than I do. Something has been bothering him, and he hasn't wanted to share with me. I had thought I'd let him tell me when he was ready. Now I think I need to know."

Fitch looked at the cup in front of him. "I think it started with that thug who tried to rob him the night he got back from Washington. Happened close to home, and you know how he feels about his neighborhood. He defended himself, and the gunman later died. It wasn't Jock's fault, but he blamed himself."

"I read about that," Helen said. "I knew the man. At least I knew him when he was a boy."

"You did?" Fitch said.

"He was in my school about ten years ago. I'm a middle school principal," she said to Malika. "I knew him and his brother."

Both stared at her, astonished.

"You remember kids from ten years ago? Out of what, thousands?" Fitch said.

"The Manley boys were memorable. They were a handful. Also, I don't get that many identical twins. Over the years, maybe only—"

"Twins?" Fitch said, then, "Twins! C'mon, Helen, I know Judge Boucher is going to enjoy meeting you."

Fitch had parked away from the house because two squad cars were parked in front. Police investigators were going over the exteriors of Boucher's as well as neighboring properties, looking for any physical evidence from the shooting.

"They've done this before at Judge Boucher's house," Fitch said.

"I remember," Malika said.

"The identical twin brother of the man who died. That's who shot him," Fitch said as they drove to the hospital. "He thought he'd seen a ghost. Sounds corny, I know, but ghosts have been causing folks acute stress syndrome for centuries. Helen, you wouldn't happen to know where this twin brother is now, would you?"

"They were out of our system long ago."

They made their way to his room with ease, disconcerting ease, Fitch thought. No one challenged them; no one asked for identification. There was no one else in his room. Boucher was at last conscious but dazed, staring into space. The three stood at the foot of his bed. Fitch spoke.

"Jock, we think we know who shot you. This is my friend Helen. I've told you about her. She's a middle school principal." He stepped back as if onstage, and Helen was given the spotlight.

"I'm pleased to meet you, Judge Boucher," she said, "though not under these circumstances." Her tone was soothing, as if she were consoling one of her schoolkids. "I knew Tyrone Manley, the man who tried to rob you at gunpoint. I blame myself for how he ended up as much as anyone. We failed him. We fail a lot of them. We save those we can. What I wanted to tell you is that he had an identical twin brother. His name was Peter, and he had a nickname—Pip. If you got a look at the man who shot you and thought it was Tyrone, who is deceased, then it very likely was Pip." She took a step back, ceding the stage to Malika.

"Jock," she said, "talk to me."

CHAPTER 14

F OR NEARLY A MINUTE the trio stared at Boucher. There were subtle signs that the gears were turning. His eyebrows knit together, and his lips pursed as he frowned. Finally, he spoke.

"That's possible," he said.

"It's more than possible, it's probable," Fitch said. He stepped to the bed and grabbed his friend's forearm. "You feeling better now?"

"I think I am," Boucher said. He reached out for Malika. "Yes, I think I am."

"What's all this?" The doctor entered the room, surprised and not looking too pleased at the trio of visitors.

"They're friends of mine," Boucher said. "They've helped solve a riddle that has had me somewhat perplexed."

"I'm sorry, but I'm going to have to ask you all to leave immediately," the doctor said.

"Wait a minute," Fitch said. "Your patient is obviously feeling better, and I think it's because we came to visit him."

"My request has nothing to do with you," the doctor said. "I've been asked to clear all visitors out of the hospital. National security."

"Bomb scare?" Fitch asked.

"The president. He was returning to Washington from Houston when he got word of Judge Boucher's shooting. He's ordered Air Force One to land and is coming in for a visit." The doctor walked to his patient, cuffed his arm, and took his blood pressure. "Solid," he said, then looked at his eyes, now sharply focused, not vacant. "Are you back from wherever you were?"

"Wherever I was," Boucher said, "I don't want to return." He held up a hand and motioned Helen to step forward. "I'd like to know more about these brothers when you have the time."

"The Manley twins? My information is a bit dated, but I can tell you what I knew then."

Two men in dark suits who could only have been from the president's security detail stood in the open doorway.

"Come on, people," the doctor said, "I've got my orders."

It was too late. The president entered the room. To the astonishment of all, he strode not to the bedside of the man he had come to see but straight to Malika.

"You must be Malika," he said. "I owe you an apology."

"I b-b-beg your pardon, Mr. President?" she said, flustered.

"I'm sure I ruined your Mexican vacation. I'm sorry. If the two of you are ever in Washington, I hope you will let the First Lady and me make it up to you." Still ignoring Boucher, he asked the doctor, "How's the patient?"

"He's showing marked improvement, Mr. President. I think he's going to be fine."

At last the commander in chief turned to Boucher. "You haven't come to believe that the conferring of a lifetime appointment grants some kind of protective shield or superpowers, have you? Cats may have nine lives, but federal judges get the standard allotment: one per customer. And they've got to take care of it. Okay, Judge, tell me how you're feeling, and introduce me to your friends, and tell me when you plan to get back to work."

"Mr. President," Boucher said, "I will be in my office within forty-eight hours." He introduced his group of visitors, and they all shook their leader's hand.

Then the president returned to Jock's side. "Would you folks mind if I had a private word with Judge Boucher?" The room was cleared. He pulled up a chair and bent forward, almost whispering. "Judge Boucher, I need you on the bench. I can't afford any surprises right now. I'm trying to fill a vacancy with a candidate I believe is one of the most qualified legal scholars in the country, and my appointing him to the federal bench is just a prelude. I want him for the Supreme Court at some point in the future. I'm getting a lot of pressure against this nomination. I need you to stay on board and stay out of trouble—if that's possible for you. If you ever start to have doubts again about your role as a federal judge, I want you to call me. We'll talk. Use this number and this password. That will make sure your call reaches me. All right?" He handed the card to Boucher.

"Of course, Mr. President. I'm sorry I've been such a pain in the ass."

The president smiled. "Your career has been rather colorful lately."

After his brief conversation with Boucher, the president blazed a tornado trail throughout the hospital, calling on patients young and old. All were energized by his unexpected visit, but none more so than Boucher. After the chief executive had departed, Mildred French paid a visit, and the Dumonts sent a floral arrangement that took two men to carry. It was like a birthday party, into the middle of which walked a complete stranger.

"Can I help you?" Boucher asked.

"I came to see how you were doing," the man said. He looked like he had come directly from a men's clothing store. He wore trousers that had razor-sharp creases, a spotless white cotton shirt, and a zippered brown windbreaker that was definitely a new purchase; a tag remained uncut and hanging from the rear. He was clean-shaven and sported a fresh haircut and wore canvas boat shoes—the only clue to his identity. Boucher stared hard at him.

"It's me, Judge. Fred Arcineaux." It was extreme make-over, in the flesh. The shrimper looked reborn.

"Fred, how nice of you to drop by. I have some good news for you."

Boucher told him of the job interview Ray Dumont had promised as Fitch eyed the man up and down. After Arcineaux excused himself and left, Fitch gave Boucher a wink and a thumbs-up, then left the room to take a call on his cell phone. The women were talking when he came back in. He walked to Boucher and said out of range of the others, "They found the bullet that winged you. We know the caliber. It seems the identical twin had an identical gun."

"We've got to find him," Boucher said.

"We're working on it right now."

"No. *We've* got to find him. We. Like in you and me. We have to find out where he got that gun."

Fitch shook his head. "You've been shot. You've just had a personal visit from no less than the president of the United States, who I'm sure told you to act like a judge, right? And two seconds later, you're trying to be a detective. I should ask your doc to give you another sedative. Or maybe a strait-jacket."

* * *

The doctor was firm. He would not release Boucher until the next day. Malika stayed with him. Boucher was cornered. He had to answer the hard questions.

"Why didn't you tell me?" she asked with purposeful ambiguity, hoping to sweep in anything else he had been keeping from her.

"Malika, I've never discussed my work with you," he answered with equally purposeful evasion.

"You've never discussed pending cases with me, and I've never asked. Lately, though, your work has not been like that of any judge I've ever heard of, and you seem to be going from one dangerous situation to another. I don't know what's going on with you, because you don't tell me anything. Fitch's friend Helen knows more of what's happening in your life than I do, and she just met you."

"That's not true," he said weakly, but he knew it was. He was silent for a minute, staring down at her hand holding his. "We have phone conversations. We update each other's lives in ten words or less, and one of us is always on the run while we're talking. How do I tell you in such a dialogue that my life was threatened and I put the perpetrator in the hospital, where he died? How do I tell you, as we run from one meeting to the next, that I feel responsible for his death even though the doctors tell me otherwise? Should I wait till the first night we're back together? The second night? When is the right time to turn our reunion into a reflection of my guilty conscience?"

"There's never a wrong time, Jock."

The next morning, Boucher was released from the hospital.

"No lifting, no exercise," the doctor said. "You have a sedentary profession. You're a judge. Just act like one, and you'll recover in no time."

Boucher said nothing, just smiled. He'd been lying in bed for almost three days. He'd gone into the ring with more serious injuries than he was suffering now. He and Malika took a taxi home from the hospital, and it was as if the fates were signaling their accord: when he walked in the front door, he saw the light flashing on the answering machine; his new cell phone vibrated in his pocket; and Malika's phone buzzed in her purse. She walked out onto the porch to take her call. Boucher drew his phone from his pocket. It was Fitch.

"You out of the rest home?" Fitch asked.

"Standing in the living room of my own hacienda."

"Want to rejoin the world of the living?"

"What did you have in mind?"

"I'll pass by and tell you."

He closed his cell and checked the landline message. It was Ray Dumont. "Judge, give me a call when you're home and feeling up to it. Thought I might get up a card game. Wanted to know if you're interested."

The front door was ajar. He could see Malika on her phone, pacing the porch, mostly listening. When she had finished her conversation, she came in, her expression blank.

"Something wrong?" he asked.

"I have to go to New York."

"When?"

"Tomorrow."

He took her in his arms, held her close, and felt dampness on her cheek.

"Are you crying?"

"Jock," Malika said, "when you were shot and I was lying next to you, trying to keep you warm . . ."

"You told me you loved me. I remember."

"I was wondering if it was our last good-bye. Every time I leave you, I wonder the same. I'm always afraid that someday, it will be."

Malika's phone rang again. They both shrugged. This was their life. Live in the moment, and be thankful. He saw Fitch's car pull into the drive and went out to meet him. "Let's talk out back," Boucher said. "Malika's busy with work. What's in the bag?"

"Shoes," Fitch said.

They sat at the wrought-iron patio suite in the back. "These are canvas Sperry Top-Siders," Fitch said, putting the bag on the table, "identical to the shoes your guy wore to the hospital. If we can figure out a way to get him aboard that vessel—"

"I've already done that. Dumont told me one of his off-shore vessels needed a cook when I first broached the subject. Arcineaux will say he's a cook and ask to meet the ship's captain."

"Great. Tell him to use these shoes. He knows you don't wear street shoes on a boat. Ask him to take them off as soon as he can after the interview."

"Any luck finding the shooter?"

"I went through records on the dead brother. He had an address as a juvenile in the Seventh Ward. I drove by. Wiped out by Katrina. Helen's going through old school records, but I'm sure she'll find the same address. Since there are no public records on him, he's probably homeless, like his brother was."

Boucher looked toward his house. "Malika's leaving to-morrow. I'm going looking for him after she's gone. Don't worry, I'm not planning a confrontation. I just want to see the world he lives in. The world his brother came from. If I should stumble across him, I promise to call you. I'm not going to do a cop's job."

Fitch nodded. "I know you. I've been expecting that. Also, your case got assigned to Fayette and Gough. With all the shit the department has been getting lately, an internal regulation is in force: 'Thou shalt not speak ill of thy fellow law enforcement officer.' But Fayette and Gough? If either one of them was given a new brain, it would die lonesome. This would not be a priority with them, and the guy might shoot you again before they get off their asses. Also, they are not particularly sophisticated when working with suspects from the lower economic strata, if you know what I mean. Just be careful. Don't do anything stupid."

"Thanks for understanding."

"I'm not sure I do."

CHAPTER 15

MALIKA'S DEPARTURE THE NEXT morning was understated, maybe a twinge of regret, but they'd been through it many times before. Minutes after Malika left, Mildred brought by some paperwork that kept him busy till early afternoon. Then he called Arcineaux and was told his appointment with Dumont Industries had been scheduled. Boucher offered to come out and wish him luck. He grabbed the shoes Fitch had left and went to meet the shrimper on his boat. He was pleased to see the trawler shipshape. There were no beer cans, no refuse. There were sounds of Arcineaux working below, and Boucher called to him. The shrimper came up covered with grease and grime, but it was fresh. He wiped his hands on his shirt. "Working on the engine," he said. "Come aboard."

Boucher felt ridiculous. His expression showed it.

"Something wrong?" Arcineaux asked.

"I need a favor."

"Figured you didn't drive over here just to wish me luck. What can I do for you, Judge?"

Boucher had worn a raincoat, which did not look out of place on the overcast afternoon, but then he pulled a plastic-wrapped shoe out of each side pocket, which looked weird as hell. "I'd like you to wear these shoes for the interview," he said.

Arcineaux laughed. "Could have saved you the trouble. I bought a pair just like those, and I was planning to wear them."

"These are special," Boucher said. "The soles of these shoes have been treated to pick up residue of certain chemicals. There is a law enforcement agency interested in the cargo that one of Dumont's ships may be carrying. You're going to meet the captain of this vessel, applying for the job of galley cook."

"You want me to be a spy. So this is not really a job interview at all, is it?"

"As far as Dumont Industries is concerned, it is."

Arcineaux reached out, and Boucher handed him the shoes. "If I don't wear these, do I still get the interview?"

"Yes, and I wish you luck. I just have to ask that this little conversation—"

Arcineaux interrupted with a wave of the hand. "You took me into your confidence. I don't betray a man's trust. You've been trying to help me, Judge. And you really turned my head around, you know? Here I was, feeling sorry for myself, wasting my life away . . ." He paused, staring at the soles of the canvas shoes. "I'll do it on one condition: if these things discover something, you've got to let me know what it is, and if I can help with anything else on this, you gotta give me the chance."

"That's two conditions. But okay."

Fitch was waiting in a bar outside of Gretna where they had arranged to meet. The place was dark and rank with the smell of stale beer and smoke. There was another odor, not unique to New Orleans's seedier joints: the scent of despair. Two men sat alone at opposite ends of the bar, nursing drinks and cigarettes. A muted TV made a newscaster's efforts ineffectual.

Boucher said as he sat down, "I walk into a crummy joint like this and see guys like that at the bar, and I can't help but wonder how miserable things must be for them on the outside to have to escape in here."

"Trompe l'oeil," Fitch said, "an illusion, in this instance, one fostered by alcohol. To a drunk, this place doesn't look bad. He walks in here, and he's on his way to getting plastered before his first sip. Doesn't see the filth or smell the squalor; he's floating on the memory of the last time he got loaded in this very place or one just like it, already en route to his own dreamland. It's like an opium den. They don't think much about interior decor in those places either." He looked at his glass. He was drinking soda water.

Boucher was glad to change the subject. "Arcineaux said he'd do it."

"Good."

"But he wants us to keep him in the loop."

"We'll have to see about that. By the way, Helen called me. Same address for both brothers. Place no longer exists."

"So he's homeless."

Fitch nodded. "It's probable, since his twin brother was. Most of those who lost their homes try to stay near the old neighborhood if they can, and if you were going to look for him, that would be the place to start." Fitch had certain facts and figures committed as if they'd been tattooed on his arm. "There are maybe twelve thousand people squatting in over forty thousand blighted and abandoned homes or buildings in New Orleans, four percent of this city's population." He sipped his soda water with the same lack of enthusiasm he showed for the subject matter.

"Then I guess we start with his old neighborhood," Boucher said.

"I don't know how much help I can be on this venture. The homeless have their own radar when it comes to police. You'd stand out less walking through a homeless camp than I would, and there aren't too many other ways to get close to those people. Of course, you'd have to get some old clothes, wear a hat, disguise yourself so he doesn't shoot you again. But like I said, not now; when you're feeling better. You ready to get out of this dump?"

"Yes. This place gives me the creeps."

"For me, it brings back memories of a time I'd just as soon forget," Fitch said.

Boucher's home had a study facing the street. Its custom-built shelves held a respectable collection of rare editions, but he wasn't in the mood for reading. He sat in the dark looking out over Chartres Street, staring at the parade of pedestrians passing by. There were tourists, the rich men. There were those who sold trinkets in the street, the poor men. There were shaved heads and purple-haired panhandlers the local landowners called gutter punks—the beggar men; and though he couldn't spot any as he sat brooding in the dark, he knew there were thieves in the vicinity of his castle; knew from personal experience. The walls of his antebellum home were not all that separated his world from the privation that surrounded him. The difference between him and those less fortunate added up to a lifetime of choices made. He'd come from poverty too. He'd known discrimination and the way it stripped away one's thin veneer of pride and achievement. Unlike those lost souls out there in the dark, he had overcome. But maybe—the thought seemed to crawl through his brain like some parasitic worm—maybe it was just good fortune. Maybe he'd just gotten lucky. He dismissed the thought. He knew better.

Boucher stood and moved to the back of the house and his master suite, feeling tenderness in his ribs as he walked. In this one respect, he could count himself blessed. The bullet had missed by the width of a finger, and instead of death, he had little more than a nagging bruise. It was not enough of an injury to postpone the search he knew he must begin. He would start now, this very night.

Esplanade Avenue was the eastern border of the Seventh Ward, the former neighborhood of Pip Manley. Boucher was taking Fitch's advice and beginning his search near where the twins' old house once stood. Boucher drove to the area, parked his truck near St. Louis Cemetery Number 3, and got out to walk. Those in the cemetery could be envied one thing—they had their homes: eviction-proof. If it had been daylight, Boucher would have been walking in the shadow of the 610 overpass. In the darkness, he knew its presence by the sound of cars rushing overhead. It wasn't long before he came to a derelict building, someone's former home. The doorway was open—if there was a door. He stepped inside and onto debris—splintered wood, broken glass—and thanked his choice of shoes, the pair of thick-soled chukka boots worn on his Katrina cleanup missions. They walked well over destruction. A pair of old jeans, a faded flannel shirt, and a beat-up windbreaker, and he had his basic outfit. A faux-fur hunting hat with earflaps topped it all off and helped hide his face, though his cover didn't seem much of a concern for the moment. The inside of the building was black.

"If you got nothin' to eat, you can turn yo' sorry ass around an' keep goin'," a raspy female voice said.

He pictured a toothless old hag but knew it could have been a young woman. "How many in here?" he asked, hoping for an honest answer.

"Me an' my dog. That enough for you?"

He heard a low growl. Animals weren't common among the homeless; they competed for food. But this one was real.

"I'm going. Sorry I disturbed you." He backed out, retracing his footsteps as best he could.

He walked toward the sound of traffic. He shuffled under the raised highway just like the hobos of the thirties had followed railway tracks during that earlier chapter in America's history of periodic financial disorder. The cement roof of the overpass was noisy, but it was shelter, and groups seemed to congregate every few hundred yards, small fires providing not only warmth but a communal meeting center. He passed a fire flaming from a metal drum. The sleepless hunched close to the flames. Behind them was a second tier of dark lumps: bodies lying prone on the asphalt with sour-smelling blankets covering them and whatever possessions they had. They looked like headless corpses. The bodies on the ground, the fires—the scene had an Armageddon feel. He stopped to warm himself. They made room for him but didn't say a word. These were old people, he saw from their faces. Their demographic caused them to stick together. After a few silent minutes, he left. The space they had allowed him was quickly filled in.

A short distance away, he came upon a real bonfire, wood most likely ripped from an abandoned home. There were more people gathered around this blaze, sitting on the ground, many hunched over as they passed a crack pipe. He sat on the opposite side of the circle from the drug users, but the pipe was making its way toward him. A woman sat on his left, cross-legged. She turned to him. She sniffed. She drew her face closer and sniffed again, like a dog on the scent. "You just leave the mission," she asked, "or prison?"

He was too clean. Dire poverty had its smell.

"Mission," he said, and hunched over, lowering his head, pulling his chin to his chest.

The crack pipe was making its way to him, hand to hand, mouth to mouth. There was no concern for germs passed by its communal use, but then hygiene was nowhere in evidence in this subculture. It looked like a regular pipe with the stem either cut down or broken. It was short, which meant the smoke inhaled was hotter. Intense heat burned the mouth upon inhalation, and the blistered lips of most of those in the circle attested to frequent use. All were smoking. If he refused, he was a marked man. It was enough searching for one night. He stood up and shuffled away.

Boucher returned to his truck and drove home. Though he had almost been discovered, revealed for the fraud that he was by his cleanliness, he felt dirty. He stripped off his clothes, throwing them into a pile on the bathroom floor, and took a scalding shower. In bed, he lay awake, staring into the dark, asking himself, *At what point does life become no longer worth living?* Could he endure a life of squalor as did the unfortunates whose company he had just shared? Was there some kind of perverse courage in those downtrodden homeless, or did their attitude of defeat and acceptance of privation numb the senses? Had they simply succumbed to a fate that was little more than a death sentence? He fell asleep as the phrase rolled over and over in his brain. *Dead men walking.* It seemed applicable to the wretched homeless.

"I almost got caught." Boucher sat in his courtyard the next morning, his first call to Fitch. "Soap," he said. "It's a dead giveaway."

"So you didn't find him."

"I'm going back out tonight—that is, unless your esteemed colleagues are hot on the trail."

"Not a chance. But don't get me started on that, okay?

I don't like what you're doing, but if you find the guy, you just might be saving your own skin. Just don't go Rambo on me. Don't even open your mouth."

"Fitch, I'm only there to observe."

Boucher passed the day attending to the files Mildred had brought over. She came to collect finished work that afternoon, and they had a pleasant cup of tea together. It was rare for him; he was a coffee man, and enjoying the weaker brew unnerved him a bit. He poured himself a shot of bourbon after she left, just to reassert his Cajun contrariness. The evening passed with little to do but watch shadows lengthen as the early Seth Thomas clock on his mantelpiece ticked away the seconds. He sat in the dark and waited until ten. Social activities would be winding down among the micro-communities encamped under the interstate. He would mingle unnoticed before they bedded down for the night.

He parked in the same place as the night before and again passed the cemetery. There was little use in poking his head in other abandoned houses; not even candlelight came from the dark hulks. He passed the same groups, sitting down in almost the same place amid the circle. There was no woman beside him; no one sniffed. He'd not showered today, and his clothes had lain where he'd left them the night before. It wasn't much but was all he could do. The scent of despair was rarely acquired in a day.

Again a crack pipe was being passed. Again it was coming his way.

"Hey, Pip," a voice called out, "this thing's gone out. You got some more of this shit?"

Boucher hunched over as the man approached the circle from the rear, took the pipe, filled its bowl, then passed it back, saying something about it being the last freebie. Then he returned to the shadows. Boucher had caught a glimpse. It was his man. He rose slowly from the asphalt, watching where Pip had gone.

"Leavin' so soon?" a woman in the circle asked.

Boucher nodded, then slipped away, leaving the overpass. When he was far enough from the group, he retrieved his cell phone, turned it on, and punched numbers. "Fitch," he whispered, "I found him."

Fitch yawned. "Where are you?"

Boucher read the road sign by the light of a passing car. "I'm standing between Humanity and Benefit streets, near a group of homeless under the 610 overpass."

"Humanity and Benefit? You like irony, don't you?"

"Whoever named these streets had a flair. Anyway, he's here. I can't take him on my own, but you and I can. If we're lucky, he'll be sleeping when you get here. Just don't come in like the cavalry, please."

The detective joined him in under half an hour.

"That was quick," Boucher said.

"I didn't have to spruce up for this occasion, did I? Where is he?"

"Over there. Under the expressway."

The fire was dying; only a few remained of the earlier circle. Boucher led Fitch to where he had seen the man go. He stopped. Bodies had moved and shifted in sleep. He couldn't be sure which one was Pip. Fitch whispered, "Be careful. We go kicking over the wrong people, they'll gang up on us. This is their turf and they're very territorial."

Boucher nodded, then whispered loudly, "Hey, Pip. I need some shit. I got money."

"Go away, motherfucker. I'm sleepin'."

The voice came from a covered-up lump. Fitch approached, bent over, and pulled down the blanket. He shone his flashlight in the man's face, blinding him. "You're under arrest," he whispered low. "My gun is pointed right at your head. I want you to stand up slowly and put your hands behind your back."

"Aw, shit," Pip said, but there was no resistance and no stirring from those slumbering nearby.

Fitch whipped out the flex-tie he'd stuck in his belt and bound the prisoner's hands. Boucher knelt down and bundled up the blanket, feeling for the gun that had been used to shoot him. "Got it," he said. "Let's go."

Pip Manley was hustled away in the dark. Not a single head was raised, not even out of curiosity. Though these people congregated for support and security, the fundamental law of the street was supreme. It was every man for himself.

* * *

Fitch shoved the assailant into the backseat of his unmarked patrol car. Boucher slid in next to him. "Do we have to take him straight in?" he asked the detective.

"You want to find a deserted spot and work him over a little first?"

"I was thinking about getting him something to eat. He must be hungry."

"You're kidding, right? Why don't we just get him a room at the Royal Orleans for the night? He can order room service, then clean up in the morning so he'll be fresh as a daisy when we book him for attempted murder."

"You killed my brother," Pip said.

"No, he didn't, you dumb shit," Fitch said. "Your brother died of kidney failure from drug and alcohol abuse. My guess is you won't be far behind."

"I don't use the stuff, I just sell it."

"You were giving it away earlier," Boucher said.

"I get charitable impulses sometimes."

"Yeah," Fitch said, "give 'em a taste so they'll come back for more."

"Those folks don't have money for more. I help them."

"You're a regular Saint Francis," Fitch said.

"Stop there," Boucher said. They were passing a Denny's, open all night.

"You gotta be kidding me," Fitch said.

"No, I'm not, Detective. We're going to get something to eat and have a nice civil conversation."

Fitch grumbled but pulled into the parking lot. He parked, then turned around and glared at Pip Manley. "We're going to get a booth. You're going to slide over against the wall, and Judge Boucher is going to sit next to you. I'll be sitting right across from you, staring at your ugly face. Under the table, I will have my gun pointed at the same gut you will be filling with pancakes, grits, eggs, and sausages. It would be a pity to waste all that food, so you behave yourself when we get in there. Got it?"

"I can eat all I want?"

"Let's see how our 'civil conversation' goes."

They got out of the car, and Fitch cut the flex-tie with his pocketknife. They entered, and a waitress led them to a booth. Too harried by her late-night hours to question appearances, she didn't get close enough to catch the younger man's street scent. She seated them in a far corner and took their order. When she left, Boucher spoke. "We want to know where you got the guns you and your brother used. The ones you both tried to kill me with."

"Why you want to know that?"

"We ask the questions here," Fitch said.

"I'm not sure I remember."

Steaming hot coffee was served, the aroma tantalizing. Pip inhaled. Boucher slid Pip's cup to the far edge of the table. "Try to remember."

Fitch and Boucher drank their coffee while Pip's cup sat out of reach. They removed even his glass of water. He sat, stoically defiant. Then the food came: pancakes with a caddy of six different flavors of syrup; fried eggs and sausage; grits; toast and butter, lots of butter. Pip's plate was removed from his reach. He swallowed hard and blinked rapidly. Boucher and Fitch began to eat. It didn't take long before he caved. "We stole 'em."

"Not now," Fitch said, "we're eating. Would you pass me the salt and pepper and Tabasco sauce? I can't eat eggs without Tabasco."

Pip's eyes grew wider as he watched them. Then came the giveaway. His stomach rumbled loud enough for all to hear. "This is cruel and unusual," he said. "Let me eat or just go ahead and shoot me."

"Talk first, then eat," Boucher said, wiping his lips with his napkin.

"Okay," Pip said. "You know Jackson Barracks?"

"Lower Ninth Ward," Fitch said. "Old army base, I think."

"I know it," Boucher said. "I know it well. It was built in the early nineteenth century. The original buildings remain one of the finest groups of Greek Revival architecture in the United States, comparable to the University of Virginia. As a military installation, it played a role in every one of America's military campaigns, including the Indian wars. General Zachary Taylor used the barracks to organize his troops for the war with Mexico. It was used as a hospital during the Civil War, and afterward, two of the first regiments of colored troops were based there. Many of the greatest soldiers of the nineteenth century passed through at one time or another. Since the sixties, it has been used by the Louisiana National Guard, and in 1976 it was listed in the National Register of Historic Places. It was severely damaged by Katrina. After several years of reconstruction, it was rededicated."

Food dangling from his fork, Fitch stared open-mouthed. Pip too stared in amazement. "How you know all that shit?" he asked.

"He knows New Orleans," Fitch said. "He loves this town and respects its history. Not like some."

"I walk there sometimes," Boucher said. "It has a wonderful parade ground. I've often thought what a great attraction it could be if more military bands and reenactors with period uniforms and weaponry could put on displays of close-order drill for tourists. Anyway, what were you doing at Jackson Barracks?"

"There was a lot of construction going on. Where you got construction, you got opportunity."

"To steal," Fitch said.

"Right. There was a warehouse. We thought it would be where they kept tools and shit, so Tyrone and me broke in one night. Look, I'm starving. Let me eat something. The food's getting cold."

Boucher nodded and Fitch passed the plate. Pip shoveled food in his mouth as if masticating had never been part of his intake routine. He swallowed, emptied his water glass, and reached for his coffee cup, which he likewise emptied in one continuous motion.

"Slow down," Boucher said. "You'll make yourself sick. Chew your food. If you want more, we'll get it."

"Keep talking," Fitch said.

"Yeah, well, we broke into the warehouse, only there weren't no tools. Guns. Lots of guns. I mean, the whole warehouse was filled with all kinds of weapons. Rifles, pistols, boxes of grenades. I even saw a couple machine guns. It was like war shit."

"National Guard might have had weapons stored there," Fitch said to Boucher.

"No, man, these had Russian shit written all over the boxes."

"You know Russian?"

"Hell, no. I know movies. I seen Russian writing in the movies, and there was Russian writing on a lot of the boxes. We opened a couple and found the pistols. We broke in another box and found some ammunition. We heard someone coming, so we just grabbed what we could carry and ran."

"You just took the two pistols?"

"And some ammo."

"You only broke in once?"

"We went back a few nights later with some other guys,

but they had guards, dogs, lights, and everything. There was no getting in, and we never went back."

"Do you remember anything else?"

Pip thought as he cut a link sausage in two with his fork and stabbed a piece. "I remember that Tyrone never liked his gun. Said it was too heavy. I told him he had to carry it for his own protection. You know, we get beat up out there too. The street's a shitty life."

The three sat in silence.

"You want a way out of it?" Boucher asked.

CHAPTER 16

PIP WAS BOOKED AND incarcerated. Though Pip had tried to kill him, Boucher demanded special treatment, and Fitch complied. The accused was given his own cell, the cleanest accommodations he had known in recent memory. He lay down on his bunk and was out before the count of ten.

"I'm driving you home," Fitch said to Boucher. "I'll send someone to pick up your truck, and you're going to stay in your house all weekend, or I swear I'll find some reason to arrest you and throw you in there with him. Damn it, Judge, you just got out of the hospital with a gunshot wound."

"I am feeling kind of tired," Boucher said. Fitch had to help him to the car.

Fitch did not arrange a stakeout, not exactly. He asked Helen to come over and look after him. She fixed breakfast the next morning. "I've been appointed your custodian," she said. "You are not to leave the house without my permission, and you can save your breath, because I'm not going to give it. We are all delighted your injuries are not serious, but you have been through a traumatic experience, and you need to rest. Going out on your own last night was both reckless and foolish. Are you bent on self-destruction, Judge Boucher?"

"No, ma'am."

"Don't call me 'ma'am.'"

"Sorry. 'Ma'am' is for old maids, I've been told."

In one of those speak-of-the-devil moments, Mildred French was at the door, unaware of the judge's late-night extracurricular activities. He was pleased to see her. She had brought more files for him to work on. He held the door open; she stepped inside and halted, then stopped. Part of her purpose in coming was to look after his welfare, but there was the sound and scent of another woman on the premises.

"If I've come at a bad time—" she said, then Helen stepped out of the kitchen.

"Mrs. French, how nice to see you. I'm Helen; we met at the hospital. Your boss has been very bad. He went out alone last night to try to catch the man who shot him."

"Judge Boucher," Mildred said, her tone stern.

He was caught in a cross fire of withering glances.

"Detective Fitch asked me to keep an eye on him and

make sure he stays home and gets some proper rest," Helen said.

"If I can help you in any way," Mildred offered.

"I think I can manage. I've had experience with willful children. Would you like some coffee? I just made a fresh pot."

"Why, thank you, Helen, I'd love some. Here." Mildred handed Boucher the armload of files she had brought, then went to the kitchen with Helen, the two marching in step. "Men," Mildred said. "What was God thinking?"

Federal Judge Jock Boucher stood in the foyer of his home. "We caught him," he said meekly. "The man who shot me? We caught him." But the ladies were pouring their coffee, more interested in each other's company.

So the weekend passed. His appreciation grew for the two women, who treated him like an errant schoolboy. Helen was a competent custodian, but more important, she was good company. For hours they discussed lifesaving, the rescuing of those whose lives had gone from bad to worse. The files Mildred had brought contained their own surprises. She had taken on much of the legal research herself and demonstrated an impressive grasp of fundamental principles of law, as adept as any law clerk who had ever worked for him. Malika also called several times, keeping him informed of her activities so he wouldn't think she was checking up on him, which of course she was. The combined power of these women who had taken control was too much. He succumbed and did their bidding and felt the better for it. By Monday morning, he was well rested and up and early to the office.

Judge Giordano, the only female jurist on the district bench, had sent him flowers with a note welcoming him back—a fact she no doubt learned from Mildred. The judge's note also thanked him for helping with her caseload, complimenting him on the work. He called Mildred into his office and asked her to take a seat, smiling as talcum powder wafted his way.

"Mildred, I am receiving compliments on the job I've been doing."

"That's wonderful, Your Honor."

"The only problem is, I haven't been doing it."

"But sir, you have. It's your signature on the bottom of every one of those documents."

"Yes. I have been rubber-stamping your rather impressive work. You have been a tremendous help. I just wanted to tell you how fortunate I feel to be working with you. This is a challenging time for me. Thank you. Sincerely, thank you."

"You are welcome, Your Honor. It's mostly administrative details. I'd better get back to work."

She rose and turned. It seemed she was walking on a cloud. Maybe it was the talcum powder.

* * *

Fred Arcineaux called late that afternoon. He'd had his interview.

"I'm on my way," Boucher said.

The shrimper sat on the deck of his trawler. The deck was spotless. He'd put out a folding chair for his guest and sat sipping a Diet Coke. Boucher stepped carefully onto the boat. Large steps up or down jolted his still-tender ribs. He took the seat meant for him. From a canvas tote Arcineaux pulled two clear plastic bags containing the shoes Boucher had given him.

"I met the captain of the *Gulf Pride* and was given a tour of the vessel. They treated me like a dignitary. It sure helps to have a word from the owner. I don't know if it helps, but I sketched this layout of the ship." He handed a paper to Boucher. "I went through everything, the crew's quarters, the galley, the bridge, the nav station, the hold, everywhere. I didn't see anything unusual. The hold was empty, and there were only a couple of crew members on board. They'd gotten in the day before."

"Did he say where they'd been?"

"No. He said they service offshore rigs."

"What was the job you were interviewing for?"

"Galley cook, like you said. I told him I was a shrimper, but if they brought on a store of shrimp, I could cook 'em any way they wanted. I did that bit from *Forrest Gump* where Bubba goes on about the ways to cook shrimp. The captain said that might work, because their runs are usually two days out and two days back. I thought that was curious."

"Why?"

"Two days on a vessel like that can put you several hundreds of miles out to sea. There aren't many rigs that far out. In the whole gulf, there are only two that I know of that are two hundred miles offshore. Farther out than that, and you're in international waters. You could make that distance zigzagging between wells closer to shore, but the way he said it made me think he was talking about straight out, straight back. Another strange thing—he said I'd be restricted to the galley and crew's quarters; the rest of the ship would be off-limits. You don't do that to a seaman. You never know where you might need him."

"Did he offer you the job?"

"He did. I thanked him and said I'd think about it. He won't be surprised if I say no. He knows I captain my own trawler and I'm just going through a rough patch."

Boucher looked around. "How much would it take to repair your boat?"

Arcineaux told him.

Boucher reached in his coat pocket, pulled out a checkbook, wrote a check, and handed it over. "Fix it, then have me over for dinner. Gulf shrimp, fresh-caught, prepared any way you like." He shook the hand of the stunned shrimper, then picked up the shoes. "Thanks for your help." He started to leave.

"Wait a minute, we had a deal. You find out anything, you keep me in the loop. Something funny going on, I'm on board, remember?"

"I remember. I owe you."

Arcineaux looked at the check. "I'd say it's the other way 'round. But if I can help you, I want to be included."

Boucher nodded. "I'll be in touch."

"Yeah," Fitch said, "why would they restrict an able-bodied experienced seaman to galley and quarters? Because they're hiding their cargo. That floater we found, poor guy ignored those orders, saw something he wasn't supposed to see. The trooper got his because he was going to arrest the ship and keep it in port. They had to get it out to sea. When I get back the lab report on those shoes, I think I'll know what that cargo might be."

After meeting at headquarters and dropping off the shoes at the lab, they were sharing an early dinner at Landry's seafood restaurant on Lakeshore Drive, overlooking Lake Pontchartrain. It was a family-style restaurant and packed with early diners of all ages. Boucher's cell phone buzzed. He clicked it on. "Mildred, you're not still at the office, are you? I did? You didn't have to do that. Thank you very much. I will. I'll call him this evening."

He clicked it off and smiled. "I like to believe that when you give people a chance, they will exceed your expectations.

That woman was stuck in the bankruptcy file room for over twenty years. She could run the whole district court."

"Wish I had a secretary like that. Could have saved me a lot of time today."

"Don't call her a secretary. She's my assistant," Boucher said, a little more gruff than he'd intended.

"What's the big deal? The word was still in the English language the last time I checked, and none of the president's department heads seem to take offense at it. You don't like the word 'secretary,' you could call the lady your *chef de cabinet.*"

"That's a secretary to a minister."

"Well, you're a federal official with a lifetime appointment. On second thought, that title won't work. I've seen your office. It's filled with cardboard boxes. You ain't got no *cabinet.* Anyway, it's more important how you treat a person than what you call them, and you treat her with respect. If you're not interested, I won't tell you what your poor overworked public servant found out today—without the help of an assistant. Or a secretary."

"You want me to beg?"

"Just a little. That's enough. I checked the city records to see who might have gotten the contract to do the reconstruction work on the Jackson Barracks. It turns out the prime contractor was a wholly owned subsidiary of Dumont Industries. They have a construction company in their empire too."

"So the warehouse where those men stole illegal guns belonged to Dumont?"

"As they say, if the shoe fits."

Boucher smiled. "That message from my assistant? She wanted me to know that Dumont called me this afternoon."

"What did he want?"

"He sent another invitation to my office and followed it up with a personal phone call. He wants to know if I'd be interested in joining him in a private party he's having tomorrow night on his riverboat casino. He said the guest list would be quite interesting. Mildred dropped it off at my house. He wouldn't tell her, but I'm sure he's getting together a high-stakes poker game."

Fitch toyed with his water glass, drawing lines in the condensation. "There's something funny about this picture," he said.

"What do you mean?"

"What does this guy want with you? He knows you and I discovered the body of one of his employees floating in the gulf."

"How would he know that?"

"Our names are on the report. He's a friend of the chief. Then he met me when I got sent to his house on a cleanup detail and found the bullet that killed his maid. I told the chief that the calibers are the same in the guns used in your attempted robbery and the maid's murder, and that I thought he was hiding the murder weapon. Then he invites you out, and you get shot with another of the illegal guns, which we know came from his damned warehouse! Now he's inviting you into his inner circle? Why? I'm thinkin' that for some reason, he's bustin' a gut wanting to tell you about what he's doing. And you're a federal judge. It makes no sense. I'm wondering if he's crazy. Dumont had a kid who was killed in Mexico. I remember being told it was a brutal murder. Might have made him a little nuts, you know?"

"It's not lunacy. Men with wealth and power believe they can do pretty much what they want. It's a construct as old as time. They believe they're immune to laws that govern the rest of us because they think they can control those who make them and those who enforce them, so they act without fear of consequence, with impunity. Immunity, impunity."

"And this is relevant to what I was just saying how?"

"Dumont thinks he can buy me."

"Why would he want to?"

"Maybe he collects people like he collects antiques. I'm a judge. Maybe he thinks that could be useful in some way. Maybe he just likes me."

"I ain't saying you're not a swell guy, but—"

"I kill people. That impresses some folks."

* * *

When Boucher got home, he found the sealed invitation Mildred had stuck under his door. He opened and read it, then made the call.

"Ray, this is Jock Boucher. I've been meaning to call and thank you and Elise for the flowers. They were beautiful. They were still fresh when I left the hospital, and we divided them among the patients on the floor. They all enjoyed them."

"It was nothing. How are you feeling? I heard you caught the guy who shot you; went after him yourself. Judge Boucher, I can't tell you how much I admire you. Few men have the courage to exact retribution from the criminals who plague our society. I know I don't."

"It didn't go down quite that way. How did you hear about it?"

"I've got friends in this town, you know that. Anyway, I called to ask how you were feeling and if you might be up for a game of poker tomorrow night. I know this is sudden, but a friend from Houston is flying in, and he always likes a game. There'll be a couple other friends who'd like to meet you."

"You know I haven't played in a long time."

"Good. Maybe I'll get back some of that money you won from me at the casino. So you're in?"

"Sure, why not. What time?"

"Six. We start early so we can have a bite to eat, a couple

of drinks, and plenty of time to play. It's no-limit Texas Hold 'Em. Weeknight games have a curfew, since we all work for a living. The weekenders are all-night marathons, but I don't want to throw you in the deep end yet. Come and test the waters. It'll get your blood circulating, that's for sure."

"Sounds like fun."

"Good. I'll send my car for you. The driver will drop you off at the employees' entrance to the casino, and someone will lead you to the suite."

"I hope a smoking jacket is not required. Mine is a little the worse for wear."

"We ask for a coat and tie. It's a gentlemen's game."

"Do I need to bring anything?"

"Just your checkbook. I'm looking forward to having you join us, Judge Boucher. I think you'll fit right in with our little group. By the way, are you going to be home for the next hour?"

"I'm in for the evening."

"Good. I'm sending something over. See you tomorrow, Judge."

Boucher hung up the phone thinking not about the conversation but about the finer points of poker. The last time he'd played cards, Texas Hold 'Em had been known only to Las Vegas regulars and folks from the South Texas town of Robstown, where they claimed to have invented it. He figured he'd better find a couple of websites to help him bone up if he didn't want to give his money away.

Boucher fixed himself a bourbon on the rocks, sat in front of his unlit fireplace, and began Web surfing on his iPad. The doorbell rang. It was past dusk, the last light of day below the horizon. He looked out the window. A minivan was parked out front. Dumont had said he was sending something. Boucher hadn't expected the delivery this soon.

"Who is it?" he asked from inside the closed door.

"Delivery for Judge Boucher from Mr. Dumont, sir."

He opened the door. There were two men and a very large object wrapped in packing paper and bubble wrap. "What is this?"

"It's from Mr. Dumont, sir. Here's a note." The man handed it over. It read, *Jock, Elise is always complaining I have too much stuff. I wanted this piece to have a home where it would be appreciated. I know you will enjoy it. P.S. Look in the center drawer.*

It was the campaign desk.

"Bring it in," Boucher said, and directed them to his study. He had two wingback leather chairs in front of the window and a butler's table between them. The men moved these around and put the desk in their place. It fit perfectly. He knew he had a period side chair somewhere that would be a good match. He thanked the delivery men and opened the center drawer to find a two-volume set published in

1864: *Memoirs of Lieut. General Scott, L.L.D. Written by Himself.*

Boucher called Fitch. "Not only has Dumont invited me to join his distinguished group of poker-playing buddies, he just sent me an antique desk and a rare-edition book. I might be crazy, but I think he's trying to draw me into his world."

Fitch was silent.

"Are you there?" Boucher asked.

"I was thinking. No, never mind."

"What is it?"

"I was wondering what you might learn if you let him take you into his confidence, that's all. But I'd worry too much to ask that you spy on the man. You attract jeopardy like free beer draws a crowd. But since you'll spend the evening with him anyway, just pay attention. There's something strange going on with this guy."

Jock said good-bye, then picked up the rare book and read the first pages of the autobiography of U.S. General Winfield Scott.

CHAPTER 17

THE NEXT EVENING BOUCHER was ready and waiting when Dumont's limousine pulled up front. He locked his door and held his breath. He'd made the same walk to the same car and gotten shot. He looked around as the chauffeur got out of the car.

"Can I help you, sir?" It was the same driver. He had noticed the judge's hesitancy. No doubt he'd been told about the incident.

"Thanks, I'm fine."

The driver held the door open, and Boucher got in the limo. He noticed his hand was shaking, but he also noticed the built-in bar with a bottle of Jack Daniel's Gentleman Jack, crystal highball glasses, and an ice bucket. He poured a drink to settle his nerves. There was enough time to finish it before they arrived at the casino. An attendant was waiting to walk Boucher to the employees' entrance, then through the riverboat to the second level.

They walked the covered upper promenade deck, passing doors to what may have been guest rooms. A door was opened, and Boucher entered. On the far side of the room, four men in suits and ties were standing around a serving table piled high with hors d'oeuvres and bottles of liquor, with a white-vested barman serving drinks. Ray Dumont turned and welcomed him. "Good evening, Judge. Come on in."

The first thing Boucher noticed was the thickness of the wine-colored carpet. It felt ankle-deep. The walls were wainscoted dark-stained wood. In the center of a hand-painted fresco on the ceiling hung an enormous crystal chandelier. The mahogany card table directly under the chandelier was circular. The armchairs were covered in tufted Ferrari-red leather. The smoke in the air was from cigars, not cigarettes. An offering of hand-rolled cigars from the Cigar Factory on Bourbon Street was in a glass-topped display cabinet just inside the door. This was a man cave. A rich man's cave.

Boucher was introduced to the group. Carl Benetton was the lawyer from Houston whom Dumont had mentioned as the reason for scheduling the game. The name rang a bell, though Jock couldn't place him. Jim Farmer, Louisiana's senior U.S. senator, he'd met previously. Again away from the U.S. Capitol, it seemed the senator preferred the levees of the Mississippi to the banks of the Potomac. Gary Quaid was the head of an acronym organization that Boucher had never heard of but pretended he knew, and James Daly was the president of the bank Dumont owned. Playing poker with his boss? Boucher didn't envy him. Dumont explained that his employee was a substitute for a regular player who'd had a last-minute emergency.

Dumont gave the group his reason for inviting Boucher. "Judge Boucher is the kind of man I know each one of us here respects," Dumont said. "He killed two armed trespassers on his property in self-defense a few months ago—with his bare hands. Recently, he was held up by a street criminal. He slammed the crook, who died that same night. Just last week, he was shot right outside his house. The thug got away but not for long. The judge tracked him down as soon as he got out of the hospital, and the creep is sitting in a jail cell as we speak."

Boucher recalled his earlier words to Fitch: "I kill people. It impresses some folks." Maybe Dumont's interest was nothing more than that.

Senator Farmer was the first to shake Boucher's hand, his smile effusive and phony.

"If Ray had put in a word for you back then, I assure you my vote for your appointment would have been different, party line notwithstanding."

"It's all right, Senator. I bear no grudge. Of course, if

you walk away with too much of my money tonight, that assessment might change."

"I hope not. I tend to do reasonably well at these little gatherings, don't I, gentlemen?"

"The senator's luck is about to change. Hello, I'm Carl Benetton. I've read about you, Judge. You made the Houston papers. If you keep putting down bad guys like you've been doing, you'll put us criminal defense lawyers out of business."

The lawyer wore a Zegna suit, dark gray; a white-on-white silk shirt with French cuffs; gold cuff links, mask of tragedy on the right wrist, comedy on the left; and a burgundy silk tie with a matching pocket square. He was Boucher's height, which made it easy for them to look each other straight in the eye. He had thick black hair, graying at the temples, which gave his youthful, unlined face an air of sagacity. He could have come from either Mediterranean or Latin lineage. He and Boucher were the youngest in the group by at least a decade.

Dumont dismissed the bartender, then walked over and addressed Boucher. "There's one thing I wanted to mention, Judge, before we start playing. We all have an understanding: anything we say in this room stays in this room. We are free to comment on anything we like, and at times some rather controversial views might be expressed. We share confidences. We enjoy a certain bond."

"Warning," Senator Farmer said, "sometimes the controversy is a ploy to throw you off your game."

"Speaking of the game," Dumont said, "let's get started."

They took their seats.

"The game is no-limit Texas Hold 'Em. We play till one a.m. The hand in play as the clock strikes one is the last hand. All of us have day jobs."

Dumont began dealing. Boucher sat to his left. On his left was the man who'd said little up to this point, Gary Quaid. He was a solid rock of a man, built like a refrigerator. As if to emphasize his sharp corners, his red hair was closely cropped in a fifties-style flattop, the front fringe frozen to attention with gel. The sides and back of his head could have been shaved with a straight razor. He was big, not fat, though rolls of flesh gathered like strands of rope at the back of his thick neck. His face was freckled and fair and showed the effects of much sun, and his fingers were short and as thick as the cigar he held. He was no violin player. Boucher's first impression: the man was a tank with about as much warmth as the armored vehicle.

"I'm sorry," Boucher said, "what did you say you did?"

Dumont spoke. "Mind if I tell him, Gary?" The silent man just nodded. "Gary used to run the DEA in this region. For the last several years, he has been the head of the MAFS, Multi-Agency Force South. It's an organization formed pursuant to special executive order after 9/11 revealed the lack of coordination between government agencies charged with security of our homeland. It's composed of representatives from the Departments of Defense, Treasury, and Transportation, the FBI, the DEA, the NSA, and others. His organization has liaisons with Europe and most of South America. Their main mission is international counternarcotics operations, and his command center controls deployment of aircraft and ships from the U.S. Navy, Air Force, and Coast Guard to stop the flow of illicit drugs in the southeastern U.S. and gulf coast areas. He is probably as powerful as any military commander in any of our armed forces today."

Boucher said, "Wow."

Quaid said, "Deal."

Boucher was sitting at a card table with one of the most powerful men fighting the war against drugs, and with the forces at his command, *war* was an operative word. Senator Farmer was hardly a slouch when it came to authority, being a ranking member of the legislative body. Despite the profiles of the players, the opening chatter was only poker banter.

It was soon obvious that the fish at the table was James Daly, the president of Dumont's bank. He was probably playing the role his boss had given him—designated loser, as his chagrin over his losses seemed a bit forced. After several hours, it was time for a break. Trays of fresh snacks were brought in, and the bartender returned to restock. During the break, Senator Farmer buttonholed

Boucher. He was determined to make amends for his vote against the judge's nomination, having learned to his horror that Ray Dumont, undoubtedly one of his largest contributors, thought highly of the man. Boucher nodded politely, looking over the senator's shoulder as he spoke. Quaid and the lawyer from Houston stood in a far corner, engaged in intense whispered conversation. Even in this room where confidences were kept, the topic was for them alone. They seemed to have reached some sort of agreement when Dumont called for the game to resume. They nodded to each other before taking their seats. Boucher could have sworn that the lawyer relayed a signal to Dumont, which was in turn passed to the senator. He and the banker were the odd men out.

It was Gary Quaid's turn to deal, which made Boucher last in the rotation and gave him the longest look at the cards in the flop, turn, and river, and the most time to consider his bets. Quaid was no more talkative when the game resumed. It was Senator Farmer who threw out the comment, as if tossing raw meat to hungry dogs. "I read some of those damned WikiLeaks. There was a quote from a high-level Mexican official in their Ministry of Internal Security. He said they were losing control of the border regions of their country to the drug cartels. He gave an eighteen-month deadline to turn things around. That deadline has long since passed. Nothing has turned around. Just a couple of years ago, some in our military, some of our own diplomats were calling Mexico a failed state because of its inability to eradicate the cartels."

"That's an irresponsible choice of words for a sovereign nation, one of our closest allies and largest trading partners, a country with the second-largest economy in Latin America," Boucher said.

"I agree with Judge Boucher," the lawyer Benetton said. "We'd certainly be offended if our government was called a failed state, yet there are American ranchers along the border from Texas to California, some of the most patriotic men in America, who are saying just that. They claim they are not being provided the protections guaranteed to them as U.S. citizens under the Constitution, that there is no security on our side of the border, and that a ten-mile no-man's-land exists where no American is safe, where sovereign U.S. territory is overrun by cartels conducting their illegal activities. If Mexican officials are admitting they've lost control of their border region, U.S. citizens on our side of the border are claiming the same thing. The truth is, gentlemen, both governments are failing their citizens."

There was silence. It was as if each one were hiding behind poker faces. All eyes were on Boucher.

"I was in Mexico recently," he said. "Puerto Vallarta. One of the most beautiful coastlines I've ever seen. Whose bet is it? Let's keep this moving."

"Sorry," Benetton said. "It's my bet. I raise fifty dollars."

"Anyway," said Senator Farmer, "the situation on the

border is like a cancer, and it's spreading. We need to cut it out at the source like a malignant tumor."

"I agree with you, Senator," Dumont said. "But I bet the judge and the lawyer sitting at this table would point out a litany of international legal reasons why we can't do a damned thing."

"Actually," Benetton said, "there is ample legal precedent for just the opposite, if anyone wants a history lesson."

"Can we finish this hand first?" Boucher pleaded. His urgency induced everyone to fold, and he won the pot, which should have been much larger. "Okay," he said, "continue, counselor."

"There have been incursions by U.S. forces into Mexico since the 1830s," Benetton began. "At first we chased Indians. In 1876 Secretary of State Fish stated that chasing Indians into Mexico was not a violation of the law of nations, because Mexico was judged to be without power to prevent or redress the hostile actions. In 1877 the secretary of defense gave Generals Sherman and Ord authority to occupy Mexican territory if, in their judgment, it was warranted. We entered into an agreement with Mexico in 1882 that provided for the crossing of armed forces of either side in pursuit of Indians.

"In 1914, President Wilson learned of a shipment of arms being sent to General Huerta, who had seized power in a coup aided and abetted by the U.S. ambassador, Henry Lane Wilson, no relation. The president ordered the navy to seize the port of Veracruz and we occupied it for six months. It turned out that the shipment had been sent by the Remington Arms company by way of Germany as a subterfuge. We seized a Mexican port to intercept weapons sent from the U.S. in the first place. And people think the Fast and Furious fiasco was a farce.

"Then in 1916 Pancho Villa attacked Columbus, New Mexico, and killed twenty-four Americans. General Pershing led five thousand troops across the border to find him, and that expedition lasted over a year. In 1919, after World War I, three thousand U.S. forces under General DeRosey Cabell crossed from El Paso and chased Villa's troops out of Juárez into the desert. There was a mild protest against this alleged violation of Mexico's sovereignty, but our State Department answered strongly that American lives and property would be protected. The international legal doctrine of 'hot pursuit' was used in support of this action, even though no Mexicans actually crossed into the U.S."

"No Mexicans crossed into the United States, yet we sent troops into their country in hot pursuit?" the banker asked.

"Shots fired by the Villistas reached El Paso, killing an American soldier and a civilian and wounding six others. That was enough reason to send three thousand troops across the border. It shows how little justification is needed. The principles of self-defense were deemed immutable. There is historical legal precedent that the doctrine of hot pursuit would justify chasing intruders back across the border—even occupying Mexican territory, if necessary."

"I have a question," Boucher said. "You mentioned Villa's attack on Columbus, New Mexico, that induced Pershing's expeditionary force to cross the border and chase him. Why did Villa attack in the first place? He must have known we would respond."

"There is evidence to support the conclusion that it was a gun deal gone bad," Benetton said. "A man named Ravel lived in Columbus and was said to have received payment from Villa for guns he never delivered. The first thing the Villistas did when they rode into Columbus that day was hunt for Ravel. He was out of town. Some historians suggest that Villa had some sophisticated strategy in mind, but it doesn't fit the personality of the man. In everything he did, he was a bull. He rarely employed anything like a military strategy. In most of his battles during the revolution, he massed his troops and charged. It worked for him in the early days, and then it didn't. But he never changed tactics. His raid on Columbus was in keeping with his personality. It was that of an angry bull."

"You can't seriously suggest," Boucher said, "that circumstances over a century ago have relevance today."

Benetton shrugged. "I'm sure you've all heard the saying 'Those who forget history are doomed to repeat it.' Winston Churchill also said, 'The longer you can look back, the farther you can look forward.' Those were observations of men far more intelligent than I."

"The drug cartels are no less a threat today than Pancho Villa was then, and just as out of control as the Indians were," Dumont said. "As Senator Farmer said earlier, even members of the Mexican government are admitting that they have no control over large areas of their own country. Are we going to wait until al-Qaeda and the Taliban collude with the cartels and attack us from Mexico? We've already lost American lives on both sides of the border. If you say there's precedent under international law, I say it's time we do something. What do you think, Judge?"

Boucher studied his cards. The river could give him a full house. He'd already lost the possibility of a larger pot by trying to keep the game moving and would not repeat that mistake. He took a breath and fanned his cards. "The situation in Mexico is dangerous and troubling," he said. "More than sixty thousand people have been killed there in recent years, and that's a tragedy of global proportions. We can't overlook our role. We're buying the drugs, and we're selling the cartels the guns. That's two thirds of the triangle. I agree that something must be done, but while the suggestion of precedent is interesting historically, nothing has happened that would justify implementation of hot pursuit."

"But if such an event were to occur?" Dumont pressed.

"If American lives were at risk, the president would have to weigh some very difficult options, one of which might be to send troops into Mexico," Boucher said. "And I'm sure there would be those among his advisers who would cite the historical precedents Mr. Benetton has noted. There are other factors to consider, since an incursion into the territory of a sovereign nation might be considered an act of war. Senator Farmer, I'm sure, is more of an expert on that issue than I am."

"Were you listening to what has already been said?" the senator said. "When Mexico was judged to be without power to control Indians, our incursions were not deemed to be a violation of the law of nations. Now the country has lost the ability to control the cartels. I think the precedent Mr. Benetton cited is right on point. What is being suggested would be considered a police action, not an act of war. A nation that cannot maintain civil order over criminal elements in its territory would have a weaker claim to sovereignty over that area. If we crossed the border in response to a threat to our territory or its citizens, not only would it be justified, but the commander in chief could send backup forces across the border to support the first responders. Hell, he could chase them down to Ecuador."

"Without a declaration of war?" Dumont asked.

"There hasn't been a declaration of war since 1941. Not in Korea, Vietnam, Grenada, Iraq, or Afghanistan. We sent forces into each of those countries. Now, damn it, I want to play poker."

Boucher picked up his cards. "Me too. I raise one hundred dollars."

The game recommenced, and poker trumped politics. The subject was not brought up again, and nothing of consequence was said by any one of them for the remainder of the evening. The final hour was approaching. It was time for down-and-dirty. It was time for concentration and deployment of each and every possible psychological gambit. It was time to win or be counted out.

When the counting was done, Boucher had done respectably; the senator—the biggest ego—was the biggest winner; and the banker, no surprise, was the biggest loser. They all shook hands and said good-bye, stating that Boucher was welcome back anytime. Dumont stood aside, smiling at the acceptance of his invitee. The men were met by a casino employee who accompanied each of them to waiting transportation.

"Judge, I'll give you a ride home," Dumont said. "This time I'm going to personally make sure you get safely inside."

They were ushered into the backseat of the limo. Dumont reached for the bottle and poured two glasses. "There's never a more suitable place for 'one for the road' than the backseat of your own limo." He poured two. "My friends liked you."

"I couldn't tell. They take their poker and their politics seriously—particularly, it seems, the situation in Mexico."

"I can't deny that. It has touched each of us one way or another. I lost my son down there."

"Yes, I was told. I'm sorry for your loss."

There was silence for the rest of the drive. They pulled up in front of Boucher's house.

"Sit for a minute," Dumont said. He knocked on the glass partition and motioned for the driver to wait. "You're a young man, Judge," he said. "You have achieved at an early age what, for most men in your profession, would be the beginning of the most productive phase of a career. Yet your future looks broken. You're standing at the edge of the cliff, waiting to jump—or be pushed. Am I right?"

"Leaving the bench would not be the end of my life." Boucher paused. "But I've never been less sure of my future."

"I can help you. I can make you one of the most powerful, respected men in this country—far more than any judge—and I can guarantee you the kind of wealth that will ensure that power and respect."

"Why would you do that for me?"

"I'm not sure. I've been asking myself the same question. Maybe it's the way you dispose of those who do you harm. As I told you, I find that admirable."

"Most people would call it vengeance. I'm a vengeful man who acts without thinking. I don't think that credits me."

"I disagree. I think vengeance is a trait necessary in a man of power. I remember asking my father late in his life something inane, like to what he attributed his many years of success. He said to me, 'My enemies. Every day I wake, I thank God for my enemies.' He was vengeful, and he was feared by every man in Louisiana till the day he died. But it's not just that. It's, it's . . ." He took another sip, then set the glass down in the holder. "My only son," he said. "I've been helpless to avenge his death. Maybe that's why I admire your ability to dispose of evil men."

"Ray," Boucher said softly, "I'm not proud of what I've done, and most condemn me for my actions."

"I don't. I can help you. I want to help you."

"In return for what?"

"Your loyalty, nothing more. Think about it. I don't need an answer right now. We'll have time to get to know each other better."

"To change the subject, I want to thank you again for that desk. It fits in my study perfectly. I know I'm going to really enjoy it."

"That's as it should be. I hope you enjoy the reading matter as well."

"General Scott's memoir? I can't wait to start reading it. I've scanned the first few pages. I'm afraid I've never given him enough credit. I've always been fascinated with the Civil War and remembered him only as the general who was too old when it started and had to step down."

"Some called him the equal to Napoleon and the

greatest military mind of his age. His accomplishments are still being praised today. An essay by a U.S. Marine colonel, 'Winfield Scott's 1847 Mexico City Campaign as a Model for Future War,' won a competition sponsored by the Joint Chiefs of Staff in 2009. We could use a man like Winfield Scott. Especially now, since we're . . ." He left the sentence unfinished. "We'll continue our discussion after you finish your reading."

"I'd like that. I would also like to be invited back when you get another game going. Your friends are unique individuals. I don't often get the chance to converse with men as involved with issues of the day as they are."

"Involved," Dumont said as if the word held some private meaning. "They certainly are that. Good night, Judge. We'll talk soon. You take care of yourself."

The driver had stepped out and opened the door for Boucher, then accompanied him up his walk.

"Thanks. I can take it from here," Boucher said. At his door, he turned and waved to Dumont, who raised his glass in toast.

CHAPTER 18

THE NEXT WORKDAY WAS uneventful. Boucher realized he'd had too few days like this lately. Mildred was also appreciative of a return to routine. At day's end, she stood in the doorway of his office to say good night.

"Your Honor, please tell me you are going straight home to do nothing but rest this evening."

"Mildred, I would be lying if I told you that. I am going to pay a call on a drug dealer who tried to kill me. After I've visited him, then, yes, I will be going home and to bed early. Thank you for your concern."

"Your Honor, empathy has its limits." She gave a little sigh. "But I guess little harm can come to you in a jail, as long as you remember on which side of the bars you belong. Good evening, Judge."

He smiled and nodded. A few minutes later, he locked up and took the elevator down to the main lobby. A federal marshal manning the metal scanner called to him. "Judge Boucher, I was asked to tell you, there's a parking space for you now. Please use it tomorrow."

"Thanks. I will."

Hallelujah. His assigned parking space. It was better than a presidential citation. He walked to the public lot for the last time, got in his pickup, and drove to the Quarter. Fitch had pulled strings to get Pip into a cell at the Eighth District, rather than lose him both literally and figuratively in the bowels of the midcity Orleans Parish Prison, the subject of horrendous claims of inmate maltreatment for years. Boucher was shown to the cell. Fitch was out on a call, expected back soon. Boucher asked for the cell to be unlocked. The custodian looked at him like he was crazy, but Fitch had left orders: the judge was to be given carte blanche. The door was opened, and Boucher stepped in the cell, closing it behind him. "Pip?"

The prisoner was on his bunk, his face to the wall. He turned and looked over his shoulder, then sat up.

"I just wanted you to know that we've done some checking, and we think you told us the truth," Boucher said.

"You thought I made up that shit?"

"I believe you now."

"Does that change anything? My brother's still dead."

"Your brother died because he abused his body. You want to change things? Then stop living the self-destructive life he did. Where he is now, he's regretting what he did to himself, and he wants something better for you."

Pip stood up, glaring at Boucher. "Don't you start that hosanna shit with me, 'cause that dog won't hunt. 'Where he is now,'" he spat. "What does that mean? Where *is* he now? Nobody told me what y'all did with my brother. Did you bury or burn him? What was the cheapest and quickest way for the city to get rid of the body of someone they forgot a long time ago? I know one thing—where he is now, he don't have to worry about bugs in his crotch, his hair, and his ears, havin' to live with them till winter comes and he freezes his ass off. He don't have to eat out of garbage cans no more. He don't have to worry about someone beating the crap out of him when he sleeps on the street 'cause they think he got something worth stealing or they ain't got nothin' better to do. And he don't have to go through the hell of fallin' off that cliff when he ain't able to score. That's heaven to those of us you call homeless: just getting out of this life of shit. Now get the fuck outta my face."

It was instinctive, it was visceral, and legions would have argued whether it was right or wrong, but Boucher's response was immediate. He slapped the foulmouthed ingrate. He checked his swing so that only his extended fingers struck Pip's face, but it sounded like a pistol shot, which stunned as much as the contact.

"In or out of court, no one speaks to a federal judge

like that," Boucher snapped. "Now stand up straight. You slump like you've got the weight of the world on your shoulders when the fact is, you're just plain lazy and think you can get away with crying about your miserable life rather than doing something about it. You have never exercised one tenth of your ability, because it's easier for you to grovel in self-pity. I said stand up straight. You're a man. You're a man in the greatest city in the greatest country in the world, and there's nothing you can't achieve with hard work and a sense of purpose. Do you know why you're stuck in the mud? It's because you don't have the balls to lift your feet. You just don't have the balls."

"Verbal skills," Fitch said, making his unannounced arrival and stepping into the cell with them. "I do believe that's what separated us from the animals and set us on the evolutionary fast track to the civilized species we've become. I'm not interrupting anything, am I? You comfortable in here, sir? Because if you're not appreciative of your present circumstances, I can have you moved. You might want to experience the Orleans Parish Prison while you can. I'm told a plan has been approved for a new facility more in keeping with our great city's reputation for hospitality. How you doing, Judge?"

"Pip and I were just having a conversation about the meaning of life," Boucher said.

"I thought it was something high-minded like that." Fitch looked at the inmate. "You do realize this man here wants to help you, don't you? This man you almost killed, he wants to help you make something of your life. You remember your old principal, Mrs. Miller? She'd like to see you crawl out of the slime as well."

"Mrs. Miller?" Pip's eyebrows rose. "She remember me?" He'd been rubbing his stinging cheek, as if ready to make a complaint about his brutal treatment. He dropped his hand.

"Maybe it was your brother," Fitch said. "She never could tell you two apart."

"That ain't true. Don't know how, but she always knew. Other than her, our mother was the only one could tell us apart. You know Mrs. Miller?"

"She's a friend," Fitch said, looking away.

"I'll be damned," Pip said. "You and Mrs. Miller?" He walked straight up to the detective, and for the very first time in their brief acquaintance, the young man showed a hint of backbone. "You better treat her right. She's good people."

After a long silence, Pip asked, "What's gonna happen to me?"

"Depends," Fitch said. "You could make things a lot easier on yourself."

"How? Already told you everything I know about the guns. Except . . ."

"Except what?"

Pip paced, then stopped. "I told you we went back and they had dogs and guards, right? I heard one of the guards say something about moving the stuff that was in the warehouse."

"What did you hear?" Fitch asked.

"One said that all the stuff was going to be moved to the new compound, that it wasn't a big deal because the work at the Jackson Barracks was almost finished and they'd have to move it anyway."

"New compound? Is that all?" Fitch said.

"Give him a break," Boucher said. "He's trying to help."

Fitch turned to Pip. "Okay, here's how it's going down. You're going to have a lawyer, a public defender. You broke laws, and there are consequences. But the judge here is going to speak up for you, and I'm going to say you've been cooperative. Let's leave it at that for now. I suggest that you spend whatever time you have in this little cell thinking about what you could do with your life to change it. You can make that happen. Only you."

Fitch followed Boucher to his house.

"I'd have been happy to buy you a drink somewhere," Fitch said as they walked in the door.

"I need to stay in tonight," Boucher said. "I promised. Beer okay with you?"

"Yeah, fine."

They walked to the kitchen, grabbed a couple of cans, then sat at the table.

"You know what he meant by the new compound?" Boucher said.

"Houma. Doesn't come as much of a surprise. There was a lot of work going on there about the time the Jackson Barracks renovation was completed, including a new airport. But damn, that's a big operation Dumont's got. Security's tight too."

"We Google like we did before," Boucher said.

"You ever wonder who's watching us Google? We hunt up something on a map, somebody somewhere is watching us do it. Anyway, it's a start," Fitch said. "I'd do anything before trying to get a search warrant. If I was to try and get a warrant to search Ray Dumont's headquarters based solely on the word of a homeless street punk, they'd lock me up and throw away the key. You don't piss in the yard of the most powerful man in Louisiana. By the way, I got the lab reports on the shoes your guy wore on the boat. Inconclusive. Sorry."

"What do you mean, inconclusive?"

"I mean the traces of cocaine were so small, they were inconclusive."

"Who said we were looking for cocaine?"

"We didn't know what we were looking for. What I'm telling you is that we found cocaine, but there wasn't enough of it to be significant. It was almost an anomaly; it barely registered. There was a very small amount of cocaine residue on the soles of his shoes, and I'm assuming it came from the hold."

"That doesn't make sense," Boucher said. "I can't believe Dumont thinks he's so bulletproof that he would traffic in cocaine when his close friends are in charge of the country's war against illicit drugs."

"What close friends?"

Boucher told him of the players at the poker game. Fitch frowned. "That Gary Quaid, he's big. He can move more assets than a general. What was the Houston lawyer's name again?"

"Carl Benetton."

"I know that name," Fitch said.

Boucher yawned. "Let's call it a night. I'm going to do a couple Internet searches before I go to bed."

"Check and see what committees Senator Farmer is on. I'm getting that feeling again." Fitch finished his beer. "I hope you got boots. I think you're stepping in some deep shit."

They said good night. Boucher was at his computer an hour later, when his cell phone vibrated with an incoming text message. It was from Fitch. Boucher stared at the small screen. The message was indecipherable. It read: *Not C. $$$$!*

CHAPTER 19

THEY MET FOR COFFEE and beignets the next morning at the Café du Monde before heading to their respective offices.

"I got your message," Boucher said, "but I couldn't understand it."

"I made it intentionally cryptic," Fitch said. "We're going to have to start covering our asses. There's something bigger than both of us going down." He sipped his café au lait. "It hit me on the way home." Though no one was sitting near them, he whispered into his coffee cup. "I know why there was cocaine in such small quantities. Money. There was currency in the hold of that ship, and it had been handled by men who handled cocaine. I read somewhere that ninety percent of currency in circulation has traces of drugs. You and I both probably have cocaine in our wallets right now. Gives you an oblique idea how big the business is. I asked the lab to check again for chemical traces from currency. There should be fibers from the paper and chemicals from ink. Bet you anything it's U.S. bills."

"We saw the vessel loaded before it went out," Boucher said. "It was sitting low in the water. It sold its cargo at sea, brought back cash before Arcineaux was given his tour. Dumont is shipping illegal arms right under the noses of the navy, the coast guard, and almost every national security agency we have."

"Agencies whose coordinated functions are controlled by his poker-playing buddy, the former head of the DEA. Having fought smugglers, he's one guy who knows the tricks of their trade. Did you look up that Houston lawyer?"

Boucher shook his head.

"I did," Fitch said. "He's one of the country's top criminal defense lawyers. He has a pretty impressive client list, several of whom have connections to Mexico's leading drug cartels."

"That would make him Gary Quaid's archenemy. I saw them together. Enemies they were not."

"His clients are in jail. Maybe they're singing. Maybe his representation is not what it seems. *Something* is not what it seems. Did you look up Senator Farmer?"

"I'll do it right now," Boucher said, and took out his

cell phone. "Farmer is chairman of the Senate Armed Services Subcommittee on Emerging Threats and Capabilities. Fitch, what's going on here?"

"God only knows, but the devil's in this too." Fitch's cell phone rang. He answered, listened, said thanks, and clicked off. "The lab. They confirmed that the currency on the ship was U.S. banknotes."

"At that poker game," Boucher said, "conversation was about the border, the problems on both sides, our past incursions into Mexico, and the possibility of history repeating itself."

"That's just politics. Men get together, they talk politics. Don't jump to too many conclusions, Judge. All we really know is that Ray Dumont may be linked to a couple illegal handguns, and that he has an interesting group around his poker table."

"Dumont sent me a desk that may have been owned by General Winfield Scott, the conqueror of Mexico."

"I thought that was Cortés."

"He was first. We did it three hundred years later, just didn't stay as long." Boucher put down his cup, his coffee cold. "Who's he selling guns to?"

"I can get away with that," Fitch said. "You can't."

"Get away with what?"

"Ending a sentence with a preposition."

* * *

Boucher's smile was forced when he arrived at his office and bade Mildred a good morning. He hoped she wouldn't notice that something was bothering him. He buried himself in the files on his desk. The ringing of his office phone was still a rare event, giving Mildred the opportunity to get up from her desk rather than alerting him on the intercom when a call came in.

"It's that Mr. Arcineaux for you," she said. "He sure sounds happy. It's good to hear him like that. I'm so pleased you were able to help him."

Boucher nodded and took the call. "Fred. Nice to hear from you. How's everything?"

"Everything's great, Judge. I've got something I want to show you. Can you come over?"

"I can be there after five. Is that all right?"

"Should still be enough time before the sun goes down. I have to show you in the light."

"I'll see you this evening."

Arcineaux did sound pleased. Boucher guessed he'd made the repairs to his boat.

It was a day of fudging, and he knew he must have looked guilty each time Mildred walked into his office. He was surfing the Internet rather than attending to the files in front of him. His research was more important than any of them. He looked up Gary Quaid's agency. It was a command-and-control center. Its mission was clear, and if he actually gave orders to the agencies under his aegis, then as Fitch had said, he was as powerful as any general in the U.S. armed forces; more so, because air traffic control, customs, and immigration were among other agencies whose activities he could direct when necessary. The bland government websites Boucher studied were in keeping with the transparency that was a hallmark of a democratic society, but they didn't reveal the danger of too much power reposed in too few men—the danger of absolute power. Quaid was coming pretty damn close.

Boucher's head was full, and he was more than ready for a break when the workday ended. He made his way down in the elevator reserved for judges to the underground lot and his assigned space. He left the federal building and joined the homeward-bound throng. Traffic slowed him down, but he made it to Arcineaux's marina with plenty of sun left in the sky. The shrimp trawler was nowhere in sight.

"Hey," a man yelled to him from the flybridge of a motor yacht, "it's me. Come aboard."

Boucher walked toward the craft. It was a Hatteras, over fifty feet in length. He walked the short gangway and stepped onto the cockpit with its teak deck. There was a fighting chair and two removable seats. All was immaculate.

"You like her?" Arcineaux asked.

"How did you—" Boucher began.

"It was a trade. I used the money you gave me and fixed up my trawler, then traded it for this. Got a smokin' deal. The previous owner passed away, and his widow wanted to get rid of it."

"A widow took your trawler in trade?"

"She wanted to put a family member into a new business. I didn't ask too many questions. You know what they say about a gift horse. It's in great shape: reconditioned engines and extra-large fuel tanks. I could drive this baby to Cancún."

"No more shrimping?"

"I'm getting into commercial charter fishing. I can make the money I need, and it will be so much easier. Take out a couple businessmen on a lark, maybe a family. I think I'm going to enjoy this. I only have to hire a deckhand when I need one. And I plan on paying you back, Judge, every penny. Want to take a tour?"

"Sure, Fred. Show me your new vessel."

"I'm going to have to move, find another marina," Fred said as he showed Boucher the helm and its instruments.

"You should talk to Detective Fitch about that. He's a sport fisherman. Uses a marina out near Fort Pike."

"I will. I called those folks at Dumont Industries and thanked them for the opportunity but said I was going into a new line of work. Anything happen after that interview? Those shoes I wore?"

Boucher hesitated. He shouldn't have.

"Come on, Judge. You made a promise."

"Let's take a look at your boat."

Arcineaux gave him the tour. The motor yacht was used but had been maintained with obvious loving care. The salon was small but as comfortable as a nice home's living room. Below were the galley and staterooms. They went back up to the cockpit and sat.

"I can see there's something you're not telling me," Arcineaux said.

"Fred, I know I promised, but there might be something very big going down; illegal activities on a large scale involving powerful men. You've been very helpful, but I don't want to get you involved in a situation that could put you in danger."

"Seems we already crossed that bridge," Fred said.

"Yes, and I had misgivings when I asked you. Now we know something's going on. That's all I can tell you."

"They're smuggling, aren't they? Under the cover of servicing offshore rigs, they're smuggling. Can't be drugs; that traffic goes the other direction. And if they need a boat that size, the cargo has to be—"

"That's enough, Fred."

"Guns. That's it, isn't it? You don't have to answer. Dumont's selling weapons. When I was out there trying to find a few shrimp, I asked myself—while trying to avoid collisions with those reckless bastards—where the hell were they going?" He took a sip, just a sip, of his beer and set it in the cupholder. "That's what they were talking about."

"Who? What who was talking about?"

Arcineaux looked up, rubbing his chin and lowering his head, scratching his temple at the point where his sideburns stopped. Boucher repeated his questions.

"There's a little joint just outside the Dumont Industries compound in Houma," Arcineaux said. "After my interview, I stopped in there for a sandwich and a beer before my drive home. I was sitting in a booth, minding my own business. Two guys came in. Took the booth behind me. Started talking. Foreigners. French-speaking foreigners. Not French French; I know a French accent when I hear one. If I had to guess, I'd say they were Belgians. Poor fools didn't know nothin' about Cajuns. They thought their language was their cover. They were pilots. They'd just flown in a cargo for Dumont. One was saying it was his last run. He'd made his money and didn't need to take any more risks. The other said the next flight would be his last too. Said it alone would make him rich. They were a talkative twosome."

"Did they say anything else?"

"The one planning to make one more flight has put a down payment on his retirement home in Marbella, Spain. He plans to close in a couple weeks. Guess he's coming into some serious money real soon."

"They didn't say their cargo was guns."

"Not specifically, no. But when a man spends as much time alone as I do, he can see things. Know what I mean?"

"Fred, that's called a vivid imagination."

On the teak deck of the motor yacht, the two men sat watching the sun disappear, watching the slow-floating commerce on the Mississippi. They nursed their silent thoughts and now tepid beers.

CHAPTER 20

BOUCHER ARRIVED HOME FROM his meeting with Arcineaux, poured a bourbon on the rocks, and took it to his new desk, not placing the glass on the antique wood. One-handed, he took out the first volume of General Scott's memoirs and began to read but didn't get far. His parents had raised him well, and he was bothered by the conflict rising within him from accepting Dumont's generous gift in light of his suspicions of the man. The dilemma made him uncomfortable, and he decided to do something about it. He went out.

Royal Street had its usual pedestrian traffic for early evening, most ambling in search of a place to dine, but many with money to spend on impulse purchases, justifying the antique stores staying open. Boucher passed one and studied the display window, which testified to the establishment's expertise in a specific niche of the antique trade. Antique firearms. He went inside.

"May I help you, sir?" the attendant asked him.

"A gentleman gave me a valuable antique as a gift," Boucher said. "I want to repay his generosity."

"He is a gun collector?"

"He is," Boucher said. "I know he appreciates antiques with historical provenance."

After admitting his ignorance, he was given an introductory lesson. Antique guns in the United States were those manufactured before 1899 and were exempted from the Federal Firearms License requirements administered by the Bureau of Alcohol, Tobacco, Firearms, and Explosives. Market values for the rarer and more collectible pieces had tripled, even quadrupled, in recent years. Boucher made his selection solely on the basis of price. This was payback. He knew what the desk cost, had a reasonable estimate of the value of the rare books, and selected an item that was in the same price range. An additional benefit—which he would be sure to point out in the accompanying card—it was small enough that Elise Dumont could not complain about it. His choice was a Colt Model 1851 Navy percussion revolver manufactured in 1863. It was in excellent working condition, with most of the blue left on the barrel and most of the varnish on the walnut grips. *Thirty-six-caliber* was visible on the trigger guard. It was perfect.

He gave Dumont's address, attached a card, and asked that it be delivered tomorrow. He was most satisfied on leaving the shop, his dilemma resolved. He could keep the campaign desk without his conscience bothering him. He really liked the desk.

Dumont called him the following evening.

"I absolutely love it," he gushed. "This is one of those 'if this gun could talk' kind of pieces. I don't like it that you thought you had to give me something in return for my gift, but what a fantastic choice. How did you decide on this?"

"Easy," Boucher said. "I liked it. You and I enjoy a lot of the same things. We share many of the same interests."

"Yes. That's partly why I invited you to join our poker group. There are few people I'd introduce to those men."

"Again, I'm grateful. Are you planning another game anytime soon?"

"This Saturday. The man who canceled last time will be there. We're going to have the game at my house rather than the casino. It's more private. You're invited, of course. By the way, Jock, have you read the Scott memoirs?"

"I've just started."

"See if you can finish them before we get together. There's some interesting history in there. I'll see you Saturday. I'll be using the limo for the general. Do you mind driving over?"

"Not if you don't mind a used Ford pickup in your driveway."

"It's fitting. Nothing could be more American. See you then. Seven sharp."

Dumont had assigned him a program for the remainder of the evening. Boucher retired to his study and read. Hours later, he was ready for sleep. The florid nineteenth-century writing style had demanded concentration, and after nearly finishing the first of the two volumes, he was exhausted. He set down the book and rubbed his eyes. Dumont had mentioned the rank of the new player: a general. No doubt he was an aficionado of American military history, Boucher thought. Why else would Dumont ask him to read this tome before the next meeting? Well, should the subject come up, he would be well versed on the life and achievements of General Winfield Scott.

It turned out that turgid prose was to be his lot for the remainder of the working week as well. Over the next several days, he was so overwhelmed with the arcane minutiae of jurisprudence that Scott's reminiscences seemed light fare by comparison. Friday evening he felt well enough to visit his gym. He rationalized that a half hour on the treadmill did not fall within the "strenuous exercise" parameters his doctor had told him to avoid. He didn't even work up a sweat. Later that night he read more of the general's autobiography. If Dumont had expected him to find some revelation in the writings, Boucher felt he had missed it.

Saturday morning dawned with more than a promise of spring. He took his coffee in his courtyard. No jacket was required; the early chill, the haze, and the dew were quickly burned off by the sun. The season was here, and no one hearing the songbirds could have doubted it. Over their chirping, he heard his name called, and he answered, "I'm back here, Fitch."

The detective joined him, looking every inch the role he was playing today—Louisiana sportsman ready for a day on the gulf waters.

"Sorry I'm late," Fitch said. "Do we need to call Arcineaux?"

Boucher pulled his cell phone from his shirt pocket. "Fred? Fitch just got here. We're on our way."

"If there's any left"—Fitch pointed to Boucher's coffee—"I wouldn't mind a cup before we go."

"No problem." Boucher went into the kitchen and returned with a full cup of coffee, black.

"Got him a slip at my marina," Fitch said. "He'll have some competition from other charter sports fishermen who dock there, but they're good guys."

"Arcineaux overheard some men talking in a bar in Houma," Boucher said. "He thinks they were Belgians, pilots who had just flown in a cargo that they said would make them rich. They didn't say specifically what it was. Fred suspects guns."

"Interesting," Fitch said.

The plan for the day was to motor over with Arcineaux in his new cruiser to the marina Fitch had recommended. A car and driver would bring them back in the afternoon. Fitch drank his coffee, then addressed what was on both their minds.

"I don't want this guy involved any further," Fitch said. "Hell, I'm not sure I want to be involved any further."

Boucher agreed. He paused, then said, "I'm playing poker tonight at Dumont's house. Same cast of characters, plus someone new. Should be an interesting evening."

"I don't think of you having too many dull ones. The old ennui isn't a part of your lifestyle." Fitch stood up. "Let's get started."

Fitch left his car in Boucher's drive, and they took a cab to Arcineaux's dock. Minutes later they were under way, part of the great river's caravan rolling out to the sea. It would be a pleasant trip for the short distance along the coast but not the most relaxing. There was too much traffic for that. And Fred Arcineaux was about to ensure that their attention did not stray. He was at the helm and had barely pulled away from the dock when he said, "To smuggle anything into this country by air, you've got to have some people pretty high up the ladder in your pocket, don't you think?"

Neither Fitch nor Boucher said a word.

"Guys," Arcineaux said, "don't think I'm stupid just because I made my living trying to outsmart crustaceans.

One and one is a pretty simple calculation." He kept his eyes ahead as he maneuvered the craft slowly downriver. "You asked me to wear special shoes on one of Dumont's boats. I figured you were looking for traces of drugs. Then I heard those guys talking in that bar. They come to Louisiana and don't know folks can speak French here. What idiots. They admitted they were smuggling, and they'd just flown in from Europe." He turned around to face them sitting in the cockpit. "How'm I doing so far?"

Boucher and Fitch sighed in unison. Their duet was now a trio.

"You do appreciate the danger involved here." Fitch's statement was a question.

"I do. You want me to sign some sort of release? I hereby indemnify and hold harmless, et cetera, et cetera, et cetera. I'm familiar with that language. They were trying to cram it down our throats to accept settlements from the oil spill. Detective, I'm full grown and aware of the consequences of my actions. I want to help. If you ask me why, let's just say Cajuns don't like guys who get too big for their britches. Chance comes along to bring 'em down a peg or two, count me in."

"What did you hear these fellows say?" Fitch asked.

Arcineaux repeated what he'd told Boucher. "I've got some ideas," he added. "New Orleans has free-trade zones. You know what they are, don't you, Judge?"

"A free-trade zone is an area designated to allow goods

to be brought in without duty if they're going to be shipped out again. There are several areas set aside as free-trade zones in and around New Orleans."

"You don't pay customs or duties on stuff shipped to free-trade zones, right?"

"That's usually true."

"Other regulations and stuff can be waived, right?"

"To an extent. It's an economic incentive for local businesses."

"So if the cargo that the Belgians flew in was intended for one of New Orleans's free-trade zones, someone with Dumont's connections could make pretty good use of that, couldn't he?"

"Especially," Fitch broke in, "if he has a buddy who has his finger in air traffic control, ICE, Homeland Security, you name it. May I ask you, Mr. Arcineaux, how you arrived at this conclusion? A shrimper, soon to be sport fisherman, is not usually familiar with details of international shipping and customs."

"I watched a movie on Netflix," Arcineaux said with a smile. "It was about smuggling between New Orleans and South America, and I kept sayin' to myself that Dumont must have seen the same film. We all know he's got powerful friends. So I'm asking you straight out. Is he smuggling in weapons and shipping them out for sale? I can't imagine what else it could be."

"We're not sure," Boucher said, "and we only have a

statement by a street criminal who says he saw contraband in a Dumont warehouse when Jackson Barracks was under renovation."

"We've also got two illegal guns from homeless thugs and a couple of banned-caliber bullets fired in his own home," Fitch added.

"He's smuggling in guns and sellin' 'em. Christ. How much money does one man need?"

"Like the judge said, we don't have much evidence, and you don't go after someone like Dumont ..."

". . . without your own guns loaded," Arcineaux finished. "So the shoes I wore, they picked up traces of something on that boat. What was it?"

"They had traces of drugs."

"I thought you said—"

"The soles of the shoes you wore had traces of cocaine, but the amounts were too small to have come from actual drugs. Currency in circulation has small traces of cocaine, and other tests showed fibers and chemicals used in U.S. banknotes."

"So you think maybe he's shipping out guns and bringing back cash."

"Yes," Fitch and Boucher said in unison.

They reached Fitch's marina, and Arcineaux was shown his new slip. He met his maritime neighbors, who welcomed him to their community. After a few hours of camaraderie, Fitch and Boucher said good-bye. They were silent on the drive home. When they arrived at Boucher's house, a light rain was beginning to fall. The two men walked the steps and stood under his covered porch.

"Arcineaux is right. It doesn't make sense for a man like Dumont to take such a risk." Boucher spoke the thought that had occupied them both during the drive home.

"Unless he's got partners so powerful that it amounts to immunity," Fitch said, "or he's making such a shitload of money that it justifies such a risk."

"I don't know if there is that much money. There's got to be another reason."

The rain was falling heavier.

"This downpour's going to make my evening simple," Fitch said. "It will be dinner and a movie. To be precise, pizza and a DVD."

"No plans with Helen?"

"I didn't say I'd be dining alone. You enjoy your evening with the top guns. Play smart. Know your limits. Why am I telling you this? You're a big boy; just be careful and keep your eyes and ears open. You might learn something tonight. *Bonne chance, mon ami.* I am about to get wet. Not many of us can walk between the raindrops like you." Fitch ran to his car and got soaked in the downpour.

CHAPTER 21

BOUCHER HAD NO TALISMAN, no prayer for good luck; and though he was a faithful Catholic, he felt conflicted about appealing to the patron saint of gamblers, the fifteenth-century Venetian Saint Cajetan. He hardly viewed Texas Hold 'Em as an enterprise worthy of spiritual intercession and decided, in lieu of prayer, he would just try to keep his wits about him.

There were no other cars in the circular drive before the Corinthian-columned portico of the Dumont home, and his mud-splattered Ford F-150 looked very much out of place. But an attendant appeared before he got out, ready to park his pickup somewhere less conspicuous—like out of sight. Boucher walked up the steps and rang the front doorbell. Deep and sonorous chimes rang from within, and the same uniformed gentleman greeted him. "Good evening, Judge Boucher. Would you mind waiting here in the entry hall for just a moment? I'm not sure where Mr. Dumont wants to greet his guests." He shook his head. "He's always changing his mind at the last minute."

Boucher stood in the entry. It was a round open space with circular stairs right and left climbing to a second-level gallery; a walkway with wrought-iron balustrades completed the circle. On the walls between closed doors to upper rooms were paintings and sculpture. From the center of a domed cupola hung a mammoth chandelier; perhaps a thousand pieces of fine-cut crystal. Boucher stared up at the art, recognizing several masters from the impressionist period, longing for a closer look.

"How about I give you the guided tour later this evening?" Dumont said, walking out of his library. "Jock, it's good to see you." He stepped forward; they shook hands. Dumont gripped Boucher's forearm in an emphasis of sincerity. "I'm glad you're the first to arrive. Gives us a chance to talk, and frankly, I'd like to tell you a bit about the general before he gets here. Let's go into my study. Would you like a drink?"

"No, I'm fine, thanks."

Dumont led the way to his study. A hardwood floor covered with priceless Oriental carpets, floor-to-ceiling bookshelves with aged leather-bound volumes, wood-paneled walls with wainscoting and crown molding, a massive desk beneath a chandelier only slightly smaller than the one in the entry, and French windows looking out on a dramatically lit weeping willow. Dumont walked to the window and stared out at the tree, standing with legs spread, hands behind his back, as if at parade rest, about to begin a military briefing. He spoke slowly and chose his words with care.

"General Moore spent most of his military career with the First Armored Division," he began, "and was its commanding officer when he retired from active duty. He was offered and accepted the task of heading up the Multi-Agency Force North, based at Fort Bliss, Texas."

"So he will head another regional arm of the counternarcotics organization that Gary Quaid runs."

"They are individually responsible for their specific geographical areas, yes."

"And he's at Fort Bliss? That must feel like home to him."

"What do you mean?"

"I'm retired army too," Boucher said. "Still hear from old buddies from time to time. One of them mentioned the First Armored Division's redeployment to Fort Bliss from their previous base in Wiesbaden, Germany. So this General Moore must feel like his old unit has followed him. Just like home."

"I suppose. I don't know whether the 'home' analogy is all that fitting. It seems to suggest a degree of comfort that I don't think is appropriate. This man has spent his life on the front line. He was in Germany staring down the Soviets. Now he's facing the threat on the border. From the cold war to the drug war. He's also an extremely intelligent man, a Ph.D. in international affairs from Georgetown, an alumnus of the National War College at Fort McNair, and like us, he has a passionate interest in history. Difference is, he doesn't just study history, he makes it. He is one of the few who recognize the need for a fundamental change in America's foreign policy. He's a visionary. I just wanted you to know that he's used to a bit of deference. With what he has done and is doing for this country, he deserves it."

"Yes, of course. Is that drink offer still open?"

"Absolutely." Dumont walked to a large antique world globe and flipped it open, bisecting the planet at the equator. It contained crystal decanters and matching crystal glassware. "I'll call for some ice," he said.

"That's not necessary. I'll take my first one neat."

"As will I," Dumont said. "Let's get a jump start on the boys, shall we?"

Carl Benetton was the next to arrive. When the butler showed him into the study, Dumont ordered a serving cart to be brought in. This was not to be the cardroom, just a place for drinks and conversation. Senator Farmer followed a few minutes later, and he and the lawyer began ribbing each other.

"Ah," the senator said, "here's our lawyer for the Mexican drug cartels."

"I was asked to represent a dual-national U.S./Mexican citizen," Benetton said facetiously, "who is innocent of the crimes alleged against him until proven guilty. He is a confused young man who lost his way and is now suffering unspeakable indignities at the hands of his captors in Mexico City." He punctuated his flippant remark with a quick nod.

"Do you think you'll get him extradited here?" the senator asked.

"Actually, it's a done deal. I'll be accompanying him to the maximum-security federal penitentiary in Florence, Colorado, on Monday."

"Maximum security? Is he a threat?"

"No. He fears for his life. He could be the most valuable informant we've ever had. It's for his protection."

The room turned still as a tomb when the final two guests arrived. All heads turned in their direction. For all his power, Gary Quaid seemed to walk in the shadow of General Cyrus Moore, though the two men entered side by side. The latter wore a light gray linen suit, a white cotton broadcloth shirt with a button-down collar, and a solid black tie. The general stood about six feet tall, was of medium build, and could have been well described using only metal-related metaphors: ramrod-straight backbone, gunmetal-gray hair, a steely-eyed look that would freeze lesser men in their tracks. General Cyrus Moore didn't look, didn't stare, he glared; and as he walked into the room, his glare was directed at Jock Boucher.

Dumont hastened to Boucher's side. "Let me introduce you," he said, and did.

The general offered his hand. Boucher matched the grip. "It's an honor to meet you, General."

"I've been informed of the judge's recent activities," the general said, staring into his eyes but addressing the others in the room. "Ray, I'm glad you have invited such a man to join our group." Then to Boucher: "You are most welcome, sir, and among us here, it's not General. It's Cyrus. Now I seem to have interrupted your conversation." He turned to the lawyer and the senator.

"Cyrus, can I get you and Gary a drink first?" Dumont said. "We'll be doing plenty of talking tonight, but we have to get the game started soon."

Drinks were served, and Boucher was left on his own with a moment to consider the obvious. Everyone here was deeply involved with the Mexican drug war; it was not just an interesting object of conversation among them. He looked at Dumont, the affable host to this influential group, and wondered again just how the wealthy entrepreneur fit in.

"Gentlemen," Dumont interrupted a few minutes later. "Everything is ready. Let's play some poker."

The cardroom continued the wood-dominated decor of the study but was smaller and hexagonal in shape, its dimensions proportionately larger than the green-felt-covered card table in the center. The serving cart was wheeled in behind the men, and the door was closed, the players thus insulated. It was not unlike being inside a bank vault or a military situation room. The men topped off their drinks, then took their seats. Dumont was on the button as dealer; General Moore, to his left, had the small blind and put in his chips. Boucher, to the general's left, had the large blind and followed suit. The game was under way.

These men knew one another well enough to know their style of play. Boucher was new, but his own manner was pretty quickly gleaned, he was sure. He played a tight-aggressive game, folding with bad cards, pushing with good—which didn't come his way too often. He was conservative when his hole cards were strong—hitting one monster with three kings and a pair of eights in the community flop—but believing in the maxim that the best players always know when an opponent has the better hand, he bet conservatively. He won that pot, though it was far from the biggest. But it led to his moment. Three hands later, he had nothing but king high, a pair of tens in the community. But he had instinct, and his instinct told him it was time to raise. He raised on the turn. The other players folded. Gary Quaig stayed in, holding a pair of jacks. Boucher raised again on the river. Quaig hesitated; couldn't get a read. He caved and folded. Boucher won the pot. Quaig saw his hole cards.

"You raised on *that?* Why the hell did you raise on that?"

"You paid for a look," Boucher said dryly. "Lessons cost extra."

Cyrus Moore guffawed, his loudest exclamation of the

evening. "*Cincinnati Kid*, right? I loved that movie. Damn, this is a good game."

Dumont smiled. He looked at Boucher. The initiation was over, his eyes said. Boucher was in. As if to prove him right, General Moore seemed to relax and opened a familiar topic of conversation.

"Sorry I missed the last game," he said. "Gary told me the conversation was pretty interesting; the legal doctrine of hot pursuit as justification for a U.S. incursion into Mexico."

"What do you think about the idea?" Dumont asked.

"I leave law to the lawyers," the general said. "My justification for any military action tends toward national security first and geopolitical doctrine second, not legal precedent. I assume such educated gentlemen as you are familiar with the term 'sphere of influence.'" He looked up from his cards. His question was directed to each man at the table. All eyes were on him. "You want the brief version or the unabridged?"

Boucher spoke. "General, I am very interested in what you have to say."

Cyrus Moore closed his cards and set them facedown on the table. "I'll begin by stating my case, as you lawyers say. I believe that after spending billions of dollars and far too many American lives, we have virtually no influence in the Middle East, and anyone who thinks we do is the kind of fool who believes you can pick up a piece of shit from the clean end." There were dry chuckles. "For our first two hundred years as a nation, we rose to become a global power without involvement in that part of the world. I think it's time to return to what has worked best for us."

He took a sip of his Scotch, then continued. "Our Middle East foreign policy has been confused and paradoxical for the past fifty years, and we have been at war for over two decades in a part of the world that will never be within our sphere of influence. Constant and unrewarding military conflict is ruining our economy and weakening our status as the world's dominant superpower. We have commitments we must honor, but we need to drastically reduce our follies there and focus our attention here—on the western hemisphere. From the Arctic Circle to Tierra del Fuego, our dominion over this part of the world should be predominant and unchallenged.

"To protect our access to the oil of the Arabian Peninsula, we've fought multiple wars in Iraq and in Afghanistan. For America, Saudi oil has been the most expensive source of energy on the planet—while we have abundant, undeveloped resources right here in the U.S. And in Mexico. And in Canada. Here is where we need to devote our efforts. Not the Arabian desert."

"We are already investing in Canada's oil sands," Boucher said.

"I'm not talking about oil from Canada. Canada has unlimited water in their glacier lakes. It is the oil of this century. Canada has twenty percent of the world's supply of freshwater, and they can't deny us access forever. A member of the Alberta provincial government once told me, and I'm quoting him verbatim: 'If the U.S. and Canada ever go to war, it will be over water.' The southwestern U.S. is drying up, as is northern Mexico. Drought gets worse every year. Nobody can tell me that the drought in Mexico does not contribute to economic problems there, which in turn contribute to the rise in crime. The water's in Canada; Mexico has oil and gas. Tell him, Dumont."

"There are fields in Mexico that may exceed those of the Middle East," Dumont said. "Some are in areas where the current criminal insurgency has made it impossible to even think about investment and development. My son, as I believe you all know, was a geologist and consultant. He was retained to study an area just south of the border and found what he believed to be one of the largest oil and gas fields in the western hemisphere. He was killed shortly after his discovery. Decapitated. His body heinously abused."

There was a hush that hung so heavy over their heads that it almost seemed to filter the light cast by the chandelier.

Boucher turned to Cyrus Moore. "General, Canada has made the bulk export of water illegal, and Mexico has excluded foreign investment—specifically, product-sharing agreements—from its energy sector since the industry was nationalized in the thirties. Are you suggesting armed intervention with our neighbors to the north and south?"

Moore didn't bat an eye. He glanced from Dumont to Boucher. He cracked a thin-lipped smile, then said softly with full dramatic flair, "I'm suggesting we make them an offer they can't refuse. If Canada wants to sell us oil from their tar sands, we tell them we'll buy it only in proportion to the amount of water they sell us. We build two pipelines instead of one. In Mexico, much of the northern tier of the country has been lost to criminal elements. It is a conservative estimate that more than sixty thousand people have been killed over the past six years from cartel violence in Mexico. If that number of civilians were killed in a natural disaster, like a flood or an earthquake, this country would be considered inhuman if we did not try to help. That's what I'm suggesting: help. We cannot sit by and do nothing."

"The Mexicans have a saying," Boucher said: "'Poor Mexico; so far from God, so close to the United States.' I think they have a far greater fear of the U.S. doing something than they do of the U.S. doing nothing. Recalling what Mr. Benetton shared with us at our last game, it would seem to me that our first priority should be to address the problems on our side of the border, not theirs."

"Oh?" The general's eyebrows arched as he fixed his gaze on the lawyer. "And what did you have to share, Mr. Benetton?"

"I believe I used the term no-man's-land," Benetton said. "American ranchers and farmers claim that there's a ten-mile strip along our side of the border, often crossing their land, where there is no protection, no security. Some say the Border Patrol ignores any call for help within this no-man's-land. The ranchers have pictures of trespassers carrying automatic rifles. They stumble across drug deliveries on their own ranchland. They claim cartels have set up lookout posts in the mountains on U.S. territory. And they say the U.S. government is failing them."

"And I agree with them," General Moore said. Suspended breathing resumed around the table.

"The U.S. Border Patrol as our first line of defense against territorial incursion? Who came up with that idea? Gentlemen, I grew up in El Paso. I grew up with farmers telling neighbors and friends when they were bringing in truckloads of illegal farm laborers from Mexico like they were talking about a trip to the grocery store. There is a long-standing tradition among those guarding our border of looking the other way when it serves local interests. No, we need men and women with the best training, the best equipment, experienced working in difficult terrain."

"It sounds like you have something in mind, General," Benetton said.

"I do. I'm thinking of our forces returning from Iraq and Afghanistan. What better mission could there be for these highly skilled veterans?"

"Posse Comitatus Act?" Benetton asked. All at the

table were familiar with the federal law prohibiting use of U.S. troops on state land.

"National Guard is exempt," Moore said, as if that were answer enough.

"Gentlemen, gentlemen," Senator Farmer said, "the only way you can keep me from winning my fair share this evening is to talk the night away. May I suggest that we get back to poker? Or you could just hand over your money to me now and continue this discussion into the morning hours. Whichever you prefer."

"Let's play poker," General Moore said. "I've said my piece."

The game continued with intense focus and little conversation. More than enough had been said. It was past ten when they took their first break.

"We've got snacks and a bar set up in the observatory," Dumont said, and led his guests to the glass-enclosed pavilion. He pulled Boucher aside. "Let me show you those paintings you were looking at earlier."

They walked to the front entry and climbed the circular stairway. "I keep my impressionists up here," Dumont said. "Other areas of the home are dedicated to different periods."

"Is that a Cassatt?" Boucher was drawn to a large canvas.

"Ray, can we talk?" Benetton stood at the foot of the stairs.

"Of course, Carl. Come on up. Excuse me for a second, Judge."

Dumont met Benetton at the top of the stairs, and they walked to the other side of the gallery, perhaps thirty feet away and separated by the hanging chandelier. Boucher studied the masterpiece. He was suddenly aware of another phenomenon. Though Dumont and the lawyer stood whispering in low tones on the far side of the open entry, he could hear them as if they were next to him. He looked up. The domed cupola acted like a parabola. Their voices were bouncing off the marble floor, then up to the dome, and were directed to where he stood. He remembered a schoolboy tour of the U.S. Capitol. The room off the rotunda, which had been the early chamber of the House of Representatives, had the same effect: a whisper on one side of the great hall could be heard on the other side—which the opposing political party had employed to their benefit at the time and which contemporary guides used to entertain their groups of tourists.

Boucher listened carefully. It was as if they were whispering in his ear.

"I don't like discussing our business in front of a federal judge," Benetton said.

"What business? Last week you lectured us on border history. This week the general touched on the Monroe Doctrine and his version of Teddy Roosevelt's Big Stick, if you didn't recognize them."

"It's too risky. I've received word. They want their next shipment of weapons. When can you get your vessel under way?"

"I can load tomorrow night. She'll sail at high tide. And don't worry about Judge Boucher. To repeat the general, I'm making him an offer he can't refuse."

Benetton nodded. "Hey, Jock," he yelled, though Boucher had heard every whispered word, "let's play some poker."

When the game resumed, Boucher sensed that Benetton had conveyed his concerns about him to the other players. In the forced silence, Boucher studied his hole cards. A pair of queens. Another pair of queens in the community. He took a deep breath, closed his cards, and laid them carefully on the table, then spoke.

"The president's director of intelligence has publicly stated that he does not feel Mexico presents a national security concern to the United States; that the drug lords have no political agenda and are interested only in shipping and selling the drugs, which, to our national shame, we buy and consume in large quantities." He paused. There were frowns around the table. Only Dumont kept his poker face. "I do not agree with the director's assessment. As Mr. Benetton previously pointed out, their own government has acknowledged that they have lost control of a large area of their own country; territory contiguous to our border. Mexican civilians have been shot, many by random gunfire; hospitals and drug rehabilitation centers have been raided and patients murdered. Raging gun battles have taken place outside of public schools. Law enforcement officers and elected local leaders have been assassinated, some forced to seek asylum and anonymity in the U.S. If they have lost control of their country to apolitical criminals motivated by greed, it offers fertile ground for terrorist elements intent on harming our country and its citizens. I think the situation on both sides of our southern frontier presents a clear and present danger to the security of the United States. I salute you gentlemen for giving this matter your consideration. I am in total agreement with you. My bet is two hundred dollars."

He won the hand and hoped that, with his declaration, he'd put to rest any doubts they had over him. That's what bluffing was all about.

CHAPTER 22

"**Y**OU PLAY CHESS?"

Fitch recognized the voice on the phone he had grabbed without opening his eyes, but the question didn't compute at this hour. Sunday mornings were for sleeping, not for competitive intellectual challenge. The sliver of sunlight slicing through the closed drapes made his digital alarm clock hard to read. He reached for his watch on the nightstand and frowned. "No," he said. "Or should I say hell no."

"That's a pity," Boucher said. "New Orleans and the French Quarter have a long tradition with the game that's been washed away with time and floodwaters. It's really a—"

"Jock, it's Sunday morning, and I had a late evening. I took the lady home, but if she were here with me right now and you called with such a ridiculous question at this

267

time of a new day, my tone of voice would be something different from the slightly aggravated one you hear now."

"How soon can you meet me? We have to talk."

"At my Sunday pace, probably in about an hour. Where?"

Boucher gave the address of a restaurant on Decatur with an outdoor seating area. It was fine weather for alfresco.

It had been almost four in the morning, with light rain still falling, when he left the Dumont residence. He'd driven home, and though his head was swimming when he went to bed, he had fallen asleep immediately, waking up a few hours later to finish the sentence that was in his mind when he had dozed off. He fixed coffee and sat in his courtyard. There was a clarity to his thoughts that was surprising, considering his lack of sleep. Physically, he felt better, feeling hardly any pain when he massaged his ribs. In the cool early-morning stillness, he had thought of chess, and the men he'd been with the previous night. They didn't make up a complement, but each man's moves could be compared with several of the game's principal pieces. One thing for sure—the pieces were on the move, with the game's primary initial objective easy to ascertain. They were moving to control the center of the board. But there the analogy faded. What was the board? Where was its center?

* * *

Fitch arrived at the restaurant wearing a white cotton shirt unbuttoned, a houndstooth sport coat, black slacks, and a straw fedora with black band. His shoes were polished. His aftershave was probably something of a drugstore variety. Boucher stared at the outfit. Fitch waved away his unspoken comment.

"I'm having lunch with Helen," he said. "So whatever your business is, get it over with. Meter's running."

"Sit down," Boucher said, smiling. "Relax and enjoy. Man, I love the Quarter in the morning after an early-spring rainfall."

"Good. Write a song about it. What do you want?"

Not to be rushed, Boucher ordered coffee and croissants and waited for them to be served. When the waiter left after bringing them their order, Fitch tapped his foot loudly, drummed his fingers on the table, and made an exaggerated gesture of looking at his watch.

Boucher leaned forward and motioned for Fitch to do the same. "They're loading the vessel and shipping out tonight," he whispered.

"How do you know?"

"They told me." Boucher recounted his overheard conversation. "I'm going to charter a certain sport fishing boat and follow it."

"What are you talking about?"

"Fitch, we can't touch these guys, you know that. But when they offload their cargo, there'll be a large quantity of weapons that will kill innocent men, women, and children. How long do you think it will be before Americans get caught in that bloody cross fire? Hell, it's already happening. El Paso's city hall is riddled with bullets fired from across the river in Juárez."

Fitch sighed. "Before I met you, my life was normal—nothing more than murders, armed robbery, prostitution, and small-time drug busts. Now you've got me chasing international gunrunners and drug lords who have more power than most heads of state. I really should choose my friends more carefully."

"But that's just it. We don't know who we're chasing. Benetton's mentioning a weapons shipment is the first real piece of evidence we have, but who is Dumont's buyer? A drug lord? That can't be. One of them killed his son. Is he backing a counterinsurgency group planning to take on the cartels? Before I take this any higher, I have to know more or I'll look like a fool. I'll pick you up tonight at nine."

"No, you won't. I don't want your tags spotted. I'll get something with plates that can't be traced. Now"—he stood up—"I've got a date. I suggest you call that girlfriend of yours and see if she remembers you."

"I spoke with her this morning," Boucher said. "I told her I'm going to be away for a few days, but when I get back, I want her to plan on a long visit."

"If you make it back alive," Fitch said. He gave a mock salute, turned, and walked away.

Boucher ordered a full breakfast of eggs Benedict, even treating himself to a mimosa. He ate slowly, watching a jazz quartet set up for the Sunday-brunch crowd, then catching the first set. It was, he told himself, a time to savor. When the band took a break, he called Fred Arcineaux.

"I want to charter your boat," he said. "I'm driving over to talk to you about it."

He enjoyed the coastal sojourn, windows down and radio up. The jazz station's DJ was featuring a pantheon of jazz guitar greats: Django Reinhardt and his Gypsy jazz; Charlie Christian, who took the guitar from the big bands' rhythm sections to center stage as a featured solo instrument; Les Paul's wizardry; and Wes Montgomery, the father of smooth jazz. It was music that could turn any drive into a magic carpet ride. There was a fullness to the air that rushed into the cab of the pickup, the product of the great river's confluence with the saline gulf waters, the meeting of earth and sea creating a transitional life force that altered the lower atmosphere inhaled by all living things. During the course of his brief trip, for a few precious moments of the God-given day, he was able to force from his mind all thoughts of the evil that men do.

Again he spotted Arcineaux on the flybridge; no surprise. It was like a penthouse up there, its elevation affording the best view even in port. The skipper waved him aboard, and Boucher climbed up to the catbird seat. The boat's slip afforded a view over the stern, a straight shot of open water between two piers where smaller pleasure craft were moored. The proud owner had bought a captain's hat, a definite improvement over his previous headgear, and wore a Hawaiian-style shirt, Bermuda shorts, and the same deck shoes, as if dressing for summer would hasten the season's arrival.

"Welcome aboard, Judge. What can I do for you?"

"I'd like to charter your boat, Fred."

"Day trip?"

"No."

"Where we going?"

"I don't know."

"You're going to chase Dumont's ship, right?" he asked.

Boucher nodded, then asked, "You in?"

"Told you before that I wanted to help. Yeah, I'm in. Wish I didn't have to charge you, but—"

"No. I want to pay your going rate. Also, I need to know—is this vessel insured?"

"To hell and back," Arcineaux said. "Is Detective Fitch coming along?"

"No. He'll need to stay behind."

Arcineaux smiled. "He can write the sea chanteys they'll sing about us when we're gone, right?"

"Something like that," Boucher said.

"When do you want to go?"

"Tonight. Fitch and I will do surveillance at Houma. When Dumont's boat is loaded and ready to ship out, I want to follow him. Where can we meet?"

"We'll meet at Dulac. I'll dock at a slip just off the canal. He has to pass us, so when you see him get under way, hightail it to our rendezvous."

"Is it possible you might lose him on the open sea?"

"Impossible. I'll show you why. Let's go down to the bridge," Arcineaux said, and they went below. "This is the Interphase twin scanning sonar." He pointed to the equipment. "This is the weather PC, driven by XM satellite. This, the Icom VHF radio. Here's the Northstar plotter/depth/radar. This is the autopilot. This, the Furuno GPS with computer interface. That enough for you?"

"Now, don't be offended when I ask this, but you just bought this boat. Do you know how to use all this gear?"

"Don't worry. I got all the manuals," Arcineaux said with a smile.

They spent another half hour together, the conversation taking a decidedly lighter tone. Arcineaux lifted his beer to offer a toast, saying, "You're nervous. Don't be. Everything is gonna be fine."

"I just wish I knew more about what they're doing."

"That's the reason for our little trip, isn't it?"

"Yes," Boucher said with a sigh. "But there's something else bothering me."

"What's that?"

"I've got to tell my assistant I'm taking off."

"So what? You're the boss."

"You don't know my assistant."

Boucher drove home and spent the remainder of the day sitting in his courtyard, listening to the ambient noise of the neighborhood. He stared at his stone statue of Saint Jude, the patron saint of lost causes, as if engaged in telepathic communication. He tried to plan for the coming evening but knew they would be reacting to whatever came up, and he trusted Fitch's experience with surveillance techniques. He asked himself whether he would—or could—break the law in an effort to combat an illegal activity, and he pondered, not for the first time in his career, the absurdity of legal compliance when it aided only the criminal. Would he commit trespass, maybe breaking and entering? Maybe, he decided. Maybe. Perhaps Dickens was right when he said, "The law is an ass." At times it seemed just so.

CHAPTER 23

HE WAS SEATED AT the campaign desk when Fitch pulled up outside. The sun had disappeared over an hour ago, but Boucher had no idea how dark the night was, since the lights of the Quarter provided their own illumination. He rose, exited his house, and locked up. Even in the dark, he could see that the car Fitch was driving was a wreck, and though no interior lights came on when he got in, he knew that the passenger compartment was no better.

"Where'd you get this clunker?" he asked.

"Automobile surveillance is probably the least sophisticated and the least effective of all police methods," Fitch said as he drove. "But we can't give it up. At least old wrecks attract less attention. A late-model unmarked car is not the way to go. I thought of getting a van, and painting some oil field service company's logo on it, but there wasn't enough time, and I really don't know where we're going to do our stakeout."

"So we're not going to try to get inside the warehouse?"

"I gave that some thought," Fitch said, "but not much. First, we don't know where it is. Second, that's trespassing. And third—no small detail to me—we might get our asses shot. There is one location we do know, so we're going to scope it out first."

"The other side of the canal. What good will that do us?"

"Not sure. We'll have to get a better angle than before. So we'll need to hunt up a spot nearby. Wish you were a girl."

"Why?"

"A man and a woman don't get noticed as much in a parked car. Two men, that's another story. Me and you? In the bayou? I don't think so."

"Okay. We find a spot where we have a line of sight to the loading. Again, what good will that do us?"

"The answer's in the backseat."

Boucher looked behind. A black leather case rested on the seat.

"State of the art," Fitch said. "Thermal digital cam: takes video in complete darkness. Got a second ultra-low-light camera with a full range of high-speed telephoto lenses that have excellent target recognition and identification capability. We'll be able to see the sweat on their noses."

There was silence, then Fitch chuckled. "You're disappointed, aren't you? You really wanted to do a commando number, sneak into the goddamned warehouse. Let me ask you something—do they have counseling for federal judges? If they don't, they should. Like for our troops. You guys bear tremendous responsibilities. When we get done with this, I think you should go talk to someone. You have a habit of acting way out of the scope of your judicial mandate."

"I want to catch the bastards."

"It's not your job. Take care of the job you have. Or quit. You're not exactly an indentured servant."

"I think about that all the time. I could be happy just being a judge; it's what I wanted all my life. But why does all this shit keep flowing my way? I don't go looking for it; it finds me whether I'm on or off the bench. We went fishing and found a body in the gulf. I go for an early-evening walk near my house, and some thug pulls a gun on me. I come back from a night at the casino and get shot outside my front door. I didn't start any of this, Fitch."

"I know. You're a dirtbag magnet. Forget the shrink. Go see a witch doctor. Get her to remove the spell."

They found the spot from which they previously observed the *Gulf Pride*. The ship was moored. Fitch took a pair of night-vision goggles from his equipment bag. "There's a guy on the bridge and two guards on the dock, but it's quiet. The boat is riding high in the water, so we haven't missed the loading. But we can't see much from here. We'll have to find a spot where we can look past the bow or the stern, get more of an angle."

"That means we'll be farther away."

"That's what telephoto lenses are for." Fitch backed out of the parking area, not turning on the headlights till he was back on the secondary road. They drove slowly, under two minutes. A slight curve to the road favored them. Fitch pulled over to the side as far as practical with no shoulder. There was heavy foliage between the road and the canal.

"There's bug spray in the glove compartment," Fitch said.

"That's being prepared." Boucher took it out and sprayed himself.

"Give me a merit badge. Grab the bag. Let's go."

"Yes, bwana."

"I didn't mean it like that."

"I know." Boucher punched him in the arm. "If I can't joke around with you . . ."

"Yeah, who else you got? That's kind of sad, when you think about it."

They left the car on the side of the road and pushed their way through the brush, wading through ankle-deep muck to the water's edge. Fitch stopped. "Hand me the night-vision goggles," he said. He put them on and turned his head from side to side, then took them off. "The infra-red camera."

Boucher handed it to him.

"There's something moving. It's approaching the ship." Fitch put the goggles back on. Several trucks pulled onto the loading dock alongside the ship. "I think we got lucky," he whispered. "They're using a crane, raising and lowering the cargo into the hold."

"How is that lucky?"

"The way the trucks are parked, blocking our line of sight, we'd see next to nothing if they were hand-loading by the gangplank. Just pray that the netting is coarse enough for us to see what the cargo is."

"It's probably boxes."

"Maybe the boxes will say they contain cans of carrots and peas. Maybe they'll have Russian writing all over them, like in those movies Pip watches. We have to wait and see."

From their vantage point, the loading process was ho-hum. Boxes. Lots of boxes. Yes, many appeared to be of a size that could hold shoulder-fired weapons. Others could have contained munitions. But no smoking gun. Until . . .

"Holy shit," Fitch exclaimed. "Look at that." He handed the goggles to Boucher.

"What is it?"

"I think it's an armored personnel carrier. No box for that baby."

They watched for another half hour. From the activity on the bridge and on deck, it was obvious the ship was being made ready to depart.

"Let's go," Fitch said. "Where are you meeting Arcineaux?"

"Dulac."

They had heard only one car pass. "See?" Fitch said
when they got to the car. "Nobody's interested in an old
wreck like this." He slapped his left hand with his right. "I
sure hope that mosquito repellent worked better for you
than it did for me."

It was another short drive to the small bayou town of
Dulac.

"That armored personnel carrier pretty much seals
the deal," Fitch said, "but we'll enhance the videos and the
stills. There may be more. I think we've got enough to put
Dumont away already, so why the boat trip?"

"What we just saw is the tip of the iceberg, that's why.
Where the weapons are going and to whom, that's the
next piece of the puzzle."

"*That's* your problem!" Fitch slapped the steering
wheel. "You've got a damn messianic complex. There's no
problem in the world too big for you to solve personally.
Nobody can do it like you. You're no hero, Jock Boucher,
you're an egotist. Hey, don't get pissed off at me for telling
the truth. Now that we know what the problem is, we can
begin to work on a cure. I'll start. I think you chasing this
gunrunning boat is about the dumbest thing I ever heard,
and if I had any stroke in the right places, I'd try to get
you put away for a while for your own good. Your damned

ego is also why you're about to lose that attractive, intelligent woman who thinks you hung the moon. You never consider her. You never think about what might be good for the two of you as a couple. It's 'I, me, my' with you. 'Hi, darling; call me next week. This week I'm saving the planet, but my schedule will be freed up by Tuesday. We'll do lunch.'"

All this in one breath. Fitch inhaled deeply. "Hope this doesn't end our friendship, but it had to be said."

There was silence. A minute is a long time in total silence. Boucher finally spoke. "You've given me something to think about. No, it doesn't end our friendship; quite the contrary. I'd kiss you, Fitch . . . but this is Louisiana."

"You're still gonna chase the boat?"

"I'm still going to chase the boat."

They arrived at Dulac. Arcineaux was waiting for them at a gas station.

"I'm glad to see you guys. I thought this place was open all night, but they closed a half hour ago. People here don't like strangers standing around in the dark. The ship loaded?"

"Yes," Boucher said. "It got under way about fifteen minutes ago."

"Should be passing any minute, then. Let's get to my boat; it's just a short walk from here to the dock. Sure you don't want to come along for the ride, Detective?"

"Funny thing about working for the New Orleans Police Department," Fitch said, "they expect you to show up every now and then. I wouldn't mind an ocean voyage, but my boss is a real old-fashioned kind of cop. He gets upset when I work out of my district, much less the state, much less the whole fucking territorial waters of the United States of America."

"You're gonna miss the fun."

"Yeah. Stay in touch. I mean it. You maintain communications. I need to know where you are at all times."

"Don't worry, we will."

"Then good luck and . . . God bless." Fitch got in the clunker and drove away.

"I didn't know the police department was doing that bad," Arcineaux said. "That car's a piece of crap."

They walked to the cruiser. It was docked in a small marina just off the large canal leading to the gulf. There were a couple of trawlers moored at the same dock, their bows facing outward, Arcineaux's craft sandwiched between them, using the working boats as camouflage. Approaching the stern, Boucher noticed the vessel's name, *Daddy's Little Girl*. He remembered the song. The Mills Brothers had been one of his father's favorite vocal groups.

"I ain't changed it," Arcineaux said. "This boat meant a lot to the previous owner, and he spent a lot of time on it with his family. I think I'll keep the name out of respect."

"Fine idea," Boucher said.

CHAPTER 24

THE *GULF PRIDE* PASSED fifty feet from them, visible by its running lights and illumination from the bridge. The captain of the vessel could be seen at his station, hands behind his back, chin raised, jaw jutting forward, his face in a tight frown.

"He looks angry," Boucher whispered.

"It's defiance. Doesn't matter if it's the first time or he's done it for thirty years; when a captain of a ship goes to sea, he's sayin', 'Bring it on; take your best shot.' Ocean can be a monster. There's a little bit of fear in a seaman every time he leaves the port. You don't want to see it in your captain."

They gave the ship a half-hour running start and then pulled away from the slip. Boucher was afraid they'd lose her.

"I got her on radar," Arcineaux said. "We're going to stay

out of her sight. I'll also be doing a little evasion. Remember, we're a deep-sea charter fishing vessel, a sports cruiser. We have to appear like we're looking for fish. They'll have us on their radar too. Don't worry. I know their speed and have an idea of their direction. I don't plan on getting close enough to make them wonder who we are. Another thing—we'll both be crisscrossing some of the busiest maritime routes in the world. They're going to see a lot of traffic on their screen. They won't even notice us."

"Plenty of gas?"

"Full tanks," the skipper said. "Like I told you before, I could drive this baby to Cancún."

"I hope it won't be that far."

They motored at the lowest possible speed through the canal. Boucher smelled oil and gasoline on the still night air, and their own lights reflected the sheen of muck clinging to the sides of the watery trench carved through the bayous. How much longer would this forgiving land tolerate man's abuse? he asked himself.

Arcineaux must have read his mind. "You got any kids, Judge?"

"My wife died of breast cancer. We were planning a family."

"Sorry to hear that. Dora and I thought about having kids too, then decided against it. Weren't sure what kind of a world we'd be able to leave them. Know what I mean?"

"You think we're destroying the planet."

"Evidence is there. You're gonna see some more of it on this trip. There's a dead zone out there that no fish can live in. Size of Delaware and getting bigger. Damned shame."

Boucher looked out over the side. "When we're gone," he said, "all traces that we were ever here will disappear in the blink of an eye." ·

"Hey, enough of this. We're two guys on a fishing trip. We got a good boat under us, and the weather looks clear for the next couple of days. Let's enjoy it."

"You're right. I'm sorry."

"Anyway, smell that? That's Sweetwater Pond. Then Terrebonne Bay, the Barrier Islands, and we'll be in open water. A sunrise on the gulf makes a man glad to be alive. When that sun comes up, I want to hear you say it: it's good to be alive."

Boucher smiled, recalling the downcast, downhearted drunk he'd first met, compared to the man now preaching faith to him.

Arcineaux's timing was perfect. They were passing the Barrier Islands when the sun came up. Pelicans and great white egrets mingled on the shore, the first of them shaking off their lethargy and taking flight. The egrets were as beautiful on land as in the air. Not so the pelicans. Onshore, the few moving waddled awkwardly, comically. Most still slept, their beaks cocooned in wings like a babe in swaddling. Two stretched and yawned, then attempted a takeoff from a running start. There was metamorphosis. In the air the bird was graceful, its lines sleek, aerodynamic. As two took to the sky, others shook themselves awake and joined them. Soon there was a V in the sky; a squadron of brown pelicans. Boucher counted an even dozen.

"They mate for life," Arcineaux said. "Only time you see one alone, it's lost its partner. I remember a pelican's body washed ashore during the oil spill. Its mate stood next to it, mourning, for three days." He did not look at Boucher; his eyes were on the horizon, glistening perhaps from the glare of the rising sun.

"You still have them on radar?" Boucher asked.

"Yep. Their speed's fifteen knots. 'Fraid you won't be able to do any fishing on the outward journey. Maybe on the way back. With just the two of us, this is going to be a demanding voyage. Even with autopilot and all the gear we got, we need eyes on the water at all times. You okay with that?"

"I'm good."

The morning chill was soon burned away by a blinding sun in a clear blue sky. They were out of sight of land but not far from human activity. They passed container ships, flat floating fields of steel piled several stories high with multicolored boxes that looked like a child's building blocks. The ships were as long as several city blocks and as high as midrise towers. There were fishing boats, oyster luggers, and shrimp trawlers, and there were a few sports fishermen in smaller craft.

"Told ya we'd have lots of company," Arcineaux said. "'Course, we're not that far from land. I'll head out to deep water this evening. Get us a little elbow room. And before you ask again, yes, I still got 'em on my screen."

Boucher looked at his watch. "Can I make a phone call? I've got to call my assistant. I am not looking forward to this."

Arcineaux handed him a phone. "It's an Iridium satellite phone for ship-to-shore."

Boucher called his office. "Good morning, Mildred. How are you?"

"Where are you, Judge Boucher? What's that noise in the background?"

"Mildred, there's been a personal emergency, and I won't be back in the office until . . ."

"That's too bad," she said. "Judge Giordano just called. She asked if you could hear some motion hearings she has scheduled. She wanted you to take the bench in her place. I thought it was a good sign. I guess I'll have to call her and tell her you have a personal emergency."

"Thank you, Mildred. Will you be able to—"

"I will do everything I can. There will be documents for your signature when you return. You will have a lot of work waiting for you, Judge Boucher."

She believed none of it—not a word—and told him so with her withering tone of voice.

Boucher sighed. He paced the bridge. "Can I do anything?"

"You can do pretty much what you want to. There's a TV below with a DVD player. Got some books—"

"I mean can I do anything to help?"

"Can you cook?"

"I can. I'm a pretty good cook."

"Why don't you look over the galley? I think you'll find most of what you need to throw something together. If we're still followin' them when evenin' comes, you can fix us a nice dinner instead of warmed-up beans and franks."

"Got any fresh shrimp?"

Arcineaux smiled. What a question.

That evening they enjoyed one of the best étouffées either of them had ever tasted. Boucher had set up a small table on the flybridge and timed the meal to coincide with the sunset. They were far from land, feeling alone in the world, when a fire came into view. A fire on the open sea.

"Offshore rig," Arcineaux said.

"Think they're in trouble?"

"I would have heard something on the emergency frequency. They're probably just flaring some associated gas or something like that. It should stop soon." He was right. A minute later and there was nothing to compete with the view of the sun sinking into the sea.

Unlike summer, when the sun's light seems to linger after it sets below the horizon, on this spring evening darkness came quickly. A hurricane lamp was a functional centerpiece, and they finished their meal by its light. The ship was on autopilot and the water calm. Arcineaux was relaxed, though always with an eye on the horizon.

"Damn, that was a good meal," he said. "Best New Orleans chef couldn't have done better."

"If you were to choose the best New Orleans chef . . ." Boucher said.

"I gotta say Paul Prudhomme. Man's done more for Louisiana cookin' than any man alive. More'n that, he's trained great chefs too—several named among the best in the whole U.S."

Conversation continued as the ship motored into deeper, darker waters. Donning sweaters and jackets, they remained in the open air till the brisk sea breeze drove them below.

"You get some sleep," Arcineaux said. "I'll wake you when it's time to spell me. You won't have to drive; ship's on auto. But we need eyes. You understand?"

"Of course."

Boucher slept in his clothes on top of the bedcovers and dozed soundly for several hours. The light switched on in the salon woke him.

"I'm awake," he said.

"Okay, you take her for a while. Water's calm. Just keep your eyes open. You can still see the *Gulf Pride* on radar. Wake me if she starts movin' off the screen."

"I don't know what I was expecting," Boucher said as he headed toward the bridge, "but I didn't think it would be this uneventful."

Arcineaux yawned. "Save that for when the trip's over. You know what they say—don't count your money when you're sittin' at the table."

"Right. Sleep well."

"I generally do when I'm at sea."

It was a gently rolling ocean, and *Daddy's Little Girl* was making good speed. It was a stable craft and rode well in the water. Boucher stood with his hands on the wheel even though gyros and magnets, springs, pinwheels, fly-wheels, propellers, and satellite-connected computers actually controlled the vessel. He looked at the radar screen but could make out nothing. Radio frequencies were silent. He had only one function, to keep his eyes on the horizon—which he couldn't even see in the total darkness. At least the black void meant they were not on a collision course with another traveler in the night.

WHUMP!

The ship struck something with such force that Boucher's hands were shaken from the wheel and he almost lost his footing. His first thought was that they had run aground; impossible, at this distance out to sea. He'd kept a lookout and seen nothing. He ran to starboard and port and looked over the sides. Arcineaux rushed up, rousted from his sleep. He dashed to a storage shelf next to the wheel and pulled out a flashlight. He ran to the stern and scanned the beam over the water's surface.

"I thought so," he yelled up to Boucher. "One of those damn containers got loose. It's out there afloat. I gotta check for damage to the hull." He went below, then came back up minutes later and joined Boucher on the bridge. "Everything seems okay," he said.

"I'm sorry, I was watching. I just didn't see it."

"No way you could've seen it. It's pitch black out there. Rolling sea and just the top corner of the damned thing is above water. Loose containers are one of the greatest dangers on the ocean. They are designed to sink when they fall overboard, but sometimes they can stay afloat a pretty long time. Anyway, I didn't notice any damage. Why don't you make some coffee?"

Boucher brewed a pot and came back up to the bridge with two cups.

"I see them," Arcineaux said, taking the cup and pointing to the radar screen. "They're not slowing down. I got a feelin' this might be a long journey. End of this day, if you still say this trip is uneventful, I'll be a happy camper."

CHAPTER 25

THEY CRUISED AT TOP speed for almost six hours. All that time they saw no other vessel on the water. Finally, Arcineaux pulled back on the throttle. It was midafternoon, the sea calm, the sky a hazy blue-gray. Arcineaux had the *Gulf Pride* on the radar as well as another blip they assumed was the second ship. Theirs was the third point of the triangle. There was not another ship in the ten-mile radius but several just outside the perimeter, their speed and direction indicating that they were going about their business. "Where are we?" Boucher asked.

"About fifty miles due east of Matamoros, Mexico."

The ship's phone rang and Arcineaux answered. He handed it to Boucher.

"It's Detective Fitch," he said, and listened to a series of *uh-huh*s. Boucher told Fitch their location, then handed

Arcineaux the phone. "You gonna keep me in suspense?" Arcineaux asked.

"Fitch was looking at the enhanced videos and photos we took. All the boxes were clearly marked in the Cyrillic alphabet. He says there's enough in that one shipment for a small war; AK-47s, shoulder-fired missiles, machine guns, and an armored personnel carrier; much of it made in the seventies for the Russian invasion of Afghanistan. He says most of it was crap when it was made. A lot of Russians were killed by their weapons blowing up on them in the field. Wonders if that's Dumont's real plan: kill narcos with their own weapons. He was joking."

"Well, black-market shit don't come with no Good Housekeeping Seal of Approval," Arcineaux said. "How close do you want to get to these guys?"

"I'm expecting they'll get side by side to transfer cargo, bow and stern pointing same direction. They'll be busy with the loading. One pass by the stern, close enough for me to get a photo with the names of the ships."

"You bring a camera?"

"With telephoto."

"If you'd had the coordinates, you could have saved yourself a lot of time and money. There's this company in Colorado that sells satellite images. You could have bought some satellite pictures."

"I did," Boucher said. "It's been tracking us since we left Dulac and the eye is in the sky as we speak. But it's fifty miles straight up. No guarantee it could catch names on the bow or stern. Besides, there's nothing like an eyewitness."

Arcineaux laughed.

"What is it?" Boucher asked.

"The legal profession. We got us hundreds of millions of dollars' worth of technology up there, and you still believe in eyeballs. I ain't been in a courtroom lately. You guys still wear black robes and powdered wigs?"

"Just the robes. Supreme Court Justice John Marshall ditched the wigs at the beginning of the nineteenth century."

"But you get my point."

"I'm not sure I do. The legal profession has modernized in significant—"

"What the hell?" Arcineaux said. He was looking at the screen.

"What is it?"

"We might have us another player. Look at this."

He pointed to the screen. Another ship seemed to be heading to the rendezvous area. It was moving slowly, as if it didn't want to be seen.

"I don't know what that is," he said, "could be anything. This might get interesting. I got a feeling that today's not going to be as 'uneventful' as yesterday."

They held their speed. Arcineaux turned over the wheel and told Boucher to hold it steady.

"I'm going to bait some hooks and throw out some lines. We're supposed to be sport fishermen, remember?

I got some whole red snapper in the galley, gonna put a couple in the deck coolers. We get stopped, say you caught 'em yesterday."

"We're not going to get stopped."

"No, I think it's more likely we're gonna get our asses shot out of the water. Then what damn good you gonna be as an eyewitness?"

The rolling water, maybe the familiar act of setting out fishing lines, had a calming effect on Arcineaux. After minutes of scurrying about the deck, he returned to the bridge and again stared at the radar screen. They watched as two blips came closer, then seemed to become one. The skipper took the wheel.

"Okay," he said. "This is where the rubber meets the road. I'm gonna make a single pass close enough for you to snap your picture. Get up on the bow and grab something to hang on to."

Boucher did as ordered, leaving the bridge, holding on to handrails as he made his way along the narrow walkway to the bow. He seated himself on the foredeck area and bent over, protecting his camera from sea spray, which soaked him as the vessel sliced through the water. He was drenched and cold before he saw the vessels' names, the *Gulf Pride* the larger of the two. It was obvious at first glance that the transfer had not gone as planned. The two ships were ten or fifteen meters apart, and between them, hanging in midair over the sea, was the armored personnel carrier. There was no crane or winch; they had counted on nothing more than cables and pulleys, arms and backs. Someone had miscalculated. He was close enough to see men grouped on the vessels and could almost hear them yelling and cursing at each other. He took out his camera from inside his jacket and started shooting, protecting the lens from sea spray as best he could. Through the lens, he saw one man look his way, pointing. The APC suspended between the two ships fell and crashed to the sea. The vessels pulled apart. Arcineaux again opened the throttle, and Boucher had to crawl as the boat's bow raised and crashed on rolling seas while speeding away from the scene.

"You get your pictures?" Arcineaux asked.

"Yes."

"Then get outta them clothes right here. I don't want you dripping wet all over the salon and staterooms."

Boucher set down the camera and started to undress.

"Uh-oh," the skipper said. "I take back that order. You might wanna keep them clothes on a bit longer. Look behind us."

Boucher turned around. The *Gulf Pride* was heading away and already almost out of sight. The second boat was following them, coming on fast.

"I'm thinkin' that one can outrun us," Arcineaux said. "I don't think our fish story's gonna do us much good. I got a feelin' they might not want an eyewitness seein' what just went down. Ya know what I'm saying?"

"Can we alert the navy, the coast guard, anybody?"

"This ain't exactly downtown New Orleans. It's just us and them out here. By the time help arrived, there wouldn't be an oil slick left of us. Remember those guns they got on board? They're probably thinking this might be a good place to try 'em out."

The prediction came true soon enough. There was an explosion and then a plume of water five hundred yards behind them.

"They're sighting in, getting the range. Shit. We're target practice. And don't ask. I can't go any faster. Running these engines all out for as long as I have, we might not need them to blow us out of the water, we might do it to ourselves."

Another explosion. This one was closer.

"Will you look at that?" Arcineaux said. The computer screen showed another boat giving chase. It was the third boat they had spotted earlier. "We end up in the drink, maybe that guy will come to our rescue."

There was a whistle over their heads, low enough to make them duck instinctively, then another explosion, this one under twenty yards off their bow. The bow of their vessel raised out of the water with the blast, then slapped down, hard.

"Judge Boucher, it's been nice knowin' ya. I think they got our range."

Boucher jumped at the wheel, pushing Arcineaux

aside. He spun it to port as hard as he could. The vessel barely moved.

"This ol' gal don't turn on a dime," Arcineaux said. He pulled back on the throttle, idling the engines. "Wasn't a bad idea, though."

They heard the whistle of another projectile and stared into each other's eyes. Boucher stepped toward Arcineaux and offered a handshake. He took it. At that moment the explosion came. *Daddy's Little Girl* rocked like its namesake in a baby's swing. But they were not blown out of the water. They turned and looked astern. Orange flames and black smoke shot into the sky. They saw the loaded ship explode with such force that it raised in the water as if it had struck a mammoth wave. It crashed back to the surface, ocean spray covering it in a momentary mist—but not enough to douse the flames; they raged higher and higher. Then there were other blasts as munitions exploded and arced in a 360-degree plume, crashing to water in a wide circle. They watched in stunned silence. Then Boucher broke out laughing. Throughout the fireworks display, he and Arcineaux had held their handshake. Now he pulled the man to him and they embraced, slapping each other's back. They sheepishly separated after the exuberant display.

"Fitch was right," Boucher said.

"About what?"

"The weapons they bought. It was all a bunch of crap. Something misfired when they shot at us, and they had a cargo hold full of explosives blow up."

"Could be something else," Arcineaux said. He stepped back to the radar screen. "The other fellow's getting outta town too."

They watched the blip. The third vessel was making a tight turn. It was leaving the scene and not wasting any time.

"Did they do it? Did they sink that ship?"

Those who knew the answer to that question were now asleep in the deep. Boucher and Arcineaux motored from the scene.

"Outrunning pirates always makes me hungry," Arcineaux said half an hour later. "You take the wheel and I'll throw together some sandwiches."

"Aye-aye, captain. I wouldn't mind a beer—hell, rum, if you've got some on board. I think a toast is in order."

"Not a bad idea. I'll be right back."

That plan was dumped. Boucher heard Arcineaux scream. "Get down here. Quick!"

Boucher jumped from the bridge to the deck, then from the deck to the galley below. He landed in ankle-deep water.

"We got a problem," Arcineaux said.

"Were we hit?"

"Could have been shrapnel." Arcineaux was bustling, tearing through compartments as he answered. "Or the hull lost integrity when we struck the container last night and cracked from the force of whatever they fired at us. Let me check the bilge."

A leak in the hull, far out at sea: a nautical nightmare. The first thing Arcineaux did baffled Boucher. He grabbed at the upholstery, pulling a cushion from a bench. This he pressed against the leak. In the salon, he unscrewed a teak table from the floor, turned it over and pressed it against the pillow, then piled chairs on and against it. Water was still coming in through the leak.

"Gotta get the pump goin'," he said. He rushed below to the engine room and returned with a pump and connected it. He ran the hose to a porthole and turned it on.

"We're taking on a lot of water. This pump has limits. We can stay afloat if the crack don't get much bigger. Lemme see if I got anything else." He ransacked drawers, cabinets, and cupboards. From a drawer, he pulled out a photo. "If this is on board, we can use it. Help me find it."

Boucher stared at an old photo that had to be the former owner and his wife. They were smiling at their young daughter, selling lemonade from a stand set up on a pier under a tent. The Hatteras could be seen in the background.

"You need a lemonade stand?" Boucher asked.

"No, damn it. I need the tarp they used for cover. It might still be on board. Check the storage compartments in the bow."

Boucher climbed into the small compartment in the bow of the vessel. No space went unused. Two foam mattresses followed the shape of the bow with a small space between them. Shelves and storage compartments were built above the beds. He rummaged through one, then another. "I've got it," he yelled.

He crabbed out of the bow space with a rolled-up blue tarp and handed it to Arcineaux.

"C'mon," the captain ordered, and climbed up to the deck. He gave Boucher one end to hold, took the other, and unrolled the tarp. "It has grommets. That'll help. Might be long enough. Gotta find some rope."

"Long enough for what?"

Boucher's question went unanswered. Arcineaux found several lengths of rope, then went to the helm and shut off the engines. The boat bobbed on the surface. "C'mon," he ordered again.

Boucher followed along the narrow starboard foot-path, grabbing rails to keep from being pitched overboard. Arcineaux stood on the foredeck, unrolling the tarp, tying one end to the railing.

"What are you doing?" Boucher asked.

"I'm going to run this under the keel and tie it on the port side. It's like putting a Band-Aid on a gutshot, but it might help stem the flow of water. Acts like a compress."

"How are you going to get it under the boat?"

"I'm going in." Arcineaux began taking off his shoes.

"No," Boucher said. "I'll do it."

Before Arcineaux could argue, he dove over the side.

The cold water shocked him, drove the air from his lungs, and induced an instant state of panic heightened by pain from his bruised ribs. He thrashed his way to the surface, fought the terror of being in the vastness of the unforgiving sea, and swam to the hull. His fingertips were already numb.

"I'm here," he yelled up. "I'm right below you. Drop the tarp over the side."

"Okay. Here comes."

Boucher grabbed the loose end of the tarp. His teeth were rattling so hard that it was difficult for him to open his jaw wide enough to take a deep breath, so he gritted his teeth and inhaled through his nostrils. Then he dived. He guided by keeping the hull against his back as he dove down, under, then up the other side. Pulling the tarp was like wrestling a large fish, but he made it to the port side and broke the surface. "I'm here. How am I going to get it up to you?"

"I've got a gaff," Arcineaux said. "I'm leaning over the side. Try to put the hook of the gaff in one of the grommets."

"Move a few feet toward the bow."

It was like threading a needle but with hands shaking uncontrollably. Boucher fitted the hook of the gaff into a grommet, and Arcineaux lifted the tarp. "Got it. Get back on board. Swim to the stern. I'll be there."

There was a platform for swimmers at water level across the stern. Boucher tried to hoist himself onto the ledge but was numb with cold. Arcineaux grabbed him under the arms and pulled him up. "Go below. I'm going to secure the tarp."

Boucher toweled off, put on dry clothes, and sat still until his shivering ceased. He joined Arcineaux at the helm as he started the engines.

"Thanks," Arcineaux said. "You did a good job."

"Will it work?"

"In principle, it should help some. The water pressure pushes the tarp against the cracks so it limits the flow. But it ain't a tight fit. We're cutting through water, and it's going to seep in between the hull and the tarp. But it's something."

"We need to call for help."

"Dumont's ship is still in the neighborhood. They'll hear an emergency call and recognize our call letters as comin' from New Orleans. They might come running out of curiosity if nothing else. I don't want the kind of help we'd get from them when they see our faces. The captain of that ship knows me, and it won't take too long before they figure out who you are. They can add two and two. No, we're gonna wait awhile. If we get to the point where more water is comin' in than goin' out, we call for help or we jump in the dingy. Sorry, Judge, the return voyage ain't gonna be uneventful."

"I can call Fitch on the ship-to-shore phone."

"Do that."

Boucher climbed to the bridge and called Fitch, who answered on the first ring. Jock gave him their situation and position. "I don't want you calling anybody just yet.

I don't know who the hell to trust. We're taking on water from a crack in the hull, but we've got things under control for the moment. One thing you can do is check on a vessel named *Zephyr*. It's a cargo carrier, not as big as the *Gulf Pride*. Somebody will be putting in an insurance claim on it. It went down with all hands."

"Christ. Stay in touch and stay dry."

Boucher hung up and went below. "Fitch is monitoring our position, and we're on the satellite. I'm hoping we'll also get pictures of the third boat and be able to track it to see where it goes."

Arcineaux was shaking his head. "I went along with this," he said. "I even asked to be included, so I have no one to blame but myself. But I gotta ask you. Seems to me all you got was the name of a ship that's now at the bottom of the sea, and you're getting all the information you need from communications satellites. Was this trip worth it?"

"I'll make sure you are fully compensated for —"

"I'm gonna throw you overboard if you finish that sentence. Answer my question."

"Probably not," Boucher said. "It was foolish. It was reckless. I'm sorry."

"What are you really chasin', Judge? You got any idea? I'm just a Coonass water rat, and God knows I've made mistakes of my own, but I'm gonna leave you watching a hole in the boat that shouldn't be there—one that might end our lives a lot sooner than either of us planned—just because you wanted to play eyewitness. You might give that some thought." He stared over the wheel and out to sea. "Now go below and keep an eye on that leak."

Boucher went below and scavenged the boat's complement of fishing gear. He found a pair of waders, sat on a bench, and put them on. He was reasonably warm and dry and could sit in relative comfort while the water rose around his legs and he watched the leak that might doom them. He thought about what Arcineaux had said. Fitch had told him much the same. Impending demise does concentrate one's focus.

He found a wooden spoon for mixing salads in a galley drawer and used it as a gauge to measure the water. After several hours of slow cruising, it had risen several inches. He called for Arcineaux to come below.

The skipper looked at the rising water. "I'm on a heading for Port Isabel, Texas. I think I oughta call in our situation."

"You must. Dumont's ship isn't anywhere near us now. We're headed for Texas, and his ship's returning to Houma as fast as it can. We should be fine."

"I ain't been worried about him for a while now."

"Then why haven't you called for help?"

"Salvage laws. I call for a tow, I might be givin' up my boat. You know anything about salvage law on the seas, Judge?"

Boucher nodded. For centuries courts had favored

those who engaged in rescuing lives and property at sea, and the definition between rescue and salvage could be a fine one. Professional salvors were generously compensated. Arcineaux might lose his boat to a salvor successful in bringing it in. It was a tough call. He was weighing the odds as he examined the damaged hull. "If the hull splits, there might not be time for you to get on deck. I'm gonna call for help."

Arcineaux got on the radio's emergency frequency. There were a number of fishing boats close enough if they had to abandon ship. With a salvor, he had a chance.

"When the salvage boat gets here," Boucher said, "let me do the talking. We'll set a fee and sign a contract. I'll tell them I'm a judge. I'm not going to let them take your boat, Fred."

Arcineaux shrugged. "Might help."

Boucher then called Fitch. "Three nearest airports from Port Isabel are Brownsville, McAllen, and Corpus Christi. There are several smaller regionals. Don't know when I'll hit land, but I'll get the first flight back. Skipper's going to stay with his boat, bring it back when repairs are done. I'll have a lot to talk to you about."

"Got some news for you too," Fitch said with a dry laugh. He hung up.

Boucher joined Arcineaux on the flybridge, the better to look out for boats in their vicinity. Within no time they spotted several, then several more.

"Some are Samaritans," Arcineaux said, "some are scavengers waiting to see if we go down. All types of men are called to the sea; all types."

Boucher had drafted a contract before the salvage vessel found them. He introduced himself and presented the document. The numbers were agreed upon. All were satisfied. There was no more time to waste; *Daddy's Little Girl* was listing badly. The wounded craft and its rescuer were joined, and additional pumps were brought aboard. The cruiser began to right itself. At that point another sport fisher pulled alongside and asked if it could help. It was headed to Port Isabel.

"Catch a ride," Arcineaux said. "There's nothin' you can do here, and somebody needs to know about what went on out there. I'll be all right. Let you know when I'm back in port."

"Give me a call if you need anything," Boucher said.

"You can bet I will. Have your checkbook ready."

CHAPTER 26

WHEN BOUCHER PULLED INTO Port Isabel, he compensated the charter fisherman who'd given him the ride by buying a tank of fuel, which he put on his credit card, then set off in search of an ATM. He bought some comfortable clothes, rented a motel room for long enough to shower, then checked airline schedules on his cell phone. The best route was a flight out of McAllen to Houston, changing planes to New Orleans. There was a drive and then a layover, but he'd be home tonight. He found a taxi for the drive to McAllen. A trip of seventy miles, it was probably the best fare the driver had seen in a while. The woman was short and thin to the point of emaciation, but ebullient.

"How you doin'?" she gushed. "First time here?"

"Yes, I'm going to McAllen to get a flight back home to New Orleans."

"Pity you can't stay awhile. McAllen's a great place to visit. It's not New Orleans, of course."

"This close to the border, with all the drug violence, I would think business would be down," Boucher said.

"You would think wrong. Tourism is down, but otherwise, business is booming. Trade with Mexico is at an all-time high. We've got more jobs than people to fill them, and not many places in the States can say that. The drug situation is a problem, but it's a work-around. Know what I mean? There's a lot more going on between the U.S. and Mexico than the drug problem. We've even got our own free-trade zone. We also get a lot of wealthy Mexicans coming here to shop. Many of them are buying houses here because of the violence in their home neighborhoods. Nice folks. I feel sorry for what's going on other side of the border. I pray it never reaches us on this side."

Just past the halfway point of his road trip, Boucher was drawn to the sight of military vehicles being transported on a convoy of flatbed trucks. "What's that?" he asked the driver. "I didn't know there was an army base around here."

"There isn't," the driver said. "We've got a National Guard armory, but it's never had that kind of activity, and I've been here all my life. My husband and I both served in the Guard. That's how we met."

Boucher got to the airport, bought his ticket, then sat in the departure lounge doing what most of his fellow travelers were doing—making one call after another. He called Mildred. She had left for the day. He had fences to mend there. Malika seemed glad to hear from him but had to cut their conversation short. Fitch was also in a rush. Something was up with him, something not for discussion over a cell phone. Boucher had made three calls, all brief. If broadband communications were the only indicator, one would be tempted to assume there wasn't a whole lot going on in the life of Judge Jock Boucher.

The flight from McAllen to IAH was barely long enough to serve drinks to the few passengers. As Boucher walked through Houston's mammoth airport, his growling stomach was a reminder that he had not eaten all day. He opted for Starbucks, coffee and a sandwich. He seated himself at a small table and engaged in the only activity still enjoyable in airports forever changed by high-security concerns: people-watching, maybe the chance of catching a celebrity on the move. One guy was a double for Denzel Washington. Boucher had spent very little time in Houston and did not expect to see anyone he knew. But there he was, speed-walking to his departure terminal, the poker-playing lawyer Carl Benetton. The lawyer wasn't looking around, absorbed in a cell phone call.

"Lord, say it ain't so," Boucher whispered.

He finished his coffee and sandwich and walked to the gate. Boarding had commenced. The flight looked full. The lawyer was nowhere to be seen. Maybe he was already aboard, first class receiving first call. Boucher was dressed in a twenty-dollar outfit he'd bought at Target. What reason could he have for traveling in what amounted to a laborer's work clothes? He boarded the plane. Benetton sat in first class, reading a newspaper. The lawyer looked up as he passed.

"Carl?" Boucher said. "Is there a game I wasn't told about?"

The lawyer was surprised to see him and at a loss for words. "Judge Boucher! What are you . . ."

Benetton sat next to the window, the aisle seat vacant. Boucher sat down and began to whisper conspiratorially. "I got a call this afternoon about a 1960 Mercedes convertible for sale in Houston at a great price. When a rare model comes on the market, the race is to the swiftest. I flew in to take a look at it." He brushed his fingers down his newly purchased casual outfit. "When I'm trying to get a deal, I dress down. Will you be seeing Ray?"

"Yes, I will."

"Give him my best and ask him to call. I'll be in my office tomorrow."

"I will tell him. Good to see you, Judge."

"You too."

Boucher stood and walked to his seat at the rear of the plane. The lawyer was making an emergency trip in to see Dumont. Dollars to donuts, it was to discuss the escapade at sea.

* * *

It was late when Boucher finally walked through the door. The red light on his landline's answering machine was flashing, but first things first. He showered. Then he grabbed a toothbrush. Then a robe. Then a bottle of bourbon and a glass. He emptied the glass and followed it with a second before he went to the phone and checked his messages. There was only one. Fitch. "Call me," it said.

"What's up?" Boucher asked when Fitch answered, but the detective hung up on him.

Boucher stared at the phone in his hand and was about to call back when he heard his cell vibrating on the coffee table. The detective's text was a message from someone severely afflicted, or whose opposable thumbs were too chunky to manipulate a cell's minute keyboard: *ate d bk dr*, it read. Boucher stared and frowned. It was gibberish. The technology of texting was beyond ham-fisted Fitch. He stared at the text: *ate d*. Not ate. Eight. It meant eighth, as in Eighth District, the detective's home base. Knowing the first clue, the second was easy; *bk dr* meant back door. Fitch wanted to meet.

The Eighth Police District served the French Quarter, and it was just a short walk from Boucher's house to the historic building where it made its home. Boucher found a back entrance. Fitch was outside having a smoke.

"Why the text message?" Boucher asked.

"I need the practice."

"I won't argue that. Thought you quit," Boucher said, pointing to the cigarette.

"I did, and I'll probably quit again. I like to have a cigarette when I try to predict the next way you'll decide to place your life in peril. You could be the cause of an unshakable habit." Fitch took a drag and exhaled, then flicked the cigarette and ground it into the pavement. "So what happened?" he asked.

Boucher related the activities at sea. "There was another ship following the one that was firing on us. I don't know where it came from or where it went. I didn't see it do any shooting, but it might have. If the weapons were as old as you said—"

"They were old," Fitch said. "The boxes had dates. No way of knowing how they'd been stored over the years, and there might have been flaws in their manufacture. Disarmament investigators use flashlights when they look at Russian nuke storage facilities. They're afraid if they flick on a light switch, they might set off a detonator. Firing missiles from a ship loaded with forty-year-old black-market munitions? That's like dropping a match into a cellar full of fireworks."

"There were plenty of fireworks."

"Did you get pictures?"

"Yes, names of both ships clearly identified. I even got

a shot of the APC falling into the drink. I also ordered satellite imagery."

"Dumont's ship should be coming back into port. We could arrest it."

"Forget it," Boucher said. "They'll have transferred the cash to another ship."

"Do you think this is just about gunrunning?"

"No, I don't. I'll be damned if I can figure out what their game is. But I might find out soon enough."

"I'm not as optimistic as you. By the way, Pip's at Harahan city jail. It ain't the Royal Orleans, but I had someone check on him. He's okay."

"Fitch, I owe you a lot."

"Yeah, you are racking up debts, aren't you? You owe that shrimper fellow too. Big-time. Risked his life, wrecked his boat. I keep asking myself, why do we fuck with you?"

"To see justice served?"

"Bullshit." Fitch went back inside.

Boucher went home. Exhausted, he fell asleep quickly. In the morning he went to the Federal Building. The office was empty, but the scent of talcum powder was strong. On his desk was a high pile of documents with a Post-it note from his assistant saying they required only his signature. She had added a postscript at the bottom: *Trust me.* There was another note placed front and center: *Chief Judge Wundt wants to see you. Call him personally for your appointment. At* the bottom it read, *Sorry.* The chief judge of the Eastern District of Louisiana had placed him on probation only because he could not fire him from the lifetime appointment. Boucher knew the meeting would not be to discuss the weather.

"*Que será, será,*" he whispered.

By midafternoon he had signed all there was to sign. He left to keep a promise.

The Harahan jail was no pleasure palace, but it didn't have the reputation of the Orleans Parish Prison. Boucher was accorded the privilege of an interrogation room. The prisoner was brought in. It looked like he had gained a couple of pounds. One's life was pretty bad when a prison provided better nourishment, Boucher thought.

"Are you doing okay?" he asked.

"I'm fine. Wonderin' what's gonna happen to me."

"That's why I'm here. I'm going to talk with the prosecutor and try to help if I can. There are programs that offer supervised living and the chance to learn a profession. Are you interested?"

"I got supervised living in the joint. If I want to do laundry the rest of my life, I got a profession too."

"Then"—Boucher rose from his chair and walked to the door—"enjoy."

"Wait. Wait a minute, Judge. I'm sorry. I got attitude. I know it. I need to get over it. Please."

Boucher returned to his seat.

"I almost killed you," Pip said. "Why would you help me?"

"I almost killed your brother," Boucher said, then stood, turned, and left.

He went home and called for an early dinner reservation at Brennan's. The temperature pleasant, the humidity low, he decided to spend the afternoon in his courtyard and pulled a chaise lounge out from winter storage. He remembered the Winfield Scott volumes. He'd finished the first. If tranquillity were granted, he could finish the second. He retrieved the book and settled in for a comfortable afternoon. This time he did not notice the old soldier's florid writing style. He was gripped by the briefest episode of the hero's life and read the account several times. Congress had declared war with Mexico. Winfield Scott was given command. His success was admirable; his governance after victory over the foe was evenhanded and lauded even by the vanquished. His pacification order treated Mexican and U.S. citizens equally and martial law was imposed to prevent looting, rape, murder, and other crimes. As the military commander and governor of Mexico City, General Scott established order exceeding that of Mexican rulers prior to the war. In fact, he restored peace so effectively that a delegation of Mexicans asked him to assume the role of leader of the nation. He might have done just that if the jealous president, Zachary Taylor, hadn't called him back to Washington, fearing the general's growing popularity and recognizing a potential political rival.

But Boucher recalled that the war was one of the most controversial and divisive of all U.S. conflicts. It was called unjust and opposed by many, including Lincoln and Grant. History was a two-sided coin.

He lay back in his lounge and closed his eyes, then opened them wide. He stared at the sky. Catchphrases uttered by Dumont played in his head. "Read Scott's bio," Dumont had urged before his first meeting with General Moore. Moore, with the 1st Armored Division in Germany. To its new home at Fort Bliss. From the cold war to the drug war. He felt a cold chill. The sun had gone behind the clouds. He got up and went inside the house, trying to convince himself that his hypothesis was not ridiculous but was the plan of determined men.

CHAPTER 27

BOUCHER'S DINNER AT BRENNAN'S the evening before had been topped off with Bananas Foster, the restaurant's signature dessert. He'd come home barely able to get his clothes off before tumbling into bed and falling asleep. He was barely awake after two cups of very strong coffee. He opened his iPad and read several online newspapers. The device reminded him that there was a trip he needed to make.

Belle Chasse translated to *beautiful hunting* in English, ironic now in more ways than one. The town was home to Boucher's last living relative, his great-uncle Mose. Mose was past ninety, nearly sightless, and hard of hearing. But he was determined to stay abreast of the latest technology. Boucher had bought him a tablet computer because the gnarled old fingers could stretch the screen and increase the font size to where he could read when he held the device just beyond the end of his nose. Boucher had taught the old gentleman the rudiments of the iPad, little more than how to turn it on and off and search the Internet. It was time to check on his relative and see how he was faring with the digital world.

Boucher finished his coffee and drove to Plaquemines Parish and the old house where his uncle swore he'd draw his last breath and from which he would leave only feet-first. Boucher passed a joint forces reserve air station, a base for air force fighters and marine helicopters, and a naval reserve early-warning squadron frequently deployed to the Caribbean on counternarcotics operations. How could such a battle be lost, Boucher asked himself, with such powerful and determined forces arrayed against it?

Boucher pulled up in front of his uncle's ramshackle house and climbed creaky steps to the porch. Uncle Mose had refused all efforts to pay for remodeling the run-down home, but he did allow his nephew to come over with his own tools and make needed repairs. It was time for such a visit. The door was open, and knocking on the front screen was useless because the old man wouldn't hear it. But he did feel vibrations on the warped wooden floor and turned from his armchair and smiled.

"Don't get up," Boucher said loudly, then walked to his uncle, bent over, and kissed him on the top of his bald head. "I wanted to see how you were doing with your tablet computer."

"It's hardly out of my hands," the old man said. "Even take it to the bathroom."

At that moment Boucher's phone alerted him to an incoming e-mail. He took it out of his pocket, read the screen, took a short, sharp breath, and put it back. "I just came over to check on you. Everything's all right?"

"Everything's fine. Thanks for comin'. I know you're a busy man, and I ain't even got iced tea made, so you get along. You can come over next week and see to the porch steps if you want. There's a loose board or two. Mailman almost broke his neck deliverin' me a package."

"Package? What did you get?"

"I ordered me a cover for this iPad thing on the Internet. Don't want it gettin' scratched, I'm usin' it the whole damn day. You know, I can even listen to college professors teachin' their students on this thing while I sit right here in my livin' room. A man can get about as much education as he wants, and he don't—I mean he does not—have to leave his house. Glorious days are comin' if we can fix some of the other problems in this mixed-up world."

"I'm glad you're enjoying it, Uncle Mose."

"I am. You get along, young man. I know you've got things to do."

"I will be by to fix that porch."

Uncle Mose nodded, picking up his tablet, returning to his self-educating endeavors.

When he got in his pickup, Boucher raised the windows. He turned on the air conditioner, pulled out his cell phone, and turned up the volume. The message he'd received was an audio MP3 transmitted by e-mail. He began the playback. The voice was that of the lawyer from Houston. Boucher could picture the two men, Dumont seated behind the French provincial desk in his study, under which Boucher had placed the bug prior to the last poker party. The state-of-the-art device was no bigger than a matchbox; voice-activated with a microprocessor that recorded conversations, it converted them to MP3 files, then transmitted the files to a designated e-mail address. Boucher listened intently. The prelude to conversation was the sound of chairs being brought into position.

"Would you care for a cocktail? Perhaps brandy and a cigar?" The voice was that of Dumont.

"Perhaps later. I wouldn't mind a cigarette," Benetton said.

"Help yourself. They may not be fresh. I don't use them. The occasional cigar is all I allow myself."

Boucher pictured the burled walnut cigarette box on Dumont's desk. He heard the striking of a lighter, then inhalation and exhale.

"He's pretty pissed off over losing that vessel," Benetton said. "That was a big investment."

"He had an incompetent crew," Dumont said. "That's no fault of mine."

"He bought a shipment—"

"Which was delivered."

"Which is at the bottom of the sea. Ray, we are dealing with a homicidal maniac here, a narco-terrorist who would kill a man—or a woman—for spilling coffee on the floor. He kills when he's angry. He kills when he's frustrated. Hell, he probably kills to get rid of his headaches. Questions of fault and liability are concepts beyond him. He paid for something; he doesn't have it."

"What does he expect me to do, send him another arms shipment for free?"

"I'd rather you did that than have him send a hit man to your front door. That's the only response he knows. Anyway, he said he'd pay. It's not like money's a problem for him."

There was a pause, then the sound of tapping; perhaps Dumont's manicured fingernail on the arm of his chair. When he spoke, his voice was firm. "It's time for the end-game," he said. "If this psycho wants another arms delivery, he's going to have to cross the border to get it. We'll drop it at an isolated spot on our side of the river, but he has to pick it up."

"He'll suspect a trap."

"Of course he will. He's paranoid. But we've baited this trap long enough; it's time to spring it. Everything we've promised him, we've delivered, all to this end. He'll be sus-picious, but from his side of the river, he can watch us fly in and make the delivery. He can't afford not to take the chance; he needs those guns. You've told me yourself that he's trying to expand his territory while others are trying to take it from him. Sweeten the offer. Tell him we'll include the latest technology, new weapons that will guarantee him supremacy over his adversaries. He'll have to lead his men over because he can't trust them not to steal the guns and use them against him. He'll do it. He'll cross the Rio Grande."

"I'll deliver the message. Has Cyrus told you what he has planned?" Benetton asked.

"Yes. General Moore is in close contact with the governor of Texas, who can call out the National Guard, as well as with the commanding officer of the guard unit based in McAllen. He will also alert those in command at Fort Bliss and Fort Hood, two of the largest army bases we've got—homes to infantry, armor, and cavalry. They have rapid-response teams experienced in counterterrorism. With the scenario that will be reported by Senator Farmer, Chairman of the Senate Subcommittee on Emerging Threats and Capabilities, the president will have no choice but to deploy troops to the area, including SOCOM, the Special Operations Command. Quaid, Moore, and Farmer will be pressing the DOD and the White House for enough resources to prevent a similar occurrence from ever happening again. That means boots on the ground in Mexico."

There was a pause before the lawyer spoke again. His

tone of voice had changed. It was most apparent to Boucher, listening only to the audio.

"I've studied this group you've put together, each man's motivation. Senator Farmer is easy. You've had a ring in his nose since he first ran for public office. He'll do whatever you ask, and he comes cheap. Quaid is more complicated. He's seen the war on drugs march through the terms of eight presidents, over forty years. What does he have to show for a lifetime of effort? The demon he's fought most of his life just gets bigger and stronger. But he's like a faithful dog, and you've dangled another bone in front of him. He wants to go out with a big show, and this incident is his trophy. He's tried to warn of the danger of Mexican cartels crossing over and has been ignored. This will be his chance to say 'I told you so.'"

"You're rather loquacious tonight, counselor," Dumont said.

"I'm not finished. General Cyrus Moore? He's perfect for his role in all this: respected, with invaluable contacts, and you've utilized him brilliantly. The chance you're giving him—to influence U.S. foreign policy—appeals to his deepest ambitions. For both Quaid and Moore, the motivation is the belief that they are serving their country."

"You underestimate the roles of these men. Senator Farmer can pick up the phone and call any corporate executive in this country, and before the smoke clears on the Rio Grande, he will have done just that. The president will be besieged with calls from leaders of the defense, energy, heavy equipment manufacturing, agribusiness, and too many other economic sectors for me to count, all with interest in a secure and peaceful southern neighbor, all imploring that he take decisive action. Gary Quaid's contacts include the leaders of every federal law enforcement agency there is, and he has cultivated those relationships in preparation for whatever may be necessary. Many of these men have been working with their Mexican counterparts for years. The foundation for collaboration between our forces and theirs has been laid. And General Moore—you think this is just an ego thing with him? The men and women coming home from Iraq and Afghanistan are facing a battered U.S. economy that doesn't have enough jobs to offer those already here, much less tens of thousands of returning warriors. He doesn't want to see them go from the front line to the unemployment line. If this becomes the police action they envisage, these soldiers will have an opportunity to continue to serve. That's why he's in the game."

"Then there's you," Benetton said. "Tell me, Ray, what do you get? What has driven you to conceive, organize, finance, and conduct this fantastic scheme?"

"My enemies," Dumont said. "Every day I wake and thank God for my enemies."

"Well, sir, I will do everything possible to avoid ending up on your enemies list. Avenging your son's murder will provoke an incident that will have international re-percussions. It sounds inconceivable that the death of one man could lead to war until you recall the shot fired that afternoon in Sarajevo, 1914. The inconceivable is never the impossible."

"Now, you," Dumont said. "What's your motivation? You'll make a fortune, but at what cost? When El Jimador is caught, your relationship will be exposed. No more cartel clients. You'll be their target, not me."

"I don't deny it; I'm in this for the money, and you've made it worth my while. I know how to disappear, and I will have the necessary resources. Thanks for your concern."

Their voices faded when the two men got up and walked from the study. Boucher closed his phone.

He drove home and tried to call Fitch, but his cell phone was turned off, which meant he was with Helen, which meant he didn't want to be disturbed. Boucher called Malika. She was spending a quiet Sunday in her Manhattan apartment.

"I've got *The New York Times* spread out all over the floor," she said. "I just picked up some fresh bagels from the deli down the street. Wish you were here."

"I wish I were too."

"What's wrong, Jock? There's something in your voice."

"Really?" he squeaked, trying to change his somber tone.

"Something's bothering you."

"Maybe it's that I'm missing you."

"You know what to do about that. Say the word and I'm on a plane. I could be there before these bagels are stale. Or you could come here. There's a concert tonight in Central Park."

"I've got a meeting with the chief judge tomorrow morning," he said.

"I know what he's going to ask you."

"What's that?"

"He's going to ask why you can't just do your job."

"It's not something I can talk about right now, that's all. Judges can't talk about their work. You know that."

"Do you think I'm going to taint the jury? Leak to the press? Jock, you're on probation, and you're being given busywork to ease the load of other judges. If you can't even do that, and it seems you can't, I think you should step down. I don't think you're doing anyone any good right now, least of all yourself, and that's all I care about. You. Whatever you're doing or not doing, it's keeping us apart."

He ended the conversation on a weak note. The matter would be resolved soon. They'd be together. Soon. Malika had said little more, but he heard it in her voice. They might go their separate ways. Soon. He thought about the other men involved in the stratagem he was uncovering. Did they talk to their wives, their partners, about a scheme that might involve the occupation of a friendly nation and ally? He doubted it. He knew he lacked what men with such ambitions possessed. Sangfroid. He lacked the cold blood. It was his weakness. One of many.

"Come in and sit down, Judge Boucher. Thank you for being on time."

Boucher took the seat across from Chief Judge Wundt's desk, as he'd done months before when he was placed on suspension. The senior jurist did not look good. He was even more overweight. His cheeks and nose were red from rosacea and there were new liver spots on his temples. It seemed the skin on his face was melting; the bags under his eyes were purple. Jowls hung from his chin, and when he coughed, he wiped his mouth after each wracking explosion. He did not warm up to his subject but jumped right in.

"I'd find a way to get rid of you," he said as if picking up the conversation from months earlier, "and every judge in this district would back me up except one. But you've got a friend up the ladder. I have no idea why the president thinks so highly of you, but he does."

"It's not that. He appointed me. I'm an embarrassment to him that he's trying to keep quiet until he can get one or two more judicial nominees confirmed. That's all. If this is a dressing-down, you don't need to waste your time. I'm—"

"Shut up. I'm your senior, and you're going to show me the respect I have earned and deserve. We do that for each other, we jurists."

"Judge, I'm sorry, but—"

"Will you SHUT UP! I'm trying to, I'm trying—"

Judge Wundt began coughing. Something viscous was lodged deep in his chest, but efforts to expel it went no deeper than his throat, and what he couldn't bring up was choking him. He covered his mouth with his handkerchief and bent over his desk, his head bobbing with each cough. Then he raised his head and tried to draw a deep breath, difficult for him even when he wasn't choking on phlegm. His face was turning purple. Boucher jumped from his chair and ran to the older man. Wundt was practically laying his chest on the desk, and Boucher slapped him on the back. His sternum hit the desktop and he coughed again into his handkerchief. Then he sat up and breathed deeply through his nostrils, the crisis past. He looked into his handkerchief and quickly folded it, crushing it in his hand. Boucher had gotten a quick glimpse of the blood and sputum.

"Judge, let me call a doctor," he said, but Wundt waved him away. He took another breath as Boucher poured him a glass of water from the pitcher on his credenza. He drank slowly, then spoke.

"That's another reason I can't let you go," he said. "I could be dead before the day is out. Christ, we had one judge die and another impeached, I've got one foot in the grave, and you have about as much judicial responsibility as an alley cat. Oh, and your 'oversight' of the administration of the oil-spill funds. How is that going?"

"I have found some irregularities."

"That, when you point them out, will encourage more litigation."

Boucher said nothing. He did not want to be the cause of another fit.

"Have you even spoken to the judge who's been overwhelmed with oil-spill lawsuits?"

"He has not contacted me."

"That's foolish of him. If that's the level of maturity I'm surrounded with, God help us." Wundt sighed. "Go on, get out. Try to remember what you're here for. That's what I called you in to say. We're swamped, and the situation is critical. I have no choice but to restore you to full active status. You will begin receiving cases immediately."

"Your Honor, I—"

"Please go before I start coughing again."

"You should see a doctor—"

"And you should see a psychiatrist. Now go on, get out."

Boucher returned to his office.

"Good morning, Judge Boucher," Mildred said coolly.

"Mildred, I'm sorry, but I was involved in something that I really can't talk about, and it was necessary to—"

"Your Honor, please excuse me for interrupting, but I

work for you. You are a federal judge. You don't have to explain anything to me."

As he entered his absurd little room with the walls lined in cardboard boxes, he heard her mumble something. "What did you say?" he demanded.

She lifted her chin and looked straight into his eyes. "I said you're acting like you need to explain something to somebody."

Yes, he needed to explain something to somebody, and that somebody probably was sitting at his or her own desk in the same building at that moment. Every government acronym imaginable was represented in this complex. There might be someone he could trust, but whom? Was there an agency that had not already been co-opted by Gary Quaid? That was the question, but he had no time to ponder it.

"Oh, Mildred," he said, almost as an afterthought, "I've been restored to duty and told to move back into my chambers. You feel up to a move?"

"Oh, sir. Yes, sir."

Boucher's focus and energies were demanded for the move. Between their cubicle and his chambers, they logged lots of elevator time. Several of his judicial brethren passed as he unpacked boxes, welcoming him back into the fold. One of them must have known that Mildred was on temporary assignment and offered to refer a more experienced office manager.

"I wouldn't give up my assistant for all the shrimp in the gulf," Boucher said, loud enough for her to hear.

With help from the maintenance staff, they finished the move that afternoon. Dark-stained wooden cabinets replaced cardboard boxes. A minimum of photographs and framed diplomas marked the territory as that of an occupant, not a transient. Boucher surprised Mildred with champagne, and they toasted their new quarters. "Here's to your next twenty years." Boucher raised a glass.

"On the government payroll? I don't think so," Mildred said. "You've got me for a few more years, Judge. Then I'm retiring."

"What will you do? You'll still be a young woman."

"You're just being kind. I'll get some traveling out of my system, then who knows? I might even go to law school."

"I would look forward to you trying a case in my court."

"Your Honor, I'd have to ask you to recuse yourself. What I know about you would embarrass both of us."

CHAPTER 28

"**Y**OU DID *WHAT?*" FITCH exploded.

The two men sat in Boucher's courtyard early that evening, having finished their day jobs.

"I placed a voice-activated bug under Dumont's desk the last time I was there. He obviously doesn't use his study that much, because the first recording I got took place a couple of nights ago. That lawyer from Houston came to see him."

"Do you know how many laws you've broken?"

"I'm not going to use it. Who could I tell? Nobody would believe me."

"Nobody would believe that Louisiana's leading businessman and a group of national security experts are trying to incite a war with Mexico? I can't imagine why you would have a problem selling *that* story!"

"We don't know the when and we don't know the where," Boucher said. "That's why I can't sell it."

"You forgot one—the why. Why would sane, responsible men try something so preposterous? You're suggesting that the gunrunning wasn't for the money?"

"No, it wasn't. That's the key, and you described the players perfectly. Moore and Quaid are national security experts. They see the border with Mexico as one of our country's greatest areas of vulnerability. Armed scouts and drug runners are in the Arizona desert by the hundreds, directing smuggling operations on American territory; American civilians are protesting the failure of our government to protect them. Look at history. The U.S.-Mexican War in 1846, Pershing's expedition in 1916, both preceded by Mexican incursions into the U.S. It's going to be déjà vu all over again. Dumont and his cronies plan to provoke an incident. There will be a rush to judgment and a hue and cry for retaliation. We occupied Veracruz in 1914. Pershing was pulled back in 1917 without finding Pancho Villa, because World War I changed priorities and he was needed for the war in Europe. In 1919 three thousand U.S. troops went into Mexico and pushed Villa's gangs into the desert. This time, if we go in, we may stay."

"We secure our borders. We get rid of the cartels. That would be a bad thing?"

Boucher shook his head. "It's not who we are," he said.

"You just told me it's exactly who we are. It's who we

have been numerous times in our history. It's a new century; maybe it's time to repeat the dance. I for one am proud to live in a country that actively protects the interests of its citizens."

"But innocent people will be killed as a part of this plan."

"Yeah, there is that."

Boucher heard the front door ring and went into the house to receive a FedEx delivery. He called Fitch to come in from the courtyard. Together they reviewed the satellite photos. Boucher was pleased that he could tell Arcineaux their trip had been justified. Accurate identification of the two vessels engaged in the arms exchange at sea was impossible from the photos. Those he'd taken were the only proof. He could see the transfer of the weapons, then Dumont's ship heading northeast, the chase, and the explosion. The third ship was tracked a short distance, then lost, but with the satellite's orbital movement, its name did become visible on both bow and stern, *Estrella Mar*. Sea Star.

"If Dumont was selling inferior weapons that blew up in their faces," Fitch said, "he might not be all that bad."

"What are you saying? Dumont smuggled guns and ammo that were stolen by criminals who used them on our streets, remember? You called the bullets cop killers."

"There's that too," Fitch said. "So what are you going to do?"

"I think my role in this little drama has played itself out. I've been told to go back to work. They're going to start assigning me cases to adjudicate. I'm going to have a brief talk with a friend of mine at the FBI, then I'm going to walk away from this, take your advice, settle down, and do the job I've been given."

"So you're going to exchange your Superman cape for a judicial robe and stop trying to save the world? Hope you can settle down to the nine-to-five."

"I have never known a judge who worked nine to five in my life," Boucher said. "It's more like seven to eleven."

"No wonder so many of them are such cranky bastards. Anyway, here's to humdrum. You've earned it."

Fitch had plans with Helen and refused the offer of a drink. Boucher wasn't hungry and realized he hadn't done any exercise in a while. He enjoyed the gym he belonged to because that's what it was, a gym—not a spa, not a wellness center. It had new equipment that made the place look like the set of a science fiction film, but it also had the two pieces Boucher used, which were getting harder to find—a heavy punching bag and a speed bag, essential tools of the boxer—though he still couldn't use them with his bruised ribs. Another thing he loved about his gym was its location at the far end of an older strip mall. Parking was never a problem; he could usually park his pickup right outside the door. This convenience meant he could leave from his home in his workout clothes, return in the same, and use his own shower. He drove to the strip mall. He did a half-hour easy walk on the treadmill and was persuaded to sit in on a yoga class. Leaving the gym wearing only shorts and a T-shirt, he walked out to his truck. It was gone. There had been plenty of traffic into and out of the gym, to say nothing of shoppers. He cursed and turned to walk back inside. He hadn't brought his cell phone and would have to use their line to report his vehicle stolen. But before he could enter, there was a flash of pain, searing light, then blackness. He was dragged a few feet and shoved into the backseat of a vehicle he would have recognized, had he been conscious. He was laid out on a floor not wide enough to accommodate his height, but his legs were folded in, and there was plenty of room. Many would have found traveling in such a fine vehicle tolerable even in this constrained posture, because most folks only dreamed of riding in a stretch limousine.

Jock Boucher regained consciousness and raised his head. He stared into the barrel of a gun he recognized. He had already seen the distinctive piece pointed at him not once but twice. He looked above the barrel into the eyes of Ray Dumont, who in one hand held the gun and, in the other, a crystal fluted glass.

"Champagne, Judge? It might help your headache."

"No, thanks. I had some earlier," Boucher said.

It was a rhetorical question. His hands were bound behind his back. He pulled in his knees and twisted so he could sit with his back against the jump seats across from Dumont.

"What insolence," Dumont said. "Bugging me, of all people. Did you really think I wouldn't have my home swept? When I found the bug, I backtracked and came to you. The night before our poker party—you and me in the study."

"I don't know what you're talking about. Plenty of people have been in your house."

"Yes, that's true, and others may have had an opportunity. I did lose some sleep over it, but I kept coming back to you. Benetton told me you were on the same flight from Houston and that you had gone there to look at a rare Mercedes. I thought it odd that we had discussed a mutual passion for antiques but you had never mentioned automobiles, and your only vehicle is a rather ordinary Ford truck. I had your flight schedule traced. You flew to Houston from McAllen with no prior flight. 'What on earth was he doing in McAllen?' I asked myself. An investigator found out that a federal judge had negotiated a contract with a local salvage company to tow a boat into nearby Port Isabel for repairs. And where was that boat from? Right here. My, you were busy, weren't you?"

Dumont sipped his champagne and set the pistol in his lap. Boucher eyed it, his thoughts obvious. "Don't even think about it," Dumont said. "I could fire without even picking it up. And it would make a terrible mess of the upholstery."

"You know you're going to have the whole U.S. government on your back, kidnapping a federal judge? Even your friends won't be able to help you."

"You have no idea who my friends are. I assure you, I can get just about whatever help I need whenever and wherever I need it, and there will be little concern over the disappearance of a federal judge who has proved to be nothing but an embarrassment. There are those who are wishing for your disappearance even at this moment. To me, you've become more of a disappointment than an embarrassment. I brought you into my little circle of friends. I told them they could trust you. How wrong I was. I was ready to let you play a part in what will be the next great chapter in American history."

"You mean the next slaughter of innocent people; the next unnecessary shedding of blood; the provoking of hostilities with a neighbor, friend, and ally."

"Again, how I misjudged you. I thought you were a man of vision, a man who appreciated the lessons of history."

"What has history taught us recently? We're finally learning that war without end can bankrupt an entire global economic system."

Dumont poured another glass of champagne and toasted. "Here's to a war we can't lose," he said. "We need one. It's been too long."

"You're mad," Boucher said.

"If you mean that in terms of angry, you're right. I'm angry that crime and anarchy reign all along our southern border. There is a vacuum down there. I propose we fill it before we start finding headless bodies on our side of the river. Yes, I'm angry. I hate waste, and there is an intolerable waste of resources there."

"It's sovereign territory. The people there don't want us."

"Those constraints didn't keep us out of Iraq and Afghanistan. It's a new world, Judge Boucher. We eliminate heads of state inimical to our interests. We send troops where our interests are threatened. A secure and tranquil northern Mexico is in our national interest." Dumont took a sip.

"Is the destruction of a democratic government in our national interest?"

"We will be aiding a democratic government, not destroying it. Mexico has always had trouble controlling its northern territories. Pancho Villa came from the north. They were never able to control him; they had to massacre him. If old Pancho were alive today, he'd be the biggest drug lord of them all. He'd have his own country, like he did a hundred years ago. Did you know he even printed his own currency? Hell, if Mexico had been able to control its northern states, we wouldn't have gotten Texas, New Mexico, Arizona, and California as easily as we did. It's simple, Judge—lack of control is bad for business, and it's bad for our national security." Dumont set his champagne glass down and bent forward, his face so close that Boucher could smell the sparkling wine on his breath.

"My son, Charles, God rest his soul, was a geologist, not a robber baron. He helped discover fields that rival those of the Middle East. What is being done with them? Nothing. My son was killed in Mexico while he was helping that country." He leaned back in the seat. His shoulders slumped. "I see his death in nightmares. I see his murderer in my sleep and wake in cold sweats."

"Revenge," Boucher said. "Revenge and greed. That's how you honor your son?"

"No. Seeing the discovery he gave his life for come to fruition: that's how I will honor my son."

"I suppose you're going kill me too. What's another murder to you? You killed that man whose body I found floating in the gulf. You killed that trooper."

"I killed no one. The body you found, that was a horrible accident. He fell overboard. I paid his family a fortune in benefits after he worked for me for just two days. The trooper? He died in a car wreck. Was it the accident, a heart attack, the chemo, or too many beers? See, I made the effort to learn a little about the unfortunate young man, but I had nothing to do with his death. Do I need to teach you the law, Judge Boucher? I have killed no one."

"The illegal arms you've transported certainly have."

"Show me. Show me one victim. I made a few shipments of substandard armaments. They killed only the criminals who bought them."

"A few shipments?"

"Those were all that was necessary. The first established the relationship. The last shipment, you know what happened to it. The next, and final one, we will make tonight. It's the bait. The trap is set. They will cross the border, and we will chase them to hell and back. I did not traffic in guns; I baited a trap."

"You're an innocent man. So I'm going to be the first to die at your hands?"

"For the moment I just want you secured and out of the way. I don't want you playing Paul Revere. We'll decide what to do with you later. It's not my decision. My partners have a say in the matter. So lean back and enjoy the ride. Oh, I'd better put these on you. Don't give me any trouble, Judge. I don't want any bodily harm to come to you—not in my favorite limo."

Dumont placed blinders over Boucher's eyes. The smell of Dumont's wife's perfume on the mask was nauseating.

Boucher had no idea how long he'd been unconscious but guessed it was brief. He knew their starting point, the strip mall. Unable to see, he tried to picture their route, differentiating the sounds of the road. They came to a bridge; driving over the Mississippi, obviously. He figured the bridge was part of Interstate 310. They turned off the interstate on the other side of the river. That would put them on Route 90, which would make sense, he thought. They were heading to Houma. He estimated speed and distance. With a federal judge bound and blindfolded in the backseat, they were not going to go over the speed limit. It was an easy calculation: fifty-five miles to Houma at fifty-five miles per hour. He counted off seconds and minutes in his head. An hour passed. They were still traveling. They slowed to a crawl, then stopped. He heard what sounded like a garage door opening. The limo drove maybe twenty feet and stopped again. The door closed. The motor was turned off. The passenger door was opened, and Boucher smelled oil. Not motor oil, but something else familiar. Rough hands reached in and grabbed him by the shoulders. With resistance futile, he helped as best he could to exit the limo. He was pushed and prodded across a smooth concrete floor. The soles of his gym shoes squeaked as he walked. A key was placed in a lock, a door was opened, and he was shoved into a room. Or maybe it was a closet. Thrown off balance, he hit a wall that kept him from falling. The door was closed and locked. The space wasn't large. His hands were still bound, his eyes still blindfolded.

He heard the garage door open, the limo's engine start, and the car drive out. The door closed. He walked around the small space. It was some kind of a storage closet. If it had been in use, it was cleaned out before his arrival. There was that oily smell he knew but couldn't identify. It was from a long time ago. He sniffed the air. Of course. It was gun oil: solvent for cleaning and lubricating firearms—and storing them. He knew where he was—the warehouse where Dumont had kept his cache of smuggled weapons.

Elise Dumont's sleep mask was driving him crazy. Her stale perfume and gun oil were a repellent mixture. With his hands still bound, he rubbed his head against the wall until the mask slid off and fell to the floor. It didn't help; he was in total darkness. But at least her scent had been replaced with one more tolerable. Right up there with the manly odors of leather, pipe tobacco, and brandy, gun lubricant wasn't all that bad.

His wrists were tightly bound with flex-ties. He pulled against them but gave that up when the plastic edges began cutting into his skin. Though he was not into pointless suffering, he could endure pain with purpose. It would hurt, but there was a way. He kicked off his shoes, then leaned against the wall and lowered himself to the floor till he was sitting. Then he leaned sideways, slowly, till gravity pulled him down to the concrete. He landed hard on his shoulder and tried to keep his head from snapping onto the floor. He failed. His head hit hard, and he was dazed for several seconds, but he was lying on his side, his objective. Boucher stretched his arms as if trying to pull them from their sockets, lowering his bound wrists down to his buttocks. He brought a knee to his chest. He pointed the toe, trying to flatten his foot against his butt cheek. His muscles and joints were flexible for a man his age, but Boucher was not a teenager. He strained, pulling and stretching, the pain almost unbearable. Then he felt the flex-tie slide over his toe and up his instep. He wanted to scream with pain but didn't know if he was under guard. The plastic cuff flayed skin off his bare shin as he scraped it toward his knee, that pain exceeded by the pain in his shoulder joints. Further movement was impossible. The tie was stuck at his knee and wouldn't budge. In an effort to snap the plastic, Boucher tried pressure, leg muscles being stronger than arm muscles, but it held. He was trussed up like a roasted chicken, panting, sweating . . . and surrendering. It couldn't be done. They would find him like this and have a good laugh. No, he decided, one more try. He expelled every last molecule of air from his lungs, gritted his teeth, and pulled. The tie slipped over his knee. One leg was through the loop. Now the other.

It was no less painful slipping the second leg through, but he was bolstered by the knowledge that it was possible. With both legs through and his hands in front of him, he broke through the cuffs. His hands were free.

He was still in the dark in a locked room. He felt for the doorknob and twisted it. Maybe it was nothing more than optimism, but it felt like a cheap doorknob, and a cheap doorknob meant a cheap lock. But it was still a lock, and unless he planned to ram the metal door with his throbbing shoulder, he was still imprisoned in a dark room. He brushed his hands along the length and breadth of the floor, feeling for anything, anything at all, but the surface was clean. He ran his fingers under the door, then laid his head on the floor. There was no light coming from the other side. The warehouse was deserted. He sat down, his back against the wall, and thought of his shoes, the well-worn Nikes he had slipped off before contorting out of the flex-ties. They were so used that he'd even worn out a pair of shoelaces, replacing them with the steel-tipped variety because an attractive young saleswoman had told him they expressed personality. He had admired her spunky salesmanship. Personality in shoelaces? He unlaced the shoes. His dentist would have cringed, but Boucher stuck the end of a lace in his mouth and pulled the metal tip off with his teeth. Then the other end. Then the other pair. The four tips, placed end to end, were about four inches in length. Again using his teeth, he crimped the end of one into another till the four tips were one length of metal. This he flattened, biting down hard with his molars. A half inch at one end he bent to a ninety-degree angle. He fingered his creation in the dark. It felt like a skeleton key—of course darkness heightened imagination. He felt for the doorknob, then the keyhole. He stuck the crude piece of metal in the lock and jiggled, determining the direction of the cylinder, feeling for the pins, pushing them up till they set. He took a deep breath and turned the knob. The door squeaked open.

Boucher put his shoes back on, inserted and tied the laces, then stepped out of the storage closet. In the pitch black, he walked like a zombie, his hands in front of him and feeling the air in a wide arc, his shoes sliding along the floor so as not to bump into anything. He took ten steps and saw a hint of light. It was coming from higher up. He carefully walked toward the light. His foot hit something, and his hand touched something metal—a bar or rod. A stairwell with a banister. There was a second story, probably some kind of an office with a window. The dim illumination was ambient light from outside. Boucher climbed the stairs. He reached the second landing. There was an office. He could see desks, chairs, and filing cabinets. The door was locked, but the screened windows were open. A screen held no risk of noise or lacerations. He broke through with his fist, ripped it out, and climbed in. A desk was situated right under the window, and he climbed onto it, then stepped to the floor. He felt the desktop. Nothing. No computer. No phone. Nothing. This room had ceased functioning as an office. In the far wall was a window about eight feet up from the floor; the source of the ambient light. It was for ventilation only, about three feet long and maybe two feet wide. It was open, and he could see that it was awning-style, hinged at the top and opening inward. He picked up the desk and moved it under the window, stuck his head under the open glass, and looked out. The moon and stars lit up the sky but didn't do much for the earth below. He couldn't see a thing.

Boucher thought he'd been brought to a warehouse in Dumont's compound in Houma. His calculation of the distance while blindfolded in the limo seemed to indicate so, but the compound would have had security lighting, and outside, it was pitch black. There were no other buildings near. It didn't matter. What was important was that there was an escape, through the awning window. Boucher tried to lean out but couldn't. The open windowpane was in his way. He got off the desk and began feeling around the room in the dark but soon gave up the foolish task of looking for tools conveniently left behind. He climbed back up, took the window in both hands, and pushed it up till its hinges broke. There was a loud crack. If they had left a guard, he would come running now. Boucher didn't wait. He climbed through the window. It was too small to bring his legs through and slide out sideways. There was no choice but to climb through and drop headfirst. It didn't matter what was below; hard ground or soft, he'd break his neck. But there was no choice. He went through, head, shoulders, chest, waist. Halfway out. The exterior was corrugated metal, and the ribs fit into his hands. He spidered down the wall as his thighs, then shins, slipped through the window. He was hanging by his insteps, the muscles in his legs and feet straining. He kicked away from the window ledge. He gripped the ribs of corrugated metal for a fraction of a second, then pushed away, attempting a reverse somersault upside down from the side of the building.

It was a three-point landing; right heel, leg fully extended; left foot with knee flexed; and rump. Both cheeks. Make that a four-point landing. It knocked the wind out of him, and pain shot through his body, but he did not fracture his skull or break his neck. Breathing heavily, he felt around. He'd landed on grass, wet grass, maybe moss. He blessed his home state of Louisiana, where hard, dry earth was so rare.

The blessing was brief. Dumont could return any minute. Boucher stood up, leaning against the building for support. He tried to walk. His left ankle hurt, but the pain would have to be endured. He crept around to the front of the building. There was a blacktop surface in front of the warehouse and a two-lane road. There were lights to his left. To his right, the road led into darkness. It led, Boucher knew, deeper into the bayou. He turned toward the lights and began to walk. After a minute, the pain in his left ankle subsided, and he began to jog. He was properly attired for it.

CHAPTER 29

BOUCHER RAN ALONG THE two-lane blacktop. There was bayou on both sides of the road, built on a levee. He could smell the bayou, could see the reflection of the moon on the water and hear frogs croaking all around him. A moonbeam penetrated the branches of mangroves hung with drooping Spanish moss that glowed white in the night's light. Another beam pierced through the canopy and illuminated several turtles resting on a half-submerged branch. They looked like huge brown cabochon star sapphires with the glint of moon on their moist shells. Several hundred yards later, he could see the lights of an oncoming car. It was approaching fast. Boucher jumped from the road, sliding down the embankment. Hunched over, he continued running at the water's edge. He was running blind—if you could call it running. No illumination from any source filtered down to the muddy waterline, and he sank in sludge above his ankles with each step, laboriously lifting his feet. Then something grabbed his left ankle. It tightened its grip and pulled him down. Boucher lay for a second in the muck, then whatever had a hold on his leg began pulling him into the water. He fought, grabbing whatever he could, but his fingers only clawed at mud. Boucher flailed his arms, splashing as he was tugged away from the bank into deeper water. He gasped as he was pulled under the surface, but in his panic he had failed to draw a complete breath. Submerged and being pulled deeper, he reached down for his left ankle. Already there was no sensation in his foot. He felt along his leg, expecting his hands to be severed by whatever had him in its death grip. The ringing in his ears seemed linked to the searing pain in his lungs. Deprived of air, the sacs in his chest seemed to be unnaturally expanding, as if ready to explode. In contrast, his head seemed light, his cognitive organs shrinking in his skull as he surrendered to the void. His extremities went limp as he lost consciousness.

A viselike grip held the top of his head and turned it roughly to the side.

"You prob'ly gonna puke now. Keep your head turned so's you don't swallow 'n' choke."

The prediction proved accurate. Boucher tried to take

a deep breath and vomited. Dry heaves. There was nothing in his stomach to throw up. He heaved again, gasped for air, and knew from the musk he sucked into his mouth that he was still on the bayou. The hand that had held his head helped him to sit. He sat up and began a paroxysm of dry heaves, coughing and gasping for air, interspersed with none too gentle slaps on the back.

"You back from the dead, you know that?" the voice said. "I'd be int'rested to know if you saw a white light or that tunnel leading to the beyond, 'cause you surely had crossed over."

Boucher stared at white eyes and teeth, the only features visible in a face as black as the swamp night. He was breathing now, short convulsive breaths. "Where am I?"

"Oh, you ain't too far from where you started out. You stepped on my line and disturbed the gator what had my hook in its gut. He was jest tryin' to get away; you was caught in the loop. Gator dragged you down. I'd a never knowed, but he came up to the surface, and I had to dispatch him then and there. Normally, I'd a waited till mornin' when I check my trap."

"Dispatched?" Boucher wheezed.

"Yeah. That's him next to you."

Boucher looked down at the nine-foot beast next to him. It had three eyes.

"Weren't no easy shot," the hunter said.

"It's . . . not . . . season."

"Well, I was hopin' I might count on your discretion on that point, seein' as how I saved your life an' all. I was also thinkin' that with you runnin' around these parts at this time of night in your skivvies, maybe you jest might appreciate a little discretion on my part as well."

Clouds cleared, and a ray of moonlight shone on a wizened black face framed by short white hair that almost glowed in the dark. There was enough light from the moon to recognize a smile.

"Name's Crabb. That's with two *B*'s; not that I expect you gonna be writin' it down."

A gnarled hand was offered. Boucher took it, feeling the poacher's callused palm. "You saved my life," he said.

"Seems I did that," Crabb said, "but I been sittin' here askin' myself—for how long? What kind of fix you get yourself in, son?"

"I'm a federal district judge and—"

"You a *what?*"

"I'm U.S. District Judge Jock Boucher. I was assaulted and kidnapped earlier this evening . . ." He couldn't finish the sentence. In the inky, desolate darkness of the bayou, the old poacher was laughing hysterically.

"I caught me a judge!"

"Quiet! They'll hear you."

"Yes, sir. Your Honor, sir."

* * *

Edgar Crabb was a smudge on the notable record of the Louisiana Department of Wildlife and Fisheries, its alligator conservation program a model for similar crocodilian-species management programs all over the world. Unregulated hunting since the 1800s had, by the early 1960s, threatened the species, which had thrived for over two hundred million years. After hunting was banned for a decade, in 1972 a sustained-use management program was introduced, which promoted survival of the species, economic benefits, and maintenance of the natural habitat. But Crabb was bayou-born and had hunted gators long before the respected program was implemented, and he was too ingrained with a manner of life handed down father-to-son for generations to care much about government regulations he couldn't read anyway. He was as antediluvian in this respect as the reptile he hunted. "License?" If asked, he might have retorted by paraphrasing the banditos in the John Huston movie: "Ah don't need no stinkin' license." Fortunately for the gators, he was among the last of a vanishing breed.

"You can help me get this critter into my boat, then I guess you can go wherever you want," Crabb said.

"Where are you going?" Boucher asked.

"Gotta get it back to my place and harvest it." The use of the words *dispatch* and *harvest* were clues that he wasn't entirely ignorant of the existence of the Department of Wildlife and Fisheries.

Boucher grabbed the tail to help him move the dead creature. "You sell the hide?" he asked.

"Mebbe. Mostly, I eat him. Gator makes a good gumbo. You ever eat gator meat?"

"I grew up on it," Boucher said, one bayou man to another. "It's good for you. Less cholesterol than chicken."

Crabb chuckled. "Don't tell the gators 'bout no cholesterol. I use chickens to catch 'em."

They loaded the gator into Crabb's pirogue. He grabbed his pole and made ready to shove off, Boucher standing in knee-deep water.

"Aw hell," Crabb said, "get in. Guess I gotta feed you now that I saved you, right?"

"I won't get far tonight," Boucher said.

He got in the bow of the boat, straddling the deceased beast's snout. Crabb poled the craft away from the shore. In the middle of the bayou, water came almost to the gunwales.

"We be okay," he said, "if you stay still. Otherwise we be some gator's meal 'stead of t'other way round."

Silently, they slid along the smooth surface of tranquil waters, disturbing only the mirrored image of distant stars and a half-moon. Crabb bent over to avoid low-hanging mangrove branches as they approached land.

"You can step out now. Water ain't up to your knees. I don't gotta warn you 'bout snakes 'n' such, do I?"

"I'm mindful of them," Boucher said. He stepped out and onto the soft bottom, trusting timing, location, and prayer to keep the water moccasins and coral snakes from his path. Crabb got out, and they both grabbed the bow and pulled the boat onto the muddy bank.

"Stay right here. I gotta get somethin' wet to cover this gator with. I'll do the harvestin' in the morning." He was gone under a minute, then came back with a long piece of cloth that he dampened in the water, then spread over the carcass. "Okay, now follow me. Stay close. Trail's a bit tricky."

Boucher knew that a step off the beaten path might be an unpleasant one. Here in the bayou, man lived cheek by jowl with deadly predators, and any truce was temporary at best. He walked in lockstep, less than an arm's length behind the old man, trying to place his feet in his footsteps as they walked under a canopy that blacked out the meager light from the sky. When Crabb stopped, Boucher froze.

"This is ma' place," Crabb said. "Stay here. I'll go on in an' turn on the lamp."

He walked up three creaky stairs. A door squeaked open, then slammed shut. A flickering light from a match lit a lantern, and the flame was adjusted. Boucher could see Crabb's outline through the screen door. He looked around. It could hardly be called a clearing; mangrove branches brushed the walls and ceiling and hung over the roof of the one-room hut. A front porch with a single-rail banister ran the entire width, which could not have been much over ten feet. Boucher walked up the steps. Crabb was lying on a sagging metal cot.

"I'm gonna sleep now," he said. "This evening's activities done aged me somethin' considerable. Make the best of whatever you find, then turn down the lamp. See you in . . . the . . . mornin'."

And with those words, he was out, sleeping like a baby.

Boucher looked down on the old man, seeing him for the first time in the dim and flickering light. Crabb wore a tattered T-shirt and patched jeans that did not reach his ankles; his pink-soled black feet were bare. If there was a picture of serenity, this was it. In sleep, the wrinkled face smoothed out some, almost forming a smile. His breath was shallow but even. Though the eyelids twitched, it was obvious that his dreams were untroubled. Not just an observation, Boucher realized, this was recall. Before him lay his grandfather's kindred spirit: a man of the bayou, disdainful of society and its interference with a lifestyle unchanged for centuries. Boucher foraged and found a couple blankets. One he spread on the floor, the other he bunched up as a pillow for his head. They smelled and were probably bug-ridden, but on this he did not dwell. He lowered the lamp, as instructed, reclined on the pallet on the floor, and was soon asleep.

He woke to the sound of humming and splashing of water, got up, and walked to the porch. The sun had not yet risen, the sky a predawn gray. Crabb had a length of garden hose that descended from the roof, and with the water spurting from it, he was taking a shower. The naked brown body spraying water over itself looked like a leafless tree in a rainstorm.

"Got me a tub on the roof," he said. "Collects rainwater for drinkin' and washin'. I throw the ol' hose in it, then suck the end, like siphonin' from a gas tank. Come on, I'm done. Wash up, an' I'll throw some breakfast together." He handed Boucher the hose.

The shower was heaven. The soap was lye, something Boucher hadn't used since he was a boy. He washed his gym outfit and set it on the banister to dry, wrapped a towel around him, and entered the shack. Crabb was heating water for coffee over an old can of Sterno. Breakfast was on the table: beans. A fork stuck out of each can. Crabb poured boiling water from a pot into two cups, then served teaspoons of instant coffee. Crabb sat down and started to eat without a word. Suddenly, there was a roar over their heads. The old shack shook and felt for an instant like it would cave in on itself.

"Goddamn it!" Crabb grabbed the table to steady it. "Guv'ment comes after me 'cause I catch a gator to skin and eat it. Them bastards built 'em a runway right in the bayou, they killed more gators buildin' the damn thing than I would in ten lifetimes, an' they scare 'em away with those damn planes landin' whenever they want. You're a judge. Tell me, where's justice in that!"

"That was an airplane?"

"Yeah. Big sucker too. They got 'em that landin' strip, an'

they built 'em a road through the bayou to Houma. They the ones got no respect for wildlife, not me."

"Do you know whose plane it is?"

"Ain't for people, that's all I know. Comes in right over my head, usually at night. Trucks be waitin' to unload, then the plane takes off again. Curious, if you ask me, curious."

"Where is this landing strip?"

"I can practically spit at it from here. That's why the plane nearly takes my roof off every time it comes in for a landin'."

"I need to see it. Now."

"You sit there an' finish breakfast first. Damn, yo' mama raised herself a boy with no manners at all."

Boucher wolfed down his beans, gulped his coffee, then sat while the old man calmly finished his.

"Man in too much of a hurry gonna get to the end of his life a lot quicker than a man who takes it slow," Crabb said as he rose from the table. He went to a chest and opened a drawer. "You take these. You can't be runnin' around in what you wearin'. It's unseemly for a man your age, especially bein' a judge, if that's what you really be." He handed Boucher an old gray cotton work shirt and a pair of patched bib overalls. "They'll fit you good enough to get you to a store. You can bring 'em back someday if you got the time."

"I . . . I don't know what to say," Boucher stammered.

"If your folks taught you anything, they taught you to

say thank you, right? That's enough. Now come on. You're the one who's got the itch all over him."

They walked to the pirogue and unloaded the dead gator onto the bank. Boucher stared again at the creature that had almost taken his life in trying to save its own. It looked no less threatening in death. Anticipating another slog through the swamp, he was wearing his gym outfit in an effort to keep the clothes Crabb had given him clean and dry as long as possible. He got in the boat, and Crabb poled away from the bank. In minutes they had crossed open water and stopped a few yards from a man-made embankment.

"Far as I can take you," Crabb said. "Water's too shallow to go closer. When you get to the bank, climb up. You'll see the runway."

Boucher stepped out of the boat, then shook the old man's hand. "Thank you. For everything."

"Good luck to you," Crabb said. He shook his head. "Damnedest judge I ever heard of." He pulled away, turned, and headed for his home.

Boucher watched him go and promised himself that he'd see the colorful coot again. There was something of himself in that grizzled old man, something he'd lost long ago.

CHAPTER 30

BOUCHER BEGAN WADING, TRUDGING through sludge. The bottom had been churned up from the construction of the landing site, and his feet were sucked into the muck with every step. It was tough going. In seconds he was covered in mosquitoes, which began buzzing around his eyes and ears and feeding on his arms. He reached down to the bottom, brought up fists of mud, and plastered his skin from head to toe. When the exposed areas of his body were covered, the mosquitoes left him alone. Still, he wanted to scratch himself raw in about a thousand places. He reached the stone-covered embankment. The sun was rising, and visibility was clear, which meant he could also be seen. He climbed up the rock face. Finally out of the mud, Boucher slipped the denim overalls and shirt over his gym outfit.

Lying on the extreme end of the runway, he could

see the plane at the far end. It looked like a C-130. The rear hatch was down, forming a ramp, but nothing was being loaded on or off. He could not see anything inside the dark, gaping maw of the aircraft. A group of men sat at a small wooden table, employing the shade of a wing. Boucher couldn't make out what they were saying and crawled closer till he could hear the voices. Dumont was there, of course, and he recognized Moore and Quaid. The lawyer from Houston was also in the group. Boucher inched forward.

"Landing will be west of the Santa Ana National Wildlife Refuge," Benetton said. "It's two thousand acres of several different climate zones, a migratory location for a number of bird species, and home to the Texas ocelot and jaguar. The location is a few miles south of Alamo, Texas, right on the river. Just west of the wildlife preserve is an old cemetery that's rarely used. We've cleared a temporary landing strip on the other side of the cemetery. The weapons will be placed in the graveyard for pickup; after unloading, the plane and crew will take off immediately."

"Alamo? Santa Ana?" Dumont chuckled. "Who is going to tell me history doesn't repeat itself?"

"Alamo is a small town in Hidalgo County, Texas," the lawyer continued. "It was named for the Alamo Land and Sugar Company back in the twenties and has a population of around fifteen hundred. I have given coordinates to the cartel where they cross the Rio Grande into the park.

They think the national park is perfect for the pickup. In fact, they've used it before. The drought has been very serious, and there are large irrigation diversions upriver that will be employed and will have temporarily reduced the flow in this area to a shallow depth. It's only about fifty feet from bank to bank at the crossing point and the cartel has a new toy, one you should appreciate, General. They've built a pontoon bridge. I hope you've planned a proper reception."

"I have," General Moore said. "The Texas National Guard will be waiting: citizen soldiers, one of our country's proudest traditions."

"You know there are going to be casualties," Benetton said.

"Yes. That's unfortunate, but if we want the response we are hoping for, there must be loss of American life. No one who wears a uniform is unaware of the risk taken every time they put that uniform on. Today they are soldiers. Tomorrow they might be the honored dead. But we are doing everything possible to minimize casualties. We are going to employ weapons of war that will strike terror into the hearts of these invaders. My fear is that they will turn tail and run as soon as they see them, before they fire a shot. We'll be using robots."

"What?"

"Remote-controlled robots. When aimed, they do not miss."

"That's good," Quaid quipped. "We don't want stray

shots hitting any of the CIA, DEA, or Special Ops forces probably already hiding in the bushes across the river." This brought on a round of knowing laughter.

Moore continued. "The controller observes from a position of safety and operates the portable control unit, which contains video screens and joysticks. These weapons will engage the terrorists. They can operate in up to six feet of water and will chase them back across the river. Gentlemen, if we do our jobs in Washington, after the National Guard, the next wave will be the U.S. Army. But initially, the robots will ensure that our casualties are minimal."

"What documentation does this plane have to fly to Texas?" Dumont asked. "I only had clearance to get it here."

"She's getting a paint job," Quaid said. "New call letters, new air operation certificate, and new crew. Tell those guys in the cockpit their job is done. Pay them and get them out of here. I don't want them to see us painting the bird. They know too much already."

Boucher watched as the arrival flight crew was released. The paint crew arrived. Four men were engaged in painting the phony call numbers, two of them on the fuselage, two on the tail. One of each team held a stencil, the other a can of spray paint. This took under an hour. The paint was still wet when an SUV pulled up and parked next to the open ramp. The new crew got out and climbed up. Seconds later, Boucher observed them enter the cockpit.

Dumont spoke. "General, how will you confirm when the terrorists are on U.S. soil?"

"We will have satellite pictures," the general said, then laughed. "You're a history buff, Dumont. You remember what William Randolph Hearst said to his reporter before we went into Cuba? 'You provide the pictures. I'll provide the war.' I'm going to provide the pictures *and* the war. Once again, history repeats itself."

CHAPTER 31

BOUCHER CRAWLED TOWARD THE plane till he was parallel with it. Dumont and the others had walked back and were inside a shed near the beginning of the runway. This was his chance. He crawled over the tarmac, under the wing, then under the fuselage until he was at the ramp and open rear bay of the aircraft. Then he just stood up and walked into the plane. He climbed over cartons and crates as far into the interior of the aircraft as he could go, then nestled between boxes, pulling one over him. It took no effort. It was empty. He pushed at other crates. They too were light. They too were empty. The shipment was a ruse. Hidden among the fake cargo, he had nothing to do but wait. And pray.

The bay door was raised and locked in place. Engines turned over, and props sliced the humid air of the marshes. The plane lumbered to a slow taxi to the end of the runway, turned, and prepared for takeoff. The whine of the propeller blades pitched higher and higher. The aircraft lurched forward and began controlled acceleration. Though the runway was smooth, the contents of the cargo area rattled and vibrated. Boucher had to hold on to the crate covering him to keep it from sliding. Then they were airborne, above the bayou. He pictured the old man paddling below in his pirogue and wondered whether he looked up and waved a final farewell.

Boucher was beginning to feel his muscles cramp when the plane finally banked and the descent began. They'd been in the air under three hours, by his reckoning. The landing jolted him. This was not smooth tarmac but hard-scrabble desert. It had been cleared but was rocky and pitted. They came to a stop. Like a hound that had run till it was out of breath, the huge aircraft seemed to sink into itself as if collapsing, the slowing of its props like some final gasp. There were several minutes without any motion, then the rear hatch was opened. Even cocooned by cartons, Boucher could feel the rush of dry desert air. He heard one of the men descend the ramp, then climb back up.

"Are we in the right place?"

"Ask the pilot."

Boucher peeked from behind his barricade. There

was a set of headphones with mike hanging on the wall with which one could speak to the flight deck.

"Are we in the right place?" There was brief silence. "Roger that." The man hung up the headphones. "Pilot says we're where we're supposed to be. We landed in the strip they cleared for us. We're next to a cemetery. We have to pile the stuff there, then get the hell out."

The four men began to unload the crates.

"Hey, some of these things are empty," one said.

"Not our problem. Let's dump this shit and get out of here. Whatever's going on here, I don't want to be a part of it."

The men were independent agents, interested only in getting paid. Boucher watched and waited as they carried the first load over to the cemetery. He crept from his niche and walked to the ramp. They were about fifty yards away, with their backs to him. He ran down the ramp and away from the plane, then dove to the ground as the men returned for the final unloading. The cargo was stacked at the edge of the cemetery, maybe fifty yards from the river. The plane's engines started. A dust cloud consumed the aircraft. The men climbed inside; the ramp was raised. The plane again taxied, then turned, revved its engines, and began takeoff. Boucher could clearly see into the flight deck as it passed him, the plane's front wheels inches off the ground. The big bird lumbered into the air, and dust settled slowly. Jock Boucher stood alone on a desert plain, on the fringe of the Chihuahua desert, on the banks of the Rio Grande.

He faced the river. The water was slow-running. There was desert sand beneath his feet, the land around him covered with scrub brush. To his left was the cemetery where the weapons were stacked. Recalling that there might be eyes on the landing site from across the river, he bent over and ran to the graveyard. He crawled through the cemetery, reading the names on the tombstones. Names like Pharr, Briscoe, Duval, and McAllen were known throughout South Texas. Names like Hinojosa, Garcia, and Martinez were not as well known but staked no less a claim to the ground. There was no time to give the dead their due; he had to find a way to stop the carnage about to begin.

The cemetery had been built on a hill that sloped down to the river. Over the crest of this hill, Boucher saw an old man standing at a grave site, head bent, hat in hand. He walked slowly toward him, winding his way between headstones. When he was close enough, he spoke in a low tone. "Sir, there are armed men coming here. It's going to get dangerous. You must leave."

The man, dressed in jeans, boots, and a western shirt, looked to be a local farmer; Hispanic, this discernible by his features and the name on the gravestone before which he stood. He did not respond. Boucher scanned his limited Spanish vocabulary. "*Por favor,*" he said.

"I speak English. I'm American. You look like you've been rolling in pig shit."

Boucher sighed his relief. "Sir, could I borrow your cell phone?" He nodded at the device hanging on the man's leather belt.

"Local call?"

"Actually, no. I need to call the White House. Sir, I'm Federal District Judge Jock Boucher."

"Pleased to meet you. I'm George Washington," the man said.

"No, really, I'm Judge Boucher."

"And I'm really George Washington. George Washington Hinojosa. Here. Give the president my regards. Talk all you want. I've got extra minutes." He retrieved his cell phone from its case and handed it over.

Boucher could not recall the direct number the president had given him, and dialed the main White House number. "I'm Federal Judge Jock Boucher. This is a matter of national security. I must speak with the president. My password is *gavel.*"

"Password?" the operator said. Boucher held the phone away from his ear. Her laughter sounded like the breaking of crystal on the still air of the South Texas morning.

But he was ultimately connected to the president. "Jock, you haven't been shot or shot anyone this morning, have you?"

"No, Mr. President. But the day's not over yet. Sir, I'm

calling from a borrowed cell phone. I'm standing on the banks of the Rio Grande. I don't know if GPS—"

"We've got you, Judge. Look up and wave. Eyes are on you right now. My God, what have you done with yourself? You look like shit."

Boucher looked up and saw only a clear sky of robin's-egg blue. His summary of events was terse.

"Mr. President, a group of men has dropped a cache of illegal arms here on the U.S. side of the river. A Mexican drug cartel will be crossing to claim it, and they will be met by a contingent from the local Texas National Guard, who I understand have orders to chase them back into Mexican territory. Sir, a violent encounter with loss of life on both sides is expected." There was silence on the other end of the line. "Mr. President?" he said.

"Okay," the president said, "get yourself out of there. We'll take it from here."

Boucher clicked off and returned the phone to its bemused owner. "Sir, you need to leave now."

"Drug runners, huh? Glad to see someone's doing something about them. Good. I'll be going."

Boucher watched the man drive from the cemetery. Then, defying a presidential order, he walked back up the hill and chose a spot that gave him cover and line of sight to where the weapons lay waiting for collection. It was now late afternoon, the sun high and hot. The air was still. Even the birds in the neighboring wildlife sanctuary had ceased calling out. They'd given their warnings; all that was left to do was wait. Boucher had gotten little rest the harrowing night before and was exhausted. He chose a double headstone and read the briefest of family histories before sitting down and leaning against it. Stanley Archer was buried beneath where Boucher took his rest, and had walked this good earth from 1880 to 1950, had been a beloved husband and father. Agnes lay beside him; devoted wife and loving mother, she had survived him by five years. There were no signs of children in the neighboring plots, and Boucher wondered if they were among the living or had long ago left this small Texas town, leaving their parents alone in their golden years with only each other. Trying to imagine their lives put him to sleep.

A whisper of a breeze woke him. He opened his eyes and looked around. Evening was on the land, the sun less than an hour from setting and already painting the sky with deepening colors of red, orange, and purple, portending the coming of night. Had he slept through it all? He peeked around. No, the arms lay stacked and untouched. The cartel had not arrived; neither had the U.S. forces scheduled to meet them on this side. But there was something new in the neighborhood, and it was most bizarre. Midway between him and the arms cache were two objects that looked like large lawn mowers. They had not been there when he fell asleep and could have dropped from the heavens above, perhaps even from another planet. They definitely looked otherworldly and lethal. They just sat there, silent as the tombstones.

Then he heard the noise of automobile engines. He sat up and peeked over the headstone. A narrow, floating, temporary bridge now spanned the river, and vehicles were crossing from Mexico. The first one drove slowly, the driver testing the stability of the pontoon bridge, but when he made it to the American side, those following sped across. There were Hummers and late-model pickups. They drove to the pile of weapons and stopped. The doors of the Hummers opened, and men poured out. The pickups also discharged passengers. One spoke, and laughter broke the evening silence, maybe a joke about the ease of entering the country with which they'd had a love-hate relationship all their lives. They'd approached the stacked boxes, preparing to load them, when another sound was heard. A separate caravan was crossing, following the trail just blazed. There were curses as the men ran back to their vehicles and grabbed their weapons. They didn't wait for the interlopers to reach the riverbank but began firing immediately. Automatic rifle fire was returned. The new arrivals fanned out when they'd crossed, a second convoy of late-model SUVs and trucks. Boucher recognized a black Cadillac Escalade in the second oncoming group. All the conveyances were favored rides of narcos. There was much shouting and screaming in Spanish between the two gangs, as if the epithets could do as much damage as the bullets. Boucher realized he was viewing a firefight between competing drug cartels. Someone else had gotten word of the treasure trove waiting to be plucked up and had come to claim it. But where was the Texas National Guard?

Hundreds and hundreds of rounds were fired, with few apparent casualties but no small amount of damage to the vehicles. Some new-car dealer would receive a windfall when this pitched battle was over. Bullets whistled past Boucher and struck neighboring headstones. He received a minor flesh wound to his right forearm, not from a bullet but from a chunk of granite chipped off and flung from a grave marker. Then the gunfire abated. There were shouts of confusion. He took a peek. Crossing the river was what looked at first like a tank on wheels. It came closer, and he could see it was another pickup, one with plates of metal welded to its exterior, forming a V in front, like the bow of a ship. The windshield was covered with a protective iron shield, slits cut for visibility. It was a homemade armored vehicle. Above the cab, standing in the bed of the truck, was a man with a weapon. A flash erupted from the muzzle of a shoulder-fired grenade launcher, and one of the Hummers was hit. It exploded and several men were incinerated; several more ran from the wreck like flaming torches. Shots were fired. They were put out of their misery and fell dead on the ground, their mortal remains still burning.

Through all this, Boucher could see no one defending against this armed intrusion into territory of the United

States of America. Where was the defense against these insurgents? There was no sign of the Texas National Guard or any other U.S. force.

Then it happened. The homemade tank on the pontoon bridge exploded in the middle of the river. There was a shrill whistle just before it was hit, the sound unmistakable to anyone who had ever heard one. It had been struck by a precision-guided missile from above, though there was nothing to be seen in the evening sky. Boucher guessed that the weapon had been fired from an armed drone, no doubt the first ever unleashed over the U.S./Mexico border. He realized that, as of that moment, as Yogi Berra had said, the future would never again be what it used to be. Still there was no sign of U.S. troops.

A command that could have come from God Himself was heard booming above the spit and crackle of gunfire. No U.S. forces were visible anywhere, but unseen megaphones boomed orders in English and Spanish. The invaders were directed to lay down their weapons. There was a brief moment of silence during which Boucher heard yet another sound—the whirring of an electric motor. He peeked over the tombstone. The two lawn mowers were moving toward the invading gunmen. The order was repeated. It was again ignored. He watched as a shooter took aim at the small machine and fired, the rounds bouncing harmlessly off its metal shell. Jock took a closer look. Affixed to the remote-controlled device was a machine gun.

The barrel swiveled, and it fired off a single round. The man who had shot at the robot, his weapon still pointed, fell to the ground. The second robot whirred into action. Its weapon was aimed and fired, and its grenade launcher destroyed the Cadillac Escalade and those inside. Out of anger that superseded their limited if not totally absent judgment and reason, several others fired on the robotic weapons. The one with the machine gun did the heavy lifting, firing single rounds and not missing a target, all shots in the kill zone, center chest, as if the insurgents had been wearing bull's-eyes. They finally got the message. Some turned to run, keeping rather than surrendering their weapons; these men too, the robot dropped like flies. Once more the order to drop their weapons was repeated. This time the command was obeyed: they were cast to the ground. To convince them that the futile mission was finished, the robot grenade launcher aimed, fired, and blew up the weapons cache. If anyone was surprised that the store of munitions did not make a bigger bang, they didn't show it.

Finally, men in military fatigues of the U.S. armed forces appeared, coming over the hill behind and approaching the unarmed intruders with M16s in ready fire position. As astounded as he had been while watching this *War of the Worlds* spectacle play out on the banks of the Rio Grande, Boucher was equally amazed when Ray Dumont walked across the open field toward the surrendering and now unarmed cartel members, accompanied by several Texas

National Guardsmen. The soldiers wasted not a second covering the captured trespassers with their own weapons and ordered them to raise their hands high. Several more guardsmen collected the discarded guns of the cartel members. Boucher stood and walked toward them, joining a major heading that way, and he introduced himself. If the major disbelieved him, he had the good sense not to show it. "Yes, sir" was all he said.

Boucher pointed to Dumont. "What is that man doing here? He's not one of your troops."

"He has valid press credentials. I think he's really CIA. They tag along sometimes too."

"Those things," Boucher said, pointing to the remote-controlled weapons that had won the conflict with limited loss of life. "What are they?"

"They're SWORDS, special weapons reconnaissance detection systems. They've been hugely successful in both Iraq and Afghanistan. One is loaded with a fifty-caliber machine gun, the other with a forty-millimeter grenade launcher. They have five mounted cameras, including a target acquisition scope, a 360-degree camera, and wide-angle zoom lenses. At twelve hundred feet, a SWORD can identify the make of an enemy's weapon, even determine whether the selector is on fire or safe. When aimed, it does not miss."

"I'd like to meet the operators; tell them what a great job they did."

"How's your Spanish?" the major asked.

"I beg your pardon?"

"We've been training members of the Mexican military in unmanned weaponry as part of the Merida Initiative, a security cooperation agreement between the two governments. We let them handle this one. They'll get the credit for it."

"No kidding," he said.

"Yes, sir. No kidding. This is their fight too."

Boucher shook his head.

"What is it, sir?"

"We trained their special forces a decade ago. They became the bloodiest cartel of them all. I was just worried about someone going rogue and turning those robots on us."

"We can override any command," the major said. "Plus, I removed these." He opened his palm and showed two small fuses. "The babies are asleep."

They walked to the National Guardsmen covering the unarmed insurgents.

"Sir, what are we going to do with the prisoners?" one asked.

"Keep them covered. A team is on the way to take them into custody," the major said. "Be careful. These men are violent criminals."

"I don't think we'll have much resistance, sir. Several say they've been praying they'd end up in a U.S. prison, that it's the only way out of the life. They said they've been waiting for us to begin the fight and asked why we've taken so long. Several told me we're their saviors, not their captors."

Obviously, the president had countermanded General Moore's battle plan. Boucher's call had saved American lives.

Ignoring Boucher's presence as if he'd expected it, and seemingly unconcerned that his grand scheme had been foiled, Dumont walked to the group of insurgents and stared into each face. "¿*Quien es* El Jimador? Which one of you is El Jimador?" he asked. There was no response. "I will give one million dollars to the man who points him out to me." He stopped before one man who had half his right ear shot off, an old injury.

"*Tú*," Dumont said. "The witness who saw you murder my son said you had an ear missing. It's you." From his belt, Dumont pulled the pistol Boucher knew all too well and pointed it at the man's face.

"Ray," he yelled, "don't! Put that gun down. It's over. It's finished."

"It's not over while this bastard is alive. He killed my son," Dumont said. "He—"

The narco grabbed the gun from Dumont's hand, spun him around, and pinned him by his neck in a choke hold. Holding his hostage in front of him, he moved away from the group. One foot behind the other, he backed toward the river, the barrel of the pistol pointed against his captive's temple.

"You found El Jimador, *amigo*," he said. "Where's my

million dollars?" As he waded into the river using Dumont as a human shield, he was laughing.

"Can't anybody take him out?" Boucher asked.

"We don't have snipers," the officer said. "The robot might have a shot, but I disabled it."

The laughter of the man reverberated across the Rio Grande as he reached the far bank and disappeared.

"Aren't you going after him?" Boucher asked.

"We have no authority to cross into Mexico," the officer said.

Boucher hesitated for just a second as he looked toward the river, then ran. He ran without forethought. He ran out of compulsion, not understanding why. The water was deeper than it had been earlier. He was up to his waist upon reaching midriver. The irrigation diversions upstream must have been reopened, allowing normal flow. Still, the Rio Grande was not more than chest-high at its deepest. He reached the far bank quickly, rinsing the dried, caked mud off his body as he crossed. He had kept his eye on where the narco holding Dumont had disappeared into the brush, and he headed for that spot. He followed the tracks into chest-high reeds, turned back, and took a final look. Law enforcement teams had arrived, and the prisoners were being led away. Only the National Guard officer looked his way, shaking his head in disbelief.

Jock Boucher had invaded Mexico.

CHAPTER 32

Madness was upon him, he was sure. Of all the reckless, compulsive acts ever undertaken by Jock Boucher, this outranked them all. Alone, unarmed, knowing hardly a word of the language, he had done the most absurdly futile thing ever. Certain in his own mind that he was crazy, he began talking to himself. Sitting on the bank of the Rio Bravo—the name those on this side gave to the riparian frontier that divided their nations—he attempted to rationalize the insane action he'd just undertaken.

"He's not going to kill Dumont," Boucher convinced himself. "He's a kidnapper too, and Dumont offered a million-dollar reward, so he knows he's got money. He's going to hold him for ransom, maybe start sending over body parts as proof that he's alive. If he finds out Dumont's identity, the ransom will be astronomical."

"Okay, smart guy," his alter ego said, "so he's got Dumont hostage. What are you going to do? You're in his country—enemy territory. You don't even have a gun. You're a fool. A damned fool."

Boucher walked from the reeds, rushes, and small trees on the riverbank. The growth was dense only near the river. Less than twenty yards from the water, the topography changed to flat, dry farmland. As the sun slipped below the horizon, he could see several structures: barns, storage sheds, and small houses. He stepped back into the brush, sat down, and continued his conversation with himself.

"The night is my ally," he said. "And I will find others. I'm not in enemy territory. Those farmers whose land and homes I just saw, are they my enemies? Am I a threat to their families? Or is it the monster I'm chasing, a beast who would decapitate a young man just to terrify those same farmers' wives and children?"

His alter ego answered. "Stop talking to yourself."

Boucher waited only till it was dark enough to walk the open fields without being seen. Though he did not want the trail to grow cold, neither did he want to get shot in plain sight. He headed toward the lights of what he guessed was a home; he could see a family seated at dinner. Now it would get dicey. He had no strategy but the truth. He walked to the small wooden structure and knocked on the front door. A woman came, took one look at him, and called her husband. A man walked into the room and stood beside her.

"¿Qué es lo que quieres?" the man asked, his voice gruff but not entirely masking a fear of strangers in the night.

"I'm sorry, I don't speak Spanish."

"Carlos," he yelled, "ven acá."

A boy of about fifteen joined the couple. "What do you want?" he asked in English.

"I am looking for a man called El Jimador," Boucher said.

Either the door would be slammed in his face, or he would receive heaven-sent confirmation that he was doing the right thing. The boy muttered to his father. The mother gasped and took a step back. The father spoke, and his son translated. "What do you want with him?"

"I am an American judge. I want to see him brought to justice. He is a bad man."

This was translated. Words flew among the man, his wife, and son, no translation necessary. They were arguing the age-old question of one's duty in the face of evil. Perhaps, Boucher mused, with all the violence rampaging around them, not for the first time.

"I saw him earlier," the boy said. "I know where he went. I can take you there."

"No. I don't want to put you in any danger."

"I will only show you where he is. Then I will run. I will hide. These things I do well—and often." There was another flurry of Spanish. "My father asks if you need a gun," the boy said. "My mother asks if you are hungry."

"If your mother could make me a sandwich, I would be grateful."

"*Torta*. The word for 'sandwich' is *torta*."

"*Torta*," Boucher addressed the mother, "*por favor*."

The gun, well, that was something he did not expect. The simple farmer brought him an AK-47, the most popular weapon among Mexico's criminal insurgents, called almost lovingly *cuerno de chivas*, or goat's horn, for the curvature of its magazine. Had this man of the soil retired from a more violent trade?

"This gun belonged to my older brother," the boy said. "He is dead." The three words spoke volumes. "There are no more bullets; only those in there." He pointed to the magazine.

His sandwich ready, Boucher and the boy left the house.

"How far is it?" Boucher asked.

"Not far," the boy answered.

"I doubt he'll still be there."

"He will be there. Where would he go?"

"This is a big country."

"But it is not his. He is *jefe* only in a small area. He leaves it, he is dead."

"*Jefe?*"

"It means 'boss,'" the boy said. "You should learn Spanish."

It wasn't far. They had walked under half an hour, crossing farmland and desert; it was difficult to tell one from the other, particularly at night.

"That is his house," the boy whispered. "See? He is there. The lights are on. He usually has many guards, but you are lucky. His men went with him this afternoon, and none of them came back. I wish I could go with you. Tonight would be a good night to kill him. I will see if there is a guard."

"No. I don't want you in danger."

"This man killed my brother. I must help you kill him. It is my duty to my family. If there is a guard, he will talk to me; I am just a farmer's son. Come, we go."

"No," Boucher whispered harshly. "You are right. Your duty is to your family. You have already helped me enough. Now go."

Reluctantly, the boy slid into the darkness. Boucher crept toward the house. Luck. He had it. The boy was right. The assassin had taken his men with him earlier, and now they were sitting in a jail in Texas. This was the opportunity of a lifetime—the opportunity to end a lifetime. The house was far bigger than he'd expected. When the moon came from behind a cloud, he could see it was a cross between the Taj Mahal and the Alhambra. All that drug money had to be spent on something. Would there be entrances on the

sides as well? Perhaps guest suites with patios and sliding glass doors at ground level? No. He got close enough
to see barred windows throughout the house; no side entrances, just front and back. Though large, the home was
one level, not counting the domed cupolas and minaret
towers, the architect going for a Granada theme. Boucher
inched closer. What he feared most was a dog, but there
was no barking. Again, the *jefe* used men as dogs, so why
bother with the care of a four-legged beast? Tonight he
had neither. He crawled around the entire perimeter: no
guard. Maybe the last of his men had heard of the debacle
at the river and seen an opportunity to run, to leave their
master and this road leading only to death.

Boucher stopped, twenty feet from the side of the
house. Lights were on throughout, but there was no sound
of any kind. He had two choices: front door or back. He
studied the windows. One-story living, lots of rooms. The
front entrance would lead into a salon and maybe a dining
area. El Jimador would not be in the living room right now,
Boucher knew, because he would be trying to extract from
Dumont his identity, and if he had learned it by now, he
was likely causing the American enough pain to wish he
were dead, a wish the *jefe* would grant soon. *So,* Boucher
concluded, *he is not in the front of the house. That is where his
best furniture is—probably matching sofas and chairs in white
calf's leather; he wouldn't want blood all over them. There is no
basement, so he has Dumont trussed up in a room at the back.*

Boucher crept around to the front of the house, his automatic rifle pointed. He walked up marble stairs onto a marble porch between marble columns and opened a double door ten feet tall, made of an exotic heavy wood he did not recognize. The huge room was empty, at least of anything human. He'd guessed right about the furniture; everything in the room was white. Dark souls prefer light decor. He'd guessed right about something else—at that moment he heard Dumont scream.

Most men do not scream well. There's something about the larynx, the vocal cords, the physiology of the male voice box that makes nearly impossible a masculine-sounding emission forced out under extreme pain. What comes out is more like a shriek or even a squeak, hitting a high pitch unattainable under normal circumstances. For some reason, most men don't holler when pressed to the limits of their tolerance. So it was a horrible, ear-splitting screech that caused Boucher to run to the rear of the house and fling open the closed door.

Dumont was tied to a wooden chair. It had no armrests; his wrists were secured to the legs just below the seat. Blood dripped down the legs of the chair and puddled on the floor. Several fingers on both hands had been severed, the digits neatly placed in a small ice-filled Igloo cooler, probably to accompany ransom demands long after death. But those wounds had been inflicted earlier. The current source of the man's agony could be seen from the blood gushing down his neck and chest. The sadist had been busy hacking off Dumont's right ear. Nearly severed, the cartilage hung loose and vibrated like a tuning fork.

And yet he was conscious. The recognition of Boucher, the realization of what he was doing, registered in Dumont's eyes. There was a message in those eyes: *He's behind the door.* Boucher turned and emptied the AK-47's magazine into the door. There was a clang of metal as the machete was dropped, then the body of El Jimador fell forward. It was impossible to know how many bullets had penetrated his body. He lay there twitching, still alive. A raspy, breathy sound was emitted, but not from the monster on the floor.

"Please," Dumont rasped. He drew a deep hoarse breath. "Please let me."

"Let you what, Ray?"

Dumont nodded toward a table. On the table was a pistol. His pistol. His head practically lay on his shoulder, his neck muscles barely able to support it. His eyes implored. Boucher realized what he was asking and ripped the rope from his wrists, picked up the gun from the table, and put it in Dumont's mangled, bloody hand, steadying it to compensate for the lack of digits, helping him place a remaining finger on the trigger. He helped Dumont aim at the body quivering on the floor. The gun fired a rifle caliber adapted to a pistol. The cop-killer bullet blew the narco-terrorist's head off.

At this death, Boucher felt no remorse.

From the next room, he grabbed a sheet from the bed and wrapped it around Dumont. From the adjoining bathroom, he wet and then wrapped facecloths and towels around his mutilated hands and head. With a hand towel, he carefully picked up the severed fingers from the cooler and put them in his pocket, though the ice had probably destroyed too many cells for reattachment to be possible. He gently lifted Dumont, whose shirt had large bloodstains at the waist and several more seeping through from the rib cage.

"How bad are you hurt?"

"Bastard kicked the shit out of me. Look at his boots."

The toes of the dead drug lord's cowboy boots were gold-tipped, the jeweler's ornate design accented in dried blood. Dumont's blood. Internal bleeding was a certainty. Boucher carried him from the room toward the front of the house.

"Wait," Dumont gasped, gesturing behind them. "Down the hall." With a feeble head movement, he indicated the door to a closed room. Boucher carried him there, set him down against the wall, and opened the door. The room might have been built to serve any number of purposes. Though it was devoid of furniture, it was not empty. It was full of stacks upon stacks of hundred-dollar bills, piled from the floor to shoulder height.

Dumont whispered, "That might be five hundred million dollars."

"We're not taking the money."

Dumont shook his head. "Don't take it. *Burn it!*"

Boucher stared at the paper fortune; cellulose pulp, created from wood, rags, and certain grasses with an ignition point of 451 degrees Fahrenheit. The stuff of dreams, the root of evil; it was easy to torch.

"Do you have a match?"

"Look in the kitchen."

Boucher ran to the kitchen and quickly returned. He struck a match and threw it on the pile. It caught; the flame burned slowly for an instant, then burst like spontaneous combustion. He backed into the hall, bent over, and picked up Dumont. They stared for a moment longer, then Boucher raced to the front porch and out to the garage. It was almost as big as the house and filled with exotic automobiles: Ferraris, Lamborghinis, all with keys in the ignitions. When you're the top dog and surround yourself with pit bulls, no one is going to fuck with your toys. But the top dog was dead. The pit bulls were caged. And all these luxury cars would soon be engulfed in the flames destroying the house. Boucher carefully lifted Dumont and placed him in the front seat of a jet-black Hummer.

"I'm going to get you home, Ray," he said, "but you're going to have to hang on."

"Take me home, Jock. Take me home."

Minutes later, as Boucher crossed over the Rio Grande into the United States, the flames could be seen and explosions heard in the distance: the devil's domain destroyed.

CHAPTER 33

TWO WEEKS LATER, FITCH and Boucher strolled through Jackson Square. "We sure pegged Dumont wrong," Fitch said.

"What do you mean?"

"I spoke with the medical examiner about that body we found in the gulf. He said he gave his honest opinion, and I believe him. The death of the ship's cook was an accident. The guy just fell overboard and hit his head on the way down. Then Trooper Freeman got suspicious after questioning a single crew member and jumped to conclusions. The guy was coming from the dispensary after getting a prescription filled and ran into a state trooper. I think his nervousness had more to do with the nature of his prescription than the death of a fellow shipmate. Freeman was going to tie up the ship. I think they were going to kidnap him to keep him from interfering with Dumont's plan. I don't believe they meant to kill him."

"That's what Dumont said to me before he died," Boucher said. "He confessed that the whole thing was to avenge his son. It was a calculated ruse to get the murderer onto U.S. soil. When Moore told him that innocent Americans would be killed, he blew the whistle on himself and his team. I had thought it was strange that when I called the president, he already had a satellite on me. The drone was in position, and the Texas National Guard was in place with orders from their commander in chief, not some renegade retired general."

"Another thing," Fitch said. "We ran a check on the third ship that showed up on the satellite, the one that got away. It flies a Panamanian flag and is owned by a company in Malta whose registered owner is a lawyer who handles the international affairs of Dumont Industries. So I'm wondering, with all that we're finding out about Dumont's motives, whether he had that shipment of weapons blown out of the water."

"Maybe. It was the loss of that shipment that he used to get his son's killer to cross the river," Boucher said. "That money the cartel paid Dumont for the shipment that sank, he told me he had it dumped into the sea. I believe him. We burned up half a billion dollars of narco cash ourselves."

"To avenge his son, he was going to start a war with Mexico. How did he ever come up with such a crazy idea?"

"He believed that history would repeat itself, if he gave it a little push."

"So we've got a happy ending?" Fitch said.

"I don't know. I really don't see that the exercise, with all its grand intentions, accomplished much of anything. It was all a game. A blood game."

Walking home from the meeting with Fitch, Boucher got a call on his cell from a man saying he represented Ray Dumont. It was an unexpected request but one the judge could not refuse. He was asked to meet with Mrs. Dumont. He drove to the mansion on Saint Charles Avenue. Black crepe was draped over the entrance to the house. He rang the bell and was admitted by the same butler, who once again showed him to Dumont's study. Elise was on the settee, elegantly dressed in black. A gentleman whom he had not met was seated at a chair in front of the desk. Familiar with the breed, Boucher didn't need to be told he was meeting the family's lawyer. Jock paid his respects to the widow. "I am so sorry for your loss, Mrs. Dumont."

She nodded in silence, leaving her lawyer to do the talking. Just as reticent, he handed Boucher a letter. It was from Ray Dumont. It read:

Jock,
If you're reading this, then I have avenged my son, our little campaign is finished, and history will judge us to have been heroes or fools. Whatever the verdict, I can say we meant well. I did what I had to do.

The man giving you this letter is the executor of my estate and he will have carried out my instructions prior to contacting you. Certain assets have been disposed of in order to care for my wife in comfort and luxury to the end of her days. She and I discussed this and she does not wish to remain in New Orleans without me. I expect that New York, London, or Paris will be her choice of retirement residence, maybe all three. We have not sold the house. I know you love the Quarter but I hope you will give the Garden District a chance. Its charm is unique and a grand part of the city you and I cherish. Our house is yours. If I may say so, it is more secure than your own. You need to think of such things.

You recall I asked you to consider a job as general counsel to Dumont Industries. I am now asking more of you. Please accept the position of chairman and chief executive officer. The company is also yours. My lawyer will discuss with you all details. Despite my dear wife's declarations of my financial ineptitude, I have managed affairs reasonably well and my bequest to you is quite generous. I know you have been less than happy on the bench. I hope the legacy I leave you will resolve this conflict. Should you find you don't like being a captain of industry, then of course you can sell it. You can do anything you wish, but you don't need me to tell you that.

I ask that you think of our neighbor to the south. With the discovery my son made, Mexico's oil and gas industry will thrive. If men like you, with talent and drive, focus upon a solution to the critical water shortage, then agribusiness on both sides of the border has a most promising future. The fastest-appreciating real estate in the U.S. today is farmland. If there is water, it will be the same for our neighbor.

Why am I doing this? Because I have no heir, and because I have admired and emulated you. Impressed with your penchant for vengeance, I thought I'd give it a try. The peace I am finding at this moment in planning to avenge my son may be short-lived, but it is the only peace I've known since his death. I have you and your example to thank for that.

I'm going to be watching you, Jock. I'm curious to see just how you deal with the temptations that come with great wealth and power. As they say down south, buena suerte. Good luck.

When Ronald Reagan left office, his final words to the marine saluting him as he boarded the helicopter to be taken from the White House for the last time were "Carry on." I ask you to do the same on my behalf. You are now one of the wealthiest and most powerful men in the state of Louisiana, indeed, in the United States.

Now, carry on, Jock Boucher. Carry on.

Ray Dumont

"I'm sure you have questions, Judge Boucher," the lawyer said. "If I can help you in any way—"

"Yes," Jock said. "Could I have a glass of water? And a couple of aspirins?"

The lawyer assured him he had time to think about it. Elise Dumont implored him to accept the bequest. Boucher was numb. He asked if he could leave his truck and have the chauffeur drive him home. Elise took that as a good sign, but it was not that. He was simply too dazed to drive. He got home, seated himself in his living room, and called Malika. They talked into the evening, then through the night. In the early hours, he had made his decision.

"I'm going to call the president in the morning," he said. "He deserves to hear it from me personally."

"Can I meet you in Washington?" Malika asked.

"I was hoping you would."

Dinner was served in a small dining room that looked over the Rose Garden, the White House grounds, and the Washington Monument. The dress code was "nice restaurant" attire, a bit up the scale from "friends over for dinner." There were no pretensions, and their hosts made every effort to make Jock and Malika feel comfortable. The menu was embossed with the White House seal and meant as a memento, but Malika didn't slip her copy into her purse until invited to do so. The fare began with peanut soup, a Colonial Williamsburg recipe; iceberg lettuce with blue cheese dressing; and roast beef au jus dusted with fennel pollen and served with twice-baked potatoes. The wine was a Cakebread cabernet sauvignon; dessert was a deceptively simple-looking strawberries and cream, but the cream was white-chocolate mousse with a hint of cinnamon and spearmint. With a nod to Boucher's background, coffee was served with chicory.

"Do you know what amazes me about tonight's menu?" the president asked. "That peanut soup. I really liked it. I thought I'd eaten enough peanut butter in law school that I never wanted to taste peanuts again. But that soup, that was really good. Jock, would you mind stepping outside with me? There are a few things I'd like to discuss with you in private."

They excused themselves from the table and stepped outside under a covered, colonnaded portico. "This is good right here," the president said. "We need to stay where we are visible from inside."

"Security?" Boucher asked.

"No. My wife thinks I'm sneaking out for a smoke. I need to stay where she can see me. I tell you, any man who thinks he can sneak around on a woman with her own Secret Service detail is deluding himself.

"Anyway, let's talk about Mexico. The first thing I want you to know is that the Mexican president and I were in direct communication the whole time we were monitoring the incursion of the insurgents. Though we didn't have to—they were committing hostile acts on our territory—we sought and received his accord before taking any action. We decided it was prudent to let the Mexican military take the shots against their own criminals, using our robots."

"Mr. President, are you saying that Dumont and the others had authority to do what they did?"

"Gunrunning and the sale of illegal arms? Of course not. Those men were trying to usurp a presidential prerogative. I'm the one who decides when to send troops onto foreign soil, not some band of misguided mercenaries, however noble they think their objective might be."

The president looked toward the Washington Monument. "There are no better friends and allies than the U.S. and Mexico," he said, "but . . ." He paused. "Do you know the Latin phrase *si vis pacem, para bellum*?"

"Yes, sir. It means if you wish for peace, prepare for war."

"Some think that glib, ancient axiom can define a nation's entire foreign policy. It's never that simple. But let no one ever doubt that we are prepared."

"I got a glimpse of that preparation on the banks of the Rio Grande," Boucher said.

"You got the slightest of hints, nothing more. Dumont and his cronies were right about one thing: if that genie ever gets out of the bottle, it will be hard to put it back in. Damn the drugs and gunrunning. With Mexico, we need to be partners in progress, not partners in crime." The president then added, "Jock, you could put your assets in a blind trust and stay on the bench. It wouldn't be the first time."

"I don't think that will work, sir. Dumont Industries has its fingers in too many pies. Even with a blind trust, I'd spend all my time defending myself against charges of conflict of interest. Besides, I've been thinking of things I could do with this opportunity for New Orleans, for my state. To tell you the truth, Mr. President, I'm kind of excited about it."

"It does provide us a way out of our dilemma, doesn't it? Congress can't blame me because good fortune has changed your life's path. Are you starting right away?"

"No, sir. Malika and I are flying down to Puerto Vallarta and finishing our vacation that, you may recall, was unexpectedly interrupted."

"You'd better be careful down there. I mean it, Jock."

Boucher gritted his teeth. This lecture he did not need.

"Mr. President, in the past few weeks I've been held up at gunpoint a few blocks from my home, and shot right outside my front door. I'm not going to live my life in fear. I'm going to Mexico to sit on a beautiful white, sandy beach, to relax, to forget about recent events and hopefully work out some kinks in a rather strained relationship. Don't worry about me. I will be perfectly safe."

"I was only going to warn you about the dangers of too much sun. Skin cancer is dangerous. Don't think your Cajun genes and thick hide give you extra protection. Your thick head won't do you much good either. Enjoy your vacation. You've earned it. Just be mindful of the tropical sun. That's all I was trying to say."

"Oh. I'm sorry, sir. Thank you. I'll be careful."

"But don't think I'm letting you off that easily. I'm still your president and there's still something you can do for me."

The commander in chief spoke in low tones as the two walked the covered portico.

"Mr. President, you want me to do *what?*"

Jock Boucher's screech was heard all over the White House grounds.

EPILOGUE

FOR SEVERAL WEEKS, BOUCHER waited for the call from the White House he hoped would never come. There were many administrative details involved in his departure from the bench, and Mildred took care of them as she transitioned onto the staff of Judge Giordano. Unable to begin his new corporate life until his judicial mantle had been officially passed, Boucher was in limbo with nothing to do. Still, he rose before dawn. His first cup of coffee with chicory made in his French press was ready to sip by the first light of day. He could have slept till whatever hour he chose, but out of habit, Judge Jock Boucher rose early. Soon his judicial title would be only honorific. Jock could count the days until his tenure as a federal district judge was over.

Sipping his coffee, he read online versions of newspapers from all over the country. An article from a Texas publication caught his attention, and he reviewed it several times, carefully. Airline schedules were checked. Calls were made. There was no second cup this morning. Boucher dashed to the airport. After a brief wait, he was in the air. A short flight later and he was on the ground, in a rental car, driving across South Texas, toward the Rio Grande, the border with Mexico.

Maria Aguilar had made no special plans for this day. She'd heard the rumor but discounted the repeated speculation. She had tried to convince her foolish husband, who still believed in the dream, that hopes once dashed do not take root in such arid soil as surrounded them. As always, she wiped down the few plastic tables and chairs and mopped the floor of the family cantina, one of the last businesses remaining in the small, forgotten town. Throwing the water out to settle the dust, Maria almost flung it into the face of a stranger walking her way. He was handsome, his posture erect and self-assured. She saw no car in the empty street and the visitor's clothes—and his shoes—were not dust-covered. The rare traveler to this piece of dirt next to nowhere had to come quite a distance to arrive here, and the demands of the journey were always evident. But not on this man. He could have dropped from the sky. He smiled as he entered, took a seat, and asked for a beer. She was happy to serve him. It was a rare occurrence. She asked where he came from, speaking English in her establishment for the first time in over a decade.

"Texas," he said. "Your husband rowed me across the river and told me to come here."

"You mean it is true?" she asked.

"Yes. The river crossing reopened today. I wanted

to be one of the first. There are more people behind me."

Maria stood in the doorway. She saw a group walking down the street. There were faces she had not seen in many years and she ran to greet them. The few others still living in the dusty and nearly deserted Mexican town heard the noise and ran from their homes to greet the arrivals. There was laughter. There were earnest embraces in the middle of the main street of the *pueblito*. After sharing hugs they walked to the cantina.

"But I don't have enough to serve you all," Maria said.

Two men in uniform, one an officer of the U.S. Park Service, the second from the U.S. Border Patrol, carried a cooler.

"I hope we're not committing a customs violation," one said, "but we brought some beer to celebrate."

"There's no violation if you share it," their Mexican counterpart shouted.

The small, remote crossing with no bridge, not even a ferry, was one of several authorized international crossings on the Rio Grande that had been closed by the U.S. government more than a decade earlier as part of tightened border security. Visitors to parks on the Texas side of the river and tourists who rafted down the riparian frontier had once included stops in Mexican towns on their agenda, but the tourists and their business dried up with the border closings. The towns lost their economic sustenance, and friends separated by the river lost contact. Maria's husband, who rowed visitors across the river, lost his sole source of income. Years of effort on both sides had finally brought about the crossing's reopening, but a major impetus had been the recent death of a local drug lord whose criminal enterprise had rampaged across the region. A large number of known and violent criminals had also been captured, the circumstances mysteriously not covered in the local media. The narco's death had brought stability to the area. Boucher had read of the inauguration of the crossing, not far from where he had recently entered Mexico in a much different manner, and decided he had to be there for the event.

"Hey, Rigoberto," someone yelled out to Maria's husband as he shared a beer with a border patrol officer, "don't you sing anymore when you row your customers across?"

The burly man blushed as the cry was taken up.

"It has been a long time," he said in Spanish, then stood and began a familiar *ranchera* ballad.

Jock recognized the tune and asked Maria its name.

"'*Volver, Volver.*' It is about a man returning to his lost love."

"Does she take him back?"

"With open arms." Maria smiled. "With open arms."

Jock's cell phone vibrated in his pocket. He took it out and recognized the number on the screen. His smile vanished. There was a look of grim determination on his face as he answered the call he had dreaded.

"Yes, Mr. President."